MW01167162

MURDER IN SHAWNEE

Two Mystery Novels of the Alleghenies

MURDER IN SHAWNEE

Two Mystery Novels of the Alleghenies

SHAWNEE ALLEY FIRE

A 1987 Detective Classic

and

HAUNTS

Revisited and Revised 2008

by

John Douglas

RAMBLE HOUSE

ISBN 13: 978-1-60543-188-8

ISBN 10: 1-60543-188-5

Cover Art: Gavin L. O'Keefe
Preparation: John Douglas and Fender Tucker

INTRODUCTION

WELCOME TO SHAWNEE

I guess it was natural that I set two of my mystery novels in a fictionalized version of Cumberland, Maryland since I spent most of my childhood there. In fact, the alley of *Shawnee Alley Fire* was my playground, and photographer Jack Reese's three-story house was the house I lived in until age 13. The descriptions of the place and Reese's memories of his family are pretty much real, if you substitute my family for his.

When I sat down to write a mystery novel and try to break into print in early 1985, I began with two things—the railroading neighborhood I grew up in and a dream I'd had of a mysterious woman who keeps returning to Jack Reese to be photographed in sexier and sexier costumes. When she disappears, the police visit him. I soon realized he didn't have the wherewithal to solve the case, so I came up with Detective Edward Harter. While Reese had a lot of my younger self in him, Harter had a lot of the older me—a skeptical attitude and an edge from years as a reporter. I gave him an apartment not far from Reese's house and had him go to the hotdog stands, hoagie shops and other places that I frequented (and still visit when I return to Cumberland).

Searching for a name for my city, I landed on Shawnee since the Shawnee Indians once claimed my region of Appalachian Maryland, West Virginia and western Pennsylvania. After all, the city wasn't really the Cumberland of the 1980s, but was the Cumberland of my boyhood, projected into the future, with a few West Virginia ingredients stirred in.

Partly due to its portrait of a recession in a mountain town and partly due to the sexy photography scenes, *Shawnee Alley Fire* became a minor hit in the summer of 1987. Rereading it for this edition, I realized how much I still like the book. I've always had a soft spot for it since it brought me a little acclaim, was nominated for a Shamus award and helped pay some of my sons' college bills. *Shawnee Alley* even earned me my first trip to Europe after rights were sold for foreign editions in France, Italy, Germany, Argentina and Spain.

I was finishing up *Shawnee Alley Fire* in November, 1985 when the events took place that inspired *Haunts*, my other novel set in the same city with the same detective. The spark was the reporting I did on the Flood of 1985 as news editor of *The Morgan Messenger* in Berkeley Springs, West Virginia, and *The Hancock News* across the raging Potomac River in Hancock, Maryland.

The flood unearthed some bones upriver in Hampshire County, West Virginia. While these turned out to be Indian remains, leading to an archeological dig, I wondered what would happen if a more recent burial had been uncovered. A story developed, again set in a blue-collar section of Shawnee. This time the neighborhood was close to the Chesapeake & Ohio Canal and the B&O Railroad shops where my grandfather worked. In my books, the canal is known as the Shawnee & Chesapeake and the railroad is renamed the Shawnee-Potomac.

Haunts, like *Shawnee Alley*, is full of descriptions of my version of Cumberland and the surrounding region. It begins with scenes of the 1985 Flood, including lines straight out of my newspaper reporting, and has its own set of social concerns. *Haunts* is as much a mountain family saga as a mystery and it's quite different from *Shawnee Alley*. If anyone ever cares to compare the original *Haunts* of 1990 with the 2008 version in this volume, they'll find it's now a tighter, tougher, darker story, as it always should have been. *Shawnee Alley Fire*, on the other hand, is as it was in 1987. I hope it speaks to today's hard times.

After *Haunts*, I faced the question of whether to try to do a series of Edward Harter mysteries set in Shawnee. Two of my favorite writers—Ed McBain and Arthur Conan Doyle—had done this, with McBain's 87th Precinct novels and, of course, Doyle's Sherlock Holmes. But others who influenced me, like Dashiell Hammett and James M. Cain, had avoided a series. I'd tried to avoid one too by writing *Blind Spring Rambler*, an historical mystery set in a 1923 coal town, between the two Shawnee books. Deciding against a third Shawnee novel, I pretty much put mystery writing aside in the early 1990s.

Since then, I've made a career of journalism and followed my head. I'm now editor of *The Morgan Messenger* and my editorials have won awards in a couple states. I've written thousands of words about American music and folklore, and I've done two books with regional themes. I've also written assorted ghost stories and a few other tales, which may be collected in book form one of these days. I haven't lost any sleep thinking too long or hard about Shawnee and Edward Harter.

Yet people still ask me about getting copies of the two Shawnee books and they still wonder when my new mystery novel will come out. So, to solve the first problem, here are *Shawnee Alley Fire* and the revised *Haunts* in one volume. As for when my next detective novel will see light, or if there will ever be another one, who knows? It's a mystery.

—John Douglas
Berkeley Springs, W. Va.
November 2008

SHAWNEE ALLEY FIRE

For men and women are not only themselves, they are also the region in which they were born, the city apartment or the farm in which they learnt to walk, the games they played as children, the old wives' tales they overheard, the food they ate, the schools they attended, the sports they followed, the poets they read, and the God they believed in. It is all these things that have made them what they are and these are things that you can't come to know by hearsay, you can only know them if you have lived them.

—W. Somerset Maugham, *The Razor's Edge*

JACK REESE

I

I'M ONLY HUMAN.

I noticed her nylon-brown legs before I saw her face.

I don't like to admit it, considering everything that's happened since that morning.

But I can plead partly innocent. I didn't notice her legs first simply because I like women's legs, which is no crime, or because she had fine ones, which she did.

You have to picture the scene to get it straight.

The house is built into the mountainside in such a way that the fierce slope of the fire-escape hill in front means you have to walk down five steps from the pavement to the level of the front porch.

I was standing on the porch, sifting through the bills the postman had brought, hoping for that check in the mail, when I heard her heels strike the sidewalk.

I glanced up just in time to see the bend of her knee as she stepped down. Not used to visits from classy ladies, or from ladies at all, for that matter, I wondered what was going on.

I'm not positive I ever got a reasonable answer.

You have to understand, I probably wouldn't have taken her job if I'd known what it involved.

No, that's not exactly right. Words give me trouble. That's why I'm not a writer.

Try again: I probably wouldn't have taken her job if I'd known what it involved—*and* if I hadn't been scrambling to make some sort of a living, waiting every day for that elusive check in the mail.

It was a hard-times fall, that fall of 1982. Not just for me, either. Shawnee, and most of the country, was sunk in a recession. They never called it a depression, though I can't explain the difference to you.

In the midst of it, she sneaked up on me.

Or *snuck* up on me, as Tattoo would say.

She came down the steps from the street and my eyes took her in like a camera panning upward.

High-heeled brown shoes strapped across trim ankles.

Loose tan skirt ending at mid-knee, above those good legs.

Chocolate sweater hiding the fullness of her breasts.

Tan jacket, matching the skirt, adding a businesslike reserve to her outfit.

Red lips, makeup immaculate, green eyes.

Brown hair to her shoulders and sort of flipped under at the ends.

"Are you the photographer, Jack Reese?" she asked in a calm voice I couldn't quite place. She had a certain Shawnee tone but it was overlaid with a studied precision, like she wanted to make it clear she knew her ABCs.

"Yeah," I answered. "What can I do for you?"

"Are you a *good* photographer?" she asked, giving me a wise smile to show she saw the ridiculousness of her question.

"On par with Ansel Adams." I smiled back.

Actually, I've never claimed to be the best camera clicker around. I'm surely not the most successful. Nor am I one of those guys who loads you down with chatter about shutter speeds and exposure times and darkroom expertise. I just do what I have to do to get the image I want on film. Then I do what I have to do to make a decent print of it. At these tasks, I'm more than competent.

"I probably don't need Ansel Adams. I'd just like a passport picture taken," she said.

"Sounds simple enough. Just a head shot?"

"That should do," she replied, her voice turning more like business.

"Come on in and we'll try it."

I opened the screen door and motioned her to enter. I was immediately embarrassed about leading her into the front room. Until I saw her standing in it, I'd forgotten the shape it was in. Not only did it need a new wallpapering, but the room itself was a full-scale mess. I'd furnished it sparely with secondhand odds and ends. Photos, books, magazines, catalogues, newspapers, and old mail were piled all over. A coat of dust was beginning to cover everything.

"I'm still getting set up," I explained.

"Did you just move in?" she asked. "I only today noticed your sign."

A month before, I'd attached the sign, rather like a shyster's shingle, to one of the wooden columns that held up the front porch roof. I'd been careful to hang it high enough so it could be seen from the street.

"I moved here in early August," I told her, deciding to cut short a story I'd been shortening with each retelling. "I used to live in this house when I was a kid and I recently came back to Shawnee." She didn't need to know more about me.

I led her around the staircase that rose up through the middle of the narrow house, bisecting each of the three floors into front and back rooms.

"The studio's a little neater," I said, flipping the light switch. "You can sit on the stool over there."

With careful steps, she crossed the worn rug to the stool. She scooped in the back of her skirt with her right hand and knelt to place her purse nearby. Then she seated herself on the stool, crossing her legs away from the camera and smoothing out her skirt. She moved like a woman used to wearing a dress, not jeans.

As she waited in almost formal silence, I went to work adjusting lights, until there were no shadows on her face or on the screen behind her. I'd done my best to make a simple studio out of what had once been a den and, in later years, a TV room. I'd left the space mostly empty of furniture and covered the windows so natural light didn't confuse the artificial light.

"How long will it take for you to have the photograph ready?" she asked, breaking the silence.

I stopped focusing the camera and looked out from behind the tripod. "How soon would you like it?"

"Tomorrow?" She folded her hands and rested them on her knee. She wore no wedding ring.

"No problem." I wasn't exactly overburdened with work. "I'll take three or four shots and you can pick out the one you want. Passport size, right?"

She nodded.

"Are you going away real soon?" I asked, trying to relax her.

She didn't answer, and I thought I sensed her tense. I guessed she just wanted to get the picture-taking over with. Some people are like that.

Her smile for the camera was different from the rather sly one she'd flashed when she'd asked if I was a good photographer. It was almost as demurely frozen as Mona Lisa's. Behind her eyeshadow and lashes, there was a wariness in her eyes that I'd seen before, that every camera clicker has seen at one time or another. The camera changed her personality. I could tell she didn't feel natural in front of its cocktail-party gaze.

"You really hate getting your picture taken, don't you?" I said after I'd clicked the fourth shot.

"Do you require a deposit or anything?" she asked, stepping off the stool.

"No, just a name."

"I'll be back tomorrow afternoon," she said, bending to pick up her purse.

Then, rapidly, she walked out, making her way without escort through the front room's rubble.

2

TATTOO WAS COMING up through the hilly yard when I went out onto the back porch that evening. A brown bag was swinging from his only hand.

He'd been nicknamed Tattoo by his railroad buddies because he'd come home from the Navy in World War II with a tattoo on his left forearm. It was of a girl in a slinky dress. Her body rippled when his muscle tensed. May had never liked it.

I only remembered the tattoo vaguely. I was still in elementary school when he'd lost the arm that some Tokyo artist had affixed it to.

"May had a craving for some ice cream," Tattoo called to me as he climbed the steps on his side of the porch. "You want some?"

"No. Thanks I just ate."

"Whatever you say," he said, opening his door and disappearing into the kitchen.

Tattoo and May had lived in the other side of the house since I'd been a kid. They were like uncle and aunt to me.

We often entered through our back doors because cutting through the alley and up the backyard eliminated a block of the steep, rising sidewalk out front. Besides, the old country people usually lived in their kitchens. Tattoo and May, like my grandfather and most of my older relatives, had come to Shawnee from the hills and hollers to work for the railroad years before. They'd brought with them a lot of ancient mountain ways—more than I'd ever been able to fathom.

I guess you'd call the house a "duplex," though I'd never heard the word until I was older, just as I never remember hearing the word *Appalachia* until I sat in a boring sociology class and listened to a flatland college professor play expert about life in the poor-man Appalachians. We ourselves always said we were from East Shawnee, or just Shawnee, or maybe "from the mountains," or—if really pressed—"from the Alleghenies."

I stepped off the porch and walked down through the yard, past the line where my mother had once hung out clothes. She'd always been so careful to bring in the laundry as soon as possible so the grit of the city and the tracks didn't cover it.

At the foot of the yard, by the alley, I leaned against the rusting Ford that had brought me home to Shawnee. The car sat in a space I had cleared and leveled for it. Once a fence had divided the yard from the alley, but it had tumbled down long ago.

The landlord should really rebuild it, I told myself.

Yet I hadn't.

Though it was well before seven, the streetlights in the alley were already fighting the dark. The October days were shortening toward winter.

Looking down the narrow blacktop-and-brick alley, I saw old Daniel sitting on his swing, as he often did. Past my house, the alley they officially called Baxter Street broadened out a trifle, and the lay of the land changed enough to allow a few houses to be built in a triangle between two more major streets. Daniel's was the nearest of the alley houses.

He'd seemed old as long as I could remember—so old I was surprised he was still breathing when I'd returned to the city. I imagine he'd only been in his late fifties when I was a kid playing ball in the alley, but to a kid, late fifties is ancient.

Shortly after I'd come home to Shawnee, I'd spent an August afternoon sitting on his porch swing with him. Daniel, maybe eighty-five, had watched the occasional car go by, momentarily breaking up the games of another generation of kids. That afternoon he'd spilled out one tale after another, some pretty salty. He was not at all the drab old man I'd once thought he was.

Slowly I'd tried to convince him to let me take his picture. He had been reluctant at first because he didn't understand why, but he finally gave in. I'd been happy with the portrait, with the way the lines were strip-mined into his face while the eyes retained a coal-hard purity.

He was a proud man in the way that old working-class mountaineers could be, like my grandfather had been, like Tattoo was. He was also lonely. He had no May, and no relatives came to visit, only a few old railroad pals and, a couple of times a week, the woman who drove a van around Shawnee, delivering hot lunches to the elderly for the Commission on Aging.

He'd told me he hadn't wanted the lunches at first, not liking the idea of someone taking care of him. But then a pretty young girl had come and talked to him and told him how he'd worked and paid taxes all those years, so he might as well enjoy it. Railroad retirement not being exactly the top-of-the-line executive plan, he'd given in.

I looked away from Daniel's porch and turned toward my own house, studying its outline against the darkening sky.

I'd inherited the three-story structure from my grandfather. It was laid out in such a way that if you entered through the back door, you were in the kitchen, which was below street level on the front side. Tattoo's half of the house was a mirror image of mine.

Off the kitchen was the bathroom, installed indoors about the time I was born. Aside the kitchen was a half-basement. Dug right into the mountain rock, it got wet in heavy storms. I'd jerry-built a darkroom in the basement, using the old laundry tubs.

Up the dark staircase and you got to the main floor, where I'd been trying to establish the photography business.

Up the final flight and there were two bedrooms, one on each side of the steps, not a safe arrangement for sleepwalkers.

The house was the reason I'd moved back to Shawnee after fifteen years of living away. The house and the recession.

I'd lost a good chunk of my income in May when the small magazine I'd been working for had folded under the weight of lost advertisers, fewer readers, and postal-rate hikes. While the magazine had never paid me a fortune, it had given me a small base income to operate from, as well as the excuse to go places and the time to freelance. Over the years, I'd managed to find a string of publications, mostly tiny and specialized, to sell photos to. Still, without a regular paycheck coming in, it was hard to keep up with big-city costs. I grew to depend more and more on the rent checks from my grandfather's house in Shawnee.

Then, in mid-July, I'd gotten the letter. The guy who'd been renting one side of the house had been laid off from Shawnee Steel with no prospects of being called back. He'd decided to pack up his family and head for the Sunbelt—Florida, Texas or California. He wasn't sure where. He just wanted to get out before his savings disappeared and winter struck.

So he'd played Okie and driven off.

Spurred by the moment, I'd decided to move too. I had nothing to lose. With a place to live for free in the mountains and a few magazine contacts, I figured I'd wait out the depression. Shawnee beckoned.

Since then, I'd eaten a lot of tomato sandwiches, as my grandfather told me they had in the 1930s Big One. The tomato plants had been left by the former tenant.

I'd tried to be frugal. Ben Franklin would have loved me. About the only luxury I spent money on was film, and that's hardly a luxury to a photographer.

I spent a lot of my days simply roaming Shawnee, clicking my camera at old railroaders like Daniel, at unemployment lines, at derelict buildings, at everything I saw around me. I was determined to document the Shawnee of the 1980s in the same way Walker Evans the Miraculous had once pointed his camera at the stoic faces of dust bowlers and sharecroppers and allowed their black-and-white angularity and their proud, scared eyes to speak for themselves.

Nothing *fancy,* you understand. Nothing too slick.

I clicked roll after roll, at first not sure what I'd ever do with them. They all blended, click after click, frame after frame, in my head, like photos in a Muybridge series.

Eadweard Muybridge is another of my black-and-white heroes, even if he spelled his first name weird.

Story is, he was hired to settle a bet by the governor of California. (Not Ronald Reagan—this was in the 1880s.) Muybridge was asked to prove if there really was a moment in time when all four hooves of a racing horse were off the ground. He clicked one shot after another of a running steed with a contraption he had devised for the occasion, showing how each motion flowed into the next.

Muybridge went on to trap other animals, including people, in action. He did a series of a naked lady kicking a pith helmet, which I like to pretend was his social commentary on Queen Victoria's British Empire. The lady faces us—faces Muybridge's camera—full sex, full pubic hair, long before *Playboy*—and raises high her fleshy thigh, and her breasts bob slightly and the pith helmet flies away from her foot and finally falls to the floor, like Newton's apple. Then she turns away from us—away from the camera—and picks up the helmet and kicks it again to show off the flex of her buttocks.

Take any photo from the series, let it kick on its own, and you can imagine the motions that came before and after.

Any picture could really be the start or the end.

Just actions trapped in time and space by the camera.

Like words, time and space give me trouble.

My problems with words, space, and time only grew more complicated after I moved back to Shawnee.

3

"AIN'T IT A MANGLED, screwed-up mess?" declared Tattoo.

I mumbled agreement but kept on peering through the camera hole, trying to line up a good shot of the scrap-metal engine, the twisted track.

"Why bother with the picture?" he asked. "They won't use it anyway."

"Then why did Metling call me out of bed to run out here?"

"They're just going through the motions, Jack."

I looked out from behind the camera. "Tell me what you're trying to say. I like it much better when you're blunt than when you hint around."

While Tattoo could ramble on with the best of the old railroaders, he could also be damn blunt.

He scrunched up his lips and rubbed at the stump of his left arm before he spoke. "I've lived in this city all my life and I know the Shawnee—Potomac don't get no bum publicity in *The News*. Notice they sent you out here, not one of their regular camera wielders. They'll only put your picture in the paper if they can pin this wreck on some poor working slob. Employee error, they call it, like some fellow made a crap wheel on purpose, or some engineer set out to kill hisself. If it turns out this thing was caused by bad tracks, the company'll get touchy and nothing'll be in the goddamn paper."

"Not my decision," I said, clicking my third shot of the flopped over, partly crushed diesel. "I'll get paid whether they use my photos or not. Besides, the engineer didn't die. No one died. Tell the truth. Have you got a grudge against *The News?*"

"I remember too good all those damn editorials they used to write when the union went out on strike. You'd think we was communists. It's the kind of thing stays with you a long time, like a fierce burn. When you think back on it, you get hurt and mad all over again."

"I never wrote any of those editorials. I doubt Metling did either. He's not that old."

"But would he?"

I had no answer. I didn't know what Metling would or wouldn't write, or what *The News* would print if labor troubles arose.

Labor troubles: no such thing, the old union men used to say. There are only capitalist troubles. Fat chance of there being capitalist—or labor—troubles in 1982, when half the U.S. feared joining the unemployment lines even if they were *complacent* employees.

Still, the old men remembered the old times and I should have remembered they remembered. Their anger burned with a low flame that could be turned up at the flick of a hand.

I maneuvered away from Tattoo so I could catch the engine at a different angle. I wanted to show the cab on its side, with the arching loop of ribbon rail pushed out from the ties behind it.

I was glad I hadn't had to decide whether or not to show the bleeding, moaning engineer being removed from the wreckage. Maybe that's why I wasn't a world-renowned photographer. I don't normally go for the blood. I can't stand the television footage of the wailing masses at Mideast funerals, or the newsman who pushes a microphone in some griever's face and says, "What did you think when you saw your husband crushed in the garbage compactor?"

I'd had no regrets that the state police and railroad bulls had kept us back from the wreck until there were no accident victims to see.

The police had said the engineer was the only one seriously hurt, that the others had walked away under their own power. The engineer had been ambulanced to Shawnee City Hospital. I guessed Metling would send a *News* reporter there to learn his condition, and that someone was already working to uncover the story of what had caused the derailment in the first place.

I snapped another picture.

"Didn't your Grandfather Reese die in a train wreck?" asked Tattoo.

I nodded. He knew the story but he was always asking questions like that. Whether he was trying to fill in gaps in his knowledge or rubbing the scab off memories to make people remember the wounds, I didn't know.

Actually, Tattoo probably knew more than anyone else about the histories of Shawnee's railroading families. He'd worked hard for the union much of his life, though he'd never held a cushy leadership job. After he'd lost his arm in the accident, he'd had plenty of time to collect his data.

They'd gotten him back to work as fast as they could. Shawnee-Potomac policy was that it was better for a man to sit on the job all day than to sit at home. There was always some chore even an injured man could do. Maybe sort out a bin of screws and bolts. By keeping them on the job, the company could point to signs proclaiming **THIS DIVISION HAS LOST ONLY 9 MANPOWER DAYS DUE TO INJURY OR ACCIDENT THIS YEAR.**

At first they'd installed Tattoo in one of those shanties by the downtown tracks, where, for eight hours a day, he sat and talked with the older railroad men who dropped in. The only time the conversation stopped was when he had to step outside and hold up traffic to let a train go through the heart of town. Then, in the early 1960s, they'd replaced the signmen with traffic lights and assigned them to odd jobs until they could take early retirement or disability or whatever.

"How did your grandfather die?" probed Tattoo.

"You know it better than I do, I'm sure. It was long before I was born. Not long after World War One. Not exactly the stuff of Casey Jones ballads."

"They didn't write no ballads about most men," he said.

"Well, they tell me he was an engineer. He never got out of the South Shawnee yards that night. Somebody had switched two freights onto the same track. It was a head-on collision. They weren't going fast, but I suppose it was fast enough that the engines were melted together by the heat of the blood."

I walked away from him again.

From straight in front of the long freight, I aimed down the right side, trying to capture the accordion folds of the upset and tilted cars. At the far end of the camera's depth of field, a new Japanese truck was hanging two wheels off the upper deck of an automobile carrier, ready at the slightest tremor to kamikaze into the gravel alongside the tracks.

This was the photo.

I clicked again to cover myself. Then again.

If Metling didn't like it, if Tattoo was right that he'd be careful about what he used, then I'd find another market for it. Since August, I'd sold a few photos to a small rail-lore magazine.

Another possible project had also begun to grow in my mind: *a book.*

Much worse photographers than I had put out photo books on every inconceivable subject in the last decade. Some of them had so little reason.

So why not a picture book about trains or Shawnee railroaders or 1980s' hard times?

Maybe.

At least it gave me something to pretend I was doing, when what I was really doing was biding time, walking the streets, clicking a camera and hoping that if I walked long and far enough, I'd get somewhere.

Lifting the camera from around my neck and then slipping the strap over my shoulder, I turned to Tattoo. "You ready to go?"

"I been ready," he said.

We walked through the weeds toward the Ford parked at the edge of the highway.

"Is it ten yet?" I asked. I don't wear a watch myself.

In one of his odd quirks, he raised his right wrist to eye level rather than look down. "Just after."

"Good, I've got plenty of time to get these pictures made." Being a morning paper, *The News* didn't really get serious until after supper.

"Give my best to kindly Mr. Metling when you deliver them," Tattoo said sarcastically as we climbed into the car.

I started the Ford up. After making a U-turn onto the highway, I accelerated toward town, thinking about how visiting the wreck had brought back so many buried things—the oral traditions of head-on tragedy, the anger still inside the old men. I seemed to always be digging up buried elements as I made my way around Shawnee.

I'd only driven a mile or so when suddenly, on impulse, I stopped the car, grabbed the camera from the seat beside me, and climbed out. Tattoo hung his head out the window and watched me.

For some reason, I took a photo of a black-and-white sign:

SHAWNEE

Shawnee was established in 1754 when
a fort was built to protect settlers from
raids by the Shawnee Indians who hunted
and camped here before the white man.
During the Civil War, Shawnee was
crucial to the Union because *of its rail*
and canal industries, and because Shawnee
offers the easiest land route through
the mountains to the West.
Long the railroad hub of the Alleghenies,
Shawnee was the second largest city in
the state until 1959.
The Chamber of Commerce
Welcomes You

4

THE FORD WAS running fine for a seven-year-old car with over 125,000 miles on it. It had had plenty of rest. I'd only driven it a couple times a week since coming back to Shawnee. I had little need for a car, though I knew life would be tougher without one.

I also knew life would be cheaper without one.

When I was a kid, we'd survived without wheels. It was possible to walk anywhere in Shawnee worth going to. We'd walked up the fifty-percent grade to school. We'd walked downtown to stores and movies. We'd hiked through the patches of woods in the unusable gullies between hillsides. If we went far enough through the tunnel of trees, we'd come out the other end into the orchard countryside, where we'd swipe Stark Delicious apples, the ones with the bumpy bottoms.

Shawnee was—*is*—a small city with less than forty thousand people. Twenty years before, there'd scarcely been any suburbs, though it had sprawled some since, as all towns seem to have. The guts of the city hadn't physically changed so drastically in the years I'd been away, though.

Driving up the Avenue that Tuesday morning, I noticed the old ladies still wore flowery housedresses and rested on their stoops with brooms in their hands. I wondered if they still baked bread. Probably, like May, only rarely. My great-aunt had been one of the last of the great household bakers. She'd make loaves all day Thursday, and I'd deliver them for her after school, collecting a quarter from each customer.

The Avenue, the main drag between the South Shawnee rail complex and my neighborhood, was still lined with narrow brick row houses, two or three stories tall. I'd been born in one of them.

No, that's not true. I was really born in Shawnee City Hospital, where the wounded engineer had been taken. I was born premature, they tell me, and I was only moved into the row house when they let me out of the hospital incubator. A couple of years later, after my father was sent to Korea, my mother and I moved up the hill to share her father's house.

At the traffic light, I turned the corner where her father, my grandfather, had sometimes boarded what he never stopped calling "the streetcar." It took him to his job repairing railroad cars in the South Shawnee shops.

A short distance up the grade, I turned right again, into the alley, steering the Ford past a few small backyards until I reached my own. I pulled out of the alley and into my parking place. I climbed out from behind the wheel and gave the car a pat for its good work.

Tattoo gave a right-handed wave to old Daniel, who was already out on his porch for the day. Then we hiked up the hill toward our common back porch.

"You want to come in for coffee?" he asked me. "May might take pity on you and feed you some breakfast."

He was always offering me breakfast, or ice cream, or dinner. Maybe he thought I was too skinny. Or maybe it was just the way the old people had of making food a communal event, of always wanting to feed you a piece of cake or a cookie. It had been so all my life.

"No, I've got a pot full at home. There's a woman coming to pick up a passport picture sometime today. And I better get these negatives started for the paper," I said.

We split up at the porch, him going left and up his steps, me heading right and up mine. I began feeling guilty about turning him down twice in a row. Just before he went in his door, I called, "How about breakfast tomorrow? Can you swing that?"

"Possible probable," he said in a gruff put-on voice. "If you ain't over by nine, I'll rise you up."

He obviously knew my sleeping habits.

I WAS SITTING in the front room at the scratched-up table I used for a desk, writing a letter to send with my next batch of photos to the railroad magazine, when she rang the bell.

She was wearing a trench coat, or whatever the female version of a trench coat is called. It made her look even more businesslike than the matching skirt and jacket of Monday.

"Are my photos ready?" she asked.

"Yeah."

I picked up an envelope from the table and handed it to her. She opened the flap carefully, as if she were dreading it, and took out the prints. Tilting each one toward and away from the light, she looked them over slowly, as customers often do when they're studying themselves trapped on paper.

"I imagine they look like me," she finally said.

"You look better in person, but they're not bad. You're just a little nervous around the mouth."

'They could be worse. How much do I owe you?"

"Pick the one you want. For a photo I usually charge—"

She cut me off. "I'll take them all."

Good deal. I needed more customers like her.

I told her the grand total and she placed her handbag on the table, took out her billfold, and counted out the cash.

"How does one stop being 'a little nervous around the mouth' in photographs?" she asked as she put the photos and her billfold back in her purse.

"I suppose by losing the fear that many people have of the camera. And by seeing yourself look good in a photo for a change."

"How does one go about losing the fear of the camera?" she asked, glancing at me as she closed her purse. All those *one*'s she used made it seem as if she were speaking about someone else.

"You could get your picture taken more often." I laughed. I sounded like a salesman.

She never cracked a smile. "Can you take some more now?"

"Sure, that's what I do."

Without another word, she led me back to the studio. There, she put her bag on the floor by the wall and took off her coat. After searching for a clean place to stow it, she simply dropped it on top of her purse.

I was amazed how different she looked now than she had the morning before. No longer the prim businesswoman, she was costumed like a young girl. But not like a modern girl. Like a Victorian one almost. No wonder she'd come in wearing the trench coat.

She was wearing a white dress that ended just below her knee. The loose top disguised her bustline. Above her breasts and at her wrists was lace. Her stockings were a sheer white, allowing the flesh of her legs to shine through just a little. She had on flat silvery slippers. Her makeup, too, was lighter, almost nonexistent, though there was a sort of silver sheen around her green eyes.

She reached up and brushed her hand through her hair so it fluffed a little and appeared less perfect. Looking slightly embarrassed, she said, "I always seem so hard and angular in pictures. I wanted to try something else."

"You're paying," I said. "It's your business. Some people dress up like cowboys and saloon girls and get their pictures snapped in a booth at the beach. If you ask me, this is much classier."

"Can you get all of me in?" she asked, ignoring my comments.

I looked through the camera. "As long as you stay around the stool at that end of the room."

She slid up on the stool and turned to her left a bit. She knew her best side.

"Stop worrying about the camera," I said as I lined up the shot. "Just forget it. You know what you want to look like. Just act it out. Choose a position, an angle, where you feel comfortable, in control. Don't be afraid to smile or move or throw your head back or anything else. Movement takes the self-consciousness out of it."

While she was looking my way, I clicked the first picture. I knew right off she wasn't ready. The moment she saw me move, her slight embarrassment had become outright camera shyness.

"Don't flinch," I said. "Remember, you want a picture of yourself. Help me out."

"Can't I be the one to say 'Cheese'?" she asked distantly. "Can't I tell you when to do it?"

"Sure," I said, realizing immediately it was a game I might be able to use again.

She looked to her left again, showing off her profile. Settling herself silently, she rested her hands in the lap of the white skirt and modestly crossed her ankles.

"Now," she softly instructed after a minute or so. "Take my picture now."

Click.

"Again."

Click.

Without budging her body, she tilted her head toward me, lifted her chin high, and flashed me a smile that was close to the wise, almost cynical one she'd first showed me the morning before.

"Now."

Click.

Lowering her chin and positioning her mouth into something of a pout, she almost commanded, "Now."

Click.

Then she gently slid off the stool and stood beside it, her right hand resting on the seat. She crossed her right ankle lazily in front of her left.

"Now."

Click.

Another minute went by while she stood there, obviously figuring out what to do next. Then, moving into action, she crouched down behind the stool. Her hands gripping the rungs, she said, "Now."

Click.

She poked her head out from behind the left side of the stool.

"Now."

Click.

Playing hide-and-seek, she moved her head behind the stool once more and then inched it out on the right side.

"Now."

Click.

She stood up and climbed back on the stool slowly, balancing herself so she could raise her heels to the seat. The white skirt slid playfully up her thighs. She put her pale arms around her white-stockinged legs and pulled them tightly toward her.

"Now."

Click.

"Again."

Click.

She lowered her legs and stared spacily in my direction for an instant. Then she squirmed on the wooden seat, adjusting her legs until they were hanging down on either side of the stool.

Facing me head-on, she said, “Now.”

Click.

She began swinging her legs, like a bored little girl, swinging them higher each time, higher and higher, until she was kicking like a cancan dancer, bad little girl in white, lips separated so that her white teeth showed.

“Now.”

Click.

Kicking higher and higher, her bare thighs flashing with each kick.

“Now, Jack Reese.”

Click.

“Again.”

Click.

She stopped kicking, stopped moving altogether, and fell into an almost meditative calm. Eventually she climbed off the stool and picked up her coat.

“I’ll be back for my pictures tomorrow,” she said as she covered her costume with the trench coat.

She reached for her pocketbook and left.

I stood behind the camera, confused.

5

I WAS STILL ASLEEP when the phone rang Wednesday morning. How many times the thing had rung, I had no idea. The sound had begun somewhere deep down in my dream, like a fading ambulance siren or a distant fire alarm.

"You coming over for breakfast or not?" Tattoo growled after I'd managed to struggle down the steps to the phone.

"On my way," I mumbled.

Back upstairs, I put on the uniform I'd worn all fall—khaki pants and a flannel shirt. I hurried down to the kitchen and into the bathroom to splash water on my face, brush my teeth, and run a comb through my hair. I stared at the face reflected in the mirror. I looked almost awake. No better, no worse-looking than usual.

Then I went out my back door and walked around to Tattoo's, going inside the kitchen after I'd given a hard rap to announce myself.

He was puttering around with coffee cups and May was hefting a heavy iron skillet, about to pour bacon grease in a can.

"Knew I'd have to call you," he said, handing me a cup before I even sat down.

"That's what phones are for, I guess." At least that was why I had one, though like the old Ford I could scarcely afford it. Modern conveniences cost a bundle.

I sipped at the coffee and felt my head begin to clear as soon as the liquid slid down my throat.

"Were you up late?" asked May as she cracked an egg on the edge of the skillet and artfully dropped the insides onto the hot black iron. The orange yoke remained unbroken and bravely rounded, not like some of the things I do to eggs. "You want one or two?"

"Two eggs. Yeah, I was up a lot of the night. I ended up walking around downtown for hours after I delivered my pictures to *The News.* When I got back, I couldn't sleep, so I worked in the darkroom a while."

"Something special?" she asked.

"No," I answered, deciding not to tell her about the woman in the trench coat.

"Downtown's not the same as it used to be, is it?" She carefully flipped over one of the eggs in the skillet. "It's downright sad down there."

I took another sip of coffee. "It's surely not the same as when I was growing up, when my mother worked at Levine's."

"Levine's is long gone," Tattoo said grumpily, pouring himself another cup of what he often called "mocha java." He filled mine to the top again. "All the stores that didn't close up altogether moved out to the shopping center ten years ago. You can hardly buy a pair of shoelaces."

"They asked me if I wanted to work in the store at the shopping center when the drugstore closed two years ago," said May. "I told them I was old enough to retire and get my Social Security. I worked in that store downtown for over forty years. Didn't want to have to worry how I'd get out to the shopping center every day. It's hard enough to get out there to market once a week."

She lifted the skillet and brought it over to the table. With a metal spatula, she placed two perfect overlight eggs on my plate beside four strips of bacon. Then she put eggs on Tattoo's plate and her own. Tattoo spread butter on the last two pieces of hot toast and handed them out.

"It really is hard on people now that all the corner groceries are closed," said May, sitting down. "I don't know what we'd do without you and your car. Can't walk any place anymore. I used to like to walk. Your mother and me'd have a good old time jabbering about our day when we'd walk home together."

"I remember."

I could still picture her stocky body moving up the long hill of Thomas Street after the downtown stores closed at five o'clock. Sometimes I'd meet my mother and her at Bernhardt's, at the corner of our street and the Avenue. Bernhardt's stayed open until six so people could buy groceries on their way home from work. My aunt worked behind the counter and filled in as butcher when Bernhardt was on a drunk. Sometimes I'd earn movie money by stocking cans on the high narrow shelves or filling up the bins of kidney beans, rice, flour, fig newtons.

Christ, only thirty-four and already nostalgic.

"You're awful quiet this morning," said Tattoo between mouthfuls. "I guess you seen your picture on the front page of *The News?"*

"No. You got one?" I asked.

May turned her thick body and grabbed the paper off the cupboard behind her. There at the top of the front page was the photo of the train wreck that Metling had liked.

The evening before I'd spread my shots across his desk and waited for a response. "Pretty good," he'd finally said, which was heavy praise from him. Only about forty, he had the cranky manner of a newspaperman who'd been at it a long time and wasn't easily impressed. "I like the one with the truck hanging in the air. I'll see you get a few extra dollars for running out there."

"The story ain't good, though," said Tattoo, rapping the page with his index finger.

ENGINEER INJURED IN DERAILMENT read the headline. According to *The News,* the engineer—one Harry Bryson, age thirty-one—was in stable condition at Shawnee City Hospital. The information was sketchy at best. Maybe that's how Metling had intended it. Bryson's injuries weren't spelled out. Nor was the cause of the accident, which was said to be under investigation by Shawnee-Potomac authorities.

"That's the last we'll hear of that story," proclaimed Tattoo.

"You know him—Harry Bryson?" I asked.

"I know the family. Used to work with his daddy."

"His mother worked awhile at the drugstore with me," said May.

"Any idea how seriously he's hurt?"

"He's lost a leg," said Tattoo.

I looked across the table at him. Him, with his arm missing from another railroad accident. I didn't know what to say and he volunteered nothing further.

"You going to be working full-time now for the newspaper?" May asked me.

"I don't plan to. No one's asked me to. Metling only calls when he can't get one of his staffers to do a job. I get most of the junk work. Last night he gave me an assignment I really don't want."

"What's that?"

"Hell, tomorrow night I'm supposed to get a picture of some preachers giving an award to their favorite congressman, Charles Whitford Canley."

"Son of a bitch, just like his daddy was. They kiss rich asses and hand the job down, father to son."

"Someone votes for them, Henry," said May. She always refused to call him Tattoo.

"You don't have to complain to me," I said. "I don't want to do it, but I don't know how to get out of it, short of putting myself out of any future jobs with *The News.* My grandfather's probably screaming at me from his grave."

"Why's a picture of Canley and some preachers have to be in the paper anyways?" asked Tattoo.

"Metling had mixed feelings, he said, but he guessed it was news," I answered.

"I told you about that paper! All them politicalized preachers ain't nothing but Sadducees and Pharisees like in the Bible. Those Billy-Sunday boys used to preach against the union like we was godless heathens. They probably still do."

"God knows the good preachers from the bum ones," said May.

"I hope he can tell the difference," said Tattoo.

"Reverend Ruffing's a good man," she said.

"He's all right," Tattoo admitted.

Reverend Ruffing was the pastor at the Methodist Church down the street where May went each Sunday morning, where I'd gone as a kid.

"He's started a food bank to help out-of-work people," she said.

"Somebody's got to help them," said Tattoo. "What's the president done but toss out a little cheese and butter that the taxpayer's already paid for?"

I recalled the long lines of people waiting for cheese and butter outside the handout center, which had once been the biggest movie theater downtown. The theater lobby had become a registration room, while the aisles contained boxes of surplus dairy products. I'd clicked my pictures of the line from the other side of the street, not really wanting to show faces in close-up, but only to show the scope of the hard times. Once a line like that would have been waiting to see a CinemaScope blockbuster. Now it was waiting for charity.

"We're lucky we all ain't back in sweatshops," said Tattoo angrily. "These young guys that work for the railroad now, they don't remember. They all voted 'servative 'cause they liked all that talk of cutting taxes. But whose taxes got cut? The big shots. Those boys don't remember the old battles. They think there always was decent wages and benefits, since there has been as long as they been around. Well, it's all ending. Look at Shawnee Steel, all those men who worked there all their lives out of work. And what do they tell them? Go to computer school. There's plenty of jobs in *The Washington Post.* There's lots of service jobs. *Service jobs,* they call them. I call them servants."

"Calm down, Henry," said May, staring across the table at the man she'd lived with for thirty-five years. "You're retired now. God is good."

"Yeah, they can't take the railroad retirement or the Social Security or the Medicare away. They can call Roosevelt the devil all they want and blame him for everything that's gone wrong for fifty years, but where would we be without him? He wasn't just no tin man with an actor's voice. FDR had a heart. He didn't make men waitresses. He put them to work building power dams and making parks. What if he hadn't started Social Security and the farmer subsidies that paid for all them goddamn five-pound hunks of cheese? And Eleanor, they make fun of her, but she'd go all over helping people. She'd go to coal towns and square dance with the miners at night. We ain't got no one like them no more. Instead, we got flag-wavers dressed in evening gowns standing in pulpits."

As his face grew redder and his voice got louder, I felt crummier and crummier that I'd let Metling con me into taking a picture of Congressman Charles Whitford Canley getting patted on the ass by a group of ministers.

When I got the chance, I said my good-byes and went next door.

6

I'D JUST ABOUT GIVEN UP ON HER.

The streetlights were on and it was almost completely dark. I figured she wasn't coming.

Waiting for her, I'd whittled away the afternoon. For a while I'd sat on the front porch, but I'd gone inside when all the school kids started pouring down the hill like gutter water in flood season, with all their horseplay and clatter and their contagious happiness about being out of prison for the rest of the day. It just hadn't fit my mood.

Inside, I'd spent a good hour trying to straighten up my desk and the clutter of the front room to make it more presentable to her . . . and to other customers.

Waiting, I'd looked again through the photos of her in the white little-girl costume. For a moment, I'd felt a little like Charles Lutwidge Dodgson, alias Lewis Carroll. Aside from writing *Alice's Adventures in Wonderland* and *Through the Looking Glass,* that Victorian gentleman was known to dress up little girls and click their pictures in his studio at Christ Church.

I won't comment on his motives, but he wasn't a bad photographer. His girls often illustrated literary scenes. One was caped as Little Red Riding Hood, with no wolf in evidence. In another, Alice Pleasance Liddell, Carroll's inspiration for the famous Alice, was done up as "The Little Beggar Maid," ragged child of working-class English streets. The rags hardly clung to her shoulders, leaving her chest almost naked.

But, unlike Carroll, I was not fascinated by little girls. I'd dressed up no one. I'd merely hung out a shingle and she'd come to me, whoever she was.

Why? What kind of fantasy was she working out?.

Shaking off the questions, I'd gone downstairs, cooked myself a couple of sausage-and-egg sandwiches, sat at the kitchen table a while, and flipped through the latest crop of magazines to see if I was missing any picture angles. Then I'd cleaned up my mess and stepped into the basement to sort through the negatives on the darkroom drying line.

WHEN SHE FINALLY SHOWED UP, she was wearing the same coat as the day before. She seemed slightly ill at ease as she looked through the prints of Tuesday's session. She stared a little longer at the one of her legs lifted high in the air. Then she hurriedly stuffed the photos in her purse, paid me my fee in cash, and stood there silently, like she was deciding what to do next.

"Are the pictures okay?" I asked, prodding her.

She nodded. Then she softly said, "You didn't give me the negatives. I'd like *all* my negatives, always."

"I'll be right back."

I went downstairs, pulled the negatives from the two sessions off the clothesline, slid them in a glassine envelope, and headed back upstairs.

She was no longer in the front room. "I'm back here," she called when she realized I didn't know where she was.

Again she surprised me.

She had taken off the trench coat and was standing on stiletto red heels in the middle of my studio. She was wearing a pink dress.

Not just any pink, but the pinkest blushingest pink.

Not just any dress, but one of those sheeny tight-fitting ones with a low-cut top, straight out of the late fifties.

I was at a loss for words as I handed her the negatives, and simply stared at her new costume as she carefully bent down, her knees together, and placed the glassine envelope in her bag.

She couldn't help but notice my stare. "This dress was my mother's," she explained as she stood up. "I always liked clothes like this. They were made for women's bodies."

I chanced it. "It certainly looks like they were made for yours . . . Who are you anyway?"

"Just a woman paying you to have her picture taken, as she wants it taken." There was no hint of nervousness in her voice. "Don't ask any more questions. You do have film in your camera?"

"Always. I take one roll out and put another in."

Her tongue flicked out to wet her shiny red lips and her green eyes grew serious beneath the dark eye shadow and long lashes. "Let's not waste time then."

"Whatever you say."

I went over to the tripod, adjusted lights, and began to slowly focus the camera while she turned away, stepped to the stool, and positioned herself on the edge of the seat, her thin red heels jabbing into the threadbare carpet. Her costume was perfect in every detail, right down to the seamed stockings. Had she found those in her mother's closet, too?

"Aren't you ready?" she asked, tenseness starting to creep into her voice.

"Yeah. Tell me when."

"Now."

Click.

She slid up onto the stool and crossed her legs inside the tight skirt. Looking straight at the camera, with not a glimmer of softness or smile, she said, "Now."

Click.

She moved a little so that what she believed was her good side was in profile. Her skirt rode above her knee when she moved.

"Now."

Click.

She raised her right arm so that her long red fingernails rested gently against her powdered and rouged right cheek. Light reflected from the large bracelet on her thin wrist. Whether the bracelet was real or costume, hers or her mother's, it went well with the dress, as did the long glittering earrings.

"Take it now."

Click.

"Again."

Click.

Holding down her skirt, she slid off the stool and moved behind it, folded her hands, and calmly positioned them on the seat in front of her.

"Now."

Click.

She leaned forward so that her elbows rested on the seat.

"Now."

Click.

Her breasts swelled out from the top of the pink dress.

"Take it now."

Click.

With small steps, she walked around to the front of the stool, turned her back to me, and rather coyly stared over her bare shoulder toward the camera lens.

"Take it now."

Click.

She turned once more and carelessly slid up onto the stool, her skirt rising high on her thighs, the dark rings at the top of her stockings showing.

"Take it now."

Click.

She hooked her high heels behind a stool rung, her knees moving apart.

"Now."

Click.

For a long moment, she seemed lost in her thoughts, in her fantasies. Then she reached behind her, her breasts pushing forward with the action, and unzipped the dress, letting the top of it fall toward her waist. A sheer pink strapless bra held back her breasts.

"Take it now."

Click.

She slid off the stool and pushed the tight dress down to her ankles. A lacy pink half-slip covered her from waist to knee As she lifted her right leg to step out of the dress, she said, "Take it."

Click.

She bent down, her breasts almost tumbling out of her pink brassiere, and tossed the dress on top of her coat and purse. Then she slid the slip off, added it to the pile, and turned back to face the camera.

"Take me now."

Click.

She reached up and fluffed her brown hair. She stood so that her legs made an inverted V and put her hands on her waist, on the elastic waistband of pink lingerie-catalog underpants, slit open at the sides. *Her mother's?*

"Take me now."

Click.

Sitting on the stool again, she angled her body to the left, crossing her legs so that the slit underpants fell open at the side. The black strap of her garterbelt stretched across her white thigh.

"Take me now."

Click.

Moving again, she slid off the stool and turned her back to me, bent her leg at the knee, and glanced over her shoulder and then down at her calf, as if to see if the fine black line of the seam was straight. The stockings were so sheer that only the seams and the dark rings around her white thighs gave away the fact she wasn't barelegged.

"Take me now."

Click.

Reaching behind her, she slid down the slitted panties so her buttock showed, her upper thighs white against the black garter strap.

"Now."

Click.

She turned to face front. Her long thin fingers pushed the right side of her panties to the left, exposing just the slightest curl of dark brown pubic hair. She slid her red-nailed fingers inside the silk.

"Take me now."

Click.

"Take me again."

The camera wouldn't click.

I tried again. No luck.

"I've got to change film," I told her.

As I rewound the roll, she stood in place, her hand inside her panties, eyes closed, legs apart, swaying on her high red heels.

I took the first roll out and hurried to put another in, not wanting to break her mood, not wanting her to stop. But I was either too slow or she had second thoughts. From across the room, I could almost feel her relax.

Opening her eyes, she asked, "Where's your bathroom?"

"Downstairs, off the kitchen."

She picked up her slip, her dress, her coat and her purse, and almost ran from the room. The sound of her heels grew more distant, until I heard the bathroom door close.

Feeling a little weak, I crossed the room and sat on the stool, waiting for her to come back. Finally, I heard the bathroom door open, then footsteps cross the kitchen linoleum. Then the back door opened and closed.

I didn't react for a minute, but eventually I stood up and ran down the steps and out the kitchen door and down the hilly backyard toward the alley.

I couldn't see anyone.

She'd certainly disappeared fast enough. Either she knew the alley as well as I did, or she had a car nearby. Or she could fly.

I stared up the alley toward old Daniel's porch, wondering if he was sitting there alone in the dark, if he'd seen her run by, if he could tell me the direction she had fled. But he wasn't outside. The downstairs lights were on inside his square two-story frame house. He was probably watching TV or doing whatever old men do at night.

Just as well. I didn't want to have to explain anything to him. I hadn't mentioned her to Tattoo either, except to say I was making a passport photo for a woman.

Passport photo. Was she really going off to some exotic land, or had that just been to check me out? I was fairly sure I knew the answer.

I was also sure she'd be back. Without a doubt. She'd been careful not to leave any of the first batch of negatives. She wouldn't think of leaving behind tonight's.

I paused for a moment and pondered it. If she weren't so damn serious, it could almost have been funny. Then again, perhaps a whole new field of endeavor was opening up for me. I should change my sign:

SPECIALIST IN CAPTURING FANTASIES
Come as you are, or as you would be

A car turned into the alley, its headlights swinging with the turning vehicle until they were shooting straight down the much patched and potholed lane. I watched it come closer and closer, not realizing until it was even with me that it was a police car cruising on night patrol. The cop looked my way as he drove by.

So, they still did that.

When I was a kid, a police car had come down the alley nearly every night shortly after ten o'clock, the city curfew for kids under sixteen. Summer nights we'd still be out playing at ten, so when the cop came through we'd scurry into backyards or slide into dark garages through holes in the rusting metal walls. When the cop was gone, we'd get back to Jailbreak, our nighttime game.

The neighborhood was younger then and there were more kids. We'd divide up into two teams—the crooks and the cops. The crooks would hide under porches or in shadowed crevices and the cops would fan out to find them. The streetlight pole was the jail. Once caught, you'd stand next to it and hope another crook would creep into the circle of light and tag you free.

Being a crook was always more fun than being a cop. My punkier impulses must trace back to those alley nights. The hiding and the breaking out were always more exciting than the finding and putting into jail.

In our imaginations we would disappear into the night, never to be found.

Like she had.

Who would have believed such a job would come my way in Shawnee? How could I begin to tell the old men about her?

Crazy, but they just might understand.

Tattoo, who'd worn a picture of a sensuous woman on an arm he'd once possessed.

Daniel, who'd told me how he'd paid a friend a dollar to introduce him to his wife-to-be in 1924, flapper days.

The old men admired pretty legs and valued the feel of cock in cunt as much as any other sensation in life.

"I've lived a hell of a long time and yet I've only learnt much about two things," Daniel had told me one hot afternoon. "Railroading and fucking."

Railroading & Fucking. As good a working title for my photo book as I was likely to find.

I'd put her in the book if I ever got it together. She was now part of Shawnee 1982 to me. Besides, the thing would be easier to sell with a spread of her in it.

Put a blond wig on her head and, with that low-cut pink dress, she might pass for Marilyn Monroe.

We could find a grate down by the abandoned passenger station some night and restage the famous scene from *The Seven Year Itch.*

She would stand over the grate and let the warm air blow up between her thighs and waft her skirt up above her waist. She would slam her hands toward her crotch to hold the skirt down in front while the rest of it floated above her thighs.

I smiled. Her fantasies were causing me to have fantasies. They were catching.

It was getting late and chilly. I went back inside to the darkroom.

7

WEIRD.

Monday morning she had seemed so dress-for-success proper.

Tuesday's child had been a more provocative one.

Wednesday night she had played dress up—*or down*—slipping into her mother's clothes and high heels. Her mother must have been a dazzler in her prime.

Thursday's child hadn't come.

Unless she'd appeared during the time I'd been clicking Canley and the evangelists. Quite a different job than hers.

Metling had promised me the whole thing would take less than an hour, and it had. I'd driven to the church, snapped the pictures, delivered the film for *The News'* darkroom to process, and been home before eight o'clock.

It had been the only time I'd been away from the house all day, and it must have been when she'd come by. If she'd come at all. Maybe she'd had second thoughts. Maybe she was backing off, afraid of what might happen when she again stepped into my parlor and shed her trench coat.

Her costumes seemed important somehow. Maybe because I knew so little else about her. Not even her name. I knew nothing except her fantasies. And though I was getting sucked into them, they were *her* fantasies, not mine.

What she wore was my only clue to what was going on inside her.

Weird to see a woman's fantasy but to know nothing of her reality.

She could be a market clerk for all I knew.

When she hadn't come by 11:15, I gave up on her and for once went to bed at a decent hour, determined not to wait around the next day. I thought I'd get up early and make my way out to the South Shawnee switchyards to catch the trains moving through the soft morning mist before the sun burned it away and turned the light hard. Morning was usually a good time to click frames in mountain light. Even as a kid, I'd appreciated the look of the foggy patches hunching over the ridges surrounding Shawnee.

Adjusting May's quilt over me, I decided that if all else failed, I might try marketing some scenics.

Hell, Metling might even buy a scenic to break up his gray column pages.

Lying there, I mentally kicked myself for missing her, if indeed I had. A session with her would certainly have been more entertaining, even more profitable, than the visit to the Shawnee Independent Bible Church.

The Reverend Richard Baum had come over to greet me as soon as I'd stepped into the church basement. "Are you the photographer from *The News?"* he'd asked in a genial-enough voice, extending his hand. He was wearing one of those slick pastel suits that come unslicked by the end of a hard day. It looked like his day hadn't been too hard.

"I'm the photographer," I answered.

"We're just about ready for you."

He led me toward a U-shaped arrangement of folding tables where about twenty people were seated. The room was a long rectangle with cheap paneling and a drop ceiling. They probably held Sunday school in it as well as church dinners. Three or four older women were scurrying around, clearing plain white dishes from the tables. The plates showed the remains of fried chicken and mashed potatoes.

"Would you like coffee or something?" asked Baum, motioning for me to sit on a folding chair.

"No, thanks. I've eaten."

Feeling out of place, I waited quietly.

Once the ladies had finished clearing the plates, Reverend Baum stood up and announced in a strong clear voice, "We've had a successful conversation with the congressman this evening. We're glad he was able to take time from his busy schedule to break bread with us. Soon he must go on to another event, so we'll be postponing dessert for a few minutes while we present him with a token of our appreciation for his efforts in Congress over the years."

Next to Baum, a middle-aged woman in a pale pink high-necked dress reached beneath the table and handed him an octagonal piece of wood upon which was mounted a bronze-colored plaque.

Displaying the plaque to the others, Baum said, "As you are aware, Congressman Charles Whitford Canley has long been a staunch supporter of the Christian American Way. He has sponsored legislation to put prayer back into this nation's public schools. He has opposed abortion. He has backed our beloved president in his various tax-cut measures. He has been an ardent foe of International Communism and of creeping socialism at home. Early in his political career, he stood up to the critics of the Vietnam War. I could speak all night about his brave efforts, from his campaign against pornography to his valiant words concerning the leftist anti-nuclear movement. He stands, in short, for a return to the basic Christian values that made this country great. Many organizations have recognized his dedication and his patriotism. Last week in Washington, the Daughters of the American Revolution paid tribute to him. We members of the Bible Ministers of Shawnee offer him this modest plaque, and our continued support."

Congressman Canley, a tall man in his forties, rose, took his award from Baum, gave an instantly forgettable acceptance speech, and thanked the group. I snapped a photo of him looking down at the plaque as he talked.

Then all the preachers crowded around to congratulate him and shake his hand. Baum put them in some sort of order and I took a couple photos of the group. Ignoring Baum's directions, one preacher, a big red-haired man about my age, reached over, tapped Canley on the back and crowded closer to him, not wanting to be missed. Even preachers like Baum had their problems with rank.

Soon after, Canley headed for the door. I was about to follow when Baum cut me off.

"Thanks for coming," he said softly. "You're welcome to stay for pie."

"I've got to get my film down to the office."

"You might want this," he said, offering me a slip of paper. "My wife wrote down the names of the clergymen in the group picture."

I took the paper from him. "Sorry, I should have done it myself."

"No trouble," he said, like the best of public relations men.

And that's all there was to it.

THE PHONE RANG.

I tossed back the quilt, climbed out of bed, and almost stumbled down the steps, having no idea what time it was or how long I'd managed to sleep.

"Are my photos ready?"

"Wait a minute. I'm half asleep. Who is this?"

Of course, even half asleep, I knew who it was.

"I stopped by for my pictures tonight and you weren't there," she said, a sad, stood-up inflection to her voice.

"Ah, the lady in pink."

"Don't make fun of me," she said. "I'm a customer, aren't I?"

"I'm sorry . . . you're right. What time is it, anyway?"

"Around midnight. I imagined you'd still be awake."

"Well, I am now, sort of."

"Where were you?" she asked, almost as if she was jealous.

"I had another job. I'd have told you last night if you hadn't sneaked out the back door. I'd have called you if I knew who you were."

She ignored what I'd said. "Is it all right for me to come over now?"

"Now?"

"I can't sleep. I want my pictures . . . and . . ."

"And what?"

She didn't answer, just left a long silence for me to take in as I stood there in my underwear in the darkness of the front room.

"Where are you now?" I asked.

"At home."

"Where's that?"

"I'll be there in less than an hour," she said quickly, before hanging up.

It was all getting weirder and weirder. Our next session would be in the middle of the night. There was no sense trying to guess what Thursday's child would be like. She'd arrive soon enough.

8

SHE KEPT ME WAITING.

Sitting at the desk in the front room, I felt like writing her a time-and-a-half bill for the waiting she'd put me through, and for the late-night duty.

I drained a mug of coffee, then a second, and headed back downstairs for a third. It was already after one o'clock. If I was going to be up all night, I might as well really be up all night. After she left, I would hike across town and hit the South Shawnee switchyards at dawn—before the caffeine ran out and I crashed.

I poured the mug full, put the coffeepot down on the stove, walked to the back door, and stared out the glass toward the alley. To the left of the sheet-metal garages flashed a jagged scarlet-and-yellow.

I just about threw the mug on the table. I pulled open the door and ran down the yard yelling "Fire! Fire! Fire!" as loudly as I could, hoping I would wake up the whole goddamn neighborhood.

I ran around my Ford, jumped down into the alley, and rammed my knee into the back of a parked car that I hadn't expected to be there. Backing away from the car, I stepped in a pothole. My ankle twisted, my bruised knee gave out, and I fell on the ragged roadway.

"Fire! Fire! Fire!" I screamed.

I grabbed the bumper of the car and pulled myself to my feet. My ankle ached. Unable to run, I limped toward Daniel's house.

"Fire! Fire! Fire!"

The intense heat of the flaming house kept me at a distance. The porch where the old man had passed so much of his time was burning like crumpled paper. Flames showed in every window of the two-story structure. Fire slithered up the outside wooden walls. The roof crackled like kindling. Sparks were carried by the night breeze and landed like glowing match tips on the tin garage roofs nearby.

Despite the flames and heat, I debated whether I should dash inside and try to find Daniel.

"We got to move that car before the fire engines come," said Tattoo, suddenly beside me.

"Shouldn't we try to save him?"

"Are you crazy? Look at that house a-burning! There's no way to get inside it. It's too late for him anyway. All we can do is keep the thing from spreading. May was calling the fire department when I run down. We got to move that son-of-a-bitching car so the damn fire trucks can come up the alley."

He was trying to sound reasonable, but I could tell he was as agitated as I was. He'd known Daniel for a long time.

"Come on," he ordered. "The siren's already blowing. Can't you hear it?"

The fire, the sparks in the darkness, the pain in my knee and ankle ... I wasn't sure what I could hear.

Tattoo started walking toward the parked car and I followed him. "Parked" is generous. The driver of the blue Volkswagen had made no apparent effort to move the vehicle out of the middle of the alley between my yard and Daniel's burning house. He'd just left it there.

Tattoo opened the car door and peered in. "The keys are in it." Watching me approach, he asked, "What happened to your leg?"

"I ran into this son-of-a-bitching thing and twisted my ankle," I said, borrowing his words.

"And you wanted to run in that house after Daniel? You really are crazy. If you want to do something, then drive this German monstrosity down the alley and out of the way."

Nodding, I climbed into the VW and turned the key in the ignition. The car started right up, as if the engine was still hot. I slipped the stick shift into first and began crawling ahead. I had to go forward, past the fire, or else I would have risked bottlenecking the fire trucks. I gassed the car hard as I neared the burning house, wanting to get by as quickly as possible, my head filled with visions of the sparks in the narrow alley somehow finding a way to ignite the gas tank.

When I figured I was out of danger, I let up on the accelerator and tried to calm myself. I drove most of the way down the alley until I found a place that was broad enough to park and still let a fire truck by if need be. I left the keys in the ignition and climbed out, my leg almost collapsing again when I put weight on it.

I limped to the back of the car and studied it. It had in-state license plates. I didn't remember seeing it in the neighborhood before, but that wasn't unusual. Cars weren't something I spent a lot of time noticing.

Slowly I made my way back up the alley toward the fire. The whole block seemed awake by then. Light bulbs burned in every bedroom. The night was filled with voices coming from all directions, people on back porches, people rushing through their yards to the alley. A crowd had formed a semicircle around the front of Daniel's flame-defeated home.

I pushed my way through the people until I found Tattoo. Soon a bathrobe-clad May joined us. She handed Tattoo a brown sweater to put on over his white T-shirt.

The house had started to collapse in on itself by the time the fire engines arrived. There was little the firemen could do. Some of them fought to extinguish the bed of glowing coals in what had once been the center of the dwelling. Others wetted down nearby buildings and garages, which sizzled and steamed when the water hit the red-hot metal.

The alley took on a glary, surrealistic tone, like a wartime London street after a Nazi bombing or a disastrous rock festival in the midst of its last night. Neighbors stood around in robes, nightclothes, even wrapped in blankets. The firemen, in full gear, ran back and forth. The garish streetlights, the dying flames, the smoke and steam, the swirling fire engine lights . . . Nothing seemed real any longer.

A city cop and a man with a State Fire Marshal emblem on his shirt moved through the crowd, ordered us to step further back, and asked if anybody knew anything about what had happened.

When they got to us, I told them how I'd been in my kitchen looking out the back door and seen the flames and run down and tried to wake people up and moved the car. They coolly wrote it all down, each keeping his own set of notes. Then they headed toward the fire chief.

I glanced over at Tattoo. The strangeness of the light in the alley gave his face a dark cast that would have seemed menacingly demonic if I hadn't known it was caused by sadness and sorrow.

"What do we do now?" I asked.

"I suppose we bury Daniel, if there's anything left to bury," he said.

He seemed older to me right then than he ever had before. Under his brown sweater, his usually broad shoulders looked hunched and his strong chest seemed caved in.

After a while, he reached for May's arm and led her home.

9

"WHERE'S THE PICTURES?" Metling asked.

It was Friday afternoon, about four-thirty.

"Of what?" I asked back, still groggy. I'd been asleep when the phone rang—and only for three or four hours. Getting to sleep had been an obstacle.

"The photos of the fire," he said, but he sounded like he meant "The photos of the fire, *stupid.*"

"I didn't take any."

"It was in your neighborhood, wasn't it? Didn't you get any shots at all? I figured you'd be down here with prints long ago."

"I was too busy."

"You were the one who spotted the fire, weren't you? How many Jack Reeses live up there? When you get down here, I want you to talk to a reporter. It's arson, you know. *It's murder.*"

"Christ, I don't want to talk to a reporter," I said.

"We can talk later," Metling shot back. "You get out and snap some pictures of what's left of the house or something. Get your film down here. We'll take care of developing it, like we did the roll of Canley last night"

Canley last night.

Was that just last night? My world had changed a couple times since.

Metling hung up and, though I hated doing it, I got dressed and went down to the alley. With a miserable feeling in my stomach, I stood in front of the pile of charred rubble that had once been old Daniel's home. I aimed the camera at the darkest, blackest, most burnt goddamned area. If Metling wanted a photo of the fire, then the uglier the picture, the better. I clicked five or six shots of the same thing, then climbed into the Ford and headed downtown.

It was turning dark by the time I got back to the alley. My headlights picked up on someone standing, staring, at the destroyed house.

The person turned toward me. From his odd gait, his leaning slightly forward and to the side to balance a missing left arm, I knew who it was.

"Where you been?" Tattoo asked when I climbed out of the car.

"At *The News* office."

"What do they know? What'd the police tell them?" he asked.

"It's murder. Arson. I didn't get the details. I didn't feel like waiting around. Just handed my film to a girl at the front desk and left."

"I'll get the son of a bitch that killed Daniel," he said. "You know that goddamn foreign car's still parked down the alley. Are the cops looking into it?"

"I don't know. If it's still there, it must be all right. You heard me tell the police and the fire marshal about it."

We began walking up the hill to the house.

"You had supper yet?" asked Tattoo.

"No."

"Come on in," he offered.

DINNER WAS A WORDLESS AFFAIR. Like the neighborhood around us, we seemed to have sunk into silence in the wake of the fire.

Sitting at the table, picking at a hunk of May's Poorman's Cake, I knew Saturday morning's paper would break the silence. The fire, the murder, had happened too late for *The News'* Friday edition, but judging from the urgency with which Metling had wanted a picture of Daniel's house, I knew there'd be a big spread the next day.

"When's Daniel going to be buried?" I asked.

"Sunday afternoon," Tattoo mumbled, without looking up from his cake.

"It's all supposed to be in tomorrow's paper," said May. "Reverend Ruffing's doing the service out at the cemetery. We're having a small reception here afterwards. Don't expect many. No one knows of any family left."

"He never had children, did he?"

"Not that anyone knows of."

"Sad way to end, ain't it?" said Tattoo. "With hardly a body left to bury and hardly a mourner left to see you out."

"Fires are nasty," I mumbled, realizing immediately how dumb it sounded.

"You're too young to remember the one in your house years ago," said May.

"I remember some hushes about it when I was a kid. What happened exactly?"

She slid her plate out of the way and rested her elbows on the table. "It was years before Henry and me lived here. I only know what your granddaddy and mother told me. It was back in the thirties, during Prohibition, when your mother was young. Your people was living in this side of the house and your grandfather was renting the other side out to a man who come into Shawnee from out in the mountains somewheres."

"Buck," inserted Tattoo.

"You want to tell it, Henry?" May asked him.

"No."

"Your family always felt something was strange over next door," she went on. "There'd be water running and bottles clinking at all hours. The fellow seemed to be taking out box loads of something late at night, and they'd hear his old Model T running up the hill someplace. Till one night there was a boom. Like an exploding gas tank or something. The fire swooped up the stairs from the basement before anybody knew what was going on. Your side of the house was just about gutted. Fire probably would've spread to this side too but for the brick wall between them."

She stopped, but I didn't want her to.

"Wasn't there someone killed?" I asked. "I thought someone died and that's why they never talked much about it."

"A thirteen-year-old girl. The bootlegger's daughter," answered May. "She was asleep upstairs and couldn't get down the steps and no one could get up through the flames."

"Named Mary," added Tattoo. "You ain't seen her ghost over there, have you?"

May shot him a shut-up glance.

"Whatever became of them?" I asked.

"They moved," she said. "You know your granddaddy was a teetotaler. He was an upright man, even if he never went to church."

"Church ain't got nothing to do with morals," said Tattoo.

She ignored him. "I always heard they moved to somewhere in Shantytown, by the canal. I guess they set up another still there. Your people remodeled the other side of the house and liked it so much they moved over there."

"You ain't been making home brew in that darkroom of yours, have you?" asked Tattoo. "He had his still in that basement over there."

This time, May didn't object to his remark. We all laughed and some of the tension over Daniel was relieved for a while.

10

DANIEL MORGAN JONES

Daniel Morgan Jones, 84, of Baxter Street, Shawnee, died early Friday, October 15, in a fire at his residence.

Born November 11, 1897, in Wild Stream, West Virginia, he was the son of the late Albert M. and Susan Schmidt Jones.

Mr. Jones came to Shawnee in the early 1920s to work for the Shawnee-Potomac Railroad. He retired in 1963.

He was a veteran of World War I and a member of the United Brotherhood of Carmen. He was a Protestant.

He was preceded in death by his wife, Ella Scott Jones, in 1964. There are no known survivors.

Burial will be at Rose Garden Cemetery at 2:00 p.m. on Sunday, October 17, with the Rev. Joseph Ruffing officiating.

How neatly a man's life could be wrapped up in a few paragraphs.

I read the obituary again. Not so much as a hint of *Railroading & Fucking,* or the time in 1935 when Daniel said he'd almost killed a man, raising a wrench in hot-blood against another worker who'd claimed Uncle Joe Stalin was a finer man than Franklin Roosevelt.

The obit couldn't begin to explain him.

How he liked to tell of sitting under a tree in France when he got word of the armistice ending World War I. How the doughboy beside him had been blown apart five minutes after the war was supposed to have ended.

How he fought his second war, walking the picket line with the United Brotherhood.

He was a Protestant. Sure he was. Just like my grandfather, Tattoo, and me.

I turned back to the front page of Saturday morning's *News*. There was the photo I'd taken of what had once been his home. The picture looked as gray, dark, and murky as I'd figured it would. No great advertisement for me as a photographer.

The story told how what was left of Daniel's body had been found by firefighters near dawn on Friday, and how arson was suspected.

I was named as the person who first saw the blaze. Metling was probably still fuming that I hadn't loaded his reporter up with all the details.

At least only two of us knew why I was up at 1:00 A.M., looking down into the alley. It wasn't spread across the headlines that I'd been waiting for a mystery woman.

Who hadn't come.

Hadn't come the night of the fire.

Hadn't come Friday, to my knowledge.

Hadn't yet come Saturday morning.

I hadn't heard a peep out of her since that crazy phone call. Her pictures from Wednesday night still sat on my desk.

I went down to the darkroom to pass some time. I figured, if she came, she'd see the note on the front door: *If no one answers, ring bell to darkroom.* But, as I puttered around, the bell didn't ring.

The darkroom seemed strange to me. May's story of the moonshiner and his still kept running through my mind, as it had the night before. Trying to sleep, I'd kept thinking of Daniel, and shaking off Daniel, I'd thought of the girl burned in the explosion. In the middle of the night, the rain had started, beating on the tin roof and adding to my sleep problems.

In temperamental October fashion, Saturday morning had been unseasonably warm, as if the fire at Daniel's were rising again to scorch the whole neighborhood.

Daniel.

I sorted through my negatives until I found the one of him sitting on his swing in August.

I made fresh chemicals and prepared to make a book-quality print.

I put the negative in the enlarger and focused, trying to judge the light and dark of it. His face sucked me in.

There, in reverse image, the face black as if charred, the eyes burning, its shadows and wrinkled hollows ghost white. What kind of bastard would kill him?

II

AS HE SPOKE the words he thought appropriate, I wondered how well Reverend Joe Ruffing had known Daniel Jones. The Bible verses he quoted seemed to have little to do with the old man.

Sunday's cold damp wind beat at us as we stood on top of the hill at Rose Garden Cemetery, not far from my own family's plot. It was one of those fierce fall winds that occasionally rise up to dry the mud.

The Reverend Ruffing talked in a soft monotone and I kept returning to Thursday night. To her call. To the flames I'd seen out the back door. To running down the hill, bumping into the car, twisting my ankle. To the feeling of guilt at not being able to do anything to save Daniel.

Those scenes stayed in my head the whole drive back to Tattoo and May's, and even as I reached down to the platter of little quartered sandwiches on the kitchen table.

"May's certainly gone to a lot of trouble for the few of us," said Joe Ruffing, reaching for a sandwich at the same time.

"She always does when food's involved. She loves messing around with hors d'oeuvres and cake decorating and all that fancy stuff. She missed her calling. She should have been a caterer," I said. "When I was a kid, she was always making these little sandwiches and frostinged cakes and sweet trifles whenever she or my mother had people over. I suppose she wanted to keep busy at something before the funeral."

"You've known May a long time, haven't you?" he asked.

"All my life. I grew up next door."

"She's filled me in about you," he said.

I looked down at the platter. Deciding against cheese salad, I picked up a ham salad sandwich. With my other hand I grabbed a cracker topped by a thin smear of cream cheese and a whole olive.

"She speaks highly of you," I said to him.

"I've noticed her husband doesn't bark at me anymore if I stop by."

"Tattoo's impressed by the food bank you started," I told him. "You're not likely to see him in the front pew, though."

"The food bank just came about. I saw the need and convinced some of the congregation to help. May's been one of the stalwarts. Somebody had to do something. There are a lot of people out of work, scrimping by on a few dollars a week, with no prospects for anything better. Back home, it's like that too."

"Where's back home?"

"Pittsburgh area. I grew up in a steel-mill neighborhood. It was basically a lot like here."

"How'd you get to be a preacher?"

"Went to seminary." He smiled before biting into another cream-cheese-and-olive cracker. "In seminary they always kidded me I was a social worker disguised as a minister. Take Daniel, for example. He didn't really belong to the church, but I met him last spring while I was walking up the alley. Later I called the Commission on Aging and asked if they'd deliver hot lunches to him."

"He told me about that."

"I assume they followed through."

"Over his objections."

"I guess I really shouldn't go around doing things like that," said Ruffing. "But I don't think I'm necessarily here so much to preach as I am to pastor."

"You sound out of touch with the theology of the eighties," I said. "Aren't you supposed to be laying a little guilt on people, or at least helping them realize that free-market economics and nuclear bombs are the flowering of the Gospel?"

"Jesus would overturn their tables," he said, his voice just as sarcastic as mine had been.

I looked him over closely as he picked up another sandwich. A tall bachelor, his black suit hung on his bones like a shirt on a clothes hanger, making me feel hale and hearty. I could see he wasn't all that different from me. Maybe, in another world, I'd have become a preacher.

"Actually I was hoping to meet you," he said.

"Yeah, why?"

"May's told me you take pictures for the newspaper."

"Yeah?"

He turned quiet, then began reluctantly. "Perhaps I shouldn't ask, but we wondered if you'd consider taking some photos at the food bank, and then get them in the paper. The publicity might help bring in donations. It's hard to keep going."

"No big corporate givers?"

"You're kidding." He laughed. "It's as hand-to-mouth as the people it serves."

"I'd certainly be willing to come by with my camera, but I can't promise anything for the paper. I'm just a stringer. Metling's the big man, and he and I run hot and cold. At the moment, it's pretty chilly," I said, remembering how I'd handled the pictures of the fire on Friday. "He has very clear ideas about what's appropriate news coverage, particularly with an election only a couple of weeks away. He may not want to make the economy look too bad."

"All I'm asking you to do is try," said Ruffing.

"Okay. I'll stop in this week."

"Thursday," he said, reaching for another sandwich.

"Thursday then."

"Somebody wants to see you upstairs," said Tattoo, suddenly standing in front of us.

"I hope she's pretty," I answered.

But he didn't smile. Even in the bright electric light of his kitchen, amidst the chatter of the wake, his face was as serious as it had been in the glow of the flames from the burning house.

"It's a cop," he said.

12

"YOU JACK REESE?"

"Yeah."

"You're a photographer?"

"I try."

The cop flashed his badge. "You're the one who spotted the fire and reported a Volkswagen parked in the middle of Baxter Street that night?"

"One and the same."

He stood in Tattoo's doorway and peered into the living room. "Can we talk here, or is there a better place?"

"You want to go next door to my house?" I asked.

"This may take a while. There are people downstairs, aren't there?"

"We're holding a sort of wake for Daniel Jones."

"I'm sorry I interrupted," he said. But he made no offer to come back another time.

"Okay, let's go over to my place," I finally said.

I opened the door and led him across the short length of sidewalk to my porch. He followed me silently, a slight swing to his arms. He had a large brown envelope in his hand. I wondered if he had a gun under his black quilted jacket. I guessed he did. Weren't all detectives supposed to?

I had no idea how many detectives were on the Shawnee police force, or how they stacked up against the tough plainclothes variety you saw in the movies, but the detective seemed formidable and intimidating enough to me. A child of the sixties, I could be put on edge easily by police, even when I had no reason to be.

His name was Edward Harter, and he looked to be about ten years older than me, in his early forties, though it was hard to tell from his expressionless face, a face that was starting to show lines of wear. His brown hair was shorter than mine but scruffy. He was solid enough that I wouldn't have wanted to chance finding out what kind of shape he was in. Maybe about six foot, my height, he was at least twenty-five pounds heavier.

Inside my front room, I switched on a light and motioned him to sit at the rickety desk chair. I went back to the studio and returned with the stool for myself. The moment I climbed on it, I was glad I had the high seat, looking down on him, not vice versa.

"This where you do your business?" he asked, taking in the room, from the peeling wallpaper to the pile of stuff on the table next to him.

"I use this room for an office and the back one for a studio."

He pulled a small notebook and pen from his jacket pocket. "How did you come to notice the fire?"

"I was up late and looked out the kitchen door and saw flames in the alley."

"Then you called the fire department?"

"No. I ran down to see if I could do anything. I yelled and yelled, hoping to wake people up. May, the woman next door, actually called in the fire, I think."

Harter nodded and jotted a few notes. "When you got to the alley, Baxter Street, you saw Daniel Jones' house burning, and you found a car parked in the middle of the street?"

"Right, the Volkswagen."

"Empty?"

"Yeah. I wasn't expecting it to be there. I rammed my knee into the back bumper and twisted my ankle. Turned out the keys were in it. Later I moved the thing after we decided it would be in the way of the fire trucks."

"We?"

"Tattoo and I. He's the one who answered next door when you knocked."

"The old guy with one arm?"

"Right."

"He's married to this, uh, May?"

"Yeah."

"So you got into the Volkswagen and moved it?"

"I drove it down the alley and parked it. Left the keys in it. It was still there yesterday, I think."

"You didn't notice any personal articles inside? Papers, clothing, a purse, anything?"

"No."

"Was that the only time you were in the car?"

"Yeah."

"You have no idea who the Volkswagen belonged to?"

"I don't remember seeing it before."

"You never saw Susan Maddox Devendall driving it?"

"Who?"

"Susan Maddox Devendall."

"I never heard of her."

"Never met her?"

"Not that I know of."

He lifted the brown envelope from the floor, opened the flap, and pulled out a pile of photographs. I recognized the top one even before he handed them to me. There she was ... in her little-girl costume, her legs kicking high, her white skirt flying, her thighs bare.

"Did you take these?" asked Harter, making no secret of how closely he was watching my eyes.

I flipped through the prints, studying them. I turned one over and read my name and address stamped on the back.

"Yeah. Is she this . . . ?"

"Susan Maddox Devendall. Her mother-in-law found those pictures at her home."

"I didn't even know her name. The car was hers?"

He nodded, then asked, "You took her picture and didn't know who she was?"

"That's not unusual, is it?"

"You tell me, you're the photographer."

"She came on Monday and asked me to photograph her and came back the next day for the prints. She paid in cash. What's the big deal?"

"She seems to have disappeared after she left her car behind your house on the night of the fire. Her body was discovered last night."

"Her body?"

I began to understand his visit. I glanced down at the photos in my hand and realized the position I was in. She'd disappeared and turned up dead after I'd taken some questionable photos of her. She'd turned up missing the same night as the fire down the hill from me—a fire I'd been the first to notice.

He reached over and took back the pictures. "Were these all taken on Monday then?" he asked.

"No. The ones of just her head are from Monday. She said she needed a passport photo by the next day. When she came back on Tuesday, she asked me to take the others. She was wearing that costume. She picked them up on Wednesday."

Wednesday. Christ. I remembered Wednesday's session all too well. Her in "her mother's" pink dress, stripping down.

Harter was staring at my face and eyes. I forced myself not to look toward my desk, where, amid the other clutter, the photos from Wednesday were. It was better not to tell him, unless he asked.

"Wednesday was the last time you saw her?"

"Yeah, but ..."

"But what?"

"She called me up Thursday night."

"The night of the fire?"

"Yeah."

"What'd she want?"

"To come over and have more pictures taken." And, I failed to add, to pick up Wednesday's lingerie shots.

"When did she call?"

"Around midnight."

"She called you up at midnight and asked to come over?"

"Yeah. She'd apparently been here earlier in the evening but I was out."

"Where were you?"

"I was at Reverend Richard Baum's church taking a picture of some preachers giving Congressman Canley an award."

"Preachers and a congressman?" he asked, glancing at her legs as he slid the prints back into the brown envelope.

"I work sometimes for *The News.*"

"I thought maybe you took pictures for *Playboy* or something."

I didn't like the remark. His next question was worse. "Did you ever sleep with this woman?"

"What kind of question is that?" I asked, surer than ever that I would volunteer nothing about Wednesday evening.

"A logical question," said Harter. "A married woman comes to have pictures like these taken, then later calls you up at midnight and wants to come over—and ends up murdered."

"No, I didn't sleep with her. I didn't know she was married. I didn't even know her name. I don't know how she was killed or where you found her body, either."

"So she just calls up and asks if she can come over?"

"Right."

"What happened then?"

"I made coffee and waited for about an hour. I happened to look out the kitchen door and see the fire. I ran down to see what was going on and ran into the Volkswagen. I moved the car so the fire trucks could get to Daniel's house."

I wondered if I sounded as irritated as I felt. If I did, Harter didn't care. He continued with his questions.

"Did you know Daniel Jones well?"

"Fairly well. I grew up in this neighborhood. I've talked to him a few times in the last couple of months."

"Anything strike you as particularly odd about the fire?"

"How do I answer that? The fire struck me as particularly odd. I don't normally see old men get burned alive. I guess the oddest thing was the car. I told the fire marshal and the police about the car that night. Everyone knew I moved it. Didn't you guys check into it?"

"Everyone didn't know you knew the woman it belonged to," responded Harter.

"I didn't know it was hers."

"You didn't see any sign of Mrs. Devendall or anyone else?"

"No."

"Didn't you wonder why she didn't show up?"

"Yeah, but what was I supposed to do? Call the police and say a mystery woman didn't come for a middle-of-the-night photo session? I figured she saw the fire and all the activity and decided to go home. I haven't heard from her since."

"Did you expect to?"

"I guess I did. Like you keep pointing out, she called me at midnight."

"You're telling me you never saw her that night and you didn't know it was her car and you were never in the vehicle except to move it for the fire engines?"

"That's what I keep telling you over and over. It's the truth."

"You never saw that car during any of her other visits?"

"I didn't know how she got here."

"You have no idea why she vacated her vehicle on the night of the fire?"

"None at all."

"Do you think she knew Daniel Jones?"

"I certainly never saw them together or heard them mention each other."

"Do you spend a lot of time in the alley?"

"I don't know what you're after. My backyard faces on the alley. My car's back there. We all use it as a shortcut down the hill. Sometimes I go out back in the evening. Sometimes I visit Daniel."

Harter flipped back through his notebook as if he were looking for something. Finally, he found it. "You were out in the alley last Wednesday night, weren't you?"

"Yeah. How do you know that?"

"An officer on patrol remembered seeing someone behind your house."

"Can't I be out in my own backyard?"

"What were you doing?"

"Thinking. What do you do in your backyard?"

"Was this before or after she stopped by for these photographs?"

"After. She left fairly early. I remember the police car going by about ten. I'd already been outside a while."

"You hadn't noticed anything unusual going on around Daniel Jones' house lately?"

"No."

"No strangers or vehicles?"

"Nothing I recall."

"He didn't have any enemies, did he?"

"He was almost eighty-five years old," I said.

"That's not what I asked."

"I imagine Daniel had outlived most of his enemies. I don't know anyone who hated him."

"Is there anything else?"

"What?"

"Anything else you should tell me?"

I ran the events of Wednesday night through my head again, then answered, "No."

The detective closed his notebook. "What was she like, this Susan Maddox Devendall?"

"When she was here, she was rather nervous. Reluctant at first to relax for the camera. She said that's why she wanted those photos taken in costume. She was, maybe, sort of disconnected a bit."

When I didn't offer more, he rose from the chair.

"What happened to her? How did she die?" I asked before he could leave.

"I guess you'll be reading about it in the paper tomorrow anyway," he said, his voice a little softer than it had been. "She apparently left home late Thursday night or early Friday morning, and then it's all a blank until her body was found last night in the canal. She'd been beaten. She was wearing only jewelry. A raincoat and a lot of jewelry."

"You think her death and Daniel's are related somehow?"

"I'd say I have to think so."

"Am I a suspect then?"

"Let's just say you're the only one who knew both victims." He stepped toward me and pulled a card out of his pocket. "Here, if you think of anything else, call me."

For a long while after he'd gone, I sat on the stool and fingered his card.

Had he known I hadn't told him everything? Had I given myself away?

I hadn't lied. I'd answered his questions. He hadn't asked about Wednesday night's session. What good would it have done to have shown him those photos? They would only have dirtied her reputation more. *And mine.*

Found dead in only her jewelry and raincoat. So that was Thursday's child.

I glanced at the envelope that contained Wednesday's prints. I could destroy them, burn them, cut the negatives in fragments and dump them in the trash.

But what if they truly mattered? What if they had something to do with why she'd been murdered?

How could they? I was innocent, whatever Harter believed. And what could those photos, what could she, have had to do with Daniel?

"You're the only one who knew both victims," he'd said. As if to put me on notice. He didn't have to tell me I was a suspect all right.

My head suddenly felt like someone had cracked it with an ax.

13

THE DREAM CAME for the first time Sunday night.

I was asleep in the top floor of a very old, very tall, narrow, four-story, paint-bare frame house.

I was awakened by the noise of a burglar somewhere downstairs.

So what do you do?

You brave it.

You climb out of bed and go in search of him.

You run down to the third floor, where you see a dry old wooden table with a tall thin candle on it and the candle falls over before your eyes and immediately the table starts to burn like paper and you run over and try to smother the flames with your bare hands.

Then you run down to the second floor of the dry-as-kindling house and see a dry old wooden table with a tall candle on it and the candle falls over before your eyes and the table starts to burn like paper and I run over and try to smother the flames with my bare hands.

Then you run down to the bottom floor of the old house and see a dry wooden table with a tall candle on it and the candle falls over before my eyes and the table starts to burn like paper and I run over and try to smother the flames with your bare hands.

Upstairs there is the noise of a burglar somewhere.

So I run up to the second floor of the house and see a wood table with a tall candle on it and the candle falls and the table starts to burn like paper and you run over and try to smother the flames with my bare hands.

Then you run up to the third floor and see a table with a tall candle and the candle falls and the table starts to burn and I run over and try to smother the flames with bare hands.

Then I run up to the top floor and a table with a candle and candle falls and table starts to burn and I run over try to smother flames with bare hands.

Downstairs there is the noise of a burglar.

EDWARD HARTER

14

SOMETIMES they simply lied.

Sometimes they didn't lie but they weren't forthcoming with the truth, either.

Sometimes the truth was hard to take.

Harter didn't know which category the photographer belonged in.

Monday morning at his desk, he remained unsatisfied with his first questioning on the case. Jack Reese's story was so scattershot—the unnamed woman who had posed suggestively and called him at midnight on the night of the fire and left her car behind his house and ended up dead in the canal—so scattershot that it was hard to see the target.

Susan Devendall or Daniel Jones? Which case was he working on?

The way he saw it, finding an opening in the old man's killing was a tougher proposition than finding someone to talk to about Susan Maddox Devendall. At least she had had a husband and, presumably, friends who might be able to explain her behavior.

Harter didn't know how other detectives worked. He'd spent his career as one of only two full-time investigators on the Shawnee police force. He'd pretty much taught himself. Usually he began with the closest brick when building a case. Then he reached out a little farther for the next one.

Harter moved the papers around on his desk, wondering what bricks Reese was hiding. More and more, being a cop meant moving papers. He put one batch in a desk drawer. He tossed another on Caruthers' desk. Let him move them. Caruthers wouldn't complain much. He'd already been warned by the chief that he'd be picking up a lot of little stuff.

Caruthers didn't hate the paperwork as much as Harter. A day spent at his desk filling out reports and forms was just one less day Caruthers had to be on the street, one more day on the conveyor belt to retirement. Not that Caruthers was such a bad guy, or a bad cop. He was just tired.

Harter wondered if the chief would have given him such a free hand if there wasn't a Devendall body involved.

Maybe so.

Two killings in two days threw off all the crime stats for Shawnee. Like most blue-collar cities in the Alleghenies, Shawnee usually had a low incidence of violent crimes on the annual FBI reports. The big-city people had it wrong. The working-class mountain towns weren't really so rough and rowdy, though Shawnee could get rough and rowdy enough for him.

What Harter had originally planned for Monday was a visit to the Devendall family. To meet the husband. To talk to the mother-in-law who had reported the victim missing, the mother-in-law who had found the strange photographs. But they had put him off.

Howard Devendall had called first thing to say he had only returned to Shawnee late Sunday and would be busy with family matters all day, planning his wife's cremation and setting up the details of the memorial service set for Saturday, October 23.

Devendall added that his mother was very upset and it would be best to delay speaking to her, too.

So the interview had been set for Tuesday morning. All Harter could do in the meantime was work around the edges.

He read every shred of paper about the case—the fire marshal's report, the coroner's preliminary findings, the obituaries and articles in the newspaper, even notes on the kids who'd found the body—and he was bothered by the Volkswagen. Someone had screwed up by not seriously checking into it right off. There had been a note saying who it belonged to. That was all. Probably because the weekend had come, he told himself.

He kept returning to Jack Reese, the only apparent connection between the Devendall woman and the old railroader. He reminded himself to lay off the photographer for a couple of days. A watched pot never boils, his tea-drinking grandmother had always professed. So he'd let Reese simmer some before trying to pry the lid off the pot. He'd return to the house on Thomas Street in mid-week.

Hating the waiting, he hurried out of the office and headed to Baxter Street for another look at what was left of the Jones house.

No one was in the alley when he pulled his unmarked car off to the side and killed the engine. Climbing out, he glanced at the back of Reese's house, noting the window in the kitchen door from where Reese had said he'd seen the fire. Then he lit a cigarette and studied the ruin of the burned house. The charred fragments still glistened with moisture.

Thursday night, the old man had apparently been sitting in an overstuffed chair in the living room, right off the alley, when whoever came in, came in. At least, that was the conjecture Harter had inherited from the fire marshal and the coroner. There was nothing left of the house or the overstuffed chair, and there'd been little left of the old man. Sometimes Harter wondered how such theories evolved, how anyone could be sure of anything.

Jones was believed to have been beaten and was probably unconscious or already dead when the place was doused with kerosene.

Susan Devendall had been beaten, too.

Harter dropped his cigarette into one of the puddles in the alley and it sizzled before it was soaked. Sunday night, for the third straight night, it had rained. The heavy downpour early Saturday morning had probably created the shallow pool in the canal where Susan Devendall's body had been dumped.

Dumped.

The coroner believed she'd been killed early Saturday and dropped facedown in the water.

Which meant she'd been somewhere for over twenty-four hours after abandoning her car in the alley.

Somewhere she'd stayed—or been kept—wearing only a raincoat and a barrelful of jewelry.

In all her gold and diamonds, she'd been on her way to a photographer in the middle of the night. Figure that out. His instinct told him Reese was holding back. But what—and why?.

The coroner had detected no sign of recent sexual intercourse, rape or otherwise. So, neither sex nor robbery was the apparent motive.

"Ain't you solved it yet?"

Harter turned to see Reese's one-armed neighbor standing a few feet from him in the alley.

"Tattoo, isn't it?"

"How'd you know?"

"Jack Reese told me last night."

"Name's really Henry Kendall. They call me Tattoo. You know, you got Jack upset. He didn't have nothing to do with it."

"Why are you so sure?" asked Harter, watching the older man closely.

"I know him. Knowed him since he was a kid. If you'd seen him the night of the fire, seen how frantic he was about not being able to help Daniel, you wouldn't doubt it."

"You've got to understand. I'm supposed to doubt everything, to check out everything."

"So what do you think?"

"I don't know. It's too early. You knew Daniel Jones well, I take it."

"Yeah, 'course."

"You work with him on the railroad?"

"We both worked for the railroad, but we never worked together. He worked in the shops with Jack's grandfather. I was usually out on trains as a brakeman or something, till I lost my arm."

"Any reason anyone would want to kill him or burn his house down?"

"I got none. I don't figure he had buried treasure in the place. He was too harmless to hate."

"No family, huh?"

"None anyone knows of."

"He didn't tell you of anybody visiting lately? You didn't notice anybody prowling around, did you?"

"No."

"How about the Volkswagen in the alley that night—had you ever seen it before?"

"I don't think. I don't usually keep track of the traffic around here."

"Jack Reese moved the car that night?"

"Yeah. I told him to so's the fire trucks could get down the alley."

"When did you first notice the fire?"

"May and me was in bed and heard Jack yelling outside. I got dressed and run down while she called the fire department."

"What was Reese doing when you got here?"

"Staring at the flames, trying to decide whether to go in and try to pull Daniel out. I told him there was no use."

"You didn't spot a woman around, did you?"

Harter watched as Tattoo nervously shifted his weight from one foot to the other.

"You mean the one that went with the car?"

"Yeah, that's who I mean," said the detective.

"Only thing I know about her is a day or so before, Jack told me he was expecting some woman to come pick up a passport picture he'd taken."

"He never mentioned taking other pictures of her?"

"No. He never mentioned her any other way."

"Has he been busy with his photography lately?"

"Not that many paying jobs. A few for the newspaper. We went out the other morning to a train wreck."

"I saw it in the paper."

"He's been spending a lot of time taking pictures around town since he come back."

"When did he come back to Shawnee?"

"In early August. His tenant moved and he'd lost his job, so he come here for a while."

"How long had he been away?"

"Maybe fifteen years."

"What'd he do all that time?"

"I don't know much about it. I think he worked for a magazine. I told you, you're wasting your time checking on him. He's a good boy. Like everyone else, I'm sure you can find out things about him that he'd rather you didn't know, but he ain't no killer."

"I hope you're right," said Harter as he glanced again at Reese's tall, narrow brick house. "Look, I may come back and see you in the next few days. If you think of anything odd about last week, or anything I should know about Daniel Jones, call me."

He pulled a card out of his jacket and handed it to Tattoo. Then he climbed back in his car and headed down the alley and out onto the Avenue toward South Shawnee, past the railroad yards, toward the old Shawnee & Chesapeake Canal.

He'd only seen the spot where her body had been found in the cloudy dark of Saturday night. He'd been in the midst of a candlelight dinner at

Liz's when the chief had called. They always knew where they could get him. And he always responded, even if it meant leaving a birthday meal.

He maneuvered through the cramped streets of Shantytown—or what had once been Shantytown but was now giving way to the prefab houses of a neighborhood they'd started calling Riverview. The collapsing canaller joints and shacks were, street by street, being ripped down and replaced with $60,000 aluminum-sided residences. The Shawnee city fathers and Chamber of Commerce were working on plans to turn the old canal itself into a public park. "The perfect hiking/biking trail," their brochure proclaimed. No one was anxious to save the canallers' shanties and haunts for posterity. They were too gritty for a park. They were eyesores.

He lit a cigarette as he turned onto the road that led to the arched bridge across the canal and over to the box factory. Just before he reached the bridge, he pulled off the road and parked behind a rusting Ford. He sensed immediately who it belonged to.

"You come here often?" Harter asked Jack Reese when they met on the towpath a few minutes later.

Reese, his camera hanging by a worn leather strap from his shoulder, was staring into a puddle of rainwater trapped in the abandoned canal.

"I wanted to see it. I read the morning paper and came out here." His voice betrayed an unmistakable nervousness.

"Well, this isn't the place," said Harter. He began to head down the towpath with long, quick strides. Reese fell in step alongside him.

"You been out here before taking pictures?" asked Harter. "I would think this place'd be a photographer's field day, what with all the locks and antique structures and stone walls and things."

"I haven't been here in years," answered Reese. "Not since I was a kid. After my grandfather retired from the railroad, he walked a lot for his heart. We'd come here and he'd tell me about the mule drivers and the flatboats and the winos sleeping under the bridges. He knew some people who lived in Shantytown, and we'd visit them."

"Yeah, they stayed around for years after the canal shut down, didn't they? Couldn't tear themselves away from this place. Home is home, I guess." Harter came to a stop. "Right over there's where the kids found the body."

He pointed across the canal to a small pond near a lock on the other side. Water had collected on a stone slab that was lower than the rest of the trench. The bank down to the pool was pockmarked with footprints and signs of Saturday-night activity. The kids, and later the police themselves, had mangled the muddy bank, so there was no chance of finding footprints.

"Did she drown there?" asked Reese.

"No, she was dead when she was put there. Multiple blows. The one to the head was the big one."

Harter looked sideways to size up Reese's reaction. Tattoo had claimed the photographer wasn't a killer, but there was no way to know.

Harter believed almost anyone was capable of murder once they got started. Adrenaline could make up for size and initial lack of resolve. A baseball bat could make up for soft hands—especially when one victim was eighty-five years old and the other was a slim, manicured, unmuscled woman.

"Then they had to carry the body up the towpath quite a ways," said Reese, staring at the dirty water.

"Not necessarily. Look over at the other side. That's the parking lot for the box factory over there. They could have almost driven to the edge of the canal. If it was dark, no one would have seen them."

"The cardboard box factory is closed down?"

"It's been gone since the late sixties."

"I didn't know. I was out of town then. Everything in Shawnee seems to be closing. What happened?"

"I don't know," said Harter after a minute's pause. "I'm a cop, not an industrialist. The workers there tried to start a union and the company moved away."

"Just like the steelworkers say Shawnee Steel is planning to?"

"Yeah, just like that."

"Sometime the cheap labor'll wise up," said Reese. 'They'll get tired of breaking their backs for low wages and the allure of the Sunbelt will wear off."

Harter said nothing. That was his policy: Keep your opinions to yourself. He'd already said too much. Eventually he turned away and began walking back to the cars. He barely noticed Reese had caught up with him until the younger man asked a question.

"Are you originally from Shawnee?"

"Yeah," said Harter, volunteering nothing more.

"How'd you get to be a detective?"

"I needed a job."

When they reached the parked cars, Harter lit a cigarette and got in his vehicle. He rolled down the window and said, "Don't forget to call me if you think of anything," before turning around and slowly pulling away.

In the rearview mirror, he watched as Reese slid the camera off his shoulder and began walking over the bridge, over the canal, toward the old box factory.

15

A BRIGHT SUN reflected off the roof and white walls of the Devendall mansion Tuesday morning as Harter backed into a parking spot on the street out front.

"*Mansion* is an exaggeration," Liz would lecture him. "Your class consciousness is showing. It's a character flaw. Can't you outgrow it?"

Like she had outgrown hers. Somewhere along the line, her training and clientele had erased any "class consciousness" she had—if she'd ever had any to begin with. His own training and clientele had just heightened his. Obviously, it was a sign of his origins that he'd parked on the street rather than circle up the drive to the front door.

Maybe it was best he and Liz didn't live together, he told himself.

Mansion or not, they didn't build houses like the Devendalls' anymore. For starters, you couldn't afford to heat them unless you had a hell of a lot of money to begin with. And without servants, there weren't enough hours in the day to keep such a place up. You could spend the warm-weather days just keeping the garden in shape. You could spend your winters just clearing the snow off the walks and driveway.

Carrying a brown envelope, Harter walked up the brick path past a Shawnee Historical Society plaque that proclaimed the house had been built in 1855 by one Shriver Devendall, a railroad and coal speculator who had been a state legislator before the Civil War.

A maid in a gray pinstriped dress answered his rap on the door with the knocker. Harter had seen the black maid and the spacious entry hall before.

Sunday afternoon, Amy Devendall had called headquarters to say she'd discovered something unusual in her daughter-in-law's room. When Harter had arrived, the maid had handed him a sealed envelope. Mrs. Devendall, she'd said, was in bed and didn't wish to see anyone. Howard Devendall hadn't yet returned to Shawnee.

Outside, in his car, Harter had torn open the envelope and found the photos. Jack Reese's name was stamped on the back of each one.

This time, the maid led him down the entry hall and into a large room that looked like an antique shop. Leatherbound books lined the walls. The massive Victorian furniture made it seem as if Shriver Devendall himself had just risen from his pigeonhole desk and left for a moment.

Mr. Devendall had gone to his office and would be back shortly, said the maid. Mrs. Devendall would be with him directly. Her tone of voice made it sound almost like a warning.

Harter sat down and felt even more out of place when he realized he was on a loveseat. Liz would have laughed at how he squirmed.

He placed the brown envelope on the plush material next to him and rested his hand on top of it. Through the paper he could feel the jewelry that had been taken from Susan Devendall's body.

After leaving Reese at the canal Monday, Harter had spent the afternoon showing off the necklace, bracelets, earrings, and various gold chains to Shawnee jewelers. Usually such rounds were the kind of things he tried to pawn off on Caruthers or some beat cop, but, having nothing productive to do, he'd gone to the jewelers himself.

No one could identify a thing. Could be imported, one had said. Could be made by one of those hippies who sell at craft fairs, according to another. "Custom-made. We don't stock anything like this," a third had said, holding up the largest chain with obvious distaste.

"Detective Harter?" she said before he was aware she was in the room.

He rose from the loveseat. "Hello, Mrs. Devendall. I came to ask you a few questions."

"I know," she said in a manner that somehow translated into "You may." Crossing the red swirls of the Oriental carpet, she arranged herself carefully in a chair beside the elaborate desk.

Amy Devendall looked to be in her seventies, and well taken care of. She was dressed to the teeth, false or not, and looking at her Harter figured she always was. She carried the smell of perfume with her. She said nothing. Just waited for him to begin.

Finally he asked, "Do you have any idea what may have happened to your daughter-in-law?"

"No," she said, clearly and forthrightly.

"As I understand it, your son was out of town all week," said Harter, starting with the basics.

"Howard was in Pittsburgh on business for Shawnee Steel. As you may know, he is an attorney. He's on retainer with various industries to represent them in legal matters and government hoopla. He didn't feel like staying around the house this morning, so he went to his office. We expect him back at any moment, and you may ask him anything you like."

"Susan . . . your daughter-in-law didn't usually go on such business trips with him?"

"Rarely. After the first year or two of their marriage, she usually stayed home, especially if she was working."

"Working?"

"She was . . . I imagine you'd call her a social worker, if you can believe that."

"A social worker here in Shawnee?" asked Harter with some surprise.

Her obituary hadn't mentioned a job.

"Yes. What do they call it these days? The Department of Human Services? It's welfare no matter what they call it, isn't it? She worked for the welfare department on and off for years. Until this past summer. I always told Howard the girl felt guilty about being well off. She was rebelling against her father's wealth, and later against ours, if you ask me. It was all quite ridiculous. In the early seventies she went to anti-war demonstrations and all that. Howard fell head over heels for her when they met and was a long time in realizing how different they really were."

"When were they married?"

"Oh, I imagine it was 1977. Yes, it was a week or two after the peanut farmer became president."

"She was working for Human Services then?"

"I believe that was when she first quit for a time. Then she went back."

"And she quit again this summer? Was there a reason?"

"A very good reason. A colored man tried to rape her last spring. She was never the same afterwards."

"When was this?"

"I should think it was early April. She quit in August."

"Do you know the man's name?"

"No. I'm sure the welfare people could tell you. Do you believe it has something to do with her . . . her murder, Detective Harter?"

"It's hard to say. I'll check it out. Is there anything else you know about the attempted rape?"

"Howard wanted to prosecute the man, but Susan wouldn't let him. I believe she was afraid of what would happen when she went back to the colored neighborhood. For a time, they transferred her to a position working with old people, but she'd finally come to her senses. She didn't explain it to me, but I saw signs that she was suddenly interested in clothes and social functions—all the things she'd once made fun of. Susan, you must understand, did not confide in me. I'm not sure she confided in Howard, either."

"Who might she have confided in?"

Amy Devendall folded her hands in her lap. "She didn't have many women friends. Odd, isn't it, how these attractive modern girls come and go and pride themselves on freedom, yet make so few quality friends?"

"I wouldn't know," said Harter. "Am I to assume that your son and his wife weren't very close?"

"Ask Howard."

Put off by the chill in her voice, he changed course. "When was the last time you saw your daughter-in-law alive?"

"It would have been late Thursday evening. I thought I heard the television—the eleven o'clock news—in her room when I retired. She often stayed up watching the news or movies. Sometimes she left the house at night, especially when Howard was away, though I'm sure she didn't know I knew."

"You believe she was alone at the time you passed her door?"

"Certainly," said Amy Devendall, almost challenging his question.

"Was she home every evening last week?"

The response was a long time coming. "No."

"What night was she gone?"

"She left early Wednesday night and must have returned after I was in bed. Tuesday evening she was also out. Howard called home that night and I was forced to tell him I didn't know where Susan was. I sensed he expected as much."

"You have no idea where she was those nights?"

"No. I frequently had no idea what she did."

"Did she always drive the Volkswagen?"

"Yes. Howard offered her a new sports car for running about town, but she preferred the Volkswagen. To hide her position, I believe. She didn't want her customers to smell her money."

"Her customers?"

"The welfare types."

"Her clients?"

"Yes."

"So you have no idea where she went Tuesday, Wednesday, or Thursday night?"

"I said I didn't."

"When did you decide to tell the police she was missing?"

"Saturday morning, after she'd been away two nights. Howard had called again on Friday evening to say he would have to stay in Pittsburgh longer than he'd planned. He asked about her and again I told him she wasn't home. I was worried, and on Saturday morning I called the police. I didn't know what else to do."

"She'd never stayed away that long before?"

"No," she said, biting off further explanation.

"She made no attempt to contact you or your son after Thursday evening?"

"We heard nothing until the officer came to the door Saturday night and said her body had been found in the canal. I immediately called Howard. Neither of us could begin to imagine what she'd been doing on that side of town."

"Where might you have expected her to be?"

"I certainly expected her to be at home, not out prowling the city," snapped Amy Devendall.

"Any idea who she might have been with on the nights she was out?" he pressed.

After a pause, Amy Devendall said, "I would only be guessing, and I prefer not to guess about such matters."

"Your guess could be the best lead I've got," he tried.

"Sorry, I can't help you. I'm in no position to know with certainty. Have you talked with that photographer?"

"He claims he didn't even know her name. Says she simply came and paid for some photos to be taken. Some of them may have been for a passport. Was she planning a trip?"

"Not to my knowledge."

"You found the pictures in her room Sunday?"

She nodded slowly. "I went in to look around. I was too upset to go to church. I was waiting for Howard to return home or call with word about when he would. I walked around the house, then looked in her room. I imagined I was doing the police a favor."

"Could I see Susan's room?"

"I'm sure you could force me to show you, if I said no."

"Yes, I could."

"Then I suppose we better get it over and done with."

She rose from the desk chair and began walking from the room. Harter followed her back into the hallway and down to a staircase that spiraled upward. The way Amy Devendall gripped the banister and slowly climbed the steps forced Harter to remember her age. No matter how good a job he wanted to do, no matter how much he disliked her, she *was* an old lady—an old lady who'd had to face up to the scandalous death of a daughter-in-law she obviously hadn't approved of.

Scandalous. Not a word he'd normally use. But one he figured Amy Devendall would.

Having navigated the stairway, she led him to a closed door. She pushed it open and stayed in the hall as she waved her hand for him to enter.

"Your son and his wife had separate bedrooms?" asked Harter as he scanned the light-filled room. Lace curtains covered the large windows, allowing the sunlight in. Between two of the windows was an antique canopied bed.

"Of course they each had their own room," said Amy Devendall, as if the thought of the two sharing a room—sharing a bed—had never occurred to her.

"Are most of Susan's things in this room?"

"I haven't removed anything but the photos," she said defensively.

"No, I meant she doesn't have another room for a study or anything?"

"Her things are here."

Harter crossed the lush ivory carpet and looked down at the combs, brushes, lipsticks, and makeups laid out on a vanity with a round full-length mirror.

"When you looked, did you notice whether anything was missing?"

"Taken?" she asked, misinterpreting him again.

"No. Had she packed a bag?"

Before answering, Amy Devendall came into the room and crossed to a white door. She opened it and stepped into a large walk-in closet. After some poking around, she said, “As far as I can judge, everything is here. I didn’t know she had so many clothes. I’ve never seen some of them. When she was a social worker, she always claimed she didn’t care about clothes. She almost never wore makeup. Howard and I would have to convince her to spruce herself up. Some of these things are brand new.” She reached forward, moved a pink dress, and looked down. “Her over-night case is here. We keep the luggage in the attic. I’ll have Martha check if you like.”

“I’d appreciate it,” said Harter. “Just where did you find the photos Sunday morning?”

“In the dresser . . . in her lingerie drawer. I’ll tell you, I was taken aback by some of those pictures.”

“Did you find anything else odd?” asked Harter, crossing to the dresser.

“ ‘Odd’ is such an odd choice of words, Detective. Let’s say, nothing else like the photographs.”

Harter slid open a dresser drawer and glanced down at underwear, bras, slips in all styles and colors. “This where you found them?”

“Yes.”

“You’ve looked through all the other drawers?”

“Yes.”

He turned and stared at her. “There were no notes or love letters or good-bye messages or anything along those lines?”

“No,” she answered, without half the offense he had feared. Maybe he was wearing her down.

He opened a jewelry box on top of the dresser. It was nearly empty.

“Susan didn’t wear much jewelry,” explained Amy Devendall before he could ask. “I think it was like the Volkswagen. Howard was always offering to buy her things, but she said no.”

He closed the box. “What was she wearing when you last saw her?”

She reached inside the closet and held up the sleeve of a silk Oriental robe. “This is what she had on before she came up to her room. She bought it this summer.”

“Do you know what she was wearing the other nights when she went out?”

“Not exactly. She wore a raincoat when she left the house. Just an old raincoat she’d had for years and wore to work.”

“Mother!”

Mrs. Devendall stepped away from the closet and went out into the hall.

“We’re upstairs, Howard,” she called.

Harter stood next to the dresser and waited for his first glimpse of Susan’s husband. For all intents and purposes, her *estranged* husband, it seemed. Having seen the young woman in Reese’s photos, he wasn’t prepared for Howard being as old as he was. Mid-forties at least. Maybe fifteen years older than his wife.

For a minute, he found it hard to concentrate on Howard's features. His face was so ashen and his eyes so pale that the man's head nearly blended into the light walls. His gray hair did little to destroy the illusion.

"This is Detective Harter, dear," Howard Devendall's mother told him. "He wanted to see Susan's room. I didn't think it would hurt."

"No, whatever the police want," said Devendall. The way his jaw clenched as he talked and his movements as he stepped into the room showed Harter that the pale lawyer did have some muscle attached to his rather boyish frame.

"I don't believe we've met before," said Harter. "I know most of the attorneys in Shawnee."

"I don't take criminal cases," Devendall said. Then, brusquely, he asked, "Is there anything else you would like to see while you're here, Detective?"

"I don't think I have to see any other room in the house. But I'd like to talk to you, if I could."

"Shall we go back downstairs?" Devendall asked.

"Fine."

The word was barely out of Harter's mouth before Amy Devendall was leading the way down the hall, then the stairs. He found himself feeling a little claustrophobic sandwiched in between her and her tall, pale son as they descended the curving staircase.

"We'll really have to paint the banisters and the wooden trim this year, Howard," said the old woman, fingering the railing as she neared the bottom. "You wouldn't believe how much work is involved in simply preserving one's inheritance, Mr. Harter."

"Oh, I'd believe it."

"Families that don't take care of what they have are the ones who don't keep it for long," she continued. "Whether it's a house or a reputation, one must constantly work at it." She came to a stop at the library door. "You two go in and talk. I'll leave you alone. I could have Martha bring you some sandwiches for lunch, if you like."

"That would be good," said Devendall.

"And I won't forget, Detective Harter," she added before she disappeared into the house. "I'll have Martha go up to the attic and see that all the luggage is there."

Harter was sure Amy Devendall never forgot to attend to such details. He was almost as sure all the suitcases would be in their proper places.

Inside the library again, Harter picked up the evidence envelope from the loveseat. This time he staked out the desk chair for himself.

He waited for Howard Devendall to relax into a seat before opening the envelope and pouring the jewelry onto the desk. "Do you have any idea where this came from?" he asked.

As with the luggage, he thought he knew what the answer was going to be.

16

AFTER HE LEFT the Devendall mansion—he'd stick with that word—Harter spent a chunk of the afternoon making a stream-bank check.

He had a friend who worked for the State Health Department. Sometimes, when the guy had inspected enough septic systems and taken enough water samples and bagged enough rabid animals for the lab, he'd drive out into the mountains to make what he called a stream-bank check.

Which really meant he'd sit on a stream-bank and check the state of his mind. *And body.*

Harter's stream-bank checks rarely involved much real communing with nature. Sometimes he simply drove around Shawnee, the city he knew like the brown of his own eyes. Once in a while, he would drive south of town to the overlook on the mountain. From there he would stare down on the city where he'd been born and wonder what he was doing. Occasionally, he would show up at Liz's at lunchtime in hopes she was alone and had time to hold him.

This Tuesday, however, he merely drove long through the west side of town, past the big houses, some even bigger and grander than the Devendall period piece. When he tired of the west side, he headed east, crossed the river bridge, ducked through the underpass, and headed toward downtown Shawnee from the south.

Passing the idle Shawnee Steel mill he noticed that about a dozen men were still carrying signs on the cracked sidewalk outside the huge plant building. They probably had nothing else to do. Day after day, week after week, they would picket, their numbers slowly dwindling.

Harter had seen many pickets in his day. The bitterest times he personally remembered had been during the long rail strikes of the mid-1950s and late 1960s. Some of his own relatives had even been involved. He'd seen winter days when the men built fires in oil drums to warm their hands so they could keep going. They had acted like their lives were at stake, and he guessed they were.

He had had two uncles who didn't speak for fifty years because one of them had been a scab in the twenties. Better to starve to death than to cross a picket line, his father had always said.

He didn't know what he would do if he was ever called on to move against strikers. Maybe he'd sit down, resign, or be fired. Sometimes it was strange being a cop, representing the so-called law.

The steel mill might be closed, but the big shots hadn't stopped their activity. Lights burned in some of the offices. And Howard Devendall had been sent to Pittsburgh on company business the week before. He could have been making plans to move the mill south, like the pickets claimed, or to farm their jobs out to Korea or Taiwan. He'd told Harter he'd taken a charter flight on Sunday evening, October 10. Everything had been perfectly normal when he'd left Shawnee's small airport. Whatever *normal* meant.

From what he'd heard so far, Harter didn't consider Howard and Susan Devendall's marriage "perfectly normal." They had met at her father's funeral, Devendall had told him, after they'd gotten over the hump about the jewelry he couldn't identify. Oh, Howard had seen Susan at social events before, he'd said. He'd rather watched her grow up. But it was at Mr. Maddox's funeral in 1976 that they'd gravitated to each other. Susan, then twenty-three, was alone, her mother having died when she was fifteen.

She had been close to her mother, said her husband. Probably closer than she could ever be to anyone else again. Her mother had been a nurse who'd married the president of the hospital board of directors. Susan wanted to help people too, but she didn't have the patience for nursing. So she became a social worker. At the time of her father's death, at the time Howard and Susan began their courtship, she'd taken a long leave of absence and was unsure whether she'd return to work.

She went through those periods, Devendall said. Sometimes she enjoyed spending money, shopping, and living a life of leisure. Other times she felt the compulsion of a career.

No one had expected their marriage, least of all his mother, who had never liked Susan, or vice versa, he admitted. But Susan had wanted the company and a more settled life. He had wanted a wife, and had begun to believe he wanted a son.

Before long, Susan grew bored and went back to social work. There was to be no child. They comfortably went their own ways. Sometimes they didn't sleep together for months at a stretch.

Yes, she had changed in the last year. He couldn't put his finger on it. There had been the attempted rape in April, but the change had started before that. After the rape, she no longer had the nerve to visit the Negro projects. Her opinions had grown more conservative. She'd seemed less involved in her work. Ask her supervisor at the Department of Human Services, insisted Devendall, giving Harter a name and number.

So, Tuesday afternoon, after losing a few hours on his stream-bank check, Harter sat down at his desk, called the welfare office, and made an appointment with a Linda Dean for Wednesday morning.

Then he moved the "bricks" around on his desk again. Among them now was the report on the fingerprints found in the Volkswagen. Only two sets—the victim's and Jack Reese's.

"How's it going?" asked Caruthers as he came into the office they shared.

"Could be better," Harter answered, watching the medium-sized man collapse into his chair.

Harter always described Caruthers as "medium." Medium height. Medium weight. Medium-length salt-and-pepper hair. Medium voice. Medium viewpoints. Medium intelligence. If there was such a thing as the medium American, Caruthers was him, from the informality of his sportcoat to the practicality with which he approached problems.

"If you need any help on the case, checking anything out, let me know."

"There's nothing I can't handle yet," said Harter, playing his cards close.

"That won't make the chief's day."

"What are you on to?"

"A couple of B and E's, some vandalisms at vacant warehouses. They seemed related. Probably kids."

"You'd think they'd at least have the smarts to break in someplace with something worth stealing," said Harter, lighting a cigarette. Caruthers, like Liz, hated it when he smoked. Sometimes he smoked up the room just to drive the other detective out.

"You going to Liz's tonight?" asked Caruthers, flipping through the papers on his desk.

"No, you know the routine by now. Just Wednesdays and weekends. The other weeknights she has classes."

"So you'll head back to your lonely apartment and pop a TV dinner in the oven. You two really ought to get married."

"You forget I've been married, and I don't cook TV dinners," said Harter, blowing smoke toward Caruthers' desk. "I hate the mashed potatoes and peas and the little helpings. Tonight I'll feast. One of Mattioni's deluxe hoagies."

"You'll die eating that stuff."

"You tell me what could be healthier than a chef's salad on an Italian roll. Meatloaf?" He snubbed out his cigarette butt.

"I like meatloaf," said Caruthers.

"I don't," said Harter, putting on his black jacket and heading for the door.

Outside headquarters he turned right and quickly walked the two blocks to Mattioni's. Pushing open the heavy glass door, he breathed in that spicy salami-and-olive-oil aroma. Better than Amy Devendall's heavy perfume had been, that was for sure.

The evening line was shorter than at lunchtime, when a dozen or more downtown workers, courthouse employees, street punks, and cops might crowd into the small place. Sometimes you could wait in that line forever.

No matter how long the line got, old man Mattioni kept the same pace and ignored all but the customer in front of him. One sandwich at a time. He even refused to cut a pile of thin salami ahead of time. Everything cut fresh every time, no dried edges, no brown lettuce, no waste. Mattioni had no desire to turn out less than a masterpiece. Amazingly, it was also one of the cheapest subs in town.

The old man, nearly always silent, nodded a good evening to Harter as he slid his cash across the counter. Harter picked up his hoagie, and went back to the street. At his car, he climbed in, and drove away from the downtown, across the tracks, and up the hill into East Shawnee.

He turned onto his narrow side street and slipped the stick into reverse after turning off the engine. Once inside the turn-of-the-century frame house, he climbed to the third floor.

The apartment was big enough for Harter's needs. A living room, simple, modern, angular. A kitchen, large enough to eat in but small enough to reach the tan refrigerator from almost anyplace in it. A bedroom, roomy enough for a king-sized bed, with a closet that more than held his clothes. A bathroom that worked.

He'd been glad to find the place in a rush eight years before. The living room even offered a view of the abandoned Shawnee-Potomac passenger station. He hoped they wouldn't replace it with a Holiday Inn, like the plans called for.

He put the hoagie down on the low wooden table in front of the couch, took off his jacket and gun, and went to the kitchen for a Coke. Then he switched on the evening news.

Shawnee didn't have a television station, but the Bartlesburg station, fifty miles to the east, came in on cable, and WBRT made at least a cursory attempt to cover Shawnee. It was a "Good News" station, custom-made for the eighties, given to footage of Rotary clubs, visiting congressmen, charity bazaars, fashion shows, boy scouts, and the like. For the most part, WBRT didn't cover Shawnee's crimes. So far the only reports he'd seen about Susan Devendall or Daniel Jones had been the simple facts in *The News,* and *The News* had had nothing new to say Tuesday morning. He hoped it stayed that way for a while. He was sure Amy Devendall, with her concern for her family's reputation, felt the same way.

The Devendalls must have hated even the limited publicity they'd gotten. It certainly had *National Enquirer* possibilities. **NUDE, BEJEWELLED SOCIALITE FOUND IN SHANTYTOWN.** Except that Susan Devendall might have fought being depicted as the socialite her mother-in-law wished she would be.

Amy Devendall had carefully measured her words. She'd insinuated more than she'd said. Harter had decided her message was: Susan was a social worker. *Imagine that!* She'd spent her days with the shiftless. No wonder she had nearly been raped in the projects. No wonder she'd ended up in Shantytown. She shouldn't have been there.

Shantytown. When Harter had joined the force in the mid-sixties, there'd still been an aged cop or two around to fill him up with tales of Shantytown Saturday nights, when the hootch was blinding and the gambling fixed and the women lewd. They'd told him of heads crashed in by thick brown bottles and of bloated bodies floating until struck by passing canal boats.

He'd never expected to have his own tale, his own bashed-in head, his own body in the ditch. *And a west-side body at that.*

"You really should get over this class-conscious thing, this feeling you're working-class and the west-side people are the bosses and never the twain shall meet," Liz kept telling him.

Harter swallowed his last bite of hoagie, crumpled up the white butcher paper it had come in, and took the wad to the kitchen garbage can. Back in the living room, he turned off the TV and sprawled on the couch.

He wished he could see Liz right then. He'd joked about enrolling in one of her aerobics classes so he could see her more often. In the last couple of years, she'd been busier with exercise classes than with dance classes, a trend she didn't particularly care for. But she had to pay the bills, just like everyone else.

He grabbed the paperback book off the coffee table and opened it to his place. Liz was the one who'd suggested he give up Dashiell Hammett for Sinclair Lewis, a better writer than he'd expected. She'd been high on *Main Street,* with its careful piling up of facts about a small town, like clues in a mystery that never happened.

But he could only concentrate in spurts. When he'd reached his limit, he leaned his head against the arm of the couch and tilted it back so he was staring up at the Edward Hopper print on the wall. Liz had given him the street-corner scene two years before, after he'd been drawn to it in a museum shop during a weekend they spent in New York. The brightly lit eatery in the black city night was like somewhere he'd walked into and out of many times. It could never pass as sheer decoration.

He lit another cigarette and let his thoughts drift back to a conversation they had once had.

"Maybe I shouldn't see things like I do, but I can't help it," he had said.

"With a little effort, you could help it," she'd responded.

"I keep thinking of John L. Lewis."

"Your family were railroaders, not coalminers. What do you know about John L. Lewis?"

"It's the idea. I've read that in the thirties—I don't know exactly when—John L. Lewis gave a speech about how the future belonged to the working people. He talked about the miners' children getting educations so they could become lawyers and teachers and doctors and help put the worker on equal footing with the bosses."

"So?"

"So it happened, and it didn't work. Millions of coalminers' kids and factory workers' kids and railroaders' kids have gotten more education. We became those lawyers, teachers, and doctors. We became artists, dancers, and detectives. We became middle-class. We stopped worrying about the people we came from."

"Stop feeling guilty," she'd said.

"I can't stop feeling it," he'd said. "All I can do is stop talking about it."

17

HARTER TOOK THE ORANGE PLASTIC CHAIR he was directed to and waited for Linda Dean.

He had no idea whether all days were so busy at the welfare office, but the place was certainly snapping Wednesday morning. There must have been a couple dozen people filling out forms or waiting for assistance in the Department of Human Services' downtown office. They made the storefront—an old shoe store that had been divided and subdivided into cubicles—seem crowded. Now and then a welfare worker would lead someone out of one of the cubicles and take another in.

Mostly the room was populated by women. The social workers were almost all women—at least the ones he could see. The people waiting were primarily younger women with screaming babies on their laps.

Deep down, Harter had his doubts about the welfare system, about whether it was possible to keep paying money to people who didn't work, who produced nothing but babies. He stared at the women, at the babies. It was beyond him what to do. Even if you put the kids in government day-care, it was no sure thing the mothers could find jobs these days. They looked so young, the mothers. He bet half of them had dropped out of high school pregnant.

The baby next to him was crying so loudly he didn't hear his name when the woman called it.

"Detective Harter?" she asked again, planting herself right in front of him. "I'm Linda Dean. Come this way."

He got up and followed her through the maze of cubicles until she ducked through a doorway and sat down behind a metal government desk that took up half her office.

"Like I told you on the phone, I'm looking for information about Susan Maddox Devendall," he said, sitting down.

"I was shocked when I read about it," said Linda Dean. "I don't know how Susan would have gotten herself into that situation."

"What situation?"

"I mean being found murdered in the canal."

"So I suppose you've got no thoughts on why she might have been in that area?"

"None at all."

"What was Mrs. Devendall like?"

Linda Dean nervously brushed back strands of her graying hair. "That's hard to say. I knew her for so long. I've been a supervisor for over ten years. I was the one who interviewed her for a job originally. She was fresh from college and had a definite social consciousness. I saw her moods over the years. It's hard to pinpoint the times when her personality changed drastically. I remember when she quit for a while, about the time her father died."

"Mr. Maddox died in 1976?"

"Yes. He'd been ill for months. We'd all been overworked here. The 1974-75 recession had strained us just like this one is doing. She said she wanted to take care of her father in his last illness. I thought she just wanted a break. I'd always been under the impression she and her father weren't very close."

"Her mother-in-law seems to think Susan Devendall was embarrassed about her family's wealth."

"Amy Devendall *would* think that."

"You know Amy Devendall?"

"Not very well. She isn't a fan of the Department of Human Services. From the way Susan talked about her, she wasn't a fan of Susan's, either. I shouldn't have said that. Mrs. Devendall could be right. Susan could have been rebelling against her family. Girls in their teens and early twenties do that, you know. Then, as they grow older, they often revert to the mores they grew up with. I'm sounding clinical, aren't I? Of course, her rebellious streak wouldn't have prepared anyone for her marriage to Howard Devendall."

"He was quite a bit older, wasn't he?" asked Harter.

"Yes." She seemed to calculate her words. "To be honest, I always believed she was seeking a father figure after Mr. Maddox died."

"She came back to work after her marriage?"

Linda Dean nodded. "Late in 1977, I think. I could get the exact date from her personnel file."

"I don't think that's necessary. Did you notice any change in her when she came back?"

Linda Dean considered what she was about to say. "She was still a good worker, though I believe the job wasn't as important to her. I was never quite sure why she stayed with it. The pay, of course, meant nothing. Twice I had to call her to ask her to cash her checks because the auditor was going crazy. She seemed more and more to have a split personality about her background and her job. She might have been guilty about her wealth, but she certainly wouldn't have wanted to be anything but rich. I know she'd been buying a lot of clothes, though she almost always wore an old skirt or jeans to work. She drove a Volkswagen, but it was well-equipped, a stereo system and air conditioning. You figure it out."

"I'm told she changed even more after an attempted rape on the job."

"Yes."

"A black man?"

She nodded. "Susan was visiting clients in the public housing project and apparently became involved in a conversation with the man. She came back to the office very upset and claimed he'd tried to assault her. But she didn't press charges."

"Do you know who the man was?"

"Ace Stewart. That's a nickname, of course. I'm not sure of his real first name. I could probably look it up."

"James," said Harter.

"You know him?"

"Yeah."

"Is he a bad one? Could he have something to do with her death?"

Harter didn't answer. Instead, he asked, "She went on working?"

Looking a little irritated that he'd changed the subject, Linda Dean said, "She took a couple of weeks off. After she returned, she didn't want to go to the projects again, which I suppose would be a natural reaction. She asked what other jobs were available. I found her a position as an outreach worker with the Commission on Aging."

"When did she start with them?"

"Early in May. I believe she quit altogether at the beginning of August."

"Didn't like the job?"

"You'd have to talk to them. From what I hear, they were glad she quit. Here, see this woman," she said, scribbling a name and address on a slip of paper and sliding it over to Harter. "I could call her if you want and tell her you're coming."

"That would be good."

"Shall I say you're on your way?"

"I probably won't get there until afternoon," said Harter, stuffing the paper in the pocket of his jacket as he stood up. He'd decided to drop in on Ace Stewart and had no idea how long it would take.

AS HE DROVE, he wondered what kind of reception Ace would give him once the point of his visit became clear. He'd known Ace Stewart most of his life. They'd grown up playing ball together in a burned-out lot on the fringe of what, in the 1950s, had been called the "colored" neighborhood. Amy Devendall still used the word *colored.* At least that was better than *nigger.*

When Harter was a kid, before the schools had been desegregated, before blocks of row houses had been demolished in the name of urban renewal, before the projects had been built, Dab's Chicken House, long gone, had been the dividing line. The restaurant, with its reputed bookie joint in the rear, had stood on the corner of Grant and Lincoln, open to both races.

The brick row houses on the north side of the street hadn't seemed much different from the ones on the south. Maybe they were a little more run-down, but the only striking difference was that white railroad families, like Harter's, lived south of Dab's, while on the north side of the street most of the bodies were black.

Ace's father, a stooped but dignified man, had been a porter back in the days when porters and cooks were about the only Shawnee-Potomac jobs allowed to "coloreds"—Negroes—blacks.

When he had died in 1979, Harter went to the funeral and then to the wake at the project apartment where Mrs. Stewart lived with her youngest daughter and her daughter's two children. Ace had just broken up with his wife at the time. There'd been something so melancholy about him that Harter could hardly stand it. He sensed the melancholy wasn't just Ace grieving for his father or singing the blues over his wife. It ran all the way through him.

Two years older than Harter, Ace had been the first black star of East Shawnee High's football team. That had been in 1957-58. Everyone expected he'd land a big scholarship and eventually make the pros. Somehow he hadn't. He'd gone to work for State Roads and, after the politics changed, managed to catch on with Shawnee Steel in the late sixties.

Harter dreaded what he was about to do. He didn't want to circulate through the projects looking for Ace or to knock on Mrs. Stewart's door asking about him. He didn't want to think about Ace Stewart almost raping Susan Devendall.

He turned the corner where the old black church had once been, and where he had often stood on Sunday nights to hear the rocking gospel music coming from inside. He'd never been able to relate to the neighborhood in the same way after they'd torn down the row houses and the church and put up the government housing. He wasn't convinced the projects were better than the way of life they'd replaced.

He got one break. As he'd hoped, Ace Stewart, too big for walls to hold in on a sunny day, was leaning on the mailbox in front of the projects.

Harter pulled up to the curb, reached across the seat to open the door, and said, "Climb in, Ace. Let's go for a ride."

They'd driven a block before Ace broke the silence. "We going to Jamaica?"

"I've got to ask you some questions," said Harter, glancing across the seat at the bulk of his old friend. Ace Stewart had upper arms like a woman's thighs. You had to study his face closely to notice his mustache and goatee.

"What about?"

"Susan Devendall."

"I didn't do nothing."

"I didn't say you did."

"She's got herself killed now."

"Yeah," mumbled Harter, pondering the way Ace had put it. "Let's start with last April."

"Refresh my mind."

"She claimed you tried to rape her."

"She come on to me. Don't you think I can tell when some woman comes up and's ready to rub herself all over you if you give her a shove?"

"And you gave her a shove?"

"I touched her arm. Honest, Harter, that's all I did."

"How'd you get in that situation with her in the first place?"

"You want the long or short version?"

"Try medium."

"This Devendall woman was visiting my sister for the welfare office. I'm living at home now that I'm single and laid off. So she's there and I come in and after a while my sister goes out to check on a kid or something. Mom wasn't around. So this woman asks what I'm doing home in the middle of the day and I tell her I got laid off before Thanksgiving, in the first batch of steel layoffs. After fourteen years—you believe that? So she says, You ain't been working for five months? I say, No. And she says, We gotta find you a job. And I say, Find one, I tried. She says they're hiring dishwashers at Maxi's and how someplace else needs a custodian and how I could go back to school for computer training. So I say, Look, lady, I'm a steelworker. I ain't no janitor or no busboy and I ain't good at books. She didn't like my answer much."

Ace stopped. Waiting for him to start again, Harter pulled a cigarette pack out of his black jacket and wiggled one free. "Smoke?"

Ace took the pack and pushed in the dashboard lighter. "You ain't gonna believe the rest of this, Harter. I don't know why I'm telling you."

"You're telling me 'cause I asked."

"She looks me over and says, I can see you're a steelworker. You're big and strong And I say, Bet your ass I'm big and strong. She steps closer to me and has this look like she wants it, so I reach out and touch her arm."

"And?"

"And she screams her fucking head off, that's what she does. She screams and I back off and say I didn't do nothing to hurt her, but by then she's running out the door and my sister's coming back in the room to see what's wrong."

"Nothing more?"

"Nothing more."

"Why'd you think she wanted it?"

"Come on, Harter. You can tell when a woman's on the make. You ever see me treat a woman wrong?"

"It doesn't jibe, Ace. Doesn't go with what we know about her."

"I didn't know nothing about her."

"She could have had anything she wanted. She had a rich lawyer husband and was wealthy herself. What would she have been messing with you for, and then screaming when you touched her?"

"Maybe she don't get along with her husband. Maybe it's like the old joke—she thinks she likes dark meat but when it's served up she gets scared. How the hell can I explain her? I told you you wouldn't believe it."

"You ever see her again?"

"No. Never saw her before and not again. A couple days after the thing, two guys come, say they're from welfare, and ask questions. I keep waiting for something to come of it. You're the first one brought it up in six months."

"You don't know anything about her getting killed last week?"

"Just what the news says."

"Nothing out on the street about it?"

"Not a word."

Harter hit the brakes, backed the car up in an alley, and headed back to the projects, saying nothing.

"If I lie, cut off my dick," said Ace. "Ain't that what they used to do? Like robbers, they cut off their hands, and liars they cut out their tongues, and rapists they cut off their dicks. If I lie, cut out my tongue and cut off my dick. You think I want to live without talking and fucking?"

18

SITTING in his second social services office of the day, Harter just wanted to get the interview over with and go see Liz. Ace Stewart's words careened around his brain as if it were an echo chamber. They kept sounding long after he'd dropped Ace back at the mailbox, kept sounding as he'd driven crosstown to the Commission on Aging's Senior Center in an old elementary school, kept sounding as he sat across the desk from the Commission on Aging woman.

He couldn't keep her name straight. Good thing that Linda Dean had written it down for him. He'd forgotten it as soon as he'd asked for her. He kept looking at her green eyes and green eye makeup and green dress and thinking of her as Mrs. Green. Even her hair seemed tinged with green.

"I imagine Mrs. Dean told you the circumstances of how Susan Devendall came to work here for three months," she said.

He nodded. "What did she do here exactly?"

"She made home visits to see that senior citizens were all right and to sign people up for the hot-lunch program. I've pulled out a list of the folks she visited."

Harter took the neatly typed list and began scanning the names. Mrs. Green chattered on about office policy, how each outreach worker kept a log of her or his time, and then prepared a list of the people visited each week.

It sounded like all the red tape the police department bogged you down in, he thought.

Then he hit on the name.

"Daniel M. Jones," he read aloud.

Mrs. Green didn't react.

"You don't have a file on this Daniel M. Jones, do you?" asked Harter.

"Certainly."

She walked over to a wall of cabinets, opened a metal drawer and, without much fumbling, efficiently returned with a manila folder in her hand.

"Why are you so interested in him?" she asked, leafing through the folder before handing it over.

"He died in a fire last week, a suspected arson," answered Harter "Susan Devendall's abandoned car was found nearby."

"I should have remembered that," said Mrs. Green, reaching for a paper from the file in front of him. "Susan visited Mr. Jones late in June. This is the application for hot lunches, and there should be some handwritten notes in there."

Harter found the yellow legal page with the notes. He was immediately disappointed. All Susan Devendall had written in her perfect round script was a sentence saying that Daniel Jones had been suggested as a meal client by a Reverend Ruffing and that she'd had to talk the old man into accepting free meals.

"Not much here," he said.

"The application just has information you probably already know." Mrs. Green read aloud: "Daniel Morgan Jones, Baxter Street (alley), Shawnee, retired railroad mechanic, widower, born November eleventh, 1897, Wild Stream, West Virginia . . ." Her voice trailed off.

"What's the matter?" asked Harter.

"Wild Stream, West Virginia. That's unusual."

"Why?"

"Oh, probably nothing, but I just closed out our files on another hot-lunch client who was born in Wild Stream, West Virginia . . . He died in a fire, too. In August. I'm always a little behind on the paperwork."

"Who was that?" asked Harter, blinking his eyes and trying to push Ace Stewart out of his mind.

"I'll get the file." Again she crossed to the cabinets, and again it didn't take her long to find what she wanted. "Simon Bowman," she said, returning.

"Never heard of him. Let me see it, please. You say he died in a fire?"

She nodded, looked down at the application, and read: "Simon Bowman, no middle name, Hays Trailer Court, Rural Route One, Shawnee, retired laborer, unmarried, born June thirteenth, 1898, Wild Stream, West Virginia."

"He lived outside the city limits, huh? I guess that's why I don't remember," said Harter.

"We're a county—not a city—agency," explained Mrs. Green. "That's one of our earlier applications. It was long before Susan Devendall's time. The file may be a trifle sketchy. We've gotten better at our record keeping."

Harter picked up the sheet of handwritten notes and read: "It is important only to provide Simon Bowman with food and essentials. He spends his Social Security check mostly on liquor. He'll pawn any items of value for drinking money. He is not a very nice man."

He turned back to Mrs. Green. "You don't know whether the fire Simon Bowman died in was an arson, do you?"

"No I didn't know either of these gentlemen myself. I know most of our clients only through their files—but I know their files well. That's how I remembered about Wild Stream."

"Would Susan Devendall have had any reason to visit Simon Bowman?"

"Not that I'm aware of. She didn't have anything to do with actually delivering the meals to clients." She picked up Susan's list of clients and ran down it. "Simon Bowman is certainly not here."

"Would she have had a reason to go to the Hays Trailer Court?"

"She may have. It would take me a while to find out. If you consider this a priority, I'll take her logbook home this evening and try to match up addresses."

"I'd appreciate it. I don't know what's a priority yet. It might just be coincidence, these two old men from Wild Stream dying in fires in two months. It might have nothing to do with her. I just don't know."

He handed her his card.

"I'll call you first thing in the morning, Detective."

"Thanks," he said. "These two old men are something I hadn't counted on."

"Seniors."

"What?"

"We don't call them old men and old women. We call them senior citizens, or seniors."

"Was Susan Devendall good at working with seniors?"

"I didn't have any complaints about how she actually treated people, but I certainly couldn't have given her a glowing recommendation," replied Mrs. Green. "Frankly, I was glad she quit. I'd been wondering what to do about her. She seemed to waste—or lose—a lot of time. I'd spoken to her more than once about it. How long do you imagine it would take to visit a senior and fill out one of those applications?"

"No more than an hour—maybe two if she chatted a while to build up some rapport."

"That's how I see it, Detective Harter. Yet sometimes Susan might only visit two clients in a day. It's right there in her logbook."

"She could have been making a lot of stream-bank checks," said Harter.

"Stream-bank checks?"

"Private joke."

"Well, some of us suggested she might be taking an afternoon siesta," said Mrs. Green sarcastically.

God, thought Harter, this was getting complicated. The bricks were piling up, but he still hadn't found one strong enough to begin the wall with.

19

SKY GRAYING, dead old men rising with the moon, Harter sat in his car.

Two old men, ordinary laborers, born in the same small town, in the last century, dead now in separate fires, two months apart.

It could all just be coincidence, as he'd admitted to the Commission on Aging lady.

Could be nothing more than . . . than Simon Bowman drunk and smoking in bed . . . than Daniel Jones beaten up by a punk who had then torched his place and run outside to find there was a witness, and so he had taken her with him, beat her up, dumped her body.

Yet an alley punk would hardly have kept Susan Devendall alive for two days without a ransom note, without stripping off her gold and silver, without sexually assaulting her. Unless he was a one-hundred-percent-certified sadist.

Furthermore, the odds were good that Daniel Jones knew—or at least had known—Simon Bowman. And Susan Devendall had at least met Daniel Jones on her rounds. There was a dotted circle there that might be filled in with a little work.

Work.

Harter had tried to convince himself he wasn't lazy for not going to the Hays Trailer Court immediately. He'd justified it by telling himself he'd see the place clearer by daylight.

Hell, hadn't he already called the state police about Bowman and the August fire? Hadn't they said the investigating trooper was off Wednesdays and would be back in the morning?

Sure, he could have called the fire marshal's office. But Caruthers had gone out the door at five sharp, and he'd bet the fire marshal had too, so he'd followed their lead. Not to head home, of course. It *was* Wednesday. He'd headed to Liz's.

Across the street, girls wearing coats over their leotards filed out of the studio and hopped in their mothers' waiting station wagons to be chauffered home to dinner. When he figured they were all gone, Harter took a last long puff and rubbed out his cigarette. He lifted the market bag off the seat, climbed out from behind the wheel, and made his way over the leaf-splattered street to the main door of the studio. The beige curtains covering the window walls of the corner building were backlit with fluorescent light. Sale signs had once hung in the huge windows, back when the building had housed a Ma & Pa grocery serving a modest portion of the west side.

Liz had been able to buy the brick structure for a song. No one had shown any interest in reopening a store in the residential neighborhood. The empty downstairs provided plenty of room for uninterrupted dancing and exercise. Upstairs was a rambling high-ceilinged apartment, complete with window seats and a view of the midtown bridge and the courthouse dome.

Opening the door, he was surprised to find her still at work. Weather Report, or some other electronic bass-heavy jazz, masterblasted out of the large speaker boxes on the far wall.

Liz was stretching on the wood floor, making occasional jerky movements to the offbeat while illustrating some elusive motion to a freckled young student who couldn't seem to find the right beat, much less perform to it.

"I'll never be able to do it," the girl almost whined.

"Sure you will. When I was twelve, there were loads of things I didn't think I'd ever master," said Liz, rather unconvincingly.

"You're a natural dancer, Miss McGee," insisted the girl. "Didn't you dance in New York when you were young?"

Liz stopped her demonstration and nodded at the girl. "I'm not so old now," she said with a hint of a smile.

"I didn't mean.

"I know you didn't," said Liz—almost wearily, thought Harter. She pointed in his direction. "I'm afraid I have a visitor. You go home now and practice that movement over and over again. I'm positive you'll have it down by next week."

The girl glanced at Harter for a long instant before hurrying over to her coat hanging from a hook on the wall. Slipping it on, she almost ran past him and out the door.

"Do you think she decided I'm all right for you?" asked Harter. "I didn't mean to come in while someone was here. I thought they were all gone."

"It's just as well. I wanted her to go. She needed to get out of here. Besides, it was good she saw you. Maybe she won't think I'm such a sad old spinster."

"A pretty shapely spinster."

Liz ignored him and continued, "She tries so hard. If she only had talent. Half of my girls want to be Solid Gold dancers—wouldn't that shock their moms and dads? The other half couldn't feel the beat if they were the drum."

She switched off the tape player, then walked over to him and put her arms around his shoulders. "How are you?"

"Tired and confused," he heard himself say. He fumbled with the grocery bag and she gave him enough room to put it down on the floor. When he was standing straight again, their arms went around each other almost automatically. As they hugged, his fingers rubbed down her back until they were on her buttocks, smooth and dancer-firm under her black tights.

"Not now," she said, inching away. "I need a shower."

"Then I'll start cooking. I brought dinner," he said, picking up the groceries again.

"What are we having?"

He went through the motion of peeking in the bag. "Steaks, mushrooms, tomatoes, Italian bread."

"Red meat isn't good for you," she chided.

"The mushrooms'll make up for it. They'll make us visionaries."

"You know, I'd have thought steak and mushrooms were just what you'd have wanted for your birthday dinner Saturday—*your second birthday dinner,"* she said, crossing the dance floor to the stairs.

"We can have it again in three days. I could eat steak a couple times a week. Man is a hunter," he said, flipping off the downstairs lights before following her up. "Anyway, I don't really need another birthday dinner."

"One's fortieth birthday should be a big occasion—not something to be interrupted by a call from headquarters, not a night to be tramping around in the mud looking at corpses."

"Thirty-nine, forty-one, what's the difference? Hemingway made love morning, noon, and night when he turned fifty, just to see if he still could. Who knows if he could do the same thing at fifty-one? It wasn't the first, or worst, time I'd tramped around in the mud looking at corpses."

"Macho man," she said, leading the way down the hall to her kitchen. "I think wrapping up one decade and starting another is a big event."

"Wait till you're forty and see what I do to you."

'Do I have to wait two years to find out?"

"It'll take me that long to plan it. You know how slow I am."

She filled a glass of water from the kitchen tap, sipped at it, then, after touching his shoulder lightly, went down the hall to the bathroom.

By the time the shower water was running, he'd disposed of his jacket and gun, stuck the steaks under the broiler, decided against baked potatoes as too heavy, and begun chopping mushrooms.

He'd turned the steaks and was slicing the tomato when she returned. She went to work reaching plates down from a cabinet and he found himself putting down the sharp knife and watching the backs of her legs as her skirt swayed with her movements.

"How's your case going?" she asked as she turned around. Not waiting for an answer, she carried the plates into the small dining room off the kitchen.

Strange question, Harter said to himself. She usually didn't ask about his job, though she did listen closely when he volunteered something.

He said nothing until she came back to the kitchen and started filling water glasses at the sink. "You hardly ever say much about my cases.

Why this one? I'm sure it's not just because it got in the way of dinner Saturday night."

"Partly it's your expression. You look like a wheel has fallen off and you don't have a spare. And partly, it's . . ." She carried the glasses into the other room. This time he followed her. "Partly it's because I know some of the people involved."

He leaned against the doorway and watched her take silverware from a drawer. "Who do you know?"

"Susan Devendall. I read about her in the paper. I know all the Devendalls, in fact. And a lot of their circle."

"You know Howard and the old woman?"

Liz nodded as she placed the silverware atop blue cloth napkins. "I've been to weddings, parties, and social occasions that they attended. Susan took my exercise classes now and then. Not regularly. Sometimes she'd come with a friend. I never knew when she'd show up. She paid by the class. Remember, the majority of the women in my evening classes are from the west side. Most of the girls I teach are from the west side, too."

"Who else can afford dancing lessons and exercise classes in the middle of a depression?"

"There you go again," she said.

He was immediately sorry he'd thrown a kink into whatever she'd wanted to tell him. "Forget I said that."

"It's no worse than things you've said before."

"Who were her friends?" he asked to get her back on track. "It might be helpful to talk to some of them."

"*Friends* might not be the right word. *Acquaintances* might be more like it. There was a sort of wall between Susan Devendall and most of the west-side women, even when she'd come with a group of them. You'll get to meet some of them at the Halloween party next week. You haven't forgotten, have you?"

"No," he mumbled, but in truth he had forgotten, or had tried to. He always felt out of place at parties.

"It's a costume party at the Winhams," she reminded him. "I teach their daughters. Have you thought about what you'll wear?"

"Will Howard and Amy Devendall be there?" asked Harter, ignoring her question. He didn't want to think about a costume.

"I'm sure they'd have all been there if the murder hadn't happened. Even at her age, Amy Devendall doesn't miss much."

"I can believe that. I met her yesterday for the first time. Met Howard, too. Somehow they managed to put me off for forty-eight hours. I should have seen them before, but they didn't want to be seen. The old lady is quite . . . imposing. She seems like she's had Shawnee society around her finger from the time she was a child."

"I don't know anything about her background. I don't think she's originally from Shawnee. She's the mistress of the perfect scene, though."

Harter nodded agreement, not exactly sure what he was agreeing to. He moved back in the kitchen, opened the oven, and took out the steaks. "I gather Amy Devendall wasn't fond of her daughter-in-law," he said when he realized Liz had followed him.

"True. Amy didn't approve of Susan, and Susan didn't like or approve of Amy."

"Where did Howard fit in?" asked Harter as he placed the steaks and mushrooms on a platter beside the sliced tomatoes.

"Oh, Howard can be downright charming," said Liz, opening the refrigerator. "Sometimes you can almost see what Susan originally saw in him. Away from his mother, he can come on as quite the ladies' man."

"Has he ever come on to you?" asked Harter, feeling a twinge of jealousy.

"Not seriously." She put the bread and butter on the dining room table and sat down.

"You say he's a ladies' man when he's *away* from his mother?"

"He's all propriety when she's around, like a preacher's kid."

"How long did you know Susan?"

"I'd known who she was for years. A couple of years ago some of the west-side women went on the good-health kick and began coming to aerobics classes. Like I said, she'd come once in a while. I never sensed any of the others were particularly close to her. I sensed she felt the life of a society lady was too frivolous for her. She had a job and all. She seemed to have more passion and fire than most of the others. She didn't engage much in west-side gossip. It's like some of the others only come here so they can gossip with the girls."

"Did the gossip ever involve the Devendalls?" asked Harter, cutting into his steak, then glancing down quickly to be sure it was well done.

"The gossip involved everyone from time to time," said Liz. "You have to understand, I haven't seen Susan Devendall herself since February or March. I've only heard smatterings about her."

"Okay, you've disclaimed it enough. I'm not taking notes. Go on. Tell me what was said. You can't just bring it up and then leave me hanging."

"Oh, I could."

"I'll subpoena you."

"She was having affairs," said Liz straight out.

"And it was common knowledge?"

Liz laughed. "Sometimes these women tell each other about their own affairs."

"And it's not damaging to their reputations? Amy Devendall seemed so concerned about reputation."

"It all depends on who the affair is with. Amy Devendall might even have been behind some of the rumors."

"Why would she do that?"

"To give Howard some cover." She looked at Harter over a raised forkful of mushrooms. "If Susan was running around, then Howard's philandering seemed justified. Don't you see?"

"I guess," said Harter. He was slightly amazed that Liz's daily work put her as deeply into a well of intrigues as his own. In the years they'd seen each other, they'd never discussed west-side affairs and gossip.

"Understand, it's a small circle we're talking about," she explained. "When I say something was common knowledge, I don't mean the man on the street knows it or that you should. Half the women in my classes had their flings, and the other half had wandering husbands. Sometimes the halves overlapped. They all have plenty of money and lots of free afternoons."

"Afternoon siesta," said Harter, remembering Mrs. Green's remark.

"What?"

"Just a thought . . . So, Howard was running around, too?"

"I'd say they were evenly matched. What I'd guess is that Amy spread the word of Susan's unfaithfulness to explain Howard's. All's fair in love and war."

"I never believed that."

"It doesn't matter what *you* believe."

"You know the names of any people that either of them might have been involved with?"

"Just one with any degree of certainty."

"Well, tell me."

"Charles Whitford Canley."

"The congressman?"

"The congressman."

"I guess it was Susan and not Howard."

"Don't get nasty," said Liz.

"So what's the story?"

"Congressman Canley is a widower. His wife died last year. Since then he's been spending a lot of time at a farm west of Shawnee owned by the Whitfords, his mother's family. It's a big spread, used to be a virtual plantation. Between staying at the farm and frequently visiting Shawnee to campaign this year, he's been in the area almost as much as in Washington. They say Susan Devendall volunteered time as a campaign worker. Of course, she and Canley had known each other socially a long time. The two got entwined."

"But if she was a social worker . . . if she had this streak of social consciousness I keep hearing about . . . she couldn't have found a less socially conscious congressman to work for."

"The Devendalls have always been big supporters of the Canleys. I also heard Susan quit her job after some bad scene with a welfare case."

Ace Stewart. The "attempted rape." Was Ace telling the truth? *Had* she come on to him? Was she looking for a lover? Had he scared her into Canley's arms?

"You don't know when she started sleeping with the congressman, do you?" Harter asked her.

"The rumors started late in the spring, just before the primary election."

He nodded. It jibed. "Why didn't you ever tell me about them?"

"Why should I have?"

"Do you know Canley?"

"I've met him."

"Charming fellow?"

"If you don't think about politics. He's quite a party-goer. If we go to the Winhams for Halloween, he'll probably be there, too."

"I can't wait ten days to meet him," Harter thought out loud.

"Call him up in Washington," she said. "A congressman's not hard to find."

"I may," said Harter. Then: "You said the Devendalls were always big political supporters of the Canleys. Did the affair change things?"

"I doubt it," answered Liz after a moment's thought. "On the west side, politics are kept carefully separated from the rest of life."

"Hypocrites."

"Pragmatists," she corrected. To let him know she'd told him all she could, or would, she glanced over at the clock on the wall and said, "We still have time to get to a movie out at the mall."

"Okay," he said without much zest.

Usually he loved movies, the bigger-than-life action. But he didn't really feel like it tonight, didn't particularly want to watch another mystery unfold.

He watched as Liz got up from the table and removed the plates. He watched her dancer's body, her long legs, as she headed to the kitchen.

He hoped the movie would be a comedy, a sexy comedy that would be over quickly so they could come back to the apartment and climb into bed. *The same bed.*

Not like Susan and Howard Devendall.

20

IF HAYS TRAILER COURT wasn't the ugliest spot in the universe, it was close enough to be in the running. It sprawled up a straggly shale hillside about three miles south of Shawnee. Some land-use expert on the take had apparently decided the hill was worthless for anything but propping up trailers, figured Harter. Only scroungy pastel tin cans were allowed—the smaller and rustier, the better.

On the other side of the county road was Hays Salvage Yard. Its sign boasted 189 ACRES OF AUTO PARTS.

Whether the spread of bashed-in cars and half-dismantled trucks was uglier than the slope of trailers was a toss-up. Harter sided with the trailer court. For starters, the junkyard's sign looked half-professional, but the trailer-court sign looked as if it had been created by a second-grader who'd been given his first gallon of thin black paint and a stick to use as a brush. Beneath HAYS TRAILOR CORT was the message *Aply at salvagE YarD.*

The man in the junkyard office was friendly enough. He listened to Harter and then said, "You want to see Phil, that's who. He runs that place over there." Stepping to the back door, he bellowed, *"Phil! Phil! There's a cop here to see you!"*

Phil Hays turned out to be a chubby bald fellow in a gray windbreaker and checkered pants. Harter decided that, with proper attire, he could have done business on Sinclair Lewis' Main Street.

"City cop, huh? You're out of your jurisdiction, aren't you? I thought you detectives always worked in pairs, like on 'Dragnet,' " Hays said.

"Think of me as a loner. The state police told me it would be all right to ask a few questions. They couldn't spare a trooper to send around with me."

"What's the big deal? Nothing going on here."

No stolen vehicles on your lot? Harter wanted to ask. Instead, he said, "I'm looking into a couple deaths. Last week an old man died in an arson in town. He may have known the old man who died in the fire out here. It's just a routine check to see if there's a connection."

"Looking for a conspiracy, huh? I can't believe anyone would conspire to burn up Simon Bowman. That fire wasn't an arson. If you ask me, Simon's kerosene tank leaked. It was right outside his trailer and he could have dropped a match or something. I tell those goddamned people to be careful all the time. My fire insurance has tripled since the fire. You can't make it up on what I charge for those places."

"You rented the trailer to Bowman?"

"No, he owned his, just rented the lot. I don't know where he got the money to buy it. Showed up here one day right after I started the court. Bought the trailer in cash. He paid me twenty-five bucks a month for the space."

"How long did he live there?"

"From about 1965 until he died."

"You must have known him pretty well."

"Well enough to know when to go collect my rent. There were only two times a month when he had money—when the Social Security checks came out and then around the twentieth, when he'd get a little extra from someplace. If you weren't there to collect at the right time, he'd drink the money up. Funny thing, he gave up drinking a year or two ago. Straightened up after all those years. Who'd have figured that?"

"You mean he gave up the bottle in his early eighties?"

Hays nodded. "Must have started worrying about his soul. Reverend Sam Knotts must have scared him to death."

"Who's that?"

"Sam Knotts runs a church back near the Shawnee line on Route Forty-three. You had to pass it to get here. He started with just a revival tent and built up a complex. Good businessman. He goes through the trailer court evangelizing fairly regularly. Simon probably drank for fifty years before Sam Knotts put a stop to it."

"What'd Bowman ever do for a living?"

"Got me. Never talked about it. I think he worked for the canal in the old days and maybe the railroad a while. He didn't talk much about anything. All I ever knew him to do was drink, until he got religion. I always wondered if he had a guardian angel. He never ran completely downhill. Like I said, he paid for that trailer in cash."

"No family?"

"None I know of."

"Did he ever mention anyone named Daniel Jones, someone he might have known back in Wild Stream, West Virginia?"

"Was he from there? I didn't know that. I don't think I ever heard him mention a friend named Daniel Jones. He never mentioned any friends."

"Anybody come to visit him?"

"Just Reverend Sam and the COA hot-lunch van. Sunday mornings, Knotts would send someone up to get him to bring him down to church. Sam's real organized about stuff like that. He runs his church tight."

"How'd Bowman get around the rest of the time?"

"Bummed rides or hitchhiked. He didn't go far. You wouldn't have wanted Simon behind the wheel of a car."

"Were you around the night of the fire?"

"I live across town," said Hays. "I came over when they called me, but the place was gone by then. Simon was baked inside. It was a Thursday night. I remember because it was my wife's card-party night."

"Thursday, August fifth, according to police reports."

"That must be right. You cops are always right, aren't you?"

Harter resisted the urge to punch Hays' face. "You mind if I go up and look at where Bowman lived?"

"Suit yourself. Nothing to see. The trailer's gone." Hays went over to the window, bent the Venetian blinds, and pointed to a spot partway up the hill. "There's still some rubble. You'll find it."

"Us cops always find it," said Harter.

A few minutes later he did find it, but Hays was right. There was nothing to see—except a scenic view of 189 acres of broken automotive dreams. According to the state police, there'd been little to see on the night of the fire, too. Everything had been inconclusive from the start.

Nor had the Commission on Aging been much help. Mrs. Green had called him at nine sharp. She'd gone through Susan Devendall's logs. She'd found no reason for her to have visited the trailer park.

Trailer park. What a misuse of the language. Harter wondered how much Hays charged for the air.

Suddenly, he sensed that someone was staring at him from the window of the pink can next to the rubble of what had once been Simon Bowman's home. The trailer was little more than the type of thing campers took out for the weekend. Harter walked over and knocked on the door. Though he was sure someone was inside, no one answered. He knocked again, waited, and knocked a third time. He finally gave up, climbed into his car, and, cussing the rutted road, left Hays Trailer Court.

The old men were nagging at him.

He didn't want to get sidetracked, but . . .

But . . .

Kerosene and Wild Stream, West Virginia . . .

21

WHEN HE SPOTTED the church, he pulled off the highway and into the parking lot, coming to a stop among pickup trucks that seemed to belong to the construction workers busy putting up a large brick building in a field nearby.

For a while, he sat in his car, watching the construction activity, debating whether it was worth talking to Reverend Sam Knotts, whose name was proudly displayed on the marquee. He knew *marquee* wasn't the right word, but he had no idea what else to call the bulletin board in front of the white building. It was one of those metal contraptions with changeable letters. Today it announced that Sam Knotts' sermon on Sunday would be "The City Built by God."

Surely not the Hays Trailor Cort, thought Harter.

According to the marquee, Knotts' True Church Of God kept a bustling schedule: Sunday school, two Sunday morning services, a Sabbath evening adult class, a Monday night "Faith Workshop" (whatever that was), and a Wednesday evening hymn sing. SINNERS INVITED read the bottom line of white plastic letters.

Finally Harter hauled himself out of his car and went to the side door of the church. "Anyone here?" he called as he stepped onto a ramp that led into the innards of the spic-and-span church building. Cleanliness is next to Godliness, he remembered.

"Praise the Lord, you've come," answered a male voice. Soon, a man came out of one of the doorways along the carpeted hallway.

"Reverend Sam Knotts?"

"Called and answered," the man cheerfully said.

Harter had seen such evangelical good cheer in older ministers, but found it slightly odd in so young a man. Sam Knotts couldn't have been more than thirty-five. Well over six feet tall and sturdily built, he looked like a football tackle. He wore his red hair styled and his muscular frame was covered with a yellow sports jacket, no tie this non-service weekday.

"My name is Edward Harter. I'm a detective with the Shawnee Police Department."

"Something wrong?" asked Knotts, extending a big hand.

"Not exactly. I'm working a case and was told you might have known Simon Bowman."

Knotts nodded his red head. "Is the trailer fire still being investigated?"

"Actually, we're looking for a pattern in some recent fires. There may be nothing to it."

"Some fires?" asked Knotts.

"Yeah."

"I'm not sure how I can help, but come in."

Knotts led Harter down the hall and turned into the room he'd come out of. He motioned for Harter to sit on a low orange couch beside a bookcase filled with religious-looking volumes. Knotts sat right next to him, not a foot away. People who didn't allow you room always made Harter tense, but he tried not to show it.

"As I hear it, Simon Bowman had been an alcoholic most of his life."

"I'd say that's accurate," said Knotts. "I worked very hard to help him kick it. Little by little, he opened up to me as I tried to prepare his heart for salvation. Building confidence is difficult, as I'm sure you know, Detective Harter. I remember well the day I saved Simon. You can see it in a person's eyes—you can see that leap they make when they give themselves over to Christ. He began crying and confessing and went on and on for hours. We prayed and prayed together in his meager trailer."

Harter wanted to ask what Simon Bowman had "confessed," but thought better of it and simply said, "If he gave up drinking after all those years, it sounds like it worked."

"It always works," said Knotts. "It's not a game. It's a matter of readying the person to accept the Lord. God will forgive anything if you are willing to start anew, Detective."

Harter felt more uncomfortable. Bad enough to be sitting so close to the preacher without having the soul-saving faucet turned on. The flowery speech didn't match the tough body.

"I take it you saw a good bit of Bowman after that?"

"He began coming to church on Sundays, and I'd always stop in and see him on my visits to the trailer court. There are so many lost souls there. Some of them I've yet to reach. I know they're inside, but they won't answer the door."

"When was the last time you saw Bowman?"

"I believe it was the Sunday-morning service before the fire. One of my volunteers had gone up to get him and bring him to church. I think I probably saw him the week before that, too. I usually visit the trailer court toward the end of the month, and he died early in August, as I recall."

"That's right. When you, uh, talked to him, he didn't ever mention family or close friends, did he?"

"Nobody he still had contact with. Simon was a very lonely man. Most of the people he once knew are gone."

"I'm specifically interested in whether he ever mentioned an elderly man named Daniel Jones or a social worker named Susan Devendall," said Harter, watching Knotts' face carefully.

The preacher showed no emotion. "I don't recall anything about a Daniel Jones. Occasionally he'd refer to someone he knew when he was young or whom he had worked with, but the names didn't stick with me. I know he didn't mention Susan Devendall."

"Why are you so sure?"

"I'd have remembered. I knew her."

"You knew her?"

"Not very well, but I knew her. Her husband, Howard, has done legal work for the church—mostly things to help us maintain our tax-exempt status when we started new projects. His mother, Amy Devendall, is quite a character."

"Yeah," mumbled Harter, surprised. "Are the Devendalls members of your church?" He found it hard to picture Amy Devendall and Simon Bowman sharing a pew.

"I believe they attend West Side Episcopal, but they're concerned, generous people. From my conversations with them, I know they're worried about the moral fabric of this country."

"Tell me how you met Susan Devendall," asked Harter.

"I believe I first met her at her husband's office one day, and then we all had lunch together. Later I ran into all three of them at functions for Congressman Canley. Susan's murder was such a senseless tragedy. I called on Mrs. Devendall to give her my condolences."

"How did you size her up?" asked Harter awkwardly.

"I beg your pardon?"

"What was your impression of Susan Devendall?"

"I knew her husband better through business, and I talked more easily with her mother-in-law. I'm not the person to tell you about her. Confidentially, I wouldn't say she led an immoral life, but I know her lifestyle worried her family." Knotts halted and tapped Harter's knee. "You're just fishing, Detective, aren't you?"

"Did Simon Bowman know her?" asked Harter, more uncomfortable than ever.

"I don't know why he would have," answered Knotts. "I told you he never mentioned her."

"When was the last time you saw her?"

"I'd say it was at a picnic rally for Congressman Canley in July. Yes, I'm positive that's when it was. There aren't many politicians, you know, with the congressman's backbone. I admire him greatly. I had dinner with him last Thursday night, in fact."

Thursday night. The night of the fire, the night of Susan's disappearance.

"Where was the dinner?" asked Harter.

"At Richard Baum's church in town. Our ministerial group gave the congressman an award for standing up for basic American values."

Thinking of what Liz had told him the night before, Harter ignored the testimonial for Canley and asked, "Did anything unusual happen that evening?"

"No," said Knotts, sounding put off by the question. "We ate. I got a chance to encourage him to support legislation that would give tax deductions for tuition for private and religious schools. It's important for people to be able to choose how they educate their children, Detective."

"That all?"

"He left us rather early for another engagement. After he'd gone, our group spent a few hours in fellowship. On the way home, I stopped here to check on the construction site, as I do each night. We had some vandalism early on. I came by the church about ten, then went home."

"What is it you're building out there?"

"A Christian academy. Didn't you notice the sign? The school is the next step in my dream, and a very expensive step, I might add. The congregation has really dug into their pockets and we've solicited some outside donations. It's a crucial part of my ministry to be able to educate children properly—away from drugs, evolution textbooks, secular humanism. They'll be raised as we were, Detective. Prayer, the fundamentals, proper discipline. Spare the rod and spoil the child, as they say. You know, Simon Bowman was especially excited about the school. It's a pity he didn't live to see construction begin. He pledged to donate the money he'd once spent on liquor. He believed that by raising up the children right, they wouldn't stray as he had. Mercifully, he was one of the strays I managed to collect."

"Huh," said Harter, unable to think of anything else to say.

A few minutes later, outside Knotts' church, he stared again at the school in the works.

FUTURE HOME OF OUR CHRISTIAN ACADEMY
Made possible by friends of
The True Church of God
and by a donation in Memory of A. L.
Sam Knotts, pastor

A.L.?

Probably another old alcoholic that Knotts had redeemed. But one with more moolah than Simon Bowman.

Christ, the job could make you mean. Sometimes he wondered why the hell he was a cop.

Liz would never fully understand.

JACK REESE

22

YOU RUN DOWN *to the bottom floor of the old house and see a wooden table with a tall candle and the candle falls over and the table starts to burn like paper and I run over and try to smother the flames with your bare hands.*

Noise of a burglar upstairs.

Run up to the second floor and see a table with a candle and the candle falls and the table starts to burn and you run over and try to smother flames with my hands.

Run up third floor see table candle falls table burns run try to smother flames with bare hands.

I would wake up and try to shake the dream, but when I imagined it had passed it would only be replaced by visions of Daniel's blazing house on that alley night:

I am standing outside the streetlight circle, in the stretched gray alley shadows, leaning against the Ford, watching the house burn, unable to do anything. Or I try and I run into her damn car and lose track of what's going on.

A guilt no preacher could bring about in me.

Should have turned her down when I saw how the sessions were shaping up.

Should have found some way to help Daniel.

Should have told Harter the whole truth when he came the first time.

I kept telling myself I hadn't really lied. Stared at his card countless times.

Monday at the towpath I'd almost come clean, almost poured it out. But I hadn't. For some reason, I hadn't.

"You come here often?" he'd asked, suspicious of his suspect.

"I wanted to see it," I'd answered, backing away from the full story.

After we'd split up, after he'd driven off, I'd wandered about, trying to decide what to do.

I'd walked over the bridge to the abandoned cardboard box factory and then the sign caught my eye.

Sign on the factory, near the spot where her abductor, her killer, had deposited her body.

I clicked the picture.

Later, watching it come up in the darkroom tray, I'd almost called him.

But Harter must have known about the building. He was the cop. He looked like he knew more than he showed. Or were all detectives like that? I'd never been head-to-head with a detective before.

He'd left me feeling stripped down to the itchy essentials, like being on stage wearing only a loincloth, before ten thousand pairs of hard eyes—*like his*—with spotlights illuminating every bump of me. As vulnerable as Susan Maddox Devendall had been before my camera.

And the dream kept returning.

I hadn't lied.

Day after day of nervous waiting. Waiting for him to come back. I *knew* Harter would come back.

I got everything ready for him. Put all my pictures in a pile, in order. Every one that could be considered evidence. Every one that could show what I'd been doing the week before.

But no Harter.

Wednesday night I tried to call him. They offered to take my name and message at the police department. I said I'd call back. I tried to get him at home. He wasn't there.

Thursday morning I tried again. He mustn't have gone home the night before. At headquarters, a guy who said he was a detective asked me to leave a message again. I'll call back, I said. I didn't want to talk to anyone but Harter. Didn't want to get other cops involved.

I kept staring at the pile of photos, wishing I could fill him in, remind him of the sign, tell him why Susan Devendall had called me the night of the fire.

I was innocent, even if he made me feel like a cheap pornographer.

"I thought maybe you took pictures for *Playboy* or something," he'd said Sunday evening.

You're the only one who knew both victims.

Run.

Candle falls.

Table burns.

Try to smother flames.

Bare hands.

If only the guilt would subside and the dream would begin to dissolve.

If only the fire trucks would come.

23

"THE SON OF A BITCH, the son of a bitch," Tattoo was repeating as I stepped into the kitchen at lunchtime Thursday. I hoped he wasn't talking about me.

"It's only politics, Henry," said May.

"What's the matter?"

"A piece in the paper has him all lit up," she told me.

"I'm innocent," I insisted.

"Look at this," Tattoo ordered. He shoved *The News* across the table at me, almost knocking a soup bowl to the floor in the process.

CONGRESSMAN SEEKS
RAILROAD INVESTIGATION

"I intend to expose a national scandal," Congressman Charles Whitford Canley had announced at a press conference in Washington on Wednesday. Canley claimed to have observed an upsurge in train wrecks.

A passenger train had left the rails in Pennsylvania in September, injuring a dozen people. Three chemical cars had ruptured in a Texas crash in July, forcing the evacuation of two small towns. EPA was still on the scene, spending bundles of tax dollars.

Just the previous Tuesday, Canley reported, he'd been in Shawnee when a freight train loaded with new trucks had derailed near town.

The danger was nationwide, but Shawnee—with its railroad economy—was especially vulnerable, he'd said.

The wrecks destroyed valuable goods, injured ordinary people, shook the public confidence in rail transportation, forced higher insurance rates.

Canley was sure he knew what was at the bottom of the accidents. The union bosses wouldn't face up to it, but it was drugs. Not faulty equipment, not bad tracks, not the nature of rail transport, but *illegal drugs.* High, speeding engineers who didn't pay attention to signal lights. Bombed-out mechanics who didn't care about the quality of their work.

The evil of drugs, brought into American society by the hippies and social anarchists of the 1960s, was undermining the railroad industry while union leaders looked the other way, claimed Canley. So he'd called for a congressional investigation.

The News reported the congressman would discuss the issue further at a news conference in the Shawnee courthouse on Friday.

I looked at Tattoo. "Sounds like our honorable representative has found a hot one for the last couple of weeks before the election."

"How can he get off saying Harry Bryson is a drug addict?" said Tattoo.

"Got me. That's why I'm not a politician."

"Goddamn newspaper puts trash like this on the front page and not a word about who killed Daniel."

He shot a challenging stare my way to let me know he still expected me to call Metling and get the inside dope, but he said nothing. After a while, he rose from the table and stomped up the steps.

"You want a bowl of vegetable soup?" asked May, ignoring his anger.

"No. I came over to go down to the food bank with you."

"So Reverend Ruffing asked you about taking pictures?"

"Yeah. I told him I can't promise whether they'll get in the paper."

"Just do your best." She removed the empty soup bowls from the table and took them to the sink. "Let me do the dishes and wash my face, then we'll go."

I watched her at the sink for a minute, then went upstairs to see if Tattoo had cooled off. He was sitting in his chair, stuffing a chaw of tobacco in his mouth.

"I thought you gave that up."

"Took it up again."

"May must be happy."

He stayed grumpy and didn't answer.

She hated it when he chewed, hated that stale moist tobacco odor in the air, hated it when he spit into the stained white spittoon at his feet, and missed. I pictured him younger, two-armed, gabbing and chewing on the porch with my grandfather, the two of them spitting their brown streams toward the street. When they'd run low, they'd send me down to Bernhardt's for fresh Mail Pouch, tossing in an extra nickel for candy.

I heard May's steps on the stairs. "Ready?" she asked when she came into the room.

I got up from the sofa. "You want to walk or ride?"

"Let's walk. It's a nice day," she said, slipping on her coat.

Heading down the hill, I was afraid she'd ask me about the detective or the murders. I hadn't discussed any of it with her and didn't know what she'd heard from Tattoo. But she was quiet until we passed the Listons' apartment house and their watchdog barked. The Listons had always had a vicious German shepherd. We believed they took the ones the police couldn't trust.

"You remember when their dog attacked you?" asked May.

"Sure. I was about ten. I was running down the sidewalk and it came off the porch after me. My sweater gave when its teeth pulled at it. Wasn't until I got home and my mother saw my shirt was ripped under the sweater that we realized how close I'd come to having my arm ripped off. It may be unAmerican, but I've never been able to stand dogs since."

"I don't like them neither, and Tattoo doesn't trust cats, so we never had neither. I feed him and he pets me."

We crossed the Avenue.

"You think you're going to stay in Shawnee?" she asked.

I debated lying but gave her an honest answer. "I don't know. A lot of things would make life look different—if I had a more regular income, if I had someone to date." I stopped myself from adding, *If the murders hadn't happened.*

"Used to be that young fellows would meet girls at church," she said. "I don't know what it is, though. Young people today don't seem to go to church, unless they catch religion and end up holy rollers."

"I don't know what it is either," I said, keeping my thoughts to myself.

"You have to twist Henry's arm to get him in a church. I gave up on it a long time ago."

We crossed Thomas Street, walked past the front door of the church, and went up the brick walkway that led to the side entrance.

The Sunday school room didn't look a whole lot different than the last time I'd been in it. But on a Thursday afternoon, there was no piano player to chord out "In the Garden." Every available surface—the piano bench, the folding chairs, the Sunday school tables—was filled with cartons of food.

As May hung up her coat, I scouted out the selection. Spaghetti, tomato sauce, cereal, flour, bread.

"No filet mignon," said Reverend Joe Ruffing, coming up behind me. "Mostly generic staples. We have to think about getting the most food for the money. Thank you for coming."

"I promised I would. So how does this thing work?"

"May sits at the table over by the door and has people fill out an application—things like how many are in the family and their average monthly income. She decides how much they need. She's a pro at sifting them out. She knows most of the people from the neighborhood, and she's good at reading the ones she doesn't know. We can only afford to help the really needy."

"Not just Methodists?"

"Of course not," said Ruffing. "All sorts of people. Ones waiting for their unemployment compensation to start. Ones without unemployment, trying to stay off welfare. Transients on their way south. Elderly people whose Social Security check ran out. Cases referred by the Department of Human Services. There's not much outright fraud."

"There's your first customer," I said, nodding at a disheveled woman in her seventies who stood in the doorway with an empty shopping bag in her hand.

"She's a regular," said Ruffing. "Take any pictures you want. Try to avoid faces on any that'll end up in the newspaper."

"I usually do," I said, remembering my reluctance to photograph faces at the cheese-and-butter line at the theater.

Leaving me alone, Ruffing crossed the room to greet the people who were filing in line behind the woman.

There was a black girl with an infant in her arms. She seemed hardly big enough to hold the baby.

There was a second old lady, her stockings bagging at the ankles.

There was a couple—him bearded, her with long straight blond hair—both in shabby blue jeans. They might have gone to East Shawnee High with me.

I turned away from the faces and fiddled with the camera so I'd be ready for the first shot. The lady didn't ask any questions or appear to mind when I snapped her putting a box of soup noodles in her brown bag. I moved behind her, framing her small body hunched over the canned goods.

Click.

A hand gripped the plastic wrap of a loaf of bread.

Click.

The baby's eyes stared out at me, its head resting on its mother's shoulder as she picked up a box of spaghetti.

Click.

The mother's hand grasped a white flour bag.

Click.

The couple were more self-conscious. As they made their way along the row of folding chairs loaded with boxes, his eyes never left me. I found myself zeroing in on the food and not them.

Click.

Down the line, other pairs of hands reached for containers of food.

Click.

More people, more hands.

Click. Click.

"There's a man outside wants to see you," said May, tapping my arm to bring me out of my camera-clicking trance.

I glanced toward the door but all I could see past the food cartons were more people waiting their turn. Then I saw Joe Ruffing's thin back. He was talking to someone.

Harter.

When I joined them on the brick walkway, they were in the middle of a discussion about a minister or church. It was the first time I'd seen Joe Ruffing show any discernible anger.

"He's built his empire in the last four or five years," he was telling Harter. "First the church, now the school. I've heard he came from Virginia originally. I don't know for sure. I've never had a real conversation with him. I stay away from Sam Knotts' ilk."

"How about Simon Bowman?" Harter asked.

"Draws a blank." Ruffing looked my way. "Did you ever hear of him, Jack?"

"Simon Bowman?"

"Daniel Jones never mentioned him to you?"

"I don't think so. If he was an old railroader or something, Tattoo's the one you ought to ask."

"I just came from his place," said Harter, staring directly at me. "He told me I could find you here."

"And he didn't know this Simon Bowman?"

"He might retrieve something from his memory yet," answered Harter, clearly watching his words. "He seems to think Bowman might have been a scab in the twenties or thirties and had a poor reputation among the union men. You know how that goes, I'm sure. I just figured maybe Jones had told you some story about him, or about a scab he grew up with."

I looked at the detective and he looked at me. Neither of us was anxious to get down to hard-core business while Ruffing was standing there. I knew Harter was full of questions. What he didn't know was that I was ready to tell him everything I'd done, from the moment Susan Devendall had stepped namelessly on my porch until he'd come to see me Sunday.

"You walking?" Harter finally asked, tired of waiting.

"Yeah." I looked at Ruffing. "I'll bring some pictures by in a couple of days. You can choose the ones you like. Tell May I'll come down and pick her up if she calls me."

"I'll get her home," said Ruffing.

"My car's across the street." Harter pointed as we started down the walk.

"I . . . I . . ."

"What?" he asked, opening his car door

"I've been trying to call you." I climbed in and sat next to him.

"About what?" He turned the key and the engine roared.

"I . . . I've got some photos you'll be interested in."

"Of what?"

I was still unclear exactly where to start. I decided to save the bulk of the story until I'd convinced him I was on his side.

"Several things. One of them I took Monday—after you left me near the old box factory. It's a sign on the wall there . . . You do know who owns the factory building?"

He shook his head no as he turned right into the alley.

"Howard P. Devendall," I told him. "Isn't that her husband?"

"That's her husband all right," he said, not showing half the interest I'd expected.

"Doesn't it mean something?"

"Might or it might not," he said, parking near my Ford. "It's a small town. They're a prominent family. They own a lot. What else have you got on your mind?"

"It's going to take me a while," I answered.

"I've got a while," said Harter.

He was a hard man to read. I didn't know whether I'd learn to decipher his nuances or not.

"What other pictures have you got?" he asked as we climbed the back porch steps.

Inside, I handed the whole pile over to him without comment. I turned on the burner under the coffeepot as he sat at the kitchen table and silently flipped through the prints.

When I handed him his cup, he was studying her intensely. There she was, alive, the previous Wednesday night, striking her Marilyn Monroe pose, her made-up face looking boldly at the lens—*at me*—at him—her body inside the pink fifties dress, her high heels hooked onto a stool rung.

"Not exactly Matthew Brady photojournalism," he said, lifting the hot coffee to his lips.

"No, I guess not."

"So do we play Twenty Questions or are you going to tell me?"

I told him everything I should have told him the first night but was afraid to.

I'm only human.

I wanted him to know I was no murderer.

EDWARD HARTER

24

FROM WHERE HE STOOD, Harter had a view of Charles Whitford Canley's left profile—not the congressman's most photogenic side. The news photographers and the TV crew from Bartlesburg were set up on the opposite end of the circuit courtroom and were able to capture his best side, the one in his campaign posters.

Harter might not have noticed how different Canley's left side was from his right if he hadn't spent a long time studying Jack Reese's photo of the politician accepting the evangelists' award for moral courage. Canley had managed to tilt his chin leftward before Reese had snapped. The chin almost poked Reverend Sam Knotts—who had been patting him on the back. *Good job, Congressman.*

In fact, from the rear of the brightly lit courtroom, Harter might not have even recognized Canley. It was as if someone had drawn a line down the middle of the congressman's head. His right side was smiling, but on the left his smile seemed to curve downward into more of a smirk. His right eye was alert, his left squinting. Canley's graying black hair was full and combed straight back on the right, but was receding on the left side of his part. Harter guessed that anyone with a perfectly symmetrical face was an oddity, but Canley's was so asymmetrical you might almost believe he was two people. "Stop projecting your animosity," Liz would have told him.

He thought back to what she'd said two nights before, and tried to see the charming party-goer in Canley, the man who had appealed to Susan Devendall. But all he could really see was a politician talking off the top of his head about dope rings and the deterioration of the American work ethic.

Harter imagined many of the young railroaders smoked a joint now and then, but he wasn't convinced they were all junkies. People like Canley conveniently forgot how hard the old men drank, how they used to carry flasks, how Victorian ladies became morphine addicts, how the saloons along the canal were once wild and woolly.

"I don't mean to leave the impression that I'm singling out any one railroad or any one incident," Canley had said.

Then why talk about specific wrecks? Harter wondered.

Harter could understand why Tattoo had been ranting against Canley when he'd stopped by on Thursday afternoon. The old railroader had waved the newspaper so madly that it had slipped out of his hand and flown across the room, landing on the daybed.

The reporters spurred Canley on with questions, but Harter barely listened, finding himself surveying the courtroom instead. Of course, he'd been in it many times, testifying for the state or presenting his evidence to the grand jury in the privacy of the adjoining jury room. The jury room would be the perfect spot to interrogate Canley, he decided.

The photographers' flashes were lighting up Canley's face, erasing the traces of wrinkles. Harter guessed the show was about over. He thought someone ought to tell the judge it destroyed the sanctity of the courtroom to allow snollygosters to hold press conferences there when court wasn't in session.

Some of the people began to leave. Others circled around the congressman to have a personal word. Harter slowly made his way through the spectator benches toward the front and came to a stop at the back of the clump of people, watching to be sure Canley didn't slip out on him.

Finally the TV crew packed up and the last reporter backed away. Canley picked up his speech from the lawyer's table, folded it neatly, and stuck it in the inside pocket of his slick blue suitcoat.

Harter approached. "Congressman, I'd like to speak to you if I may." He put the evidence envelopes under his arm and showed Canley his badge.

"Shawnee City Police, eh? Harter?"

"Right." *At least be could read.*

"Is there a bill before Congress you're interested in? I've always been a strong voice for law and order."

"No, I'd like to ask you some questions about a case."

"A case?"

"Susan Devendall's murder."

"Terrible thing," said Canley, as if he meant it. "One reason I came to town was to go to her memorial service tomorrow. I'm a friend of the family. I've known Amy and Howard most of my life, though I didn't know Susan and the Maddox family as well."

Harter searched for the proper attack. He finally said, "That's not exactly what I've heard, Congressman."

"What *have* you heard?" challenged Canley, his voice rising.

"Some people think you were a very close friend of Susan Devendall, an intimate friend," pushed Harter. "Maybe we can sit down and talk about it."

He pointed the evidence envelopes toward the jury room. At first he wasn't sure Canley would take the suggestion, but, almost scowling, the congressman at last turned and went inside.

"I asked what you'd heard," Canley demanded after the door was shut and they were seated around the jury table.

"The word from the west side is that you've been seeing Susan Devendall for months."

"Who told you that?"

"I thought, if you did know her well, you might have some ideas on what happened to her." That was about as diplomatic as he could be, as diplomatic as he got.

Canley was obviously irritated "The tongues on the west side never stop wagging, do they?"

Harter shrugged.

Canley didn't speak for a while. When he did, he calmly said, "Okay, I'll level with you. But get this straight. If anything I tell you ever hits the press, your ass is worse than mud. The mayor and police chief are beholden to me on more than one count. I'm no first-term novice. Most importantly, I had nothing to do with Susan's death."

"So?"

"What?"

"So tell me. I haven't heard you say anything yet."

"Why don't you forget about the chip on your shoulder and try asking an intelligent question, Harter?" snapped Canley.

"When did you last see Susan Devendall?"

"Wednesday night of last week. She came out to my farm and we had a late dinner together."

"I take it that wasn't the first time she'd been out to your farm."

"She'd been there many times since spring. She was there last Tuesday night, too. I'd called her Sunday from Washington and told her I'd cleared a few days for campaigning around Shawnee. I suggested it was time we plan a trip we'd talked about. I got into town Tuesday afternoon and she came out for dinner. She brought a photo for her passport. I was going to take care of the rest of the arrangements."

"A photo like this?" asked Harter. He opened the top envelope, pulled out a bunch of Reese's prints, and handed a head shot across the table.

Canley barely glanced at it. "Yeah."

"What was this trip you two were going to take?"

"We were going to Europe in November, after the election. She was going to tell Howard she needed some time to herself to decide what she was going to do."

"And what was she going to do?"

Canley flashed anger again "How the hell do I know? It was all just an excuse for her to get away. We talked about, maybe, her leaving him, but I wasn't sure."

"Sure of what?"

"What it would mean politically."

And this was the man with the moral backbone that Sam Knotts and the other preachers so admired, thought Harter.

"How long had you been involved with her?" he asked.

"I don't like that word—*involved,*" said Canley. "I'm not sure what business it is of yours, anyway. It's got nothing to do with her murder."

"Look, I'm not trying to embarrass you, Congressman. I'm trying to figure out what happened to Susan Devendall."

"We'd been seeing each other since May. She went to work for my campaign and we hit it off. She was at loose ends at the time. She'd had a bad time at work."

"An attempted rape?"

"So you've heard the story?"

"Several times. Amy Devendall told me first."

"Amy's a colossal bitch. She's probably the one who told you about Susan and me. We figured she'd spread rumors about us. Susan never did get along with Amy. Howard's a eunuch—Amy's the one with the balls in the family."

Wondering if rumors were still rumors if they were true, Harter asked, "Did Amy or Howard Devendall know about this planned trip?"

"I wouldn't think so. I can't imagine Susan told them before we'd worked out the details. Howard was supposed to be in Pittsburgh all last week, so I don't see how he'd have known. That's why Susan was able to spend Tuesday and Wednesday nights with me."

"Did she stay all night?"

Canley glared at him. "She never did. She always wanted Amy to know she was home in the morning."

"Tuesday and Wednesday nights were the only times you saw her last week?"

"Yeah, and Wednesday we didn't get together until after nine because I'd been out stumping in the country all day."

"What was she wearing?"

Canley closed his eyes and pursed his lips. "I don't see what that has to do with anything."

"This?" asked Harter, holding up a photo from the Wednesday pink-dress session.

"Yeah." Again Canley scarcely looked at the picture. "You don't have to show me any more photos, Harter. I know what she looked like. I've got pictures of her myself—ones I took and ones she sent me after I'd be gone in Washington for a few weeks. What of it?"

"How about this?" Harter opened the other evidence envelope and slid the jewelry onto the table.

Canley glanced at the pile of gleaming metal. "We bought that stuff at a summer festival. She came to Washington on a shopping trip—or that's what she told Howard. Susan liked jewelry and liked being photographed. What do you want me to say? Don't you have some sexual quirk? Do you like to handcuff your wife or pistol-whip your girlfriend?"

"None of my girlfriends ever ended up dead in a canal, Congressman," Harter replied. "She was wearing this jewelry when she was found."

"Look," Canley said, "I don't have to murder someone to get what I want."

"I haven't accused you of anything," said Harter.

"How can I explain to you about Susan and me? I'd been widowed for a year, and my wife had been ill for a long time. Howard hadn't exactly been captivating Susan lately. We sparked something in each other. That's all."

"You didn't see her Thursday, the night she turned up missing?"

"I wish I had. Things might have been different. She might not have driven to that alley. She might still be alive. She was upset with me. I'd called her in the afternoon and told her I didn't see how we could get together. I had to go to a dinner with some religious leaders and then on to a rally with some businessmen. She was very insistent about needing to see me. She reminded me how she'd sneaked around all summer, even taking off work on afternoons I was in town. She claimed I never changed my schedule for her. I told her I'd call her about ten if I could get away. I couldn't. After the business group, some party people cornered me and had me sit in on a strategy session till after midnight. The next morning I went back to Washington. At that point I didn't know anything had happened to her. You're trying to make me out the heavy, but Susan and I were lovers. Don't you understand?"

Harter stayed silent as he absorbed what Canley had told him. Nothing conflicted in any way with what Jack Reese or anybody else had said. Susan Devendall quite possibly had driven to the alley alone that night, frustrated by not being able to get her photos from Reese earlier in the evening, frustrated by not being able to see Canley because, for him, politicking came first. But what had happened in the alley?

"Did you ever hear of a Daniel Jones or a Simon Bowman?" he asked Canley.

"No. Should I have?"

"Susan Devendall never mentioned either of them?"

"The names mean nothing."

Harter stared at Canley's face a moment. The congressman was looking out the second-story window and, this time, Harter could only see his photogenic right profile. He began shoving the jewelry back in the envelope.

"I meant what I said, Harter," snapped Canley, turning full-face toward him. "I told you I'd level. I answered every one of your questions. If any of this shit ever comes back to haunt me, I'll bust your ass."

25

HARTER STUFFED his cigarette butt in the sand of the concrete ashtray outside the courthouse door and went down the steps to his car. He unlocked it, took one photo out of an envelope, left the rest of the evidence inside, then locked up again. With the picture in his hand, he began walking toward Howard P. Devendall's office.

It was a sunny October day, fit for making his rounds on foot. He'd hiked about two blocks from the courthouse when he saw her come out of the building. A gray-uniformed black driver opened the limousine door for the short lady in the violet coat.

Harter cut across the street, through the late morning traffic, and reached the limo right after the chauffeur had climbed in. He rapped at her window. Amy Devendall said something to her driver and the window powered down.

"Downtown on business, Mrs. Devendall?" asked Harter, catching a whiff of her strong perfume.

"Howard wanted me to sign some papers," she answered. "Then we looked over some of our buildings. My husband bought this entire block just after World War Two, shortly before he died. We've been thinking about remodeling some of it, but decided to wait to see what happens with the downtown. Perhaps some condominiums might be a good idea, don't you think, Detective?"

"I wouldn't know." Sensing she wasn't about to bring up the case, Harter went at her another way. "I've been running into a few people who know you."

"Yes? Who?"

"A Reverend Sam Knotts, for instance."

"Sam's really a client of Howard's," she said, turning her rouged cheek away from him in disinterest. "How did you happen to meet him?"

"Well, you know, this case has two parts. It's not just the murder of your daughter-in-law. An old man died in an arson, too. I've learned another old man died under similar circumstances in August. Sam Knotts was his minister."

"You've lost me, Detective."

"It might not be important, but did your daughter-in-law ever talk about either Simon Bowman or Daniel Jones?"

"I don't believe I ever heard of them." To emphasize her point, she stared directly at him. "I'll ask Howard about them, if it would help."

Harter glanced over at the building. "You don't have to. I may go in and see him myself."

"He's terribly busy. He couldn't even take time to go to Maxi's with me for lunch."

Maxi's, he thought, the place where Susan Devendall had told Ace Stewart he could get a job as a dishwasher.

"I won't take much of your son's time," Harter said. "I thought he might like to know Congressman Canley will be attending the memorial service tomorrow. I just spent most of the morning with the congressman."

"Yes, and what did Charles have to say for himself?" Amy Devendall asked in a detached manner that couldn't quite cover her curiosity.

"He's upset. Says he didn't know there was anything wrong when he left Shawnee early last Friday morning."

"No one knew there was anything wrong last Friday morning," she said. "I'm sure Howard will be glad to know Charles will be at the service. It's so nice to have friends around on such occasions."

"Are they old friends, your son and Congressman Canley?"

"They've been friends and associates in the past," she responded in a voice that showed she knew what Harter was after. "Of course, you know how associations change, Detective."

"Has anything come to mind since Tuesday, anything that might throw some light on what happened to your daughter-in-law?"

"Nothing I can think of," she said. "Now, if you don't mind, I have a luncheon engagement."

Harter backed away from the limousine, the window powered up, and the car pulled away from the curb. He rested against the parking meter a moment to collect his thoughts before going into the building.

Howard Devendall's secretary gave him the once-over when he stepped through the office door. At first she told him Mr. Devendall was in conference and couldn't be interrupted. But when he flashed his badge and mentioned the murder investigation, she hurried into the inner office. Soon she was back to usher him inside.

Devendall was seated behind an enormous polished desk. Despite the piles of legal documents and law books, there was something extremely tidy about the place. Howard, in his white shirt and gray vest, looked tidy as well. Harter felt like a hippie at a White House ball.

"I don't have much time, Detective," said Devendall. "I've been trying to catch up on my backlog."

"Just a couple questions." Harter handed the lawyer Reese's photo of the sign at the cardboard box factory. "How long have you owned the building by the canal?"

"We've owned it from the start. It was one of my father's first projects. He built it about 1910, when he was still a young man. We've leased it to a series of industries over the years. I believe it was a tannery originally."

"It's totally empty now?"

"As far as I'm aware. Why are you asking?"

"Would you mind if I looked through it?"

"I don't understand."

"You do realize your wife's body was found not far from the building, and that we believe she was held captive someplace for a day or so?"

Devendall's face became paler than usual. "I guess I didn't make the connection. Certainly you don't think—"

"I don't think anything. I'd just like to look at the building."

Devendall leaned forward and hit an intercom button. "Mrs. Jackson, would you find a master key for the cardboard box factory and give it to Detective Harter when he leaves?"

"Thanks. It'll save a lot of time."

"I told you the other day, I'll help in any way I can to find my wife's murderer. Anything else?"

"Daniel Jones or Simon Bowman? Did your wife ever bring up those names? She may have met them when she worked for the Commission on Aging."

"Truth is, the only time we talked about her work was when I'd encourage her to quit. I didn't pay attention to the names of her clients. Again, I don't understand what they would have to do with it. Now the man who tried to rape her—that might be something else."

"I've seen him," Harter said. "I don't consider him a suspect at this time."

"Whom *do* you consider a suspect, Detective?" asked Devendall, gripping the arms of his chair.

"I've nothing to say publicly," answered Harter, rising and stepping toward the door. "I'll get the key back to you early next week."

"Did"—Devendall stopped and then started again—"Did you ever find out about the jewelry?"

"Your wife got it at a craft fair in Washington."

"That doesn't help your case much, does it?"

"No." Harter continued toward the door. Just before leaving, he said, "By the way, I spoke with Congressman Canley this morning. He sends his sympathy. He says he'll be at the service tomorrow."

"You won't be, will you?" asked Howard Devendall.

"I hadn't thought about it."

LATER, sitting at the counter at the Desert Island, Harter wondered if there was any reason he *should* attend the service. Detectives always did that in the movies, but he never had. He also wondered if telling Devendall about Canley had been too low a blow.

He shook off the thought. He was trying to solve a murder, not make friends.

Two murders actually.

Maybe even three.

Everyone forgot that.

He studied the waitress' face as she slid the plate of hot dogs in front of him. He noticed that her heavy makeup was serving its purpose, swooping across her cheekbones and covering a right eye that was still bruised and a left eye that looked like it was just returning to normal.

Do you like to handcuff your wife or pistol-whip your girlfriend? A weird line coming from a congressman.

Don't you have some sexual quirk? Was Canley sending a message or mounting a defense?

From all the evidence, Susan Devendall had had unexpected sides to her personality.

What had Linda Dean said? *It was like she had a split personality.* The air-conditioned Volkswagen. The clothes buyer who wore jeans and an old raincoat to work. The woman who didn't confide in other women, yet was willing to bare herself to a total stranger's camera. Possessor of a streak of social consciousness that had dissolved enough to allow her to become entangled with the most conservative of congressmen. Resident of a west-side mansion, but found dead in suggestive attire in Shanty-town after being slugged around, no more protected than the waitress with the black eyes.

Ace Stewart could be telling the truth. She could have come on to him, then backed off screaming in fear. Within a month of that incident, she was inching away from social work and falling into siestas with Canley.

Harter hated such psychologizing. Yet he had to admit that fathoming Susan Devendall appeared to require a wall of degrees.

Still, when all the psychologizing was over, the two old men re-mained.

The dead old men from Wild Stream, West Virginia.

26

WILD STREAM 28

As soon as he crossed the river bridge, the road veered to the right through a relatively flat valley, the mountains rolling down to a nearly farmable level. The woods were autumn-thin and colored leaves dried in piles along the narrow state road.

Harter's eyes were as stuck to the road as his mind was on Liz. She'd tried to talk her way into joining him on the West Virginia trip, and he hadn't let her.

He'd laid out his plan Friday night, and she'd taken it so badly that he'd intended to slip away without waking her Saturday morning. But, as he sat on the edge of her bed putting on his shoes, her voice had broken through the early morning stillness.

"I could still put a sign on the door and go with you. We could make a weekend of it."

"Hell, you sound like Caruthers. He came in yesterday when I was calling the Wild Stream police chief and wanted to know where I was headed. Rather than tell him, I asked him how you write off champagne on police-department vouchers. He got pretty grouchy. Told me I'd get mine one day."

"I'll pay for the champagne," she'd said. "Remember, tonight was to be your birthday dinner."

He'd looked over his shoulder at her, at her gray-green eyes staring his way, at her dark hair against the pillow, at her tanned face with the covers pulled up around it.

"I just want to get there and get back. I don't even know if it's worth driving down there. I'm not really looking forward to it."

"You know you are. You'll enjoy it. You can complain about your job all you like, but it's the only thing that grabs you, the only thing that keeps you going."

"You grab me."

"Sometimes I wonder."

"I wouldn't have stayed around this long if you didn't. It's not like I have to."

"Are you positive you'll be back tonight?" she'd asked.

"I'm not positive of anything. I'll call you when I have an idea. I may be late."

"I'll wait until midnight, and then everything will turn back into a pumpkin, mice, and rags."

He'd leaned over and kissed her. "I hope I'll at least find the glass slipper."

He'd put on his gun and jacket and gone out into the brisk morning air. Liz's neighborhood had been quiet at 7:30. He'd climbed into his car, driven out of the west side, over the bridge, and headed south.

Near the South Shawnee rail yards, he'd stopped for coffee and doughnuts at a diner that always reminded him of the Edward Hopper print on his wall. The joint had been around longer than he had. His father had once had a regular stool in the place.

Crossing the Shawnee city line, he'd driven past a string of fast-food restaurants, a shopping center, the Reverend Sam Knotts' True Church of God with its Christian Academy-to-be. Then, passing the road to the Hays Trailer Court and salvage yard, he'd finally found himself on open highway between two mountain ridges.

"So the city boy will be going to the country?" Liz had lightly taunted him the evening before when he'd told her what he was about to do. He supposed he'd never told her how well he knew those mountains south of town. How many times over the years had he retreated up the north slope to the overlook and surveyed the city below him? But he'd never taken her with him.

When he'd been young, the west slope of South Mountain, above the city reservoir, had been his father's favorite camping spot. They'd pitch a tent in the old CCC camp, where his dad had worked during the Depression. Out there on the mountain, they'd haul water from an old hand pump and rough it for days. He'd wandered that hillside, every inch, just as he would later wander the city at all hours.

Someday he'd have to take Liz out on the mountain to see if anything remained of the CCC camp and that other world.

The road turned away from the mountain. To his right now, the Shawnee-Potomac mainline cut through a hollow and, two tracks wide, began to parallel the highway. He knew he'd be following the railroad, or the railroad would be following him, all the way to Wild Stream. The mainline ran its way south, then west, deep into West Virginia, the Mountain State, down past the coal mines, coal camps, those old company towns where his mother's mother had been born.

His grandmother had had incredible stories of the coal fields, of the kind of strike warfare that history classes ignored. Maybe he'd dress as his coal-mining great-grandfather for the Halloween Party.

The night before, Liz had again reminded him of the party the next weekend at the Winhams. She had known he didn't want to go. "What do you think you'll wear as a costume?" she'd asked, as if the debate was more over what to go as than over whether to go at all.

If he went, he decided, he'd rub black diamonds over his face and on the soles of his boots so they'd leave footprints on the carpet.

Coalminer blackface.

She'd hate it.

So many distances between them.

Amazing that they could sometimes reach out to one another that far.

He was racing to overcome a diesel pulling empty coal cars when the Wild Stream sign came up on him. He hit his brakes and slowed down. The freight swung off to the right, the engineer still gunning it, building steam for the mountain back of town.

Wild Stream was a small burg set for the most part in a valley, though frame cubicles rose up the hillsides around him. He hoped he was wrong, but he feared the visit might end up as clueless as his Friday afternoon tour through the abandoned cardboard box factory on the canal bank. There had been nothing inside, no signs of anyone being kept there, no recent garbage, no chains. Unless the company continued to make long-term lease payments, the Devendall family certainly wasn't bringing in much income from the dingy building.

When he reached the traffic light by the two-story brick courthouse—the largest structure in town—Harter remembered the police chief's directions and pulled into the first parking place he came to. Looking back, he saw he'd already sailed past The Diamond.

Outside, the restaurant was painted bright blue, with plenty of glass, making it the liveliest-looking spot on Main Street.

Inside, the formica tabletops sparkled. The wooden booths and the elaborate soda fountain mirror hinted that the eatery was well-established and, once, might have deserved its reputation.

Harter headed straight to the squat man with a crew cut who was sitting at the counter playing with a coffee spoon as he chatted with a waitress. "You Ben Lynch?"

The man tilted toward him so he could see his white shirt and the badge beneath his dark jacket. "Yeah."

"I'm Edward Harter from the Shawnee police."

"You don't look much like a detective," said Lynch in the kind of relaxed country voice that a city cop couldn't keep long.

"If you let me be a detective, I'll let you be a police chief," Harter replied.

Lynch cracked a grin. "Sit down. Bertie, bring this man a cup of coffee. The good stuff. From yesterday." After Harter had climbed on a stool, Lynch asked, "Any trouble getting here?"

"No. Nice drive. Gave me time to think. You got anyone lined up for us to see?"

Lynch reached into his pocket and pulled out a small notepad as Bertie put a cup of black liquid in front of Harter.

"After we talked yesterday, I made a list of a few old-timers that may know something of Bowman and Jones," said Lynch.

"Great. How about old police files? You didn't find anything, did you?"

Lynch shook his head. "I had one of my girls look through things quick. She didn't turn up nothing. That's not to say there couldn't be something in circuit court records or someplace. The old records are pretty incomplete. Nobody required half the paperwork they load us down with now."

"The good old days, huh?"

"Must have been. I'm still not clear on precisely what these old fellows have to do with your case."

Harter slowly worked at the coffee as he explained what he knew to Ben Lynch—the arson, Susan Devendall, the Commission on Aging files, how both Bowman and Jones had been born in Wild Stream, how his trip was just a long shot. He held back on Charles Whitford Canley and a few things he didn't figure the police chief needed to know.

When he'd told the tale, Lynch nodded his bristly head and tossed a dollar bill on the counter. "You ready to get going?"

"Sure."

"We'll take my car. It'll be simpler," Lynch said. He led the way out of The Diamond, down the sidewalk half a block, and stopped beside a late-model white vehicle with WILD STREAM POLICE DEPARTMENT and a town seal stenciled on the door.

"We'll start with the boys right in town," Lynch said as he pulled away from the curb. "This first one's a real old-timer. Ken Carlson's in his upper eighties. Lived around here all his life. He can be a trifle senile, I'll warn you. Some days he's sharp, others he's not."

Soon Lynch was turning the car into a driveway that curved away from Main Street and up a hill.

An hour later, as they drove back out the driveway, Harter was beginning to worry about having wasted a day.

This Saturday had not been one of Ken Carlson's more lucid ones.

He'd started out well enough: "Daniel Jones and Simon Bowman? Sure I recall them. They was in school with me. Don't know whether they finished or not."

Then Carlson had gone off on a rambling description of the one-room schoolhouse, the teachers, their chastising paddle, even the weather one January day when the kids had had to hike through snowdrifts—"not like these spoiled young ones today."

After that, there was no getting him back on track.

Lynch's second old-timer wasn't much better. Nor was the third, or the fourth. After considerable driving around, a stop back at The Diamond for lunch, and four hours of interviews, they'd learned little.

Whether or not they'd finished school, Daniel Jones and Simon Bowman had both served in France during World War I. When they'd come home in 1919, it was the old singsong—"How you gonna keep 'em down in Wild Stream?" They'd earned reputations for carousing and womanizing. Low-paying day jobs around town didn't suit them. Eventually they'd headed to Shawnee, which must have seemed like the Promised Land. After that, no one knew anything.

"Ain't coming together, is it?" asked Lynch as he drove east of Wild Stream, past a small market.

"No, it ain't coming together. Look, I appreciate everything you've done, but unless this next one knows something, I'll be heading back to Shawnee," Harter said. At least he could salvage the evening with Liz.

"Well, if Jerome don't know nothing, that's probably the wisest thing to do," said Lynch, turning off onto a rutted lane. "Jerome Ball's more or less the local historian. I saved the best for last."

Crossing the yard to the frame farmhouse, Harter hoped Jerome Ball would be forthright with them, that if he had nothing to say worth saying, he'd tell them right off and be done with it.

Turned out Ball had a lot worth saying, and he did say it right off.

"Simon Bowman was a real bastard," Ball proclaimed as he moved around the kitchen, making them coffee and bacon-and-tomato sandwiches on a cast-iron stove. "I was about ten when he came home from the war—World War One. My daddy hired him now and then to do odd jobs, so I saw a good bit of him. Even as a full-grown man, he'd throw stones at birds."

"And Daniel Jones?" asked Harter.

"Daniel was a whole other piece of cake. Nice fellow, fairly smart. You'd never have imagined the pair would be best friends, inseparable. It was like Daniel never saw just how mean Simon could be. They must have left here about 1923—I guess I was fourteen or so. They were expecting to get jobs with the railroad in Shawnee. I heard bits and pieces about it later. When Daniel would come back to town, like he would occasionally, I'd ask him about Simon and Amelia Logan."

"Amelia Logan?"

"She ran off to Shawnee with them. I'd judge she was sixteen at the time." The lines on Ball's thin face twisted into a lopsided grin. "Amelia'd been running a regular screwing business since she was thirteen or fourteen. Her mother either didn't know or didn't care. She was usually off with some man, anyway. God knows where her daddy was. They pictured themselves as what you'd call fallen elite. Traced the decline to being on the wrong side in the Civil War."

"Screwing business?" asked Ben Lynch. "You mean Amelia Logan was a whore?"

"Yeah. Story went that Amelia had a code for telling her customers if it was all right for them to come in. If she was alone and open for business, she'd hang a silk stocking on the clothesline beside the house. It's where the water plant is now." Lynch nodded. "The customer was supposed to collect the silk stocking from the line and bring it to the door so's no one else would come. They say Amelia had all the men in town around her finger. Or around her thigh."

"And she went to Shawnee with Jones and Bowman, and you never heard of her again?" Harter asked.

"Right," said Jerome Ball, leaning forward on his elbows on the kitchen table. "When I'd ask Daniel about her or Simon, he'd just grimace. No one around here lost sleep over any of them, though I kind of missed Daniel. I'm sure, with all her enterprise, Amelia took care of herself pretty well—at least as long as her looks held out. She *was* a good-looker. She probably earned herself a whole batch of stuff monogrammed A.L."

"A. L.," mumbled Harter, putting down his sandwich.

"Amelia Logan—that'd be her initials," explained Ball, as if the detective might have missed something.

27

HIS LEFT HAND resting on her smooth thigh, his knees pressed against the backs of hers, he laid still, watching the room slowly lighten.

She knew nothing of what he'd picked up in Wild Stream. When he'd arrived at her studio shortly before nine, she'd already had the wine uncorked and the table ready. They'd banished all serious talk.

Three glasses of wine later, the dishes piled in the sink, the stereo playing saxophone ballads, he had reached out to her, across the great distance, urging her toward him, undoing the top button of her black dress, sliding a hand to her breasts, rubbing gently at her knee. Women were so different.

They'd begun the slow garment-by-garment stripping of each other, the stripping away of cloth and of psychological layers, reducing the gap between them until, he inside her, she around him, there was no gap, for the moment, and he could forget his name was Edward Harter, forget he was a cop, and just roll with her, roll with her, with her.

He awoke near dawn but tried not to move, holding her instead, taking in the feel of her, staying close so the distance wouldn't widen.

His body safe and secure for the moment, his mind reviewed events of the last few days. It had only been a week since the chief had called him away from Liz to the canal bank on that dreary Saturday night. All those facts, conjectures, old tales that he'd come across since had been unknown to him only seven days before.

Susan Devendall, Daniel Jones, Simon Bowman, Jack Reese, Tattoo Kendall, Amy Devendall, Howard P., Canley, Knotts, Amelia Logan . . . all those people he was starting to know well, too well, had been strangers a short while before.

All those bricks . . . and yet he still couldn't put the building together. He had to pick up one of them and throw it and see how far it went and what, or who, it hit. He knew that. But which one?

He had to get moving.

He carefully disengaged himself from Liz and, trying not to disturb her, climbed out of bed, scooped up his clothes, and went into the bathroom. He was aware the shower might wake her, but he needed one and took the chance. When he returned to her bedroom, she was sitting up.

"Working today?" she asked as soon as she saw he was dressed.

"Yeah."

"Is it getting close?"

"Yeah."

"Call me."

"I will."

He bent over, kissed her, and then, as he had the morning before, went out to his car and drove south.

He got to Sam Knotts' True Church of God as the last churchgoers were hurrying into the white building for the nine o'clock service. He pulled onto the berm on the other side of the highway and stared at the church, then lit a cigarette and rolled down his window. Inside, faint voices rose in a hymn.

Soon the Reverend Knotts would be preaching. He might stand high in his pulpit, mouthing a silent sermon, waving an arm that ended in a bloody stub.

Christ.

Harter had pondered Ace Stewart's words several times since Wednesday. *If I lie, cut off my dick. Ain't that what they used to do? Like robbers, they cut off their hands, and liars they cut out their tongues, and rapists they cut off their dicks.*

If those ancient laws were ever enforced, thought Harter, imagine all the maimed people in pulpits, in the halls of Congress, in houses, in the streets.

His right hand slid across his black jacket until he felt his gun.

A van came down the highway, pulled into the church lot, and parked near the Christian Academy sign. *Made possible by friends of The True Church of God and by a donation In Memory* of *A.L.*

The van door slid open and a gang of kids poured out and headed around the side of the church to the Sunday school rooms.

Raise up the children right, Knotts had said to him as he'd crowded him on the orange sofa.

Harter leaned back and tapped out a rhythm on the steering wheel.

How the hell was he going to get at Knotts?

He couldn't prove anything yet.

The key—*if there was one*—was A.L.

He turned the key in the ignition, U-turned back toward Shawnee, and stopped at the diner near the railroad shops to call the chief—to disturb *his* tranquil Sunday morning for once.

Leaving the diner, he drove crosstown, up the Avenue, onto Thomas Street, and into Baxter Street. He halted a minute behind Reese's house to scout out the location. Then he headed back down the alley, past the piled char of Daniel Jones' house, around the block and up Thomas Street once more, all the way to the top of the hill, where he turned around and drove back down, pulling up to the curb across from the brick house.

Lighting another cigarette, he surveyed the steep street and the layout of the two-family house. Convincing himself that the plan would work was actually harder than convincing the chief. Harter didn't want anyone to get hurt, didn't want the house destroyed if things got out of hand.

He watched a short heavyset woman leave the house and go down the hill. *Mrs. Kendall.* On her way to church, he guessed. *Good.* Better to talk to Tattoo alone.

He climbed out of the car, crossed Thomas Street and knocked on the door. He was a little surprised when Jack Reese answered.

Reese stared at him awkwardly for a moment, then motioned him in. "How you doing? Back to see Tattoo again?"

"Yeah, we were running through some ancient history when I stopped in Thursday afternoon. I wanted to go over some of the ground again. How are *you* doing?"

"Better."

"Your dreams improving?"

"Improving," said Reese as he moved to the head of the kitchen steps and called for Tattoo.

The photographer walked back to the couch and cleared away sections of Sunday's *Pittsburgh Press.* "Sit down. Are you still tracking the Bowman guy?"

Harter nodded.

"Anything new on the case?"

"Stop worrying," said Harter.

Tattoo's slow, heavy footsteps got nearer. He had a chaw of tobacco in his jaw when he entered the living room. "You again," he said.

"Me again."

Tattoo dropped into his chair. "What can I do for you?"

Glancing across the sofa at Jack Reese, Harter decided it was safe to talk. Reese might even be an asset. "I just wondered if you'd remembered anything more that Daniel Jones said about Simon Bowman."

"I been thinking on that name, Simon Bowman," said Tattoo. "I talked to a couple old boys about it. Ain't much new. I can't recall Daniel ever saying nothing about a Bowman at any length, but somewheres it does mean something. I got it in my head Bowman was a scab, like I told you the other day. Maybe more than that, some of the old boys think."

"Like what?"

"Like, could be this Simon Bowman was a company thug or some such thing back in 'twenty-eight or 'thirty-four, or one of them mean strikes in them days. The name's got an evil ring to me. Could be that Daniel or old Jack—that'd be Jack here's granddaddy—mentioned him years ago. You know how these things are. The stories all blend together after a time, particularly when you got no reason to memorize them and you don't know the people they're about. Anyways, the bosses in them days would hire blackshirts, real criminal sorts. For all I know, the governor'd let felons out of the pen to be strikebreakers and head-bashing guards. I just wish the young ones could remember them days. There is one thing, though."

"What?"

"Devendall. Wasn't that the name? Wasn't that the dead girl's name?"

"Yeah," said Harter. He could feel Reese tense next to him.

Tattoo shot brown juice into his spittoon. "Some of the boys say a Devendall was who contracted thugs for the railroad. He used to scour Shantytown for real tough ones. His name was probably James Howard Devendall. 'Course he'd be long gone now, wouldn't he? He wouldn't have been a young man even then."

"His wife's still around," said Harter. "Susan Devendall was married to his son."

"The old lady must be quite an antique."

"I'd judge she was considerably younger than James Howard Devendall when they married," answered Harter, recalling Howard had said his father had built the cardboard box factory in 1910.

"What's it mean?" asked Reese.

"I don't know." Harter looked back at Tattoo. "Did you ever hear of an Amelia Logan? She might have come from Wild Stream, West Virginia, along with Simon Bowman or Daniel Jones."

"Don't mean nothing to me. I can't seem to dredge more up out of my head right now. I wish I could, but I can't."

"You've done fine."

Tattoo shook his head. "I wish I could help you more. I want to nail the bastard that burnt up Daniel and killed the girl."

"So do I," said Reese.

Harter leaned back against the afghan spread over the daybed. He lit a cigarette and, from the corner of his eye, caught Reese's sad expression. He wondered how Reese would react to the news that the best aid he could give would be to go away and leave his house empty for a few days.

Then he stared at the old man in the faded flannel shirt with the left sleeve pinned up. Was he ready for the danger?

After a long pause, Harter came out with it.

"There is a way you can both help."

28

"I LIVE ON THOMAS STREET, right above the alley where Daniel Jones' house was," explained Tattoo. "You'd best come see me. Daniel told me everything before the fire."

Harter, his hand over the mouthpiece of another phone, listened to the fumbling response. Sitting at his desk, Caruthers watched the old railroader and the younger detective closely, his expression betraying his doubt that the scheme would work.

"Yeah. He told me everything. All about the old days," insisted Tattoo. "All about Simon Bowman and Amelia Logan."

The old guy should have been an actor, Harter thought. He was sticking tight to the script, setting things up perfectly. Harter hoped he'd done his own scene-setting properly. He hoped they'd called the right person. But he wouldn't have bet his life on it.

"That's the name. Tattoo Kendall. I told you the address already. You'll find it. You never had no trouble finding Daniel or Bowman, did you? But I'll be ready for you. Don't try nothing on me. Just bring money. Make my retirement a load easier. I'll be alone tonight and Monday night. Don't come in the day. If you don't show, I'm sure a lot of people, like the police, would like to hear what I got to say."

The voice at the other end mildly pleaded ignorance, or innocence, of what he was talking about. Harter nodded for him to cut off the conversation.

"I ain't got time for this. You come see me face-to-face and talk it out," said Tattoo before slamming down the phone.

Harter listened and imagined he heard a long sigh before the click and the dial tone.

Hanging up, he said to the old man, "Great job."

"What if nothing comes of it?" Caruthers asked Harter.

"Then I made the wrong choice."

"Not the first time."

"You got a better idea?" asked Tattoo, instinctively siding with Harter.

"Him?" said Harter. "He's got no idea."

"So I'm cautious," said Caruthers. "I'm not into this game-playing.."

"Come on. It's already getting dark. We've got to get going," said Harter, having no heart for a debate on moderation. "You do know what you're supposed to do, Caruthers?"

"Yeah. You're lucky the chief called me up personally."

"You got more important things to do tonight?" asked Harter. When Caruthers didn't answer, he pushed in another spur. "You better get something to eat before you go on stakeout. It's bound to be a long night. Mattioni's is just down the street. Open Sunday evenings. I'll vouch for the place. Full line of hoagies—and *no meatloaf.*"

Caruthers ignored him and hurried out of the room as Harter lit a cigarette. He'd already driven away by the time the other two left headquarters.

"Your partner ain't got much faith in your plan," said Tattoo, climbing into the car.

"Ah, he's like that. No imagination. Wants everything wrapped up neat. Caruthers isn't exactly my partner. He'll do his job, though. He's competent. He's a cop despite the complaining."

He steered out onto the empty Sunday-night street. "So now we just wait?" asked Tattoo.

"Yeah, we just wait—and stay sharp. I warned you this could be dangerous."

"I made it through World War Two and plenty of other bad scenes," said Tattoo, rubbing at his stub.

Later I'll ask him. There'll be lots of time later. Harter crossed the tracks into the east side.

"How many cops you going to have planted around?" asked Tattoo.

"Three, besides Caruthers and me. The chief told me to pick who I wanted. I've got three beat cops lined up, guys who've done a good job with me over the years. Guys who'd like to be detectives. Guys who want my job, or Caruthers'."

"What if Caruthers is right? What if it don't work? What if we called the wrong person?"

Harter said nothing, and drove up the hill in silence. He didn't want to face up to that possibility.

When he reached Baxter Street, he turned the corner and drove on until he was behind Tattoo's house. Stopping, he said, "You go on in. I'll get rid of this car, check on the other guys, and be with you in a few minutes."

Tattoo opened the door with his right hand and climbed out. Then Harter continued down the alley until he spotted the unmarked vehicle with the three cops inside. He parked in front of them and, after looking around to be sure no one was watching, got out of his car and climbed in with them.

The cops in the smoky Chevy were dressed in grubby plainclothes, dark enough to blend into the chilly night. Harter carefully went over the plan with them again.

Everyone was to have a hand-held radio and report to him on suspicious people or vehicles in the neighborhood.

Clark was to give him ten minutes to get into Tattoo's house before making his own way up to Jack Reese's kitchen and stationing himself by the back-door window. Harter handed him a key that Reese had provided a few hours earlier.

Ten minutes after Clark left the car, McManaway was to head up the alley and seat himself in Reese's old Ford for the night.

Bettles was to stay with the vehicle, ready to drive wherever directed.

Harter opened the door and began walking slowly up the alley as if he were out for an evening stroll. With a radio stuffed inside his jacket, he checked out the buildings on the hillside above him, noting what lights were lit on Thomas Street.

What if he was wrong? What if it didn't work? he asked himself.

Perhaps he had rushed it. Perhaps he should have spent a couple more days on the investigation before going for the kill. He was still learning things, like the fact that old Devendall might have hired thugs. There was so much he didn't know, though he'd never have admitted it to Caruthers.

Four pork chops were sizzling in a black skillet when Harter stepped into the kitchen. Tattoo was standing at the table with a giant butcher knife in his hand, awkwardly chopping a mammoth potato. When he was through wielding the knife, he dropped the potato slices in the skillet to fry along with the chops.

"I been meaning to ask you," said Tattoo as he turned the homefries with a metal spatula. "You ain't Bill Harter's son, are you?

"You knew my father?"

"Not too good, just knowed who he was. So you grew up on this side of town?"

"East Shawnee, born and bred."

All through supper, Tattoo kept up the chatter about Bill Harter, the railroad neighborhoods, the Shawnee-Potomac. Now and then, when it wasn't too obvious, Harter studied the old man. Tattoo was finding it hard to cut his chop one-handed and finally picked it up and gnawed on the bone.

Later.

They were washing the dishes when the first radio report came in.

"Same blue van's been up and down the hill several times," said Caruthers. "Looks like it's turning into the alley."

"Coming this way slow," said McManaway. "It's passing. Looks like teenagers."

"It's going on down," piped in Bettles a minute later.

"Probably kids looking for a place to park and party," Harter said to Tattoo. "In my days, we used to go out to the overlook on the mountain."

"I guess they stopped calling that Lover's Leap. That's always been a prime parking spot. Used to be filled with Model T's on Saturday night when I first come to Shawnee. I bet that woman you was asking about seen her share of Lover's Leap."

"Amelia Logan?"

"Yeah, that one." He smiled.

Later.

Around nine o'clock, Harter went up to the dark third floor and peeped out a front window. Across the street, slightly up the hill, sat Caruthers' car. Moving to a back window, he had much the same view of the alley as Clark would. A streetlight reflected off the top of Reese's Ford. He hoped McManaway couldn't be seen inside.

Looking down the hill, beyond the metal garages in the alley, he could see the lights of cars speeding up the Avenue toward his old neighborhood. Below the Avenue, a freight cut through town.

When he went back downstairs, Tattoo was sitting in his overstuffed chair in the living room, putting a load of tobacco in his mouth. The blinds were shut and the curtains pulled closed.

"You do what you want. Watch TV or whatever," Harter told him. "I'll be in your back room so I don't have to move if anyone comes."

He walked to the next room and positioned himself in a soft chair in the dark parlor—the room where, on the other side of the house, Reese had set up his studio.

He waited.

"How late does this thing go on?" called Tattoo.

"We'll be here all night and all tomorrow night. If nobody comes by, say, one o'clock, you can go to bed if you want," Harter called back.

"You know, I already miss May. We ain't slept apart but a handful of times since we was married."

"Well, she's safer at the motel. I'll see you get out there tomorrow to visit her for a few hours. That way you won't be around here."

"There's a car . . ." Caruthers began. "Forget it."

"You asked me about my father—now let me ask you something I've wondered," said Harter.

"Shoot," returned Tattoo's voice.

"I'd be interested in knowing how you lost your arm."

"It was in . . . I was in . . . the wrong place at the wrong time, like they say."

"Where was that?" pressed Harter. It was easier to ask such questions when you weren't looking at the person, when you were in a separate room and the other person was only a voice.

"Wasn't in the war or nothing so dramatic. No Devendall thug, no Simon Bowman beat on me in a strike. Somehow I got in between two refrigerator cars a-coupling one night. I don't remember much else. I passed out from the pain and woke up in the hospital, the arm gone. Lucky I lived, I suppose. I knew a man died like that. Boxcars went together with him right between them. I heard him screaming myself. When they pulled the front car away, he crumpled to the tracks, almost in two halves, blood all over. Some people think it's weird these things happen. People think you're crazy or something, not being able to hear the trains and all. But when you live and work around them, you start to ignore the noise, or you don't hear it. Then you're caught one day."

"I know," said Harter when the voice in the other room had settled into a pause. "I had an uncle—my grandmother's brother—who got hit by a coal train and was killed years ago. Just walked right in front of it."

"Well, I lived. Armless, but I lived. Weird thing is, sometimes I feel like I got a left arm. Feels like I can flex the muscle and see the girl slink, the girl in the tattoo I used to have. But when I try, there's nothing there. Two refrigerator cars coupling one night, that's all. How'd your father die?"

Harter didn't respond for a long while. He was relieved when Bettles' voice cut in: "Man walking up the alley your way. Bag in his hand."

A minute later, McManaway reported, "I see him. Bottle in the bag. He's got an old Army jacket on. Wino going on by."

"Hasn't even been a car down the hill in almost fifteen minutes," added Caruthers.

What if it didn't work?

"You made my left arm itch and there's nothing to scratch," said Tattoo. "The itch says nothing's going to happen tonight."

A moment later, the sound of the television hit the air. Harter listened to the headlines. Sunday night, and they were still showing film of Congressman Canley's Friday press conference. Must have been a slow weekend.

"Son of a bitch," he heard Tattoo say.

"Son of a bitch," he agreed.

As the weather and sports droned on, Harter wished he was with Liz, just as he knew Tattoo wished he was with May. *There's nothing to scratch.*

He wanted a cigarette but he didn't want the smoke in the room.

New thought for the costume party: Put a shirt on over his left arm and tie up the sleeve.

29

"GETTING DAMN COLD out here," grouched Caruthers on Monday night.

"Turn on your heater," Harter radioed back, trying to sound just as irritated.

Sooner or later, he knew, he would have to face up to it.

"Nice and toasty in here," came Clark's voice from Reese's kitchen "I've got a pot of coffee on."

"Can't complain," said McManaway. "I got the front seat pushed back and a luscious blonde sitting bare-assed on my lap. Hope we're here all night."

Tense as he was, Harter almost laughed. Dave McManaway had always been his choice to replace Caruthers.

Of course, *he* might be the one who got replaced, busted down to the rank of street cop if his plan failed.

What if nothing happened?

At best, the chief would shoot him a nasty frown and grumble about his department budget not being geared to have five cops tied up doing nothing for two nights.

Caruthers would never let him forget it. He'd spread the tale around the force. Clark, Bettles, and McManaway would get in their digs whenever they saw him coming.

All that was the easy part.

He'd also have to arrange further protection for Tattoo and May for a week or so in case the bloody arsonist showed up late. Worse still, if he stayed on the case, he'd have to go at it from a whole new angle, hoping his ploy hadn't scared off his suspects.

Maybe he had miscalculated. The plan had hit him like a bullet while he'd sat in front of The True Church of God on Sunday morning. He'd gone all the way with it, uncritically. Maybe they had called the wrong person.

"Now to recap the news," said the WBRT anchorman. "A Bartlesburg couple died tonight when their pickup truck stalled on the James Road railroad crossing and was struck by a train. Knobtown High's football team has a shot at going through the season undefeated. And, with a little more than a week until election day, the local political scene is heating up."

Harter sat in the dark parlor, half-listening to a series of commercials until a voice announced that the late show starred Jane Russell, but he missed the name of the movie. Didn't matter. Then he heard a jar lid being unscrewed and the crinkle of waxpaper.

"Want some peanut butter crackers?" called Tattoo.

"No."

His stomach was so tight he couldn't think about eating anything.

"Car coming slow down the alley," said McManaway. "Late-model red Pontiac."

"Real slow," added Clark. "It's passing."

"Could be looking for a parking place," reported Bettles "No, it's turning down behind me, up to Thomas Street."

A minute later, Caruthers picked it up. "Yeah, it's coming . . . Went on up the hill. Forget it."

Harter didn't know whether to relax because the car had driven on or to tense even more because, still, nothing was happening.

"Coming back down," said Caruthers. "Heading for the Avenue."

"Lights pulling in the alley again," said McManaway. "No, it's backing out on Thomas Street and heading up."

"Same red Pontiac," said Caruthers. "Parking on your side, just below the house."

Harter pulled out his revolver and laid it on the arm of his chair.

It seemed like a year before Caruthers had anything new to add. "Okay, he's getting out. Got a stick—no, a cane—in his hand. Big guy. Looks like light hair. Coming to the door."

"I'm signing off," announced Harter. "You direct, Caruthers."

He had the gun in his right hand and the radio in his left when the knock came. Tattoo was on his feet in an instant but seemed to take forever to open up. The television died. Smart, thought Harter.

"Who is it?" called the old man after moving toward the door.

"You wanted to see me," said a voice—a voice Harter recognized. He was right on the money.

The door opened, then closed. He heard the footsteps of the two men but couldn't hear the tap of the cane. Tattoo seemed to return to his overstuffed chair. The other man, he judged, had sat on the daybed.

"Can't say I seen you before," said Tattoo, his voice surprisingly firm. The old man had guts.

"I'm answering your phone call."

"I didn't call *you*."

"Think of me as a messenger."

"I don't want no messenger."

"You wanted cash, didn't you? I've got it." Harter heard the cane scrape against the floor, as if the man had moved to take something from his pocket "I'm the payoff. But, first, you have to earn it. Tell me what you know so I'm sure you're worth it."

There was a long silence. Harter gripped his gun tightly and tried to picture the scene in the front room. He thought he heard Tattoo playing with a tobacco package. He imagined he heard the daybed springs as the big man adjusted his weight.

"What I been told is that Daniel Jones and Simon Bowman come to town sixty years ago with a teenage girl with a wide-open cunt. Named Amelia Logan. I figure she don't want to be reminded of them days no more. I know Bowman was a scab and a thug for old Devendall. Maybe like you are. I know him and Daniel died in fires that some blazer set. Maybe that was you, too."

"You old codgers. You pretend these moth-eaten stories are worth something, like the deep dark past always means something."

The voice was cool, not angry, in its contempt. No hot fire crackled through it. Harter guessed the man had been through similar scenes with Jones and Bowman. It was old hat to him. The Amelia Logan stories really had nothing to do with him anyway. But Harter knew how the earlier scenes with Jones and Bowman had turned out. He knew what the cane was for.

"Well, if my story don't mean nothing, why the hell are you here?" Tattoo asked. "Get back in your car and drive away. I'll tell it to someone else. The detective would eat it up."

"Harter?"

"Yeah, that's his name."

"Shit, you know he wouldn't pay you a cent."

"You ain't paid me nothing yet."

Harter heard the daybed springs creak as the man stood up.

"Come closer and I'll slice you up, you son of a bitch!" yelled Tattoo.

Harter was on his feet. Rounding the head of the kitchen steps. Into the living room. "Drop it, Reverend!"

The cane was held high above the man's red hair, ready to thump the old man in the chair—*the old man who held a butcher knife.*

For a moment Harter wasn't sure.

For a moment he feared Sam Knotts would follow through and clobber Tattoo.

For a moment he imagined he'd have to blow the preacher to the nearest corner of hell.

Then Knotts lowered his weapon.

"Wise decision, Reverend," said Harter, stepping into the room. "You playing Avenging Angel tonight, or just raising funds for your school?"

Tattoo let out a nervous chuckle, put down his heavy knife, and relaxed into the softness of his chair.

Knotts didn't respond. He faced the floor and squinted at the detective from the corner of his eyes.

Harter raised the radio to call the other cops in. He didn't take his eyes off Knotts for more than an instant, but it was time enough for the cane to lash out and crash against his right wrist. He heard his revolver smash into the television set and saw the picture tube explode glass into the room before he realized he'd lost the gun.

His wrist ached like it was broken. With his left hand, he started to slam the radio into the side of Knotts' head. Too late. The preacher was already bearing down with a fierce blow of the cane to his shoulder, digging into the flesh and glancing off the left side of his neck. Harter crumpled to his knees and dropped the radio.

When he saw Knotts turn toward Tattoo, he scrambled forward, trying to bring the big man down, but he let go of Knotts' legs when the cane rapped his back twice with a vengeance. Collapsing on his belly, he felt a steel-tipped boot grind into his hip.

His brain, overloaded with raw pain, edged toward blurriness.

Where the hell are you, Caruthers!

And then the weight landed on him, and then the quiet.

"You all right?" asked Tattoo, kneeling beside him and lifting his head from the floor. Harter felt the old man's hand rub the slivers of television glass from his face. There was a burning twinge when he moved his head.

"Where is he?"

"I killed him."

Harter twisted his bruised upper body and saw Sam Knotts' football tackle's frame lying across him.

"Pull yourself out from under," said Tattoo.

Only when he was standing could Harter focus on the butcher knife protruding from the red patch between Knotts' shoulder blades A pissrun of blood ran across the windbreaker toward a puddle of red on the floor.

"Let's go outside," said Harter, wanting out of the room badly.

He stepped around Knotts and, testing his arms and legs, walked slowly to the door. Outside, he waved Caruthers over. The bastard was still in his car. As the other cops showed up and went inside the house, he lit a cigarette and stayed out in the cool night. He touched his tender wrist. The cane didn't seem to have splintered it.

"I didn't know what to do," said Tattoo.

"You did the right thing," said Harter.

Caruthers came out the door. "I called headquarters and the coroner. That your killer in there?"

"One of them."

"What now?"

"You mop up. I'm going home." Harter turned to Tattoo. "Suppose I take you out to the motel to spend the rest of the night with May?"

"I'd like that."

Harter looked at Caruthers. "Tell McManaway to pick me up at my place at nine A.M. in a squad car. Tell him to be in uniform."

30

HIS BODY, welted, black and blue, made him sensitive to every bump in the road. He was tired, had only gotten a couple of hours sleep. Mostly he'd laid awake in his apartment, alternating between a yearning for Liz's salving arms and a single-minded drive to be back on the case.

"That's the house," he told Dave McManaway. "Turn in the drive. Park right in front of the door."

There was a side to him that wanted to tell McManaway to put on the siren and make a big show of it for the neighbors, but he didn't.

"You want me to come in with you?" McManaway asked as he turned off the engine.

"Yeah, I guess you better."

The maid in the gray-striped uniform answered their knock. "Mr. Devendall has already gone to his office," she said as soon as she recognized Harter.

"I'd like to see Mrs. Devendall," said Harter, stepping stiffly past the maid into the entry hall. "Tell her we know who killed her daughter-in-law."

Without another word, he led McManaway down the hall and into the library. He thought about stationing the young cop on the straight-backed chair outside the door but decided it was best for him to witness everything. Then he sat in the desk chair and waited.

Amy Devendall wasn't long in coming.

"Good morning, Mr. Harter," she said, tossing a sideways glance at McManaway when she entered the room. "Martha says you have news."

She sat on the loveseat, folded her pudgy hands in the lap of her blue dress, and waited for him to say something.

"Your friend Sam Knotts died last night."

"That's awful," she said, her face remaining a rouged blank. "Was it a traffic accident?"

"He was killed while trying to murder an old man. There was a can of kerosene in his car."

"I don't understand."

"He was about to do in a fellow named Henry Kendall, just as he'd done in Daniel Jones and Simon Bowman."

"There are those names again. What do they have to do with Susan?"

"Is the name Amy short for anything, Mrs. Devendall?"

"My name is simply Amy," she said curtly.

Her voice was deceptive in its confidence. Harter sensed she'd grown a shade paler beneath her makeup.

He started again. "Do you like old stories, Mrs. Devendall?"

"Occasionally, if they're short and witty."

"Let me tell you one. It's neither short nor witty, but I think it'll grab you."

"I'm all ears," she said with sarcasm.

"Where to begin?" he mumbled, as if to himself. From the corner of his eye, he watched McManaway watching him. "Once upon a time there was a girl in Wild Stream, West Virginia, by the name of Amelia Logan. Have you ever been to Wild Stream, Mrs. Devendall?"

"I don't recall if I have, Detective Harter. Certainly I haven't been through there for a very long time, if ever."

"Well, it's a small town. Not much industry. Not much happening. Not very rich. I can understand how a lady of your background might have missed it. You may find parts of this story rather shocking, in fact. If so, I apologize ahead of time. Seems this Amelia Logan found she could generate a certain income with her body. She was a whore. And she was apparently bright. When she learned that two young men—Simon Bowman and Daniel Jones—were taking off for the metropolis of Shawnee, she ran away with them. Bright lights, big city, I suppose."

"When did this happen, detective?"

"Oh, 1923 or so. I realize you'd only have been a teenage girl yourself. Anyway, soon after the threesome got to Shawnee, Daniel Jones caught on with the railroad and started his own life. Within a couple of years he was married and living on Baxter Street in the East End. Simon Bowman wasn't as lucky. He wasn't as hard a worker. He had a mean, wild streak. He worked off and on for the canal until the 1926 flood knocked it out of business for good. After that, he sometimes dug ditches. He was scab labor when the railroaders were on strike. For a while he was . . . let's call it a security guard. No, let's be honest. A man named James Howard Devendall hired Simon Bowman to be a thug, a strikebreaker."

"My late husband?" she asked. "Be careful how you throw around names."

"No offense. The names come with the story, that's all. Think of them as fictional characters if you prefer."

"I'd prefer you tell your story and be done with it, Mr. Harter."

"Okay. So James Howard Devendall owns a number of places along the canal, including a factory building. Simon Bowman probably lives in one of them. Off and on, Amelia Logan is with him. Now Mr. Devendall—I could change the name if it really bothers you, but it does spice things up—Mr. Devendall seems to have been taken by this lovely . . . let's call her a courtesan, not just a whore. Let's say the wealthy old gentleman falls for her hard. Maybe she convinces him she comes from a good Virginia family. Maybe she's got something on him, something she knows Simon Bowman did in his employ. Or, maybe, he really did love her. Old Devendall probably sets her up as his mistress in a classy apartment. Eventually they even marry. There's no marriage license in the courthouse, so they might have gone away for a long honeymoon before returning to introduce the transformed Amelia Logan to west-side society. She's still only in her twenties, very attractive and a fast learner. After a few years, they have a son, so old Devendall has an heir. Meanwhile, Simon Bowman is pretty much a drunk on Shantytown streets. It's easy to shut him up by sending a little bottle money each month or, when he gets older, buying him a trailer outside of town. He just needs to be reminded now and then that the gravy train ends if he ever breathes a word about Amelia Logan or any of the rest of it."

"I'm beginning to get confused, Detective. Surely these things happened almost fifty years ago."

"Yeah, but Simon Bowman lives a long time. The unexpected happens. He gets religion. Stops drinking. A preacher, someone like Sam Knotts, saves him. It's quite an emotional scene. You can probably picture it. There's poor Simon on his knees, pouring out his heart in confession to this Knotts fellow. He wants to be forgiven so badly. Some of the things he wants to be forgiven for might involve James Howard Devendall and Amelia Logan. Could be more than skeletons in the closet. Maybe there were corpses in the canal, a union organizer or two. Well, this preacher, this Sam Knotts, grasps everything quickly. He sees how damaging the tale could be to a fine old family, particularly to someone very concerned about reputation. He calls up Amelia Logan, now a widow, and—let's get down to it—he blackmails her. The man has no more scruples than Amelia Logan does. He's the greedy type, needs money for his empire, wants to build a Christian academy. He soon finds he's met his match in Amelia. She'll pay off, but demands he get rid of Simon Bowman so there's blood on his hands, too. One August night he beats the old man and sets fire to his trailer. For a little reminder to Amelia, he puts up a sign noting his school has received a donation in memory of A. L."

"You probably find all this fascinating, Detective, but I'm starting to be bored by your saga," said Amy Devendall. She turned her body slightly away from him and the movement sent a whiff of her perfume his way.

Harter looked at McManaway to see if he too was growing bored, but the young cop's eyes were pinned to her.

"I'm almost through, Mrs. Devendall," he said. "Seems Amelia Logan worried and worried about Simon Bowman's death. At some point, she realized Daniel Jones was also still around. I'm not sure how she found out. Knotts could have told her. Or maybe her daughter-in-law, a social worker, told her one night over dinner. Perhaps Susan had read Bowman's obituary and mentioned she knew another old man from Wild

Stream. It doesn't matter how Amelia Logan found out, does it? What matters is that our righteous preacher paid a visit to Jones two weeks ago and collected another donation."

"I still don't understand," said Amy Devendall. "It's Susan's death I'm concerned about, and your story doesn't seem to have anything to do with her."

"I know. I've been over and over that. It's the oddest-shaped piece, isn't it? But it has the simplest explanation."

"What's that?"

"Chance."

"Chance?"

"Like a man who gets trapped one night between two refrigerator cars coupling. Susan was just in the wrong place at the wrong time."

"You can't be serious, Detective Harter."

"Why not? Shawnee is a small city. I'm sure Amelia Logan has learned it's not nearly as immense as she once thought it was. I'd guess your daughter-in-law was acting out her urge to be photographed and was visiting a photographer on Thomas Street on the night Daniel Jones was murdered. She knew the alley from her social work, so she parked in it. Let's say our friendly preacher was running from Jones' house when she happened along. Knotts didn't know what to do so he forced her into his car and took her with him."

"Do you believe your Amelia Logan would allow her own daughter-in-law to be murdered?"

"Sure, I do. I figure it was a hard decision. Knotts probably kept Susan in his church or house until early Saturday morning when he got the word from Amelia. God knows what happened to her. When Amelia was sure Susan was dead, she called the police and reported her daughter-in-law missing."

"Strange behavior, Detective, for someone as protective of her family name as you believe Amelia Logan was."

"Susan couldn't be trusted to keep family secrets. She was about to run off with a congressman. You know, there was even a temporary side benefit for Amelia and Knotts. The death of Susan threw everyone off. The police and the press were more worried about what happened to her than about what happened to Daniel Jones. No one had noticed Simon Bowman's killing in August."

"Ridiculous. What else can I say? Ridiculous," said Amy Devendall.

Harter couldn't tell if Dave McManaway agreed with her.

"I don't think a smart young prosecutor would have much trouble putting together a case for a grand jury," Harter said. "Any one of the murders is enough to put Amelia Logan away."

"If she's as wealthy as you say, Amelia Logan could hire an equally smart young attorney to shoot your silly story full of holes."

"Yeah, but the press will blow it up nicely. A trial like that would attract reporters from all over, even New York. Shawnee would have its own Lizzie Borden. The Chamber of Commerce would erect a statue to Amelia. She'd love the publicity, I'm sure. No matter what the verdict, she'd live on in legend. The story's got sex and violence, religion and money. If I was Amelia Logan, I'd already be searching for that smart young attorney. Your son won't do. I understand he doesn't take criminal cases. Besides, he could hardly defend the murderer of his wife."

"Are you making an accusation, Detective Harter?" she asked.

"Yeah, I guess I am. Shawnee isn't big enough, is it, Amelia? I was with Henry Kendall when he called you Sunday."

"I received no phone call," she insisted.

"You have the right to remain silent," he told her.

31

WEDNESDAY MORNING'S HEADLINES in *The News* were good enough to sell some papers, thought Harter. He hoped Amy Devendall would see them.

WEST-SIDE WOMAN CHARGED WITH THREE MURDERS.

Beneath it, slightly smaller, was EVANGELIST KILLED DURING ARSON ATTEMPT.

Liz called before he'd even read the articles. She was often a faster starter in the morning than he was.

"Congratulations, you've solved your case," she said.

"Thanks."

"There's no doubt it was Amy?"

"No," he answered, wondering at her question.

"You promised you'd call me."

"I was going to today."

"Will you be coming over tonight?"

"Yeah. You herd the kids out as early as you can. I'll take you out for dinner."

"Where?"

He wondered how she'd like the diner near the railroad yards. "Have you ever been out to the overlook on the mountain south of town? They used to call it Lover's Leap."

She laughed. "Are we going to park?"

"That's exactly what we're going to do. I haven't made love in a car in years." He rubbed gently at the swollen bruise on his shoulder and hoped it wasn't an insane promise. "Wear something you might have worn to a drive-in twenty years ago."

"I'm not that kind of girl."

"Then you'll find out something new about yourself."

"I'm always finding out something new about myself," she said. "I'll see you tonight."

"Uh.

"What?"

"About the Halloween Party . . ."

"Saturday night?"

"I don't think I can go to the Winhams'."

"Do you have to work?"

"I just don't think I can go."

"We'll talk about it later."

He knew from her voice that, yes, they would talk about it later.

"Bye."

He hung up and lit a cigarette.

He wished she could understand. He'd take her almost anywhere but to the west-side party.

He inhaled and flipped through the newspaper spread in front of him. He stopped when he saw Jack Reese's photo.

The old lady, bent over, picking up a loaf of bread.

The brief caption gave the necessary details and the address of the food bank.

He took another hit of coffee and nicotine.

The train was distant at first but came deeper and deeper into the East End until, for a few minutes, it was louder than the traffic below him.

JACK REESE

32

I PUT DOWN *THE NEWS* Wednesday morning and stared across the kitchen table at Tattoo. "You're a hero."

"May called me that, too," he grumbled, rubbing at his stub like he did when he was nervous. "I don't see it that way. Harter set everything up. What'd you expect me to do—let the son of a bitching preacher bloody him up and then turn on me?"

"It was face-to-face combat," I said. "Not like pulling a trigger from a distance or dropping a bomb from the sky. I don't know if I could have done it."

"Sure you could of. Ain't much of a choice between living and dying. I told you the first day—I wanted to get the bastard that murdered Daniel."

"You did, Henry," said May. She rose from the table to refill our coffee cups.

Not only had he rid the world of Sam Knotts but he'd killed the burglar in my dream, as well—that burglar I'd been chasing up and down the dry-as-kindling stories night after night. The nightmare arsonist's visits had gotten briefer since I'd told Harter the truth the Thursday before. After Monday night, he'd completely disappeared.

"He's Bill Harter's son, you know," Tattoo said to May as she sat back down.

"I figured maybe he was."

"Don't know how he ended up a cop."

"Needed a job," I said, remembering the day on the towpath when I'd put the question to him. "He told me he became a detective because he needed a job."

"Shawnee ain't bursting with jobs no more, that's for sure," said Tattoo.

"You don't have to tell me," I said. "That's why I'm a stringer for *The News,* no matter how much you ride me about it. What else can a photographer do around here?"

"They did alright on *this* story," answered Tattoo, with the hint of a smile.

I pushed back from the table and stood up. "I've got to go to work right now, in fact."

"Congressman Canley getting his morals certified again?" barked Tattoo.

"I don't think so. I'm going to take pictures at the old passenger station. I've always meant to, and Metling wants one."

"They're not tearing it down, are they?" asked May. "They keep talking about it."

"You ain't going to recognize this city soon," said Tattoo sadly as I went out the door.

I started to cut through the yard to my old Ford, but changed my mind on the way, deciding I'd walk down the hill to the old Shawnee-Potomac station. I shook away the memory of having once considered posing Susan Devendall a la Marilyn Monroe there.

It was a non-threatening October day and it wasn't far. Growing up, I'd hiked up and down the long hill a million times in all kinds of weather—past Bernhardt's store, now gone, past the Methodist Church, now with its basement food bank, past all the houses, hangouts, lots, and alleys that formed the neighborhood I'd once been secure and comfortable in.

I didn't know if I'd stay long enough in Shawnee to feel security and comfort again.

All I knew for sure was I didn't want to live through the last two weeks again.

I wanted to get ahead of the killings, the arson, the dreams.

If some lady with good legs stepped down onto my porch tomorrow and commissioned a passport photo, I'd ask her a bunch of questions before I said yes. Might even make her fill out an application.

If she took off her coat and displayed a model's body, I'd pull Harter's card out of my pocket, hand it to her, and announce, "Get my agent's okay."

Then I'd grab my camera and go searching for a photogenic freight.

Hell, if that train stopped, I might even hop a boxcar and see where it went.

HAUNTS

for Dad

I

EVEN AFTER two or three days of downpour in the mountains, the flood still caught everyone off guard.

The West Virginia small towns were clobbered first—Marlinton on the Greenbrier River, Parsons on the Cheat, Moorefield on the South Branch. Name the town in the region, and it saw devastation. Name the river, and it was crazily over its head those terrible November days.

Trailers floated off their foundations and bobbed in the swirling brown water like toy ships in a bathtub. No plumber could turn off the faucets or cut the power to the pump. The water rose until it poured over the tub and rushed full blast across the flat floodplain.

Farmers hurried to move tractors and expensive equipment to high ground. Their pickup trucks were loaded heavy with whatever would fit, but there just wasn't enough warning, wasn't enough time.

They turned the livestock loose to fend for themselves, but even at that, a drowned milk cow, her udder bulging, was found hanging as if lynched from the supports of a Cheat River bridge two days later.

At the height of the massacre, a dog sped down the Potomac, the poor mutt on its raft of a roof, barking in fright as it tugged at the chain linking it to its doghouse.

Monday night, a young couple abandoned their car on a flooded road near Petersburg and ran inside an empty house to get away from the storm. As the water reached into the second floor, they climbed out onto the roof. Still not good enough. The old dwelling shifted and lifted and splintered into pieces. The man clutched a sycamore for hours until he was finally saved. His wife was hurled downstream and never found.

In the Eastern Panhandle, riverbank cabins belonging to weekenders from Washington and Baltimore left their posts and crashed against each other in the water. One sailed down the Cacapon River until it rammed into a railroad bridge, fitting as neat as a hard rubber stopper into the stone arch, blocking the normal water path, forcing the angered river up over the bridge, up over the tracks, and the trains stopped running.

Paw Paw's downtown was river bottom on Tuesday night. From the highway, you couldn't see the Potomac River bridge any longer. Everyone assumed it had washed out like countless others, but when the sun came up on a gloomy Wednesday, the bridge still stood, its yellow safety light bravely blinking.

At Hancock, on the Maryland banks, the Potomac crested early Wednesday morning, just about the time rescuers helped a stranded woman from her second-story window into a motor-boat that navigated Main Street.

Even Shawnee, where flood control walls had been built in the 1950s, wasn't completely spared, though it certainly could have been worse. The tall concrete walls protected the business district. They just couldn't save everything in the lower end of Shantytown, near the old canal.

HARTER COULD REMEMBER standing with his father at the West Side bridge, watching the work crews put in the massive flood control project where the creek—the *crick,* as his father called it—where the creek emptied into the main river.

Early 1950s, and the powers-that-be had promised nothing like '36 would ever come again. Man had learned to control nature, they'd believed. The ones who'd preached such a rosy sermon were the same guys who'd lectured about a future with safe, cheap nuclear power where we'd all be rich and healthy and jet about in flying cars.

Now it was thirty years later, 1985, Harter was forty-three, and they still spouted off about Progress, capital P. Now they claimed tourist dollars would resurrect Shawnee, which had been fighting for a decade to keep the lid off the coffin as, one by one, the factories shut down.

Christ. Liz would say he was getting cynical. Maybe he was. Or maybe he was only tired. This morning he felt like he was the canal towpath, all covered with water.

He had spent most of Tuesday night at the roadblock in South Shawnee, trying to keep fools and looters out of the evacuated area, thankful it wasn't an everyday part of a detective's job. He'd barely managed a couple hours' sleep before they called him out again. The flood level had dropped by morning, but it had left behind a slick layer of mud atop everything. It was all he could do to keep the car from sliding off the road.

Harter had seen his share of floods, but they'd all been back-porch larcenies compared to this bank heist. He'd never known the river to rage as high and vengeful as it had the night before. Only people who lived among skyscrapers could philosophize about the benevolence of nature, he decided. It was obvious to him that Mother Nature could turn into a mean bitch whenever she damn well chose.

Until yesterday, the worst hit he'd personally witnessed had been when a hurricane—*was it Hazel or some other witch?*—crash-landed in the city. He'd been about twelve, and even though his home on Grant Avenue hadn't been near the river or any of the places you'd expect might flood, the water had run down the hill to the yard and lain for days in low spots. The old people had watched it and announced, *Don't worry. This is nothing like '36.*

But last night . . . This one had all the signs of the 1936 flood, *the Big One,* six years before he'd been born, the one the old people endlessly told tales of.

Harter gripped the wheel tighter as he steered through Shantytown's narrow streets, past small frame dwellings that seemed to have been there forever, past yards littered with a deposit of soggy debris. Some people called the section "Riverview" now, a classier name that he'd never gotten used to. It had been Shantytown when he was a kid, and it was still Shantytown to him.

From the filthy bathtub ring on some of the walls, he could tell the flood hadn't reached very deep into the residences on the upper side of the street. But the ones on the lower side, nearer the canal, looked like they'd never be lived in again. Most of them had survived 1936, and 1924, too, when the canal had been knocked out.

From old photos, he knew the lower side of Egypt Street had been lined with homes and Shawnee & Chesapeake Canal structures until the '24 Flood had scooted some of them downriver. Then in '36 more had swum away, or been demolished later. He couldn't prove it, but he felt it was the lack of buildings near the river, not the flood control walls, that kept the destruction down in the old canal neighborhood.

In Shantytown, the river bent tight around the Shawnee & Chesapeake Canal, or vice versa, depending on which side you were on. There were places along the towpath where the canal didn't exactly mimic the river's course, but here the two just about kissed. Wednesday morning, the river still rushed over the canal path, discouraging hikers and bikers. Impromptu streams cut channels in the mudpie field between Egypt Street and the towpath. Trees along the riverbank had been leveled by the flood's force as if drunken loggers had blitzkrieged through by night.

Up ahead, he saw the parked squad cars. His tires churned the soft muck as he pulled in behind them. He noticed the heating-oil smell as soon as he opened the door. People had just filled up with fuel for the winter, and then their basement tanks had been swamped.

He hadn't taken three steps across the street before he cussed himself for not bringing hipboots. Squishing on, he headed toward the old house. If there were steps down to it, he couldn't find them. He battled to keep his balance as he slid down the bank. Near the porch he stopped and studied the high-water line on the wall. The entire first floor must have been an indoor swimming pool only a few hours earlier.

He turned left and slogged around the two-story structure until he could see the men waiting for him behind it. Beyond them, across the field, he noticed, most of the power lines were down. Where the lines still stretched taut, raggy clothing hung from the wires. Even though he had seen it himself last night, he found it hard to believe the river had gotten so high.

“What is it, Pete?” the detective asked when he was within earshot.

There were three of them—two cops in splattered uniforms and Pete Epstein, the city medical examiner. Shovels in their hands, they stood near a heap of brown, slimy earth.

The medical examiner shook his head. “You really want to know, Harter?”

“You giving me a choice?”

“We could bury them again,” said Epstein, wearily nodding toward his feet.

Toward a collection of bones.

The morning sun was as shit-tinged as everything else in sight.

2

"WHAT'S IT look like?"

"A dead person," said Pete Epstein, flashing a trace of smile.

"Thanks a lot, Doc."

"Hell, Harter, look at them. Those damn bones need a good washing before I can even handle them. Besides, we're still digging them up. I can't tell you much of anything yet."

Harter was amazed he felt nothing as he stared down at the muddy bones. It wasn't like seeing a human being mangled in a car accident. There was nothing really human about the bones at all. No flesh. No blood. No clue as to what kind of person they'd been, whether old or young, good looking or ugly, rich or poor. Nothing to be affected by. Only bones next to a hole that was slowly filling with seepage.

"How long have they been in the ground?"

The short, gray-haired medical examiner shrugged. "Long enough for the body to rot. I told you, I'm not sure of anything. This is going to take a considerable amount of work. I may have to find a specialist. You know, when archaeologists date bones, they're thrilled to be in the right century. Of course, if you want to take over this excavation, I can go back to my office and get started."

Harter sidestepped the offer. "Who reported it?"

Epstein pointed across the street to a house painted a sickly green. "Their name's Spilky. The Red Cross suggested they evacuate last night, so they slept at a friend's. When they came back this morning, they were relieved to find their place only had water in the basement. They say they decided to walk around the neighborhood and check out the damage. Apparently there used to be a shed or an outbuilding here, and they noticed it had washed away. When they came down for a look, Mrs. Spilky spotted the top of the skull shining through the mud. As you can see, the flood took off most of the topsoil between here and the river. The phones are all messed up from the flood, so they went back to their friend's and called headquarters. They were waiting for us when we arrived. Just went over to their house a few minutes ago."

"And you found the skull showing, like they said?"

"Yeah. What are you thinking? You suggesting they planted the skeleton? Go over and talk to them. You don't trust anyone, do you?"

"I try not to."

"I don't see any reason to doubt their story. The Spilkys say they've only lived on Egypt Street for ten or eleven months. However old these bones are, they're older than that. And I don't figure anyone kept them in the attic and dropped them here when the flood came along."

"So, someone buried a body here years ago in a shed that washed away yesterday."

"That's my best guess. Anyone burying a body around here would do well to put it inside the shed so no one dug it up by accident, gardening or something. Besides, bury it outside in the open and all the neighbors could watch."

Harter scanned the area. The house stood naked from three sides, with vacant lots to its left and right. Behind was a swampy field, stretching flat to the canal and the river. Epstein was right, as he often was. If a person sat on one of the porches across the street, he'd have a top-dollar view of everything that went on.

For the hell of it, Harter said, "Of course, there's no assurance the bones weren't here before the shed."

"No," said Epstein, playing along. "And they built the pyramids by chance over long-dead pharaohs, too. God, Harter, if I really wanted to dig for osteal relics, I'd pick a more exotic location. Damn, *Egypt Street.* No pyramids, lost temples, or belly dancers around here. No walls with hieroglyphics. You should at least get a jaunt to Africa out of a job like this. I just hope it doesn't rain ten more inches before we're through."

"A lot of people are hoping it won't rain for ten months, Pete. Any idea who owns this house?"

"Mr. Spilky says it's been empty the whole time they've lived over there. The kids tell tales about the place being haunted."

"Maybe it is." Harter glanced down at the bones again. "When can I expect a report?"

"One of these days."

"I'll hold my breath," Harter said as he turned and started to make his way back up to the street.

THE OLD MAN had moved a kitchen chair out on the porch and was sitting on it, watching the cops dig over at the Wilton place. Being outside wasn't too bad. It was just as chilly inside his damp house as it was outdoors. The electricity was dead, and down in the basement, the furnace had flooded. At least the temperature had inched near fifty, so he could live with it without his blood freezing solid.

Curry was sure the guy walking up the bank to Egypt Street was a cop like the others, even if he wasn't wearing a uniform and his car didn't have a "Shawnee Police Department" symbol. The fellow had on jeans and a black jacket, but the old man recognized the gait of a policeman in the way the erect six-footer carried himself. The guy seemed to be heading toward the McCoy house—*no, the Spilky house now.* Curry never could keep it straight. He still wasn't used to his new neighbors.

The cop was hiking across the muddy street when he looked up and made eye contact with the old man. He immediately changed course and headed toward the porch. "Terrible day, isn't it?" he asked as he neared the messy steps.

"I'm too damn old for high water," said Curry.

"Everyone's too old for high water. Looks like you made it through all right."

"No heat, no lights, no phone, and a cellar to pump out, but, yeah, I made it. Always have."

"Did you spend the night here?"

"No. The Red Cross came and got me and took me up to East Shawnee High School. I slept on a goddamn cot in the gymnasium and came home this morning. Wasn't the best night I ever spent."

"I suppose not. I guess you've noticed all the activity across the street?"

"Been watching it," mumbled Curry. He knew the small talk was out of the way and the cop was settling down to business.

"My name is Edward Harter. I'm a detective with the city police."

"Matt Curry. It's Matthew Mark Curry, if you want to be formal. My mother named me for the gospels. If I'd had a brother, she'd have called him Luke John."

"What's happened is we've found a body over there," said the detective, this Harter. "Actually, I can't say it's much of a body. We found some bones. They've apparently been in the ground a long time. Any idea who owns that house? 1 could look it up on tax records, but I figured you might know."

"Guess it's still owned by the Wiltons."

"The Wiltons?"

"They've owned it as far back as I remember. Old canal family, like mine. That started out as a company-built house, like most everything else on the lower side of the street, not that there's much still standing on the lower side of the street anymore."

"There's less now, isn't there? Didn't there used to be a shed back where they're digging?"

"Until last night there was. I helped Wheat Wilton build the thing myself. Must have been the spring of 1941 or so, a year or two before he got married. You could have guessed we put up the shed after '36. It never would have withstood that flood, either."

"So, Wheat Wilton lived over there?" the cop asked.

"His real name was Bartley, but he hated it, so he always went by his middle moniker, Wheat. It was his mother's maiden name."

"Is he still alive?"

Curry nodded.

"Does he live around here?"

"Last I knew, he was staying with his daughter on the Avenue. He moved in with her about five years ago, after he retired from the railroad."

"So, what is he, seventy, seventy-one?"

"Yeah. Same as me, give or take a year."

"Are there other Wiltons around—people who would have lived over there? Children, maybe?"

"There was the daughter, and a boy, Roger. He left town in the sixties and I haven't seen him in years."

"What's the daughter's name?"

"Dorothy. Dorothy Merrill, it would be. Husband's Bill, if I recall. His daddy used to work on the railroad with me. I think Bill caught on at the steel mill. Don't know what he does now that the mill locked its doors."

Curry watched Harter take a notepad and pen from his jacket pocket and scribble *Wheat Wilton, Dorothy Wilton Merrill, Bill Merrill, Roger Wilton.* When he was done writing, the cop asked, "So you worked for the railroad, too, Mr. Curry?"

"Most everyone around here worked for the Shawnee-Potomac, or had some connection with the railroad, didn't they?"

"I guess they did."

"Me, I used to be a conductor," Curry volunteered. It was neutral enough ground. "At least I was until my last few years, when they stuck me in an office over at the yards. Wheat Wilton and me retired about the same time."

"And his house has been empty ever since?"

"Well, for a while they tried to rent it, but they kept getting unreliable people, so they gave up. Then they tried to sell it, but that old house in the floodplain wasn't what anyone would call prime real estate. One day they took the 'For Sale' sign down and boarded up the windows like you see it."

"I understand the kids in the neighborhood claim it's haunted."

"I don't know what the kids say anymore. Hell, it ain't haunted to me, if that's what you're interested in. I remember when the place was filled with real, live, flesh-and-blood folks."

"Whatever happened to Mrs. Wilton?"

"She died in Nineteen sixty-seven. It's not her in the ground over there, if you're leading that way. She was hit by a truck. Right in the middle of Egypt Street. They never caught who did it."

The detective's pen was scratching again. When he looked up, he asked, "How about the people next door? They're the ones who found the bones. Apparently they came home this morning and noticed the shed had washed away, so they went over for a look-see. I take it they've lived in Shantytown less than a year."

"Can't quarrel with any of that. Me, when I came back this morning, the police cars were already parked out front and men were digging. You'll have to go talk to the Spilkys yourself."

"I plan to." Harter flipped his notebook closed and returned it to his pocket. "Look, I don't mean to sound stupid, but you've lived here a long time. You don't have any idea who might be buried over there, do you?"

Curry shrugged. "Depends."

"On what?"

"On how long those bones have been a-moldering in the ground. You could have someone who died in a canal feud a hundred years ago, or a person drowned in the Nineteen twenty-four Flood when there were loads of canal people out in the water, trying to keep their boats from propelling downstream. Whether anyone was stuck in the mud in that very spot, I can't tell you. I was just a kid."

"Remember, the body was buried *beneath* the shed."

Curry went on just the same. "Christ, you could even have what's left of some hippie hiker. Ever since they made the towpath a park, there's been all sorts of strangers hiking and biking it. Any one of them could have buried a body beside that vacant house. God only knows some of the things that might have happened in Shantytown down the years. Of course, this isn't the same place it used to be, if you ask me. Hell, Shawnee as a whole isn't what it used to be, either. They're turning the passenger station into a museum, like they turned the canal into a park. That's what they do when things die, isn't it? Why, they'll probably turn this whole section into a Shawnee Flood Museum some day."

Harter smiled. "Maybe they'll hire you as a tour guide."

"Why not? Give me a chance to earn a little money. See that mud line on the step, just below the porch?"

Harter nodded.

"You probably can't make it out good, but beneath all the garbage is a mark my mother scratched in 'thirty-six. And just below that's another she scratched in 'twenty-four. Last night the water got to exactly the same spot it did fifty years ago. No, it'd be forty-nine years ago, wouldn't it? Saint Patrick's Day, Nineteen thirty-six. If this goddamned flood could have held off four more months, we could have had a real fiftieth-anniversary celebration. In Nineteen thirty-six my mother stood on this porch and tried to sweep the water away. She got pneumonia and died."

The detective was silent for a moment. He probably didn't know what to say. Then, he reached in his pocket, produced a card, and handed it up to Curry. "If something happens to come back to you, Mr. Curry—something that could have to do with the bones—get in touch with me."

"I will," the old man promised.

He was still reading Harter's title and phone number when the cop walked across the yard to the McCoy place—*no, the Spilky place.*

3

MATT CURRY felt like he'd made some progress by the end of the day. The electric company men had been on the scene fast and had repaired the downed lines by dark. While they'd worked along the river, a fire truck had showed up and firemen had pumped out his basement. The utility inspector, who'd come to check the wiring in his house, reported it was okay to use the lights, but warned against using the furnace until it got a good once-over. Word was, the phone company would have things going in a day or two.

About 9:30 a Red Cross man knocked on his door to offer a ride back to the high school gym for the night. Curry turned him down, and before long the guy was back with a small electric heater that he said could at least heat the bedroom. He promised a volunteer crew would arrive in the next few days to help with the house and basement.

Upstairs, as he plugged in the heater, Curry wondered if he was getting all this attention simply because he was old. Space heaters, volunteer work crews, cots in high school gyms . . . It hadn't been like that in 1936. Then, they'd had to fend for themselves.

He told himself he could still fend for himself. The house might be cold and damp, a disaster zone to the Red Cross, but it was his home. He didn't intend to spend another night tossing and turning in a gymnasium, a few feet from someone he scarcely knew or didn't know at all. Besides, if everyone left, Egypt Street would be a sitting duck for thieves and vandals. They hadn't had as much of a crime problem in 1936. People were different then. He hoped the cops still planned to patrol the area. Whether or not they did, no one would break into his house without a fight.

Most of the other dwellings on the street had been dark for hours, their owners choosing to sleep in more comfort. The Spilkys had puttered around for a while after the detective left, but before the weak sun had given up altogether, they'd departed for the night.

Curry climbed into bed fully dressed and pulled the old quilts up over him. He knew he'd be tossing and turning again, even in his own bed.

He'd been outside trying to clean off the porch steps when the diggers had left the Wilton place. They'd carried a green plastic garbage bag to the police car, and Curry had known full well what was in it. *The bones.* The past was surfacing. The detective knew it would. That's why Harter had left his card and asked him to be in touch if he recalled anything. Cops had their tricks.

Harter had said the kids believed the Wilton place was haunted. He guessed, in some way, they were right. *It was haunted.* But not by a ghost. Not by some mysterious lantern-swinging headless specter along the canal.

Like his own, the Wilton house was one of those 1890s Shantytown frame structures, two stories high, built by boatmen and mule drivers so they could stare out on the towpath, their livelihood, just as railroaders once built homes facing the tracks.

Shantytown. The name had been coined by people who'd lived in more prosperous sections to designate the conglomeration of buildings where the canal families lived and labored. The place had never been as shabby as its name. Wheat Wilton's house wasn't anything Curry would call a shanty, and neither was his. Shanties didn't last a century and survive floods.

The houses had actually outlasted the Shawnee & Chesapeake Canal Company itself. Sometimes Curry wondered whether he'd have ended up working on the canal if it hadn't been knocked out of business by the 1924 Flood. Or so went the story. Hell, the flood hadn't been the culprit. The railroad was. The canal just couldn't compete and had been in decline for years by 1924. As far back as Curry could picture, hulls of rotting flatboats laid along the towpath. He and Wheat had played among the Shawnee & Chesapeake rains, pretending to be flatboat captains.

Curry's father had been a real captain. Then, one day, his old man hadn't returned from a trip downriver. The boat had come home, but no one had any notion what had become of his father. They'd never heard from him again. Maybe he ran off to California. To Curry, anyone who up and left beat it to California. He'd been six years old at the time. His mother, who'd always had a Bible-quoting streak, suddenly came down with religion and suffered waves of its attacks for the rest of her life.

Curry would have loved to have been a boat captain. Would have loved to work on a Mississippi steamboat like his hero, Mark Twain. Envied his father the chance to jump ship downriver and go off to see the world. Go off to California. But the canal shut down, so when it came time to get a job, he signed on with the Shawnee-Potomac Railroad, the canal's nemesis. He hadn't seen the world, but he had seen a lot of whistle-stops.

Wheat, too, had gotten a railroad job, but now the railroad seemed to be going the way of the canal. If he was a young man, Curry guessed it would be tough to get a good Shawnee-Potomac job. The station was going to be a museum. The detective hadn't sounded like he liked the changes much, either.

Curry turned onto his side and closed his eyes to make another stab at sleep.

He'd never become a captain, no matter what he'd dreamed when he was young.

WHEN HE WAS YOUNG.

When he was a boy, there was a house he'd believed was just as haunted in its own way as the Wilton place apparently was to kids today. This one had been just outside the city limits, and three old people had lived in it. Two aged men, probably brothers from the look of them—both tall and creaky—and an equally old woman, short and plump as a Thanksgiving turkey. He could never decide which of the brothers the woman was married to, if, indeed, she was married to either.

The house was a bare wood thing with that century-old, seen-it-all air, and the three old people were just as weathered.

The woman always had on one of those homemade dresses with little pink and white checks and an apron tied over it. The men wore overalls, no matter what the season. Sometimes in summer they'd be bare bony-chested, like maybe they weren't wearing anything beneath the denim. Out in the mountains, he'd seen old boys who went around like that, no underwear or anything. He guessed those guys were really a pair of old country boys, and the place was really a farm, or had been once upon a time, but even sixty years before, Shawnee was encroaching on them, city houses nibbling away at their hilly pasture.

On Sunday afternoons, his Uncle John would take Curry and his own kids for a ride out to the woods, and whenever they passed the place, one of the old trio was outside. Wood smoke always poured from their chimney, for heat in icebound January, for cooking in dog days July.

What struck him—what he still remembered—was that the three never seemed to move. He never saw one of them flex a muscle. It was like they were frozen in place on their porch, or rooted in the ground halfway to the woodpile, or standing on the path to the outhouse, like wax figures in a boardwalk museum.

Even as a kid, he'd known those old people had to move. They were alive, weren't they? They weren't wax figures. After all, when Uncle John's Model T passed them again, the one he'd seen frozen on the path to the outhouse would now be locked in a new position on the way to the chicken coop or somewhere.

He'd been a smart kid and he'd come to understand. Those old people were moving through another time and world, the city be damned. They were moving so slow, like in a dream, so slow that someone young like him, tearing along in a Ford car, was simply traveling too fast to be able to spot their movement.

Hell.

Now he was old, and his house was an old house, its cellar flooded too many times. The kids thought the people and places he'd known were haunted.

Those kids, if they bothered to notice him at all, probably glanced over and wondered, "Doesn't that son of a bitch ever move?"

He was the one frozen on the path to the outhouse.

Not always so.

WHEN HE WAS YOUNG.

She was wearing a dress so thin you could set her body move through it. She smelled so clean.

4

"I SHOT HER."

Too damn early for this confession stuff, thought Harter, taking a hit of coffee to sharpen himself up. Wednesday night, for the second night straight, he'd volunteered to guard Shantytown streets against the crazies. It seemed like he'd hardly gotten home before Herr, the desk cop, had called him down to headquarters.

"I shot her."

Darrell Phillips had simply strolled in that morning and announced he'd murdered his wife. The guy's voice was amazingly calm, but his fingers gave away his nervousness. His pale, puffy palm was cupped over his face like a prayer cloth, shielding his eyes. The fat fingers kneaded at his forehead, over and over and over.

"Drink some coffee. It'll help bring you around," said Harter, pointing across the table at a white Styrofoam cup. He didn't know if it was really possible to bring Phillips around, to clear his brain, or not. He had no idea how much Phillips was going to tell him, or even if he'd understood the rights that had been read to him. He just hoped he could keep Phillips talking until McManaway came back with a report on what he'd found.

Phillips kept his face low as he moved his hand away from his forehead to reach for the cup. Still, Harter managed to snatch a flash of his dazed eyes. *His completely dazed eyes.* Odds were, the man didn't even realize he was sitting in the interrogation room of the Shawnee Police Department.

"Okay, let's start again. You run an appliance store by the viaduct, and you live in an apartment over top of it, right?"

Phillips' head bobbed like he understood. His fingertips rubbed at the Styrofoam cup like they were still rubbing at his own skin.

Harter figured the appliance dealer was in his late thirties, but it was hard to judge. Phillips' heavy belly and balding dome made him seem older. He'd probably looked middle aged since his twenties.

"Why did you shoot your wife?"

Phillips' fingernails grated lightly against the Styrofoam.

Harter tried again. "The two of you have a fight? Were you drunk?"

Nothing but that damn dazed—*dazing*—stare. You couldn't even call it glassy. Plastic was more like it.

Sweat was rolling down the guy's face, though the room was far from hot. Phillips didn't even lift his head when the knock on the door came and Dave McManaway finally peeked in.

"You been to the apartment?" Harter asked the beat cop.

McManaway nodded and motioned the detective out into the hall. As he rose from the table, Harter told Phillips, "I'll be right back. Try to relax."

He'd barely stepped into the corridor and shut the door before McManaway was saying in a weird tone, "Detective Edward Harter, meet Mrs. Darrell Phillips."

"Vi Phillips," she said, without extending her hand. "Is my husband in there?"

"Your husband?" Harter didn't believe it.

"Darrell."

"Darrell? Yeah, he's in there." He glanced over at McManaway. It was surely too early in the morning for this damn charade.

"I didn't know what to do," explained McManaway, "so I brought her to headquarters with me. I sent Clark and the others home."

"I'd like to see Darrell," said Vi Phillips.

"Wait a minute. Let me get this straight. You do understand your husband has confessed to murdering you last night?"

"The officer told me. Obviously, Darrell didn't murder me, Detective."

"He says he shot you. He didn't wave a gun around or anything, did he?"

"Darrell doesn't even own a gun. I hate them. I won't allow him to keep one in either the store or the apartment. He doesn't have one with him, does he?"

"No," mumbled Harter, turning back to Dave McManaway.

"We didn't find a gun or any evidence of shooting. We didn't find anything unusual at all. When we got there, the store and apartment were locked up tight and the lights were off. Mrs. Phillips was still in bed. We woke her up, and while she dressed, Clark and I scouted the place. Everything appeared to be in order."

"Everything *was* in order," Vi Phillips piped up, her irritation showing. Her eyes were a little red, like she'd been jolted out of a peaceful sleep and into a nightmare. She'd clearly dressed fast. Underneath her coat, the top button of her floral print dress was unfastened. Her dyed red hair was uncombed. She was in her thirties, Harter decided, confirming his estimate of her husband's age.

"Was your husband at home all last night?" he asked.

"Except when he was at the warehouse."

"The warehouse?"

"We lease a building by the river in Shantytown, or Riverview, or whatever they call it these days. We keep extra appliances in it and do some of our repair work there. The building flooded Tuesday night, along with everything else. Darrell spent most of yesterday checking on the damage and trying to salvage what he could. He came home about nine."

"Was he upset?"

"Of course he was. He said we'd lost thousands of dollars' worth of stuff. And it wasn't insured. Flood insurance is expensive, and when was the last time the area flooded like that? Darrell was real depressed when he came back to the apartment."

"When he got home, did he start drinking, or was he testy, trying to pick a fight?"

"Darrell hardly ever drinks," she said, arching her back again at the suggestion that anything serious might be wrong. "I don't see what business all of this is of yours."

"Look, I didn't call up your husband and invite him down here and suggest he cook up a story about shooting you. He did it on his own. I'm trying to find out why. Is he violent? Has he acted strange before?"

"How do you define *strange,* Detective?"

"However you'd define it, Mrs. Phillips. You know him better than anyone else."

"He can be moody, if that's what you mean."

"Moody?"

"Depressed, that's all. It's like something will trip him, a bit of news or something. The flood was just too much. But, no, he isn't violent. He's simply been under a big weight lately, trying to keep the business going. All these big discount stores make it hard on little stores like ours. I've told him, if worst comes to worst, we can close up and find other jobs, but you know how it is. Once you've worked for yourself, it's difficult to consider working for someone else. His father started the business, and Darrell feels like a failure because he hasn't been successful with it."

"What does he do when he gets depressed?"

"He might just stare at the TV, or sometimes he talks about Vietnam."

"What about Vietnam?"

"About how much he hated being there in the war. Look, Detective, can I see him? I'd really like to take him home and put him to bed."

"I'm not sure that's smart, Mrs. Phillips," said Harter, stalling for time to decide what to do. "I've got to consider your safety, and the safety of others."

"No one has anything to fear from Darrell. You can see he didn't kill me. He's never raised a hand at me. I've told you he doesn't own a gun. You haven't charged him with anything, have you?"

"Not yet."

"So you've no reason to keep him locked up."

"He's not exactly locked up. He's sitting in there, drinking coffee."

"Do I have to call our lawyer?"

"I think he needs a doctor more than he needs a lawyer. He could have a mental problem."

"Not Darrell," she insisted.

Harter pictured Phillips sitting tensely at the interrogation table, rubbing his forehead, rubbing the Styrofoam, talking about murdering his wife. He played out the bluff. "We could send him over to Shawnee Mental Health Center for a day or two of evaluation. I'd feel better not just letting him walk out on the street without some assurance that he's not going to do something."

Vi Phillips' eyes were wide open now and Harter felt McManaway staring at him, too.

"He won't do anything terrible. I'll see to that," she said.

"I don't want to be the one to vouch for him."

"Darrell—" She broke off whatever she was about to say and seemed to reconsider. "It's only stress. He's . . . He *has* been seeing a doctor off and on . . . a psychiatrist. . . I'll set up another appointment."

"Soon."

"Soon," she agreed. "Now, will you let me talk to him? Can I take him home?"

Before he showed his hand, Harter made her wait two more long, silent minutes to let the seriousness sink in. Then he slowly opened the door to the interrogation room. "Mr. Phillips, your wife is here."

He watched the guy's face carefully for a flinch, for a reaction of some sort. What happened surprised him. Darrell Phillips raised his head and was open-faced and smiling. "Hi, Vi," he said as he stood up.

"The car's outside," she told him.

As the couple walked down the hall, McManaway asked Harter, in a voice that was almost a whisper, "You think you did the right thing?"

"How the hell do I know?"

"You sure she'll take him for treatment?"

"I'm not sure of anything."

"Pretty crummy way to start the day."

"I guess the day has to start some way," Harter said as he lit a cigarette.

5

SKELETON UNCOVERED BY FLOOD

FROM ACROSS the desk, Harter read the upside-down headline in the newspaper that Dave McManaway was devouring. Pete Epstein always had been a publicity hound. He should have seen it coming.

McManaway caught his stare. "What do you think of all this?"

"I think it must sell papers. Now that the river's gone down, it gives reporters something to write about. As many people will read that story as read about the flood in the first place."

He reached over, took the paper, and studied the front-page photo. The soggy old Wilton house looked gray and gloomy enough to be haunted. His eyes ran down the column, seeking facts, but found none, only the tabloid headline. Epstein had told the press that the bones were those of a woman, but other details would have to wait until an expert from the state university came to Shawnee on Saturday.

"It'll take all the expertise I can gather to pinpoint this thing. We need good leads before we can check dental records and that sort of thing. It's quite a mystery," Epstein the Showman was quoted as expounding. "There's such a margin of error when dating old bones that we're still only guessing. It's all ballpark stuff, but I'd be looking at from about Nineteen forty-five to Nineteen seventy. The police should be sifting through reports of missing women from that time period."

Topnotch advice giver, Pete Epstein. *The police should be sifting through reports.* Harter inhaled more coffee and glanced over at the gray metal filing cabinets lining a wall of the office. Hell of a lot of reports to sift.

McManaway must have been watching him, for he asked, "How do you go back and decide what happened so long ago?"

"Got me."

"I bet you wish Caruthers hadn't taken the month off."

"I don't give a damn. I'm glad he's taking his sick leave and vacation time. I won't cry when he retires December thirty-first."

"You really don't like him, do you?"

No, Harter didn't like Caruthers and never had, but he hadn't realized his distaste for the other detective was so apparent. He wondered how many of the other beat cops were aware of it, and whether it was a hot topic of conversation.

Year after year, as they'd shared an office, playing detective, his dislike for Caruthers had deepened. He knew it was irrational. He'd tried to dampen his smile when Caruthers had announced his retirement and lit out for Florida to eat up his accumulated leave.

"He left you at a rough time, didn't he? Now we've got a flood and an old mystery," said McManaway, trying to open Harter up.

Harter lit another cigarette and stared again at the filing cabinets that Caruthers had so diligently filled with paper. He'd been great at the red tape, more than making up for Harter's hatred of it. If he'd been there, Caruthers would already be sifting through old reports for accounts of missing women, as Epstein had suggested.

"You did put in for Caruthers' job, didn't you?" Harter asked McManaway.

"Yeah."

"Good."

Ever since the young cop had first helped Harter on a stake-out, Dave McManaway had been his first choice for detective. That was why Harter had delegated him to lead the team who'd gone to the Phillips apartment that morning. He wanted to ease McManaway into detective work, wanted chances to praise him to the chief.

"Did you read about the teenagers?" asked McManaway, changing the subject. He must have realized he'd hit a dead end with questions about Caruthers.

"No."

"Seems a seventeen-year-old boy and a sixteen-year-old girl were parked by the river on Tuesday night when the water came up. They felt their car lift off the ground and start to float away. Somehow they managed to roll down the windows and jump out. When they got to high ground, they ran to the nearest house for help. Must have been a sight when the people opened the door. All the boy had on was his socks, and she wasn't wearing anything. They claimed they stripped so they could swim better."

Harter laughed. "God, imagine telling your father how you lost the car. Expensive date. I remember how hard it was just to explain how the radio antenna caught on a tree limb and snapped off one night when I parked in the woods. Those kids must have been cold. It was down in the thirties Tuesday night."

McManaway tossed his Styrofoam cup in the trash and stood up. "Could have happened to me when I was seventeen. Could have been me parked along the river with Sally. Funny, what stays in your mind."

Harter watched the younger cop go out the door. *Funny, what stays in your mind.* McManaway was right. His mind was certainly crowded with junk. He was sifting through the debris when the first call came.

The guy's voice had the creak of age in it, and for a second he thought it might be Matt Curry—Matthew Mark Curry of biblical name. But it wasn't Curry with some retrieved fact. It was another old fellow who, without prodding, poured out a saga of the Shawnee & Chesapeake Canal so rapidly that Harter was immediately confused. He managed to rein the guy to a halt and back him up for a cleaner start.

"They're my brother's bones. He fell off a canal boat in Nineteen fourteen, when he was twelve. We always were told it took place near Shawnee. They probably buried him along the towpath. Jimmy was taken on by a boat captain to drive the mules, and it was only his second trip when he fell off, hit his head, and drowned. My mother keened for weeks. She never got over it completely."

"I'll take your name and number, but I have to tell you, we believe it's a woman's skeleton," Harter said when he could pry in a word. "We don't think the bones are that old, either."

No matter, the guy launched into the tale anew with a few fresh details. "A young fellow like you's got no notion how it was along the canal," the old boy informed him.

When he was tired of listening, Harter pulled his perennial con game of saying he had an emergency call on another line, and hung up. He had the feeling the trick would come in handy over the days ahead.

He learned from callers that the story had already been carried coast to coast on the wire service that morning. Hundreds of papers had printed it under headlines like MURDER VICTIM UNCOVERED BY APPALACHIAN FLOOD. Who cared if there was no proof whether the woman had actually been murdered?

Harter found it irritating that at least three dozen people had drowned, been washed away, or were still missing in what they'd taken to calling the Killer Flood of '85, yet less than two days later the headlines were grabbed by an unknown skeleton that had been buried for twenty, thirty, maybe even forty years.

The phone rang again. A nearly hysterical woman from Chicago said her daughter had hiked the Shawnee & Chesapeake Canal in 1975 and had never returned. The family lived in Baltimore then, and her daughter would have been thirty. She'd had a string of bad luck—an abusive husband, a divorce, arguments with relatives, finally an accident that had left her crippled. She'd been determined to hike the entire towpath as a test of survival.

Harter groaned. Old Matt Curry had said the bones could belong to a hiker, and, now, here one was. The worst possible case. God knows what kind of crazy bastard she could have met along the line.

He immediately called Pete Epstein and repeated the woman's story.

"She's not the one," Epstein assured him. "This was a relatively young woman and I haven't seen any sign of an injured leg. I don't find any evidence of broken bones at all. Besides, Nineteen seventy-five is probably too late, unless I'm way off base. Like I told the papers, I should know more Saturday."

"Great of you to tell the press before you told me," said Harter.

"Hell, they called me. Don't bitch. I run an open office. This isn't national security. If a reporter asks me a question, I answer it. I like to stay on the good side of those people. Didn't anyone ever tell you not to argue with folks who buy ink by the gallon?"

"You still interested in politics, Pete? Building up points? What are you running for? President or just governor?"

"I want to be king," Epstein said.

When they were through firing volleys, Harter dialed the woman in Chicago and informed her the bones weren't likely her daughter's. That chore out of the way, he sorted through the names and numbers piling up on his desk. Amazing, how people in the Midwest or New England had ties to Shawnee, with its population of less than forty thousand and dropping each day as jobs dwindled. Amazing, how many people felt the unexplained tragedies of their lives might have something to do with those bones.

He knew the chief would love the long distance bill this case was going to rack up. He could already hear the clamor. The chief was so budget conscious these days that he'd refused to even consider hiring a replacement for Caruthers until he had worked off all his leave time. So Harter was left to answer the phone alone.

And the phone rang.

Caller after caller convinced him that, no matter how plain the facts in the news might be, people would read whatever they wanted to read into them. If they knew of a missing boy, they ignored the fact that the bones were those of a woman. If they knew of a disappearance in 1925, they ignored Pete Epstein's estimate of the date. If they knew of a girl who never came home from a hike on the towpath, they forgot the damn canal was more than 180 miles long and Shawnee was just a port on its western end.

A college student verified the theory. He was positive the skeleton was of an Indian, a Shawnee or a Delaware who'd died three hundred or more years before. Turned out the flood had uncovered what was believed to be an Indian village on the South Branch of the Potomac in West Virginia, and the student figured it might have done the same in Shantytown. He wanted the inside track on studying the remains.

"I doubt it was Pocahontas in the shed," said Harter, almost slamming down the phone. A minute later he felt bad about his anger. He usually wasn't as clipped and angry. The flood, the skeleton, the sad and crazy appliance dealer, the calls, the hours of night patrol . . . they were getting to him.

And, always these days, he couldn't avoid the fact that Liz was getting to him, too. Or that growing distance between them. He tried not to talk or think about her, but every time his mind wasn't on work, it was on her, and what was going wrong. Not that he could put what was going wrong into words. He'd stopped talking about her to friends because they all expected him to give some reason why things were stormy. But the words were only about symptoms, not causes, and so he just kept them in. Early on, someone had told him, "Time is a healer." People always seemed to have an old saying or an easy platitude to pass on. *Time is a healer,* and maybe it was at times, but sometimes time was nothing but time. Just as well they kept calling him out to work. Just as well he didn't have long hours to sit in his apartment and think about her.

Harter got up, walked over to a filing cabinet, pulled open a drawer, stared at a row of files. Caruthers would have relished the chance to stay off the street a while. There was no danger in the office. He had actually enjoyed sitting at his gray metal government desk and filling out reports. But Caruthers was gone, and Harter tried to convince himself that sifting through files was a small price to pay. *A small price to pay for not thinking about Liz, too.*

When the phone rang again, he gave serious consideration to playing deaf. But, ever-dutiful cop, he hoisted the receiver, introduced himself, and, pen poised over notepad, waited.

"Her name was Brenda Keith, and she disappeared at the end of the war, about Nineteen forty-five."

Harter perked up. Right sex, possible year. "Why are you so sure it's her?" he asked.

"I guess I don't know for sure. I can't prove anything, but it could be her."

God, the guy's even reasonable.

"Well, what makes you think it might be this Brenda Keith?"

"I was married to her back then. When I went into the army in Nineteen forty-two, I left her in Shawnee. I never got another letter from her after Christmas of 'forty-four. She was nowhere to be found when I got home. Our landlord said she just disappeared one day. No one could tell me anything about what became of her."

"Then your name's Keith?"

The man paused a moment before answering. "Paul Keith."

"You still live here in Shawnee?"

"Pittsburgh. I read about the skeleton in the paper this morning. It's been eating at me all day. I know where the Wilton house is. We only lived two blocks from it."

"So you knew the Wiltons in those days?"

"I knew who they were. We never visited them or anything. Brenda was raised in Shantytown, so she knew most everyone. I moved to Shawnee for work during the Depression."

No one moves to Shawnee for work anymore, Harter thought. But what he asked was: "Did she know the Wiltons well? Did she ever talk about them?"

"I've been trying to remember and can't. It was forty years ago, another life ago."

"How old would your wife have been in Nineteen forty-five?"

"She was nineteen and I was twenty when we got married in 'forty-one. That would make her twenty-two or twenty-three when I lost track of her."

"Can you give me a description?"

"She was about five foot four, and blond, real blond. Look, I'm not even sure why I called. The newspaper story just drug it all back up. I left Shawnee in Nineteen forty-seven and moved to Pittsburgh to start over again. I've got a whole new family and a new life now. I don't want them to get involved in this. My wife has no idea I was married before. I just thought I should let someone know. It nags at you, year after year, never knowing. Suddenly, I'm wondering if Brenda didn't really leave me, but was killed, you know."

"Understand, we don't know how this woman died. But your wife, did she have any relatives or close friends who might still live here? You didn't have any children, did you?"

"No, no children by her. As far as relatives, she was an only child and was raised by an aunt. Brenda never mentioned her parents. I don't think she remembered them."

"What was her aunt's name?"

"Myrt. Myrtle Harris. Harris was Brenda's maiden name. Her aunt Myrt had always lived in Shantytown. She died about Nineteen forty-three, when I was in the service."

"Where did you and your wife live in those days?"

"Fletcher Street. . . One thirteen . . . God, I haven't thought about the place in years. I've tried not to."

"I understand," Harter said. "I'm sorry it's all coming back to you, but it may be of some help to us. If I turn anything up, I'll contact you."

"Don't—"

"What?"

"If my wife answers, don't tell her what it's about. I guess I might have to explain it all to her, but I don't want to if I don't have to."

Harter could hear the ache in Paul Keith's voice even after he'd hung up. *Brenda Keith.* He finally had something worth moving on. And he knew the place to move with it was where he should have gone that afternoon instead of being trapped in the office.

It wasn't yet four o'clock. He still had plenty of time to find Wheat Wilton before he called it a day.

6

TURNED OUT that Dorothy and Bill Merrill lived in one of the red brick rowhouses along what everyone in East Shawnee simply referred to as "the Avenue," the long street that linked residential sections with the South Shawnee railroad yards. If you knew what you were searching for, you could still find evidence of the trolley tracks that once ran up the broad old roadway.

The Merrill house had an archway to the left of the front stoop, much like a house Harter had lived in for a while as a kid. Behind its high wooden gate, he knew, was an alleyway that shot the depth of the building, back to the yard and the kitchen door. He wasn't sure whether to knock at the front or go through the arch to the rear. One of the curses of being a cop was constantly walking up to strange houses and being uncertain how to make your entrance, whether to knock at the living room or go around to the kitchen, where he felt he was likely to find Dorothy Merrill cooking supper.

Dorothy Merrill. Dorothy Wilton, it would have been in high school. If she'd grown up in Shantytown, she must have attended East Shawnee High at roughly the same time he had. Yet he had no memory of her. Neither her name nor her husband's meant anything to him. Not that it mattered.

East Shawnee was a large school that drew from half of the city and some of the rural areas outside. He'd never lived in Shantytown. Nor had he been what anyone would call an outgoing student or school leader. There were plenty of people his age he didn't know. If he could have foreseen he'd end up a detective, perhaps he'd have kept detailed notes on his peers. *Fat chance.* On the other hand, Caruthers might have.

He decided to attack the front door, stepped up on the stoop, knocked. The woman who answered was in her early forties and wore blue jeans and a pink T-shirt with SHAWNEE BOMBERS lettered across it.

Dorothy Merrill didn't seem surprised when he informed her who he was and why he'd come. Yes, she'd heard about the skeleton being found where the shed had washed away. The whole thing had given her a chill, but she hadn't called the police because she had nothing to say, no notion whose bones they might be. She hadn't lived on Egypt Street for nearly twenty-five years, not since getting married. Besides, she figured the police would get in touch with her, and now they had.

Harter detected no strain in her voice or manner. She spoke in a calm, efficient way that made him inclined to give her the benefit of the doubt.

The living room was small and cozy, its every surface covered with photos and knickknacks. She must do ceramics, he figured. On top of the television set was a family portrait of a younger Dorothy Merrill, her husband, and two boys, one in his early teens and the other maybe six years old. It was the kind of discount portrait they snapped in front of a screen in the corner of a supermarket. Around the room were framed school photos of the two boys at various ages. On an end table was a picture of an older man.

"Is that your father, Wheat Wilton?" he asked.

"Yeah."

"I was hoping to meet him, hoping to ask him what he might know. He lived on Egypt Street until five years ago, didn't he?"

"That's right. He moved in with us after he retired. The old house was too much for him by himself. I don't think seeing Daddy will do you much good, though."

"Why?"

"He had a stroke two years ago and can barely talk. He's up in his room."

"I'd still like to meet him if I could."

"All right," she said reluctantly. "Come on. Excuse the mess. Bill and I work odd hours, and we've still got Bart at home. You came at a bad time. I'm running around, trying to get some food together so I can get out of here. Thursday night's my bowling night. They'll all be full of questions about the body being found at Daddy's house. I wish we could have sold that place years ago, but no one bit."

Harter followed the Shawnee Bomber out of the room, down a short hall to a newel post, then up the narrow staircase. She was tall and thin, rather attractive in an untended sort of way, but there was something off center about her face that kept her from being pretty. He wondered if she took after her father or her mother. He had his answer soon enough.

Wheat Wilton was propped on pillows in a chair that was angled toward a second-floor window. He was staring out the glass, out at the Avenue—except he wasn't exactly doing a traffic count—he was just staring, straight out, at the brick wall of the house across the street. He had a full head of shaggy white hair and, like his daughter, was slim and long boned. And there was something lopsided about his face too, or had that been caused by the stroke?

The old man showed no sign that he was aware they'd entered the room, not even when Mrs. Merrill said, "Daddy, this man wants to talk to you. He's a police officer."

Harter tried to be as simple and direct as he could. "We've found a skeleton at your house on Egypt Street."

Wilton didn't budge. The lines on his pale cheeks didn't even gather.

"I came to ask if you know anything about it."

Wilton didn't budge. He might as well have been a store dummy.

"I told you it wouldn't do any good," said his daughter. "But ask whatever you want. If I can answer for him, I will, though like I said, those bones are news to me. I'm sure they are to Daddy, too."

Maybe not, thought Harter, but there wasn't much use in fishing around, so he went right to the heart. "Did you ever hear of a woman named Brenda Keith? Her maiden name would have been Brenda Harris. She was reported missing from Shantytown at the end of the war."

"End of the war? You mean Vietnam?" asked Dorothy Merrill.

"No, World War Two."

"World War Two? I wouldn't even have been two years old, Detective. What can you remember from when you were two?"

"Your father would have been around thirty, wouldn't he? He'd have a clear memory."

"But you're a little too late to tap his memory. Look at him."

Harter turned to Wilton again. "Was he in the war?"

"He spent World War Two working for the railroad. That was so long ago—why do you think this Brenda Keith has something to do with it?"

"She's just one possibility. We may come across others. She's supposed to have lived on Fletcher Street with an aunt, Myrtle Harris, before she married a Paul Keith."

Mrs. Merrill shook her head. "Means nothing to me. Surely there are older people in South Shawnee you can ask."

"Like Matt Curry," Harter said.

"Do you know Matt Curry?"

"I met him yesterday when I visited the crime scene."

"Crime scene?" Suddenly she was crossing to the old man in the chair. "Is something the matter, Daddy? Do you want something?"

Wheat Wilton had managed to move his head slightly. Had the mention of Matt Curry forced some wires to connect?

"You're upsetting him, Detective. Haven't we done enough of this? Can't we go back downstairs and leave him in peace?"

"Okay. But he seemed to react to Matt Curry's name."

Harter could have sworn the lights had lit in Wilton's weak blue eyes.

"Daddy and Matt Curry lived across the street from each other most of their lives," said Dorothy Merrill as she led him from the room to the steps. "They grew up together."

"I take it they were close friends."

"They played together, then both worked for the railroad. It's like, when you're around someone your whole life, what can you say? You know each other too well, maybe. They had their good times, I'm sure, and they had their arguments, particularly as they got older. Old men will feud."

"About what?" asked Harter, following her into the kitchen.

"Whether it's going to rain. I don't know. I told you it's been a long time since I've lived on Egypt Street."

"Has Curry ever come here to visit him?"

"No." She turned up the gas under a pot of noodle soup.

"He told me you have a brother named Roger."

"Yeah."

"I'd like to talk to him."

"You're free to talk to him all you want, if you can find him. None of us have seen him since . . . It must have been some time in 1968 when he left Shawnee."

"Any special reason for his leaving?"

"You're full of questions, aren't you, Detective? Only Roger can give you the answers to why he does—why he did—anything. I can't explain him and never could. Neither could Daddy. Roger was four years younger than me. I was born in Nineteen forty-four, and he was born in Nineteen forty-eight. Roger just took off, not long after my mother died. He went to California to be a hippie or something. That's the last we heard of him."

Dorothy Merrill had pale blue eyes like her father, and Harter could sense anger in them. It was more than simple irritation at his probing as she rushed around getting supper so she could go bowling.

"I understand your mother died in a hit-and-run. When was that?"

"It was a hit-and-run, all right. December Nineteen sixty-seven, a few weeks before Christmas. They never found the driver. Matt Curry must have told you all sorts of things."

"She must have been, what, forty-five or fifty?"

"She'd just turned forty-four. She was only twenty when I was born, and twenty-five when she had my brother."

"Your father's a good bit older. What's he, about seventy?"

"He'll be seventy-one in February. He was twenty-eight and she was nineteen when they were married, if it means anything."

"You wouldn't happen to have pictures of your mother and brother, would you?"

"Why?"

"Just wondered. I noticed all the family photos in the living room. Since I seem to be rooting around in the past, I'd like to know what the people looked like."

She ladled out a cup of noodle soup. "I don't know where any pictures would be. Probably packed away with Daddy's things." She put the cup on a tray beside a glass of tomato juice, a spoon, and a napkin. Then she flicked off the burner and turned to him again. "If you don't mind, I've got to get Daddy fed so I can get out of here. I can't help you. *We* can't help you. Honest."

"Did you and your brother go to East Shawnee High?"

"Yeah. Why?"

"Just wondered. I don't remember you. Of course, he'd be considerably younger than me, but you're only two years younger."

"Roger graduated in 1966, then went to Shawnee Community College for a while. I quit school in 1961, the start of my senior year, and got married to Bill. I never saw you before, either."

Harter guessed that explained things, but asked, "Did your husband go to East Shawnee, too?"

"Bill went to the Catholic school in South Shawnee. He's a year older than me. If you want to sit around and wait on him, I'm sure he'll be happy to talk over school days with you. He loves to rehash the old days."

"You don't?"

"No, I don't." She was getting really angry. With good reason, he supposed.

"Sorry, Mrs. Merrill. Sometimes I go overboard with questions." He reached in his pocket, pulled out a card, dropped it on the kitchen table. "If you think of anything, or if your father should say something now that I've disturbed him, there's my number. Call any time."

He made his exit through the back door and hurried around the corner of the house. He was halfway out the small alley when the gate swung open and a teenager came toward him. They exchanged hellos as they squeezed past each other.

Harter could feel the boy's questioning eyes on him as he pushed open the gate and walked through the archway to the Avenue.

7

FRIDAY MORNING, one step inside the office, Harter glimpsed the pile of fresh messages on his desk and knew he had to do something. Things were only going to get worse for a while. The evening before, two of the three television networks had reported the strange case of the skeleton uncovered by the Killer Flood. NBC had even quoted Pete Epstein, which must have made the medical examiner's year. The story was big time now.

Instead of dropping into his chair, Harter turned and headed to the chief's office. His pitch was simple: If I've got to respond to all these goddamn calls and sort through old police reports, you can count on your only detective being tied up for a week or more. When he walked out of the chief's office fifteen minutes later, he had what he wanted. Harter usually got what he wanted.

The police should be sifting, Epstein had advised, and he was pretending to when Dave McManaway showed up. "I've commandeered you," said Harter, slamming a drawer shut on a filing cabinet.

"For what?"

Harter pointed over at his desk. "See all those notes. Every one of them is from someone who thinks they can identify the bones. You're going to be my sifter. You've been assigned to me for the duration."

"What you really need is a switchboard operator."

"Or a filing clerk. Look, you wanted to be a detective, didn't you? The door just swung open."

"Sally's not so sure."

"You mean she's not pregnant?"

McManaway laughed. "No, she's as pregnant as you can get. She's not sure about me being a detective. She thinks it's too dangerous, investigating murders and all."

"Hell, you're five times safer as a detective than as a beat cop. You're more in control of the situation. You've already been through the worst of it—years in a uniform, a sitting duck for any punk, ticketing cars when you don't know if the driver will pull a gun. You've been the first on a crime scene and had the anger vented right in your face. Tell Sally to stop worrying. Tell her you've got the chance to save your back. You won't have to dig skeletons out of the damn mud. Someone else'll be doing the hard labor. You'll just have to make sense of the bones once they're dug up. There's still plenty of mud involved, but most of it's mental work."

" 'Mind Games.' "

"Huh?"

" 'Mind Games.' It's an old John Lennon song."

"Was he a detective, too?" Harter lit a cigarette and pointed to the piles of messages. "I've already done part of the sifting for you. Three stacks. This one is honest possibilities, based on Epstein's remarks—women missing between Nineteen forty-five and Nineteen seventy. You'll notice it's the smallest bunch. The middle stack may be worth returning a call. The rest are probably meaningless, though you may want to keep an eye on them as things shape up."

McManaway nodded. "So, I'm to call about the honest possibilities, and maybe follow up on some of the others?"

"Yeah. And you'll no doubt be taking new calls as the day drags on. When you need a break from the phone, I want you to look through old police reports. If *Time* magazine calls, bluff them."

McManaway's green eyes registered confusion. "Bluff them? I've never done anything like this before."

"Who the hell has? You're smart enough to play it by ear. Detectives don't get handed the sheet music."

"Damn, Harter. What old police reports am I supposed to hunt up?"

"A missing-persons report from about Nineteen forty-five, a Brenda Keith, Mrs. Paul Keith, who last lived on Fletcher Street. A hit-and-run death on Egypt Street in December Nineteen sixty-seven. Her name was—can you believe I didn't get her first name? Look for a Wilton, Mrs. Wheat Wilton, maybe Mrs. Bartley W. Wilton. Can't have been many hit-and-runs in Shantytown in 'sixty-seven. And, of course, the missing women, especially if they have some connection with South Shawnee in that twenty-five year period."

"Twenty-five years is a long time," mumbled McManaway as he scribbled notes. "Were you a detective in Nineteen sixty-seven?"

"I was still a beat cop." Harter had the feeling that working with McManaway was going to make him feel older than he usually did. "I want you to check the criminal records of some people, too. They're probably all clean, but I need to know who I'm dealing with."

McManaway picked up the pen again. "Shoot."

"Bartley Wheat Wilton and his wife, whatever her name was, and their son, Roger." Hell, he might as well have them all checked out. "And their daughter, Dorothy Wilton Merrill, and Paul Keith and Brenda Harris Keith. And Matthew Curry. He's an old guy who lives across the street from the Wilton place. Want more?"

Before the younger cop could answer, the phone rang and Harter went out the door.

Outside, the assorted light breezes had congealed into a solid wind that made the signs overhanging the street twist on their chains like condemned men jerking now and then as if they'd been shot through with electrical current, like hanging wasn't good enough and the electric chair was needed to finish them off.

Kind, gentle Mother Nature again. At least the wind would dry up the mud.

Harter guessed it was in the mid-forties, but it seemed colder. He climbed in his car, turned the key, then settled back and stared out the windshield at the bare-branch trees shimmying on the mountains. Those Allegheny ridge lines surrounded Shawnee like the rim of a bowl. Sitting downtown, at the bottom, it was easy to imagine you were drowning in hot alphabet soup and the sides of the bowl were too slippery to climb out.

He'd once told Liz how he imagined the slippery slopes, one night when they were in bed in the apartment over her dance studio, lying there, holding each other, looking out the open window at the mountain's shrouded, nighttime humps.

Liz. Damn.

He steered out of the lot, passed under the traffic light, then turned left onto the four-lane straight shot to the South Shawnee railroad complex. Past the Shawnee-Potomac shops and the long scribbles of switch-yard tracks, he turned left again, into the canal neighborhood.

A young fellow like you's got no notion how it was along the canal. Or so the old guy had claimed, the one who believed the bones belonged to his brother, Jimmy, the long-lost mule driver.

Actually, Harter did have a notion how it had been. Just as he'd grown up with tales of the 1936 Flood and the railroad's glory days when every passenger car was spit and polish, he'd heard stories of the Shawnee & Chesapeake Canal all his life. Once, Shantytown had been winter quarters for many of the canalers. It had a reputation as a beat-your-head-in-for-a-buck place. He had no doubt there were moldy corpses to be dug up along the towpath. Even when he was a kid, South Shawnee had been full of taverns and aging roughnecks. Maybe Wheat Wilton and Matt Curry were among them.

Picturing Wilton frozen in his chair and Curry upset over the flood, it was hard to think of them as young, possibly violent men. But Dorothy Merrill had said, *Old men will feud.* What, he wondered, did they feud about?

He passed several large buildings on the lower side of the street. One of them was Darrell Phillips' warehouse, which had been inundated Tuesday night, sending the appliance dealer into a deep depression.

Just before turning up the hill to Fletcher Street, he noticed a street-cleaning truck coming toward him, spraying the silt and muck from the roadway, trying to wash it into the gutter.

One-thirteen Fletcher was a one-story shotgun house covered with smeary white aluminum siding. The place surely hadn't rented for much when Paul and Brenda Keith were newlyweds, and probably was even more of a bargain-basement residence now. When no one answered his knock, he tried next door.

The lady of the house was in her late forties. Her hugeness was displayed all too well by her tight lavender pants. Her hair was short and bobby-pinned flat.

"Got me," she said loudly in response to his questions. "Paul and Brenda Keith? Myrtle Harris? Never heard of none of them. Won't do you no good to come back and see the pair that lives next door, neither. Just kids that don't know nothing from nothing. Ain't nobody on Fletcher Street lived here no longer than us. What do you need to know about these Keith people anyway? This got something to do with them bones they found down on Egypt Street?"

"Something like that," replied Harter.

"Well, you're talking forty years ago, before we even moved here."

Harter nodded and asked if she knew the Wiltons.

"Knew who they was. Had a girl and a boy, I think. That boy was always weird, like a beatnik. Remember when the mother was killed by a car or something. Don't know the details, but it certainly don't surprise me none they found a body down there."

"Why?"

"Everyone knows the damned place is haunted. Sometimes you go by at night and you see white things moving inside."

"Lights?"

"Ghosts."

Harter visited three more houses before giving up. He should have known it would be hopeless to turn up much on a woman who'd lived there while her husband was in the service forty years before. Maybe Dave McManaway was having a better day, but he doubted it.

He drove down the hill and turned the corner onto Egypt Street. Near the curb, waiting for the city garbage trucks, sat plastic trash bags, soggy overstuffed chairs, masses of pulp that had once been newspapers, magazines, books, family albums. Yards were filled with furniture, toys, boxes of stuff that people had carried out of flooded basements.

He parked in front of the Wilton place, climbed out, and started back to where the bones had been uncovered. The hole was still there, roped off, surrounded by piles of dirt. He had the urge to walk up on the porch, force open the door, go in and face down what specters might be there. *White things moving inside.* Hell, he didn't believe in such crap. He hadn't spotted anything scary when he'd driven by on patrol late Wednesday night. And if there was ever a time for a house to show its haunters, it would have been Wednesday night, after the flood, after the bones had emerged, after the grave was disturbed. But the house had simply looked sad, wet, and deserted. Like a skeleton.

He let the notion pass. Going inside would probably be as useless a gesture as the trip to Fletcher Street had turned out to be. No one had lived in the house for years, and the Wilton family had probably taken anything of value before leaving. Besides, it had been through the flood, so he'd just end up tramping around in a bog, and he'd done enough of that in the last two days. He wondered if the old floorboards would warp as they dried out, and what the Wiltons would do with the place now. Hard to make money off a flooded house with a bad reputation.

He turned away and began walking over to Matt Curry's. The night before, Curry's had been one of the few houses in Shantytown where lights had burned. Nearly everyone else had opted for warmth and dryness, but the old man was tough, not about to be frightened off by high water or howling demons.

He was ready to climb the steps to the retired conductor's door when Mr. Spilky came up from the basement of the next house. Harter changed course and went over to see Curry's neighbor. "How's it going?"

"Could be better." Spilky dropped the box of jars he'd been toting. "We have to throw away all sorts of stuff. There's things you forget you have till you lose them. We canned these tomatoes in the summer. All that work, and now I wouldn't feel safe eating them. God knows what was in the floodwater."

"God might not even know," said Harter.

"Don't be sacrilegious, Detective." Spilky ran his mud-caked paw through his wiry hair. He didn't seem to notice—or didn't care—when some of the mud flaked off on top of his head.

"Is your wife over the upset of finding the bones?"

"Not entirely. It wasn't a pleasant thing to come across Wednesday morning, not on top of the flood. Have you made any progress?"

Progress. Strange choice of words, thought Harter. "We don't know much yet. Right now, I'm digging into the past. Do you know any people who've lived around here a long time—people who might know about the Wiltons and others from years ago? Maybe they know something about Mrs. Wilton, who was killed in a hit-and-run, or about her son. Some other names have come up, too. I need someone with forty years' worth of gossip."

"We're not acquainted with everyone, particularly the older folks. There's Mr. Curry, of course, but he'll change the subject if he doesn't like the question. We try to talk with him, but I always get the feeling we'd have to live here ten or fifteen years before he'll remember our names and talk about more than the weather. Some of these people are sure hard to get to know."

Harter silently agreed. He'd lived in Shawnee all his life, but he still often felt like a wayfaring stranger traveling through this land of woe. He wondered if he would ever make it home.

8

THE AIR in the front room was chill, even though the furnace had been turned on that morning. The temperature was still in the fifties, and the house felt as damp as a barn on a rainy afternoon. Didn't smell any better than a barn, either. Matt Curry wondered if the cop was as bothered by the stench as he was.

Mennonite volunteers had helped him clean out the cellar on Thursday afternoon, but only a stretch of long dry days would remove the terrible odor of the sewage-tinged floodwater mixed with fuel oil, rotting paper, and soaked fabric. Curry hoped he'd live long enough for the air to smell clean again.

Wouldn't his mother have hated it? She'd been the sort who dusted and laundried every day. Cleanliness was next to godliness, and she'd wanted to be godly. She'd always called the front room the parlor, and had taken great pride in the furniture inherited from her family, and the neatly shelved books that had once belonged to her school teacher uncle, and the fussy curtains and doilies. Curry wasn't as fastidious. He'd stripped the room down to bachelor's quarters, putting most of the lace in a trunk downstairs. A trunk that on Tuesday had floated in the foul mixture of destructive liquids. Even after all the decades, he could still picture the front room—*the parlor*—as it had been when he was a boy.

"Damned if I remember Brenda Keith or her husband," he told Harter after the detective had worked from small talk to interrogation. "I do remember Myrtle Harris, and she did have a girl who lived with her, some relative she raised, but I can't help you there. Myrt Harris was a friend of my mother's. They were in the ladies group at the church and a couple times a year she'd come here to talk to Mother about church suppers or Bible study or some such thing. She always seemed to be laughing. Never understood why. She didn't have an easy life. Never had any money, never married, and then she had this girl dropped on her."

"So her niece never came with Miss Harris to visit your mother?"

"I don't know. I always tried to stay away from church goings-on. Mother had religion bad, and I disappeared when she got up a full head of steam. I told you how I got my name. She always wanted me to get an education and be a preacher, or a teacher like her uncle." Curry pointed to the bookshelves. "A lot of those books were his, at least the older, heavier ones. She was always after me to read them, and I was a smart kid, something of a reader, but what I read was Black Mask stories and things like Mark Twain. She never much approved. Like in *Huckleberry Finn.* You know that book? Miss Watson tried to save Huck's immortal soul—Mother used to speak of 'immortal souls'—and Huck wouldn't have any part of it. Neither would I. When we were growing up, Wheat and I used to pretend we were Huck Finn and Tom Sawyer, and that the Potomac was the Mississippi and the abandoned canal boats were our rafts. It disappointed Mother when I quit school and went to work for the Shawnee-Potomac, but times were hard after Dad ran off, and so when I was old enough, I got a railroad job. Anyway, what do Myrt Harris and these Keith people have to do with anything?"

"Maybe nothing." Harter leaned back on the daybed and stared over at the old man in the worn, lumpy chair by the window. "Brenda Harris seems to have disappeared while her husband was in the service in World War Two."

"More than one woman did that."

"Did you ever marry, Mr. Curry?"

"No."

"Hell, I've probably asked too many questions about the Keiths already. Those names are running through the South Shawnee rumor mill by now."

"I won't help spread them. Not many people ask me about anything anymore. I just don't recall the Keiths, and I told you my little connection with Myrt Harris. It's so long ago."

"I know. Believe me, I know. Can you think of anyone else who might help me?"

"Not as far as these people you're asking about, though, I should have told you before, Nan's younger brother still lives in town."

"Nan?"

"Nancy Wilton, Wheat's wife. We always called her Nan."

"Her brother lives in Shawnee?"

"Yeah. His name's David Nash, but we always called him Flathead. Lives up near the hospital. That's where Nan grew up, not down here in Shantytown. Flathead's in his fifties. He and Wheat never got along, so I don't know what he can tell you. I can't think of anyone else might know anything, but I'll keep chewing on it. I guess you've seen Wheat and his daughter. What'd they know?"

"Not much, I'm afraid. Wheat can't talk because of the stroke he had. Mostly he just sits in a chair. He did seem to react when I mentioned you, however. I guess you keep in touch with him."

"I don't know that I've seen him since he moved."

"Really?"

Curry tried not to show his hand, forced himself not to grab too hard at the arms of his understuffed chair. He didn't want Harter to believe there was bad blood between him and Wheat. He tried to sound disinterested when he asked, "How about Dorothy?"

"She claimed to have no ideas about the bones. She did say you and your old friend sure could argue."

Curry tried to be careful. "Maybe we knew each other too good."

"That's how she put it. Did you fellows have particular topics of debate?"

"I'm sure we did. Politics, the best makes of cars—of course, I don't have a car anymore. Can't afford it."

"What about the son, Roger? I'd like to track him down. You remember him?"

"Well, he did grow up across the street."

"Dorothy Merrill seems angry about him. Could just be that he's left her with full responsibility for their father, but I sensed it ran deeper."

"All families have their ins and outs."

"What do you mean?"

"I mean, Dorothy was always close to Wheat, like girls will be to fathers. If you've seen her, you know she took after Wheat in looks and temperament. Roger was more like Nan, with dark hair and fine features. She was a good-looking woman, Nan, and she had a hot streak that could flare up."

"Did Roger inherit the temper, too?"

"As I remember, he did. Like Nan—"

"Go on."

"Well, once she and Wheat had a little argument in the kitchen when she was doing dishes. Wheat told me about it later. She had a carving knife in her hand and just threw it at him. Damn thing stuck in the wall a foot from his head. No, sir, you didn't want to make that woman mad, I'll tell you. Other times, she'd be so jolly she'd break into a jig when a favorite song came on the radio, and you'd think she was the May Queen. Her emotions always ran strong, one way or another."

"And so did Roger's?"

"Never heard of him throwing knives, but you never could tell what he'd do. Totally unpredictable boy. Not that he wasn't smart, mind you. Nan was always sharper than Wheat, and like I said, the boy took after her. She spoiled him tremendous. Presents at Christmas they couldn't really afford. A car when he got out of high school. She said that was so he could travel to college, but he could have taken the bus. I know Wheat and Nan had it out plenty of times over Roger. But Nan could never see anything bad about the boy. She'd always find an excuse for him."

"And Wheat didn't see it the same?"

"No."

"Could that be why the boy left home after his mother died?"

"I'm sure Wheat made it hot for him. He wouldn't put up with half the shenanigans Nan would. I remember once he blew his stack when he and Nan came home from being out of town and some of the neighbors complained about a crazy party Roger had thrown with loud music and girls screaming."

"You remember any of his friends?"

"Never paid much attention. I suppose they were from the college."

"He went to the community college, didn't he?"

"That's what he was supposed to be doing, but from what I heard, he was pretty spotty about going to class and kept dropping in and out of school. I think he used the college mostly as a place to hang out. Nan really got on him about it, but with her, she might yell and even throw a knife, but then it was out of her system, and the next day it was all done and forgotten. I believe she'd have left Wheat before she left that boy."

"Wheat and she had problems?"

Curry sat silently for a full minute, then said, "I don't know. I didn't live with them."

"You remember when she was killed?"

"Yeah. It was December Nineteen sixty-seven. Sleeted the night before and Egypt Street was all ice. Some guy going to work saw the body and almost wrecked his car when he hit his brakes on the ice. The police seemed to think that whoever it was hit her did the same thing. Lost control, and was too afraid to stop."

"Who was the investigating officer?"

Curry shrugged. "Average-size guy with light skin and light brown hair. He came around and asked questions, like you're doing, but I never saw him again."

"Caruthers," mumbled Harter. Then he realized the name would mean nothing to the old man. "Why would Nan Wilton have been out in the street on such a nasty night?"

"You keep asking things I can't answer. I'm not the Wise Old Man of the Mountains."

"I guess Wheat took it hard."

"Of course he did. He'd worked the night it happened and showed up home when they were moving her body. It was a tough way to find out."

"And the boy?"

"Broke up."

Harter waited for him to say more, but Curry just waited, too. Finally, the detective asked, "Do you have any new thoughts about the bones?"

"Not a clue."

"We're almost in the same boat," said Harter, pushing himself up from the sofa. "Mind if I use your phone before I go? It is working, isn't it?"

"They fixed the lines a couple hours ago. Go back through that door to the kitchen. It's on the wall."

Once the cop had left the room, Curry climbed to his feet and stepped as lightly as he could to the far end of the room. His hearing wasn't what it used to be, and at first he couldn't make out more than a few words. Then either he tuned in or Harter's voice got louder.

The detective was obviously talking to someone at headquarters. He told the other cop that Mrs. Wilton's name had been Nancy, then asked what had come to light. After that, Harter fell into a series of yeah's and no's. The conversation ended so abruptly that Curry was stranded like a buck dancer in the middle of a sawdust floor when the cop returned to the front room.

He knew Harter knew he'd been eavesdropping, but nothing was said.

9

CURRY TURNED DOWN the burner under the skillet so the fresh side didn't burn. *Fresh side.* Most kids didn't even know what it was anymore, but he'd grown up with it. Hard to imagine now, but once many of the families in Shantytown had raised pigs and chickens. Sties and coops had stood in backyards and each fall they had slaughtered hogs.

He'd always liked fresh side better than cured bacon. Hard to find the stuff now. The city had an ordinance against livestock within the limits, and the meat in supermarkets came from big packing plants, not from local farmers. Young people probably believed the plastic-wrapped chickens were manufactured in Japan. Only a small butcher shop near the railroad shops still sold fresh side, and then only occasionally.

He scooped the strips of pork onto the soft bread and remembered helping his mother cut the head off a chicken. He usually held the bird by its legs as she wielded the axe. The thing's head was outstretched, resting on a stump in the backyard, and the axe had fallen, neatly severing the neck. For a short time the body would squirm and the wings would flap madly. Always amazed him the chicken didn't know it was dead.

The first time he'd swung the axe, he'd botched it. He'd missed, or rather he hadn't hit it square on. The blade had just nicked the bird's neck, and blood squirted everywhere. The chicken, a strong, fat, Sunday dinner one, had battled to get free, its head half cut off. "Hit it again! You can't do that!" his mother was screaming. "Don't make it suffer! When you kill something, do it fast!"

He swung the axe again.

The coop was gone now.

Sometimes it seemed like everything was gone. Like the passenger station. A *museum.* Earlier, as they'd small-talked, before the detective had launched into heavy questions, Harter had asked if he was going to the opening of the museum on Saturday. Curry had said he didn't know. But later, talking to Flathead, he'd decided maybe he would.

He'd tried to call Flathead Nash, Nan's brother, for hours. Flathead had been a Marine, and when he'd come home from the service, he'd continued to wear his hair sheared into a crew cut. This had been in the 1950s, when many schoolboys wore waxed crew cuts. One day Flathead had taken his nephew Roger to the barbershop and delivered him home with only stubble left on top. Nan had gone wild. If she'd been washing a butcher knife that afternoon, she would have let it fly. And if she'd wanted to, she would have hit Flathead, too, just as she could have hit Wheat, if she'd really wanted to.

But Flathead didn't answer any of Curry's calls. He was probably sitting in a tavern somewhere. Curry wondered if Harter would have the same trouble locating him. He hoped so. He wanted to talk to Nash before the detective did.

After he washed his supper dishes, he dialed Nash's number again. Flathead had a voice as thick as his bull neck, and Curry was relieved when he heard it. No, Flathead didn't want to drive to Shantytown this evening. He had to be careful. He was a little drunk, and if they picked him up one more time, he might lose his license for good. But, yeah, he'd come by in the morning and they could go to the museum opening. No, he hadn't talked to no detective yet. He'd been away all afternoon. After hearing about the bones, he'd visited Wheat, but it was impossible to communicate with the son of a bitch. Wheat just stared out the window. Then Flathead had gone for a few beers to think things through. He'd been intending to call Curry.

After he hung up, Curry went to the parlor and sat in his chair. The house still smelted like a big rat had died in the woodwork, but he tried to ignore the stench. He twisted and peered across Egypt Street at the Wilton place. There he was. In his chair. Staring out the window. Like they said Wheat Wilton did. The son of a bitch.

Everything was being kicked loose. Like rocks tumbling down a mountain.

When he and Wheat were young, they'd often played on a hillside above the tracks. There'd been an old wives' tale that a penny was all you needed to derail a train, so he and Wheat, *Huck and Tom*, had tried it. They'd put a copper coin on a rail, then scrambled up the shale bank until a freight came along. The train didn't leave the tracks. After it had passed, they couldn't even find the penny.

Later, as a conductor, he'd remembered their attempted derailment many times. *What if the copper sliver had caused the wheels to lose connection with the rail and wreck the train?* When he saw boys sitting on rocky ridges along the line, he never failed to wonder if they too had laid pennies on the tracks.

Sometimes those kids scrambled up a shale bank like he and Wheat had, and their scurrying caused rocks to come unstuck, and the rocks skittered down the hill toward the train. Seemed to him that, other times, those rocks came loose of their own accord, just popped out of their rightful places on the hillsides. Like on those mountain roads where the signs warn FALLING ROCK. AS if there was something you could do about it. Rocks falling. Coming unstuck. Someone had either kicked them free in a scramble, or the rocks loosened themselves at a predestined moment. Could cause a car to swerve out of control. Could derail a train. Could kill someone. *If you kill something, do it fast!*

She'd been lying in the middle of Egypt Street that icy morning, 1967. Just wearing her slippers and her pink robe, open to show her underthings and her thighs.

Unbelievable, that he hadn't heard a sound, not a collision, not a scream of brakes, not a yell of pain. He'd always felt guilty. If he'd only heard something, he might have run out and saved her. Might have called an ambulance. Might have gotten her to the hospital while she was still breathing.

She'd only been crossing the street. Shouldn't have been in danger.

She was wearing a dress so thin you could see her body move through it, the soft kind of dress the girls wore before the war, with shiny stockings and high-heel shoes that strapped across her slender ankles.

Curry had been heading home from work when he first laid eyes on her that warm day in 1941. She was new to him, not from Shantytown, and she was waiting for the bus to take her home. He passed her day after day, until he built up enough nerve to speak to her. It took months.

She was a secretary in the union office near the Shawnee-Potomac shops. Once he learned that, he pretended he had reasons to go in the office frequently, just to see her. Finally he asked her to go to the movies and she said yes. Nan smelled so clean as she sat in the theater seat next to him.

"Did you ever marry, Mr. Curry?" the detective had inquired.

"No."

She married Wheat Wilton, who always seemed to know what to say to the girls.

Unsure of himself, Curry's tongue had balled up whenever he was near a good-looker like Nan, but Wheat was glib as hell. Never had a problem. *Funny.* Now he was the old man who rattled on, and golden-throated Wheat had been struck dumb.

He'd known the night he saw Nan with Wheat at the ticket window that he'd lost her. Wheat, always light and joking with the girls. Curry had retreated around the corner and gone home. After that, when he'd pass her at the bus stop, he could never manage more than "Hello." He was afraid to ask her out and be turned down. Didn't want to hear her say, "I'm sorry, but I'm going with Wheat."

They married in the summer of 1943 and moved into the house across the street. Soon after, Wheat's mother went to live with her sister and they had the house to themselves. From his window, Curry would watch Nan as she hung laundry out back or sat on the front porch swing. Her belly swelled, and seven months after the wedding, Dorothy was born.

He hadn't been surprised that Wheat had taken her away from him. What surprised Curry came later.

She'd only been crossing the street. *She shouldn't have been in danger.*

10

HARTER SHIFTED in the booth and watched Al load a couple dozen of those pencil-thin hot dogs onto the cooker rollers inside the big front window, where the rotating wieners could be seen from the sidewalk. Al called that advertising.

Despite the early hour, Al's regulars were filling the stools at the marble counter and calling for hot dogs with the works. When business boomed at midday, Al would be so swamped that he'd line eight or nine buns up his tattooed arm and, assembly line style, slip the franks inside, then slop mustard on each with a flat stick, then spoon on diced onions, then cover it all with his secret-recipe chili.

Weenies, Harter's grandfather had called them, and that first Edward Harter had always ordered hamburgers—*hamburgs*—instead. Family tradition held that his grandfather's aversion to hot dogs stemmed from a pre-World War I visit to a railroad exposition in Chicago, where he'd gotten food poisoning from bad weenies in those days of unregulated meat.

Harter had more than enough dreads, but hot dogs weren't among them, no matter what Liz and the health food people warned. He could almost qualify as one of Al's regulars. Many a morning he'd eaten those wieners for breakfast, though usually, like this Saturday, he settled for coffee. Breakfast—a big victual feast of country sausage, yellow-yoke eggs, crisp hash browns, buttered toast—was his favorite meal, even if he was more likely to down it at 2 A.M. in the old diner by the South Shawnee yards than at a more orthodox time.

He lit a cigarette and stared at the local page of *The News.* At least the paper had backed off on the Egypt Street bones, though he guessed the story would be back on top once Pete Epstein and his expert were ready to say something.

The flood didn't earn much newspaper space, either. It had only been four days, and the victims were still trying to put their worlds in shape, but the sole mention of the disaster was a photo of Mennonite volunteers helping a Shantytown family, as they had helped Matt Curry. Crews of Mennonites had come out of the woodwork the day after the flood and gone quietly about their business, washing down walls, trucking away ruined goods, replacing warped doors, doing anything to make life easier for people. Where those peaceful folks lived between tragedies, Harter didn't know, but he knew his job would be a lot less complicated if everyone had their sense of moral duty.

What *The News* blasted across the headlines was the opening of the railroad museum. There had been talk of postponing the event in the wake of the flood, but the project was already running late. The 100th birthday of the old Shawnee-Potomac station had been in June, and it was now November. If they didn't cut the ribbon, the year would slip by, or at least bad weather would come and there would be fewer tourists. *Tourists.* Somehow Harter didn't believe they would satisfactorily replace steel mills and railroad shops. In a way, turning the passenger station into a museum marked its demise, too, though he was glad the building still stood.

He could see the top floor of the station from his third-floor apartment on the hill. He'd grown up near the enormous structure, which in its heyday had hotel rooms on its second and third stories. When he and his friends could find nowhere else to play, when they were tired of skinned-up knees from sliding into third base in gravel yards and alleys, they had sneaked over the wrought-iron fence into the green field near the station and used it for a ball diamond until the railroad bulls ran them off.

Like many Shawnee residents, he'd felt like an aged relative was dying when, a few years before, they'd talked of tearing the station down. This had been in 1982, during the depths of the recession, and the building had long since become little more than a holding zone for freight. Even when he'd been a kid, he'd heard how the upper hotel floors were rotting. The station's death seemed to represent everything that was going wrong.

Now the Governor, a U.S. Senator, a Congressman, and scores of state legislators and local officials were to cut the museum ribbon and announce a bright new day. The chief was worried about security, so Harter had promised he'd mix in the crowd as long as the dignitaries stayed around.

Hell, he'd probably have gone anyway. He'd asked Liz to come along, but she hadn't shown any interest. The distance between them just kept widening, and there didn't seem to be anything he could do about it. Besides, she had her Saturday morning dance classes to teach. He didn't really want to think about it. There was enough going on to pull him down without dwelling on Liz.

"Manage to get some sleep last night?"

He looked up at Dave McManaway and said, "I always sleep the same, good or bad."

The younger cop had no sooner sat down than Al put a cup of coffee in front of him. As he watched McManaway spoon some sugar into the cup, Harter had a flash of what Al's was like when he was little, when there were scratched-up wood tables, not the smooth Formica mandated by the health department. Why was he always rolling and tumbling through the past? The old wooden tables. His grandfather's distaste for weenies. The 1936 Flood. The station. The bones surfacing. All coming up like water from underground pipes.

"I waited until after five yesterday," McManaway said, "but you didn't come back to the office. I imagine you had a full day on the case."

"Full enough. Actually, I stopped in at headquarters last night. I saw the stuff you dug out and read some of the messages. Good job."

He didn't bother to tell McManaway that unable to find Nan Wilton's brother, he'd driven out to the overlook on the mountain south of Shawnee and killed time. How many hours had he wasted over the years, simply sitting in his car and looking down on the model train-layout city he was supposed to be protecting? These days, he seemed to be doing it more than ever.

"Then you saw Caruthers' accident report from Nineteen sixty-seven?"

"Yeah. I figured from what Matt Curry said that Caruthers was the investigating officer."

"Caruthers doesn't seem to have turned up much. Apparently he questioned a lot of people in the neighborhood and measured tire skids, but no one was ever charged. He believed it was a pickup truck, probably blue, based on a paint smear on Nan Wilton's robe. He kept good notes, though."

"Always did. Even back when you didn't have to do half the paperwork we do now, he was a red-tape specialist. I used to tell him he'd make a great federal bureaucrat."

"There's something to be said for good record keeping when you're digging into an accident from eighteen years ago," McManaway said.

"Guess so."

"What did you find out about the Keith people?"

"Nothing much. Nobody really remembers them. I decided to put the whole thing on hold until I hear from Pete Epstein. No sense banging my brains out until we know more about the bones."

"Dr. Epstein's promised something this afternoon?"

"Yeah. I plan to stop at his office after the museum opening. You going to it?"

"No one asked me. I promised I'd take Sally shopping this afternoon. We're working on the baby's room. It's due in ten days."

Harter rubbed out his cigarette on the lip of the green glass ashtray, then reached for his coffee. "How'd *your day* go yesterday?"

"I had a lot of callers, but not as many as you had on Thursday. I can't say there were any true leads. Confused people, aren't they? We could hand the girl's name, age, address and photo to the papers and we'd still hear from people who claim, no, it's not her at all, it's really my great-great-grandfather, who had a long gray beard and rode a big white horse. Hard to believe so many men and women have just up and disappeared without a trace, and that someone out there still wants to find out what became of them."

"Yeah. It's enough to make you as cynical as me."

"As far as those names you left me, I can't find a criminal record for any of them. I'm not saying there's nothing, but I just haven't found it. I put out requests for the whereabouts of your Roger Wilton, but it's a huge country."

"Anything else going on?"

"Usual Friday night crap. Herr says there was a bad accident out on the interstate, and a burglary reported in a West Side mansion. A drunk highway worker drove into a drainway at three A.M. and claimed he was checking culverts. A sixteen-year-old kid rammed his hand through a plate glass window downtown and set off the alarm. When Bettles showed up, the kid was frozen in place, high on something, watching the blood run down his arm."

"Friday night crap, all right. Be sure and tell Sally all the gory details. Let her know that, as a detective, you won't have to deal with half that garbage anymore."

"Yeah, but they're cut-and-dried cases, mostly. How do you even start to figure out who killed someone when all you've got is a few old bones?"

"Why do I have to keep reminding everyone that we don't know for sure whether anybody killed anybody?" said Harter. "As for learning what happened, I sure as hell don't know how to go about it. I'm not the Wise Old Man of the Mountains."

11

POLITICIANS SURE COULD TALK. Carpenters hammered, writers wrote, cabdrivers drove, engineers engineered, plumbers piped, mechanics tinkered, cops investigated, dancers danced, and politicians talked.

Harter was beginning to wonder when the hell they'd ever cut the damn ribbon. In their dark suits, they sat on the long, broad porch of the passenger station. One by one, they rose from their folding chairs and, amid applause, strutted to the podium. There was a definite pecking order. The mayor kicked off the show with a welcome, then the county commissioners waved and said a few words, then the state legislators got a few minutes to explain their role in saving the station and boosting tourism, and then came Congressman Charles Whitford Canley, who apparently had the office for life.

Whether anybody was really listening to all the glowing words was beside the point. Harter knew that what the politicians truly wanted was to be seen by voters, to make it look like they were doing something to improve the lives of ordinary people. They really wanted Jack Reese or one of the other camera-aimers to snap their pictures so they might end up on the front page Sunday morning.

Reese was a photographer for *The News.* A few years before, his angular shots had convinced everyone that the station was a monument worth saving. Now he and others pointed their cameras at the politicians on the porch. There were also television news crews from Bartlesburg, even from Washington and Baltimore. The Governor and a U.S. Senator had brought along their own photographers so they could remind voters that their benevolent realms did indeed encompass Shawnee.

The crowd of four or five hundred was turning bored long before the climax. Amid the babble of politicians, the only real puzzle was whether the Governor or the Senator would speak last. Who would get star billing?

A sizable chunk of those gathered on the station platform were old men who, Harter imagined, had once worked for the Shawnee-Potomac. But even they could stand only so much talk of the importance of the railroad to the development of the state and region, and how the museum commemorated the industry while at the same time it opened the door for a new industry, tourism, which would again bring good days. The old men shifted from foot to foot and at times would have drowned out the speakers if the public-address system hadn't been turned up loud.

The Governor got the final word. He had the good taste to inform the crowd that he and the Senator planned to tour the flood-ravaged sections in the afternoon, and that they were hard at work trying to get President Reagan to declare the region a federal disaster area. Harter wondered if, like the Mennonites, the politicos would help clear the mud away. Or would they helicopter off after an hour or so?

Finally, the speeches were over and the politicians all clumped near the red ribbon. Two pairs of oversize scissors were produced, and as the Governor and the Senator clipped, the cameras clicked. Then, accompanied by a couple of state troopers, the dignitaries filed inside for a look at what they had christened.

Harter didn't rush in. He stood on the platform awhile, watching everyone. Without doubt, this was the most activity that had taken place there in thirty years. Even his cynicism couldn't erase that fact. He was glad they hadn't torn the station down.

He'd just about fallen into a daydream about the old building when he saw the short, stocky old man climb the steps and walk across the porch toward the double doors, over which now hung the sign SHAWNEE RAILROAD MUSEUM. There was something familiar about the guy, but at first Harter didn't register it was the same fellow he'd spent so much time with in the last few days.

Only when the man turned to open the door did Harter recognize Matt Curry, dressed in his best. The dark brown suit was a little rumpled in back, but still you could have believed he was one of the special guests. Beside him was a guy in his fifties who hadn't bothered to deck out for the occasion, wearing instead blue corduroy trousers, a faded plaid flannel shirt, and a light gray jacket.

The Governor and his entourage were already leaving as Harter went up the steps. Inside the doors, other politicians congregated to shake the hands of those who came and went. Harter brushed by them and made his way to the center of the tile floor. All around him, people chattered as they studied the railroad exhibits. A man dressed in a Shawnee-Potomac conductor's blue uniform stood behind what had once been the ticket counter. Above his head was a sign that read TOURIST INFORMATION.

They'd done a great job fixing the place up. The freshly painted walls probably hadn't looked so good since World War II. The enormous waiting room, now filled with bodies and echoing with voices, didn't seem anywhere near as dingy and run-down as it had the last time he'd been in it.

He found himself gravitating to the souvenir machine near the counter, *the information desk.* The contraption was still there. They'd even shined it up. In the old days, you slid a quarter in the slot and turned a wheel to find each letter of your name, or whatever message you wanted to press into metal. Apparently the machine still worked, though the price had been upped to a buck. In a drawer somewhere he still had one of those thin, silvery disks with his name and birth date embossed on it.

Across the room, a huge, colorful map hung on the wall, and standing in front of it were Matt Curry and the other man. Harter moved over to them, but they seemed so entranced by the map that they didn't realize he was standing behind them.

"The domain of the Shawnee-Potomac Railroad, huh?" Harter eventually asked to seize their attention.

"Yeah," mumbled Curry, who didn't seem too surprised at Harter's sudden appearance. The seventy-year-old reached up and almost touched the plastic-coated map with his thick index finger. "I know all the damn stops. I spent a quarter of my life calling them out as I went through the cars punching tickets. *North Branch, Green Spring, Paw Paw, Doe Gully, Hancock, Cherry Run, Martinsburg, Shenandoah Junction, Harpers Ferry, Brunswick, Point of Rocks, Germantown, Rockville, Kensington, Washington, D.C.* Most of them were littler towns then, you understand. Hell, the Shawnee-Potomac was littler, too. Wasn't part of some national conglomerate in those days, but it was a tremendous thing to those of us who worked for it. We believed it was the most important company in the world. Anyway, we'd be steaming along and I'd call out those stops, then head back to the caboose and sip my coffee and read. Others might have drank, but I read to bide the time. They used to call me the Professor, did I tell you that?"

"I don't think so," said Harter, watching Curry closely. The brown suit didn't look as dapper as it had at a distance. Far from new, it had wide lapels and a sort of old-fashioned cut. It made the old man look hardy and barrel-chested. Such suits were back in style, Liz had told him one night, and she'd suggested he might try one.

"Washington, D.C., Kensington, Rockville . . ." Curry was running the return route west now. Harter remembered the stops, too. His grandfather had been given a railroad pass when he'd retired, and as long as Harter was under twelve, the two of them could ride anywhere on the Shawnee-Potomac for free. Once, with a chicken box lunch, they'd traveled to Washington to see the inauguration of Dwight D. Eisenhower. "*. . . Green Spring, North Branch . . .*"

"Brings back a lot," said the man with Curry. "I'm not sure I want it all to come back. Where's the pictures of the damn wrecks, or don't they put them on display?"

"They're probably tucked in a dark corner someplace," said Harter. "I don't think I know you."

"Flathead Nash," answered the guy without extending his hand. "I don't know you, neither."

"This is the detective I told you about," Curry told him. Turning to Harter, he added, "This is David Nash, Nan's brother."

"I tried to find you yesterday," Harter said.

"I'm tough to find sometimes." Nash's voice had turned gruffer. Harter guessed he didn't like cops.

"I guess Mr. Curry's told you what I'm interested in."

"Yeah."

"I know this isn't the time, but I want to come by and ask you some questions."

"Well, you can ask." Flathead Nash had a blotchy red face and all the finesse of a drunken rowdy.

"Suppose I come up to your house Monday morning. Right now, I'm waiting for a report on the bones they found at the Wilton place. Once I get it, I may have a clearer idea what I need to find out," Harter said.

"I don't know a goddamn thing about no bones. Matt says you've been asking about Nan's accident. I wasn't even in town when it happened. She and Wheat led their life and I led mine."

"How about your nephew, Roger Wilton? I've been trying to locate him."

"Ain't seen the boy in almost twenty years, not since he left home."

"You collect your thoughts. I'll be around Monday."

"My thoughts are collected, and I ain't got none," Nash barked.

Maybe he's telling the truth, thought Harter. Maybe he ain't got no thoughts. Not wanting to push it at the moment, he said his good-byes.

As he walked toward the door, he noticed the crowd had thinned out. Only one or two politicians still worked the station. There didn't seem to be very many tourists that November day, after all.

12

TURNING ONTO the street above the station, Harter could see across the downtown to the opposite hill where a steeple pierced the sky. Pete Epstein's office was only a few doors from the old church, but getting from the station to the steeple was something else again. Shawnee hadn't been designed for modern traffic. By the time you allowed parking on the hilly streets, the actual driving space was pretty narrow.

Harter couldn't remember if it had been worse in the 1950s when cars were wider and longer, but it sure was a mess now. Some high-priced traffic engineer had changed half the streets into one-way affairs. Then, in the 1970s, to create a mall atmosphere, they'd bricked in the main downtown street and diverted cars and trucks around it. The result lent credence to what the old man on a country road once said: *You can't get there from here.*

As the crow flies, it was about half a mile to the medical examiner's, but to drive it he had to turn up the hill behind the station, go three blocks, turn up another hill by the YMCA, curve around a corner, ease into southbound traffic heading back the way he'd come, wait at the crossing for a freight to pass, then bump over the tracks, turn left, then right twice, then eventually left again, and, near the flood-control walls, cross the river bridge from his own East End into the more well-to-do West Side where he roared up the hill until he came to the Episcopal Church. Luckily, Pete Epstein had a private parking lot, so he didn't have to sniff around for a spot on the street.

He stubbed out his cigarette, climbed from the car, and decided to try the small brick building where Epstein did his police work, rather than the office where he doctored his regular patients.

Epstein was smiling like he knew something when Harter walked in. "Good, you're early," he said. "I might be able to get home and watch a football game yet."

"Where's your expert?" Harter asked.

"On his way back to the university. We worked on the bones a few hours last night after Dr. Shaw got into town. Then this morning we really went at it. Come on back. I'll show you what we've got."

Epstein's short, wiry body almost leaped from the chair. He led Harter through the door to the autopsy room, a room the detective had seen more than once. Spread atop thin white paper on the table were the beige bones, now washed and sorted. When he'd seen them three days before in Wilton's backyard, Harter had found it hard to feel anything, to even accept that they were the remains of a person. Maybe it was because of all the phone calls, especially the one from Paul Keith about his late wife, Brenda, or maybe it was because the bones were now laid out into a skeleton, but he no longer had trouble acknowledging that they had once been a breathing person.

"What we've got is a young woman, like I thought," Epstein began.

"How young?"

"Twenty, twenty-one. It's easier to pinpoint the age with kids."

"How long ago was she buried?"

"We decided it must have been around Nineteen sixty-six, though it could have just as well been anywhere from, say, 'sixty-four to 'sixty-eight. Slightly unusual conditions, you understand. On the one hand, she was buried in the shed, a sheltered area, and on the other, the body was in the floodplain along the river. Given all the variables, it's hard to be much more exact. We don't believe there's any reason to doubt she was buried there shortly after she died."

"You're positive this happened in the sixties, and not Nineteen forty-five?" asked Harter, thinking again of Brenda Keith.

"There's no way we're that far off. I wouldn't want to mislead you by being so specific that you rule out good leads, but, no, it couldn't have been forty years ago. Dr. Shaw took a few bones back with him, so we might hear more from him in the next couple weeks. All I can do is help you calculate your probabilities."

"Any idea how she died?"

Epstein ran his hand through his gray hair. "Got me. No broken bones. No sign of a knife wound or a bullet. She could have been strangled, or smothered, or she could have died from natural causes."

"At twenty?"

Epstein shrugged. "I admit it's unlikely. The bones suggest she was about five-six, healthy, and probably slim, though again, that's a guess. People can put fat on thin frames."

"How about dental records? You mentioned them to the press."

"They just picked up on that. Dental records are a shell game. You have to have some notion who the victim is. You can't just send X rays to every dentist in the United States and expect them to go back and match them against their old files. Dental records only verify. Some dentists aren't good about keeping old charts, and since we're talking twenty years ago, there's no assurance the dentist is still in practice, or even alive. Still, her teeth were well taken care of. They were fluoridated at some point, which was often done to kids in the fifties. We did find one new thing."

"What's that?"

Epstein turned to a white metal cabinet, picked something up, and handed it over to Harter. "I took Dr. Shaw out to Egypt Street this morning so he could have a look at the scene and the soil and everything. He sifted a little and came up with this earring. I guess we were too busy hunting for bones the other day and, with the mud and all, just missed it."

"Doesn't look that unusual. Plenty of women have pierced ears. Hell, it could have belonged to Nan Wilton, or been dropped anytime over the years."

"Sure could have," Epstein said. "But it's still something. Besides, I'm not sure as many girls had pierced ears twenty or twenty-five years ago. I remember when my daughter had hers done. It was a big deal, and we gave her hell when she came home. Besides, that's not a dime-store earring. The little half-moon is ivory, I think. Isn't much, but it's yours."

"Any other big insights?" asked Harter as he stuffed the earring into his jacket pocket.

"Not right now. All we can do is hope to hear more from Dr. Shaw. You'll be glad to know, Harter, that so far I've resisted the temptation to inform the media. They keep calling, but I just let them talk to my answering machine."

"My God, Pete, when did you see the light? Hell, I might vote for you yet, once you decide what you're running for."

AS SOON AS he reached headquarters, Harter dug through the notes on his desk, found Paul Keith's number in Pittsburgh, and dialed. A woman answered, and he was relieved she didn't ask who he was when he asked for Keith.

Once he was on the line, Harter got straight to the point. The bones couldn't have been Brenda's. There was little or no doubt they were from the 1960s. Of course, it didn't help Keith understand what had become of his first wife, but at least it didn't open a closet of skeletons, and, anyway, he had lived a long time without knowing about her. Perhaps it was best that way.

What bothered Harter was how much time he'd wasted on the trail of the 1940s disappearance. He'd spent Friday questioning people about the Keiths, and as he'd told Matt Curry, he'd probably stoked the rumor fires in South Shawnee. He knew too well how rumors could burn through blue-collar neighborhoods. He didn't know if upper-crust neighborhoods were any different.

He reached in his pocket, pulled out the earring, and fingered the ivory half-moon. *Liz had pierced ears.* Maybe he'd see her tonight. Then he put the earring in his desk drawer and began reading the messages left for him.

McManaway had meticulously jotted down the remarks of each caller and how they related, or didn't relate, to the bones. Clearly, he was better educated than the cops of Harter's generation or the ones who had trained him.

Suddenly he saw an older detective rambling on to a young one, and he was the young one, 1968.

"First thing you got to learn, Harter, is anything can happen. Don't think just because you're in a small city in the mountains don't mean that all the big-city crimes don't rear their heads. They just don't pop up as often, which can make them trickier, since you don't always know how to solve them. Don't ever let your guard down. Anything that can happen in New York or Los Angeles can happen here. *Anything.*"

Hell, the molemen could come tomorrow.

The telephone rang.

"Are you the one investigating the bones?"

The man's voice was unaccented and bland, like he was enunciating clearly and slowly to cover up his real voice.

"Yeah."

"I would like to talk to you."

"We're talking."

"I mean in person."

"I'm at headquarters now."

"Not there."

"I can meet you someplace."

"Not now. Tonight. Somewhere no one will see us."

"Who are you?" asked Harter.

"Not right now."

"Where are you?"

"Not important. Name a place to meet."

"How about the old Shawnee-Potomac station?" asked Harter, the museum opening still fresh in his mind. "By the pedestrian underpass. There shouldn't be anyone there this evening."

"After dark."

"Eight o'clock."

"Make it eleven."

The line went dead.

The old cop was right.

Anything can happen.

13

"So, if Dr. Epstein's right, and the bones are from between Nineteen sixty-four and Nineteen sixty-eight, we're looking at almost the same time frame as the hit-and-run case you had me dig out," said Dave McManaway.

Harter rubbed his palms against the steering wheel. "Yeah, I guess we are, but don't jump to the conclusion they're connected in any way. They could be years apart."

"All of Caruthers' paperwork might help you yet."

"Let's hope he didn't toil in vain."

"You know, this is just the sort of thing Sally's worried about. I mean, us here tonight, sitting in an unmarked car in the shadows of an empty parking lot, you preparing to step out and come face to face with someone who wouldn't even give you his name."

"That's the breaks," Harter said. "Didn't you ever patrol the station platform on your beat?"

"Yeah, but—"

"But nothing. We've been through all that. Anyway, I've done dumber things. Besides, I wasn't so damn stupid. I brought you along. Keep your window down and your ears sharp. If anyone jumps me, I'll raise a hell of a fuss. I'll get off a shot or two if I need to. This guy didn't exactly sound dangerous. If you ask me, I thought he sounded scared."

McManaway laughed. "You mean you've been doing this so long, Harter, that you can tell if someone *sounds* dangerous?"

"Mind games. That's a John Lennon song, you know," Harter said. "So did you do your shopping today? Did you buy what you need for the baby's room?"

"Yeah."

"Is it going to be a boy or a girl?"

"Don't know."

"I thought all the upwardly mobile parents these days had it all checked out, so they know what to expect."

"I told Sally I didn't want to know."

"I wouldn't either," said Harter as he reached for the door handle. "Chance keeps it interesting, doesn't it?"

A minute later, walking across the parking lot, he did have to admit that he was taking a chance. You always had to wonder if you were being set up. Still, he'd picked the meeting place, and the guy had begun by mentioning the bones. Like chance, there was something to be said for nervousness. It kept you ready. He *had* done dumber things.

Once he was on the station platform, the solitary rap of his soles seemed to ripple up the concrete ahead of him until the echo was lost somewhere in the darkness. He glanced down at his watch and decided to kill the ten minutes left by sitting on the station porch. From the bench near the door, he had a clear view of the whole platform.

When he was young, when railroading was still trying to kick, that platform had never been completely empty, no matter what the hour. Now there were only two passenger trains a day—morning and evening Amtraks—and the riders went directly to the parking lot, never setting foot inside the station. No porters rushed about pushing full baggage carts, no crowds of excited relatives waited, no steam hissed out around big iron wheels. There was little evidence that this had once been the proud center of a proud city.

He turned to study the underpass. His caller, whoever it had been, might emerge at any moment. Desiring secrecy, as the guy apparently did, he might decide to park at the hotel lot across the tracks so he could come and go without Harter writing down his license plate number. Or maybe he didn't have a car. Maybe he was on foot.

Just after eleven, Harter stepped down from the porch and walked slowly toward the underpass, half-expecting the guy would come up out of the ground like the molemen. They'd become embedded in his head from a movie—*Superman and the Molemen,* or *Superman Meets the Molemen,* or some title he couldn't exactly recall. They came up from the ground in the nighttime city, out of steaming manhole covers, out of scrap-metal heaps, out of smoky pits at the dump. Only Clark Kent in his Superman guise could foil their evil designs.

Going home the night they'd seen the movie, he and Terry, his best friend in elementary school, had sidestepped every manhole cover, stayed away from every sewer grate, so as not to anger the sinister spirits. A freight had blocked the crossing and, with a curfew to beat, they'd been forced to use the underpass, the dreaded foot tunnel from downtown, under the five tracks, into their own East End.

The tunnel was always wet with groundwater and always smelled like piss, or maybe it was beer, and the winos squatted against the damp underground walls.

He and Terry were barely down into it when the dimness scared them and the dampness chilled them, and without a word passing between them, they each imagined the subterranean molemen and started running like hell, leaping over a drunk's legs so as not to be tripped, finally running up the steps, two at a time, running until they were halfway up the hill to their homes. Until they were in safe terrain. Where the molemen couldn't get them.

Anything could happen, and the nervousness kept you ready.

He thought he heard something and stopped fast.

His hand slid inside his jacket and gripped his gun.

Slowly, he turned around, checking the station platform from different angles.

He could have sworn he'd heard—or sensed—something, but there was only the empty platform.

He looked at his watch again. *Twelve minutes after eleven.*

He lit a cigarette, then headed toward the underpass, and when he reached its mouth, he hesitated only a second before he started down the steps, unsure whether he was still searching for his caller or confronting an old fear.

The underground walkway wasn't used much anymore since the crossing was rarely tied up for long, but every few years citizens demanded that the city council and railroad authorities throw the winos out and fix the damn thing up. These days the underpass was in one of its cleaner, well-lit incarnations, though it still smelled faintly of urine and spilled booze. Cigarette butts and slivers of glass littered the shattered concrete floor, but there was nothing more to be seen.

It was nearing midnight when Harter climbed back in the car.

"Well," said McManaway, "I didn't hear any shots. What'd your man have to say?"

"No one showed," said Harter. "No one showed."

14

"I SHOT HER."

Christ, here he was again. *Darrell Phillips.* Sunday morning, and for the second time in four days the appliance dealer was spouting the same confession.

Harter stared across the interrogation table and watched Phillips rub at the Styrofoam cup. "You say you shot your wife. Why?"

Somehow he didn't expect a coherent response, and he didn't get one. Phillips looked up, his weak mouth opened, and out came "Because." Then he stopped. *Because.*

The guy's head dropped, his dazed eyes lowered toward the scratched table, his puffy fingers stroked the cup, and he seemed to dive into himself. Harter wished he could come up with something reasonable to ask, but he knew there was little use. He'd just wait for the report from the apartment. This time he hadn't bothered to send anyone but Dave McManaway to the store near the viaduct. He had a pretty good notion what McManaway would find.

Phillips' face wasn't such an emotionless pancake-makeup mask this morning, or maybe Harter was just fooling himself by believing he could spot the pain in it.

He decided to try again. "Your wife says you were in Vietnam."

"My wife is dead. I shot her," Phillips said.

"I know other Vietnam vets are troubled by what happened there," said Harter, staying on the course he'd selected. "Could be you need to talk to somebody about it. The war's been over for ten years. You've got to get it out of your mind some time. We all do things we'd just as soon forget. Being a cop, I've had to shoot criminals. I've killed a few. You can only tell yourself that you were doing the right thing at the time, that you had no other choice. You *were* in a war, whether you wanted to be there or not."

Harter imagined he sensed Phillips clench his teeth, but that was the extent of it. The little sermon obviously wasn't leading anywhere fruitful. The storekeeper just seemed to retreat more. Perhaps, somewhere inside, he was caught up in his own mind games, worried about the emerging molemen with no Superman to fight them for him, facing his own haunted places, pedestrian underpasses, flooded warehouses.

Harter pushed forth a pawn. "When were you in Vietnam? The late sixties?"

The silence was becoming irritating by the time McManaway opened the interrogation room door and waved Harter out to the hall. There again stood Mrs. Phillips, alive and breathing, and looking like she'd taken more time getting dressed than she had three mornings before. Maybe she'd been getting ready for church when McManaway had arrived.

"Your husband has the same story he did on Thursday," Harter told her.

Rather than blow out the confidence she had the first time, Vi Phillips seemed genuinely confused. "I don't know what to do, Detective. I don't know what Darrell went through in the war. I don't know anything about those times, or his childhood for that matter, except what he's told me, which is very little. I'm not from Shawnee originally. I just don't know what to do."

"You promised to take him to a doctor."

"He has an appointment tomorrow." She reached up and twisted a red curl. "I told you, he's just been under so much pressure. I don't know what else it could be. I don't know if it's memories of Vietnam, or the flood caused this, or what. Sometimes it's like he's off in the wild blue yonder."

"I'd judge he's in the wild blue yonder right now, Mrs. Phillips. Did anything go wrong last night?"

She shook her head. "Everything was perfectly normal. When I went to bed, he was watching the late movie. I don't even know what it was."

"You didn't argue? He wasn't drinking?"

"I told you—Darrell's not a drinker," she said, her testiness surfacing. "He doesn't take drugs, either, if that's your next question." The red curl was now so twisted out of shape that it curved like a spike away from the rest of her hair. "Darrell didn't actually do anything illegal, did he? He didn't kill me."

"But he can't just keep walking in here and confessing to murder."

"What are you suggesting?"

"I'd like to take him over to Shawnee Mental Health Center. They have a weekend distress center. Weekends and holidays are often their busy times. They could talk to him and keep an eye on him, and you could take him to your own doctor tomorrow like you planned. You could just sign him in and out. There'd be no court orders or anything."

"Darrell hates shrinks."

"I'm not so fond of them myself, but this can't go on. It's not doing anyone any good."

"What if they decide to keep him? What if they send him to the state mental hospital at Crimpton? It's a horrible place. You wouldn't do that to a responsible citizen, a businessman, would you? You might as well put him in jail."

Harter had to agree: Crimpton State Mental Hospital was a terrible place. Once he'd taken a tour of it with a police group, and for a week afterward he kept picturing the overcrowded wards where men and women shuffled along hallways, passed their time in front of TV sets, waiting to see which one would wail out first. If you weren't crazy when you went in, you might be when you got out.

"I don't believe they'll send your husband to Crimpton, Mrs. Phillips. They don't do that much anymore, especially if you're going to get private treatment for him. I'm trying to find a way to let you avoid trouble."

Vi Phillips seemed to weigh her choices. Finally she said, "Okay."

Harter tried not to show his relief that his bluff had worked. He had no idea what he'd have done if she'd refused to take her husband for observation. And, whatever Darrell Phillips' problems, Crimpton *was* too large a specter to want to face.

A few minutes later, he stood in the parking lot and watched Mrs. Phillips drive away with her husband in the back seat and Dave McManaway next to her in the front. Harter had convinced her she ought not make the transport alone, just in case something went wrong, and she'd convinced him Phillips would be more relaxed and comfortable in their own car. McManaway riding shotgun was the compromise.

He killed a little time outside, smoking a cigarette and staring at the mountains, and then he went in and chatted for a while about Saturday night's calls with Herr, the desk cop. When he'd heard enough, he impounded the Sunday paper and slipped away to his office.

A photo of the Governor and Senator, smiling with oversize scissors in their hands, was on the front page of *The News.* Inside, a full page of the local section was consumed by the museum opening. The politicians would be in heaven this morning. He wasn't, however.

He came across a story about the state's appeal to designate the flooded region as a federal disaster area, but three sentences into it, his mind drifted and he gave up trying to concentrate. He wandered down the hall to find a cup of coffee, and when McManaway returned, he was sitting in his chair, holding the Styrofoam cup, reading the numbers on the calendar on the wall, wondering if he should go visit Liz that afternoon, or whether he should keep working and go see Flathead Nash a day early. Nash would probably be home. It was Sunday, and the bars wouldn't be open for a few more hours.

"Well, I guess that's taken care of," said McManaway as he dropped into Caruthers' seat. "You gave her a pretty rough time."

"Not as rough as if her husband had *really* killed her," Harter replied. "I don't want to be responsible for him, do you? She's not really thinking of what's best for him, anyway. She's just concerned about their reputation, their standing in the community. She'll have him signed out before breakfast tomorrow."

"Have you ever had a case where a Vietnam vet went off the deep end?"

"Not really. I don't think it's as common as TV would have you believe. Oh, I've arrested a couple guys who claimed they got screwed up in Vietnam, but I also know a guy who has never been the same since Korea."

"I probably should know more about Vietnam than I do," said McManaway. "I was still in high school when the war ended. I hear people talk about the Sixties, but I can't say I understand all the tensions there must have been."

"I don't know that anyone does."

"What do you think will become of Phillips?"

"Got me. How about this? Someday when you've caught up on the phone calls about the bones, after you've finished sorting through the files and all, suppose you try and check out Phillips' military record. With any luck, we won't see him again, but if we do, it might be useful to know more about him."

McManaway nodded agreement. "Sounds reasonable," he said, but Harter had already turned away and was flipping through Caruthers' report of the 1967 hit-and-run.

When the ring destroyed the silence, the two of them stared at each other for a moment before McManaway reached for the receiver. Almost immediately, Harter wished he'd been the one to pick up the phone. The young cop's expression had turned so serious that he wondered if Sally had gone into labor early, if something awful had happened.

Finally, McManaway hung up and looked over at him. "They've found a body."

"Yeah?"

"They think it's Roger Wilton."

15

HARTER AND MCMANAWAY were barely out of their car before Wayne Smith was crossing the parking lot toward them. Actually, he was Sgt. Wayne Smith and he headed the state police detachment in the county.

They were standing in a graveled pulloff with three picnic tables, high on the old Ohio Road atop Black's Mountain. State troopers wandered about, searching the road, the bushes, the autumn-thinned woods for anything out of the ordinary.

"Where's the body, Wayne?" Harter asked.

Sgt. Smith nodded toward a picnic table near the trees. Harter could see the gray hair of someone leaning over on the other side of the table. He recognized Pete Epstein.

"It's out of your jurisdiction, of course, but we contacted you anyway," said Smith. "I remembered McManaway asking us about Roger Wilton on Friday. I figured you'd want to be in on this."

"You know why we're interested, I guess—all about the bones in Shantytown?" asked Harter.

"Half the world must have heard that story by now."

"Seems like it."

"Are you sure it's Roger Wilton?" McManaway asked.

Smith looked a little taken aback by the rookie detective's question. "It's either Roger Wilton, or someone planned this all out and went to a hell of a lot of trouble with falsified license photos and everything." He pulled a wallet out of his pocket and handed it to Harter. "We found this on the ground at the edge of the woods. There's no money in it, but I don't see it as a robbery. Someone stole whatever cash there was and tossed the billfold into the brush. I'd say it was an afterthought. We found a checkbook, too, and it was still in Wilton's back pocket."

The driver's license was from North Carolina and showed a Charlotte address. ROGER NASH WILTON. His mother had given him her maiden name as a middle one. BORN 7/27/48. MALE. WHITE. 160 LBS. 5'11". BROWN EYES.

Harter flipped through the plastic and found a Social Security card and a telephone calling card, but no credit cards. The only personal photo was an old, creased black-and-white of a grade school boy with unruly dark hair and fine features, just as Matt Curry had described the young Roger Wilton. The boy was next to a porch swing, and sitting on the swing was a woman in her thirties. From her hairdo and clothes, Harter judged the picture had been snapped one afternoon in the early or mid-1950s. He had no doubt it was Roger and Nan Wilton on the porch of the Egypt Street house.

Odd. Dorothy Merrill had claimed she didn't know where to lay her hands on a photograph of her mother, but her brother had carried one with him all these years.

"The checkbook has the same North Carolina address as the driver's license," said Sgt. Smith. "No wife's name's on the checks. The entry book shows that two days ago Wilton wrote a check for two hundred and ninety dollars, which just about cleared out the account. We can't find a car, but it's obvious he didn't jog up here from Charlotte. No sign of keys either. I guess when we find the car, we find the keys."

"Huh," Harter mumbled, not really concentrating on what Smith was saying. Instead, he was trying to force entry into the scene of the small boy and his mother, as if it were possible to climb up the porch steps, be there with them on the swing, and overhear their conversation.

Curry had described Nan as a good-looking woman, and he'd been right. It was easy to feel her appeal, even in the worn snapshot. Nothing about her relaxed pose, however, hinted at a wild temper. She didn't look like the sort to batter heads with skillets or throw knives in uncontrollable rage, but then, you never could tell. She didn't emit an aura of craziness at all, not even the toughness that so many middle-aged South Shawnee women did. There was something vulnerable about her. And from the way she eyed her son, Harter could imagine the see-no-evil-in-Roger streak that Curry had also described.

"Can I keep this picture?" he asked.

"We'll have to follow evidence procedures," Smith answered.

"Damn, Wayne. I've been working this case."

"Come on, Harter. What do you want me to do? We must be five miles outside the city limits. This isn't your terrain. I just can't hand everything over to you. Why do you figure Wilton was out here anyway?"

Harter shrugged. "Maybe he went for a drive with whoever killed him. Or maybe someone murdered him, then brought the body out to dump. Ever since they cut the interstate through the mountain to the north, there hasn't been much traffic here. You know as well as I do that this thing started in Shawnee, no matter where the body was found."

"You sound like Epstein." Smith pointed across the lot to where the medical examiner was still hunched over the body. "He thinks Wilton was dead when he was brought here, too. If that's so, then the killer knew the area well. When he was looking for a dumping ground, he remembered this old picnic area."

"He probably used to park out here," McManaway said.

Harter handed the wallet back to Smith and moved toward Epstein. The chill November wind made him zip up his black jacket as he walked. Sgt. Smith, with his damn procedures, reminded him of Caruthers. Stick to the regulations, the book, the letter of the law. Forget the spirit. Forget you were trying to find a murderer. Harter hoped he'd have better luck with Pete Epstein, who was not so bound by jurisdictional lines since he was medical examiner for the county as well as for the city.

Roger Wilton's corpse was flat on its back, about a yard on the other side of the picnic table. "How many bodies are we going to find this week, Pete?" Harter asked.

"At least I don't have to shovel around in the mud for this one," said Epstein.

"What do you think? No doubt it's Wilton?"

"Hell, the face matches the license photo, brown mustache and all. He appears to have been shot twice in the chest at a fairly close range. There's not much blood around, so I'd say the job was done somewhere else. When you find your killer, you might find traces of blood in his vehicle. The vehicle was parked over there. You can see the marks in the gravel from dragging the body by the feet from there to here. There aren't any clear footprints or tire tracks. The mountaintop has pretty much dried out since the rains on Monday and Tuesday."

"When do you think he was shot?"

"Last night. I'd guess before midnight."

"Sounds likely."

"Why?" snapped Sgt. Smith. "You suddenly psychic?"

"It's simpler than that. A guy called me yesterday afternoon. He wouldn't tell me who he was, but wanted to know if I was the one investigating the bones and he wanted to meet me at eleven o'clock last night. I was there, but he wasn't. I'd bet the world it was Roger Wilton and the reason he didn't keep our appointment was that he'd gone to see someone else beforehand."

"And *that* someone else killed him?" asked McManaway.

"Two and two are usually four," said Pete Epstein as he rose out of his squat.

"I trust you'll see I get a copy of any report you give the state police," Harter said to him.

"It's public record. But don't expect much more than I've told you. We'll come up with a more exact time of death and some info about the weapon, but it'll most likely be pretty cut and dried."

"You still want the goddamn photograph?" Wayne Smith asked.

"Sure," said Harter. "But I'll go through procedures. I wouldn't want to rock the boat. You know me, Wayne. Yes sir, no sir, every screw turned according to the manual."

Smith pulled out the wallet, opened it and slid the old picture free of its plastic casing. "Here, Harter. Shit. Make yourself a copy and send me back the original. I don't even know what value it has."

"Neither do I," said Harter as he reached for the photo of Roger and. his mother. "I just wanted it. Maybe I'm sentimental."

"You son of a bitch."

Harter smiled. "I guess you guys are going to work the North Carolina end, aren't you? I mean, you'll contact people down there, for whatever good it is?"

"Yeah."

"And you'll keep us up to date?"

Smith nodded.

"Why don't you release the driver's license photo to the press?" Harter suggested. "Wilton's vehicle has got to be parked someplace. Someone must have seen him in the last couple days. A picture in the newspaper could cut out a lot of leg-work."

"Any other orders, General?"

"Prepare to attack at dawn." Harter turned to McManaway. 'You ready to go?"

They were halfway down Black's Mountain when McManaway piped up. "You were pretty rough on him."

"On Wayne Smith? Shit, he's been rough on me before. It all evens out. Is *rough* the word for the day? You said I was rough on Vi Phillips, too."

"So, what do you want to do now?" McManaway asked.

Before answering, Harter stared out the windshield at the road screwing down. What he wanted to do, how he wanted to spend the rest of the day, where he wanted to be, wasn't necessarily what he'd end up doing.

What he said was: "We're going to drop you off at your place so you can have Sunday chicken with Sally. The two of you won't have many more quiet afternoons together. Soon there'll be a crying, hungry, wet baby around. Once I unload you, I'll head out the Avenue to let Roger Wilton's father and sister know what happened. They shouldn't have to read it in the paper."

Then, he had a hunch he might end up driving through the West Side past Liz's studio and see if he had the guts to stop and see her. If not, he'd go out to the overlook and look down on the city for a while.

16

THE SILENCE roared so loud that it nearly gave him an earache. As he watched the old man stare out his bedroom window, Harter kept seeing the vacant eyes of Darrell Phillips, the appliance dealer who imagined he'd murdered his wife. Crazy, how a mind works overtime to fabricate connections, intertwinings between people, events, places that have nothing to do with each other on the surface, except they've crossed your life somehow, or your life has crossed them.

Wheat Wilton simply sat in his chair, his eyes hypnotized by the brick wall across the Avenue. If anything was happening inside his stricken brain, there was no way to find out. At least Harter couldn't figure out a way. He wished he could stick a needle into Wilton's thin arm and draw out facts and memories like a Red Cross nurse draws out blood.

Standing in the doorway of the bedroom, Harter felt like a cruel inquisitor. Dorothy Merrill had argued that her brother had been out of her father's thoughts for more than seventeen years and it would only harm the old man to tell him about Roger. Still, Harter couldn't shake off Thursday afternoon, when he'd mentioned Matt Curry and sensed some response in Wilton's eyes. He believed the boy's name might jar something loose, too. Eventually Dorothy had given in and slowly led him up the steps. Now, faced with the old man, Harter began to think he was making a mistake, and a harsh one at that.

At least Dorothy was taking her good slow time working up to it. She was small-talking with her father in a tone that was gentler and more soothing than her everyday voice. Now and then, she glanced at Harter to be certain he hadn't changed his mind.

Neither Dorothy nor Bill Merrill had shown much emotion when Harter broke the bad news to them. Bill had reached for the remote control and turned down the television volume, then slumped back in his chair. Dorothy had turned a bit white, then seated herself on the end of the couch near her husband. After a minute the color had returned to her face and she'd said, "So that's how it ends."

So that's how it ends. So that's what became of Roger. It wasn't like she was particularly surprised. It was like she'd just finished watching a movie.

Now Dorothy was getting to the point with her father. "You remember Detective Harter, Daddy? He came to visit the other day." The old man stared. "Well, he's come back. He says Roger has returned to Shawnee."

She stopped, and both she and Harter studied Wheat Wilson's face for some flicker.

Nothing. Nothing at all.

Dorothy's lips were beginning to form words. She was about to inform her father that Roger had been found dead. But before she launched into it, she looked again at Harter. It was too cruel a move, he decided. He shook his head to tell her not to let the words come out. Then he walked out into the hall.

He heard Dorothy say, "I'll bring you your Sunday dinner in an hour or so, Daddy," and then she too left the room and joined him at the head of the stairs. "Thank you for backing off."

"Hell, it wasn't going to do any good anyway. I didn't want to take the chance of making him worse."

"So, you have a heart after all?"

Yeah, he had a heart. Dorothy Merrill, like Vi Phillips and probably a lot of others, might doubt it, but he surely had a heart, and sometimes it hurt, though he wasn't fond of letting anyone know.

Downstairs, he sat at the kitchen table, trying to figure out what to ask next, trying to get himself back on track, while Dorothy puttered around opening the oven and inspecting the ham that was baking.

"It was probably a lousy idea to come here this afternoon," he said. "But I thought I might as well tell you about your brother myself. I bet the state police will contact you before long. They might even want you to identify the body."

"God, what an awful idea." She opened a cabinet, took down two cups, poured coffee into them, and brought one over to him. "Did you say Roger was living in North Carolina?"

"According to his driver's license."

"Was he married? Did he have any kids?"

"We don't know yet."

"I can't believe that unreliable bastard would ever settle down and support a family," said Bill Merrill.

Harter hadn't even noticed that Dorothy's husband had entered the kitchen and was leaning against the wall behind him. Luckily, Bill wasn't a big bruiser with a switchblade in his hand, hiding in a dark underpass, ready to jump out of the shadows like one of the molemen.

"You don't speak very highly of your late brother-in-law," Harter said to him.

"I've had to work for everything I ever got. Roger had it all handed to him, and he wasted it. Not that Dorothy's people had much, you understand, but whatever the boy wanted, her mother saw that he got it. All the time I was working in the steel mill and sweating to make mortgage payments on this place and raising sons, Roger was loafing at college and being handed his heart's desire. And I mean loafing. He decked out like a hippie and talked against the war and all. He was into drugs, too, if you ask me."

"You don't know that for sure," said Dorothy, cutting him off. "We never saw much of Roger. By the time he was out of high school, Bill and I had been married for years. Besides, we don't know what he did after he left home. He could have straightened up."

"I know what Wheat said about him," her husband said.

Harter wished he could disappear so he wouldn't intimidate the Merrills from really going at each other. But they were aware of his presence, and despite the hard stares they threw at each other, they fell into a silence as thunderous as the one that swirled around Wheat Wilton's head.

Odd, for Dorothy to be so suddenly protective of her younger brother. Only three days before, she'd made no pretense about the fact she had no use for him. Harter wondered if it was always like that, if people always defended their own kin, even when they felt otherwise, if the Merrills had been fighting this same argument for twenty years, or if Roger's death had merely opened some soft vein of family reveries in her.

Dorothy wasn't wearing her Shawnee Bombers T-shirt today, but rather a burgundy dress, as if she'd just come back from church. Even dressed up, she reminded Harter of his first impression of her. There was something about her face that just missed being pretty. She'd probably never been really pretty. She didn't much resemble her mother, the striking woman in the old photo in his pocket.

On impulse, to wreck the heavy quiet and start them talking again, Harter pulled out the picture. "This was in Roger's wallet," he said.

Bill grabbed it before his wife could move. "That's Roger and Nan." He walked across the linoleum and handed the photo to Dorothy. "When would you say—1955 or so?"

As she stared at it, he got himself a cup and poured some coffee. Then he leaned against the stove next to his wife.

For a moment, Harter thought Dorothy was going to cry. But, just as she'd recuperated fast from the news of her brother's death, she recovered again. She returned the snapshot to Harter and sank into a chair at the table. "I remember the day Daddy dug out his old box camera and took that picture."

"Mother and son," mumbled Harter. Then, speaking clearer: "He does look like the apple of her eye. Actually, Matt Curry said exactly what your husband did—that your mother spoiled your brother a lot."

"Matt Curry, again," she said, a little sarcastically. "But I guess they're right. She sure went out of her way to cater to Roger."

"Bent over backwards," added Bill. "You'd have thought he was her only child. I don't believe Dorothy ever felt like her mother really loved her."

Another cold stare passed between the Merrills, almost like Dorothy was angry he had divulged another confidence. This was obviously not a day she would choose to live again.

"I've met Nan's brother," said Harter, trying to steer them to a new subject. He omitted mentioning that Curry had been with David Nash at the museum opening. "What do they call him—Flathead? I'm supposed to talk to him more tomorrow. Does he keep in touch with you?"

"He came to see Daddy on Friday. I don't know the last time we saw my uncle. It was probably all the stories about the bones that made him come. He was always pretty close to my mother, but not particularly to the rest of us. He'd do things to make her happy. When he'd come by, he'd always have candy in his pocket, but he never really stayed long. He'd make other stops on Egypt Street, like—"

"Like?"

"Like Matt Curry's." Dorothy tried to change the subject by asking, "Do you know anything new about the bones?"

"We feel they date to the mid-sixties, and that they're the remains of a young woman. I figure Roger would have been in high school or college at the time."

"You think they have something to do with him?" Bill asked.

Harter shrugged. "The news probably brought him back here."

"Nothing he could have done would surprise me, not that one," said Bill.

"I keep wondering whether whatever happened is also connected with Nan Wilton being killed in the hit-and-run, or whether it's just coincidence," Harter said.

"God, it's awful to have all this stuff dragged back up," Dorothy said. "The last couple days, people seem to be looking at us different, like we had something to do with the body. I keep telling everyone I left Egypt Street long ago. Then they ask about Daddy. He'd have been there. When word gets out about Roger, people will really ask questions."

Harter thought she seemed more upset over what people might think than she had over hearing about her brother's murder. But maybe that wasn't so strange a reaction.

"What time is it?" Bill asked, like he was trying to break up the conversation.

"Almost two," Dorothy replied. "We'll have to get a move on if we're going to have dinner before you go to work."

Harter recognized his exit cue. "Where do you work now that the steel mill's closed?" he asked Bill as he stood up.

"I've got two jobs actually. Neither's much better than minimum wage. I work weekdays as a custodian and part time, like this evening, at a convenience store over on Furnace Street. Hell, I can see the mill from there. No matter what they say, it's still tough times. They may be creating a bunch of jobs, but none of them pay what the old ones did. Try and hold a family together and pay doctors' bills and all, and you'd see. Dorothy works, too. She's a waitress two nights a week. She'd work more if she could, but someone has to take care of Wheat. If he didn't get his railroad retirement, I don't know what we'd do."

"Did you work last night?" Harter asked. He knew the question was transparent, that it was obvious he was trying to find out what they might have been doing when Roger was killed.

"No," Bill said. "Dorothy did, until about ten-thirty. I was here with Wheat. We told you, we didn't see Roger. We had no idea he was in town."

Harter started for the back door and, just before going out, turned and said, "Good luck." He was nearly to the gate at the end of the alleyway when he realized he was still holding the photo of Nan and Roger. He stuffed the picture in his pocket, pushed open the gate, and stepped out on the Avenue. As he opened his car door, he glanced up at the second-floor window of the Merrill house. Inside sat Wheat Wilton, like a god-damned sphinx.

17

HE WAS UP at the overlook on the mountain, leaning against his car, surveying his domain, Shawnee, when he noticed that, down in the bottom of the bowl, the river was slowly rising, like God was ladling more milky soup into it and Mother Nature, Earth Goddess, was smiling her approval.

The thick river water was starting to wash out of its trench and over the towpath along the canal. As it slithered across the floodplain, it began to swirl, churning up topsoil, all the while making its way toward Egypt Street. It was like he had binocular vision, he could see it so clearly, so closely.

Outlined in a second-story window was an old man, and Harter had no trouble focusing in on the solemn face of Wheat Wilton staring out at the river pouring across the field toward his house. He could zero in on the old man's eyes, and as if he could read Wheat's mind, he sensed the old man knew tragedy was coming. But down on the front porch—*somehow Harter could see straight through the house with an X-ray vision like Superman's*—down on the front porch, an attractive woman sat on a swing watching a boy, and the two of them were unaware—*at least he thought they were unaware*—of the impending flood, years ahead of them.

Across the street, another man sat on a porch, and even though the fellow looked only about forty, Harter knew the solid, muscled guy was Matt Curry. Matt Curry, just staring across Egypt Street. Whether he was monitoring the river sprinting toward him or whether he was studying Nan and Roger Wilton, Harter couldn't tell.

The water rose another notch, edging closer to the shed behind the Wilton's home, and Curry's face seemed to age a year with every foot that the foul, muddy river gained on the shed. First, the smile creases near his thin lips became deeper, spaded in, and then the lips themselves seemed to drop a bit—*in sadness?*—and the eyes lost a few degrees of their sparkle, and the forehead sprang a wrinkle and elongated as the hairline receded, and the hair turned from dark to gray, strand by strand, line by line, sparkle by sparkle.

A car, a 1950s Plymouth, long and low, with sharp pointed wings, sped along the street, screeching to a halt between Nan Wilton and Matt Curry. A red-faced man with a flattop stuck his head out the Plymouth window and waved and then, as if he caught sight of the high water coming, tore away in a fog of exhaust.

By now the boy, *Roger*, was a teenager. He scurried off the porch and peeked around the side of the house, looking back at the shed, like he was suddenly aware it was in danger, like he was suddenly aware of the coming danger. He turned, called something to his mother. As his lips moved, he grew older still, his body filling out to adult size, his dark hair lengthening to a Beatles cut, then growing on past it until it is as long as a San Francisco hippie's, and it must be 1967, Roger's last full year in Shantytown, the year his mother is killed, the year all hell breaks loose, like a river overflowing its banks, and there are antiwar demonstrations and Lyndon Johnson, drawling Texan, is president and Vietnam draft calls are high. In another part of Shawnee, a young Darrell Phillips is nervously opening an invitation from Uncle Sam.

Now Roger Wilton has an earring in his hand, a half-moon of ivory, and in his mouth is a cigarette. His mother doesn't seem to notice. It is hand-rolled, a sloppy job, and he lights it and inhales deeply and it's like he lifts off the ground just as the shed is lifted out of the backyard and begins to float downstream to Paw Paw, Hancock, Shepherdstown, Harpers Ferry, and on to Washington, like stops being announced by a railroad conductor.

Everything is underwater now. All of Shantytown. Harter twists his neck so he can see upstream, upriver toward the downtown flood-control walls. He is young himself, standing with his father watching the high walls be put up, and now they are in place and the creek is rising, coming up under the West Side bridge, threatening the continental drift of one-half of the city away from the other, separating his East End from Liz's West Side.

Through the downpour, he can see Liz standing on the West Side bank. He wants to cross over to her, but the high waters turn him back, and all he can do is stand there as the river widens between them. *And now the molemen are coming.* They canoe the dangerous river like they are invincible. *Anything can happen.* They will beat him with their paddles if he tries to swim over. He knows they will beat him, but he wants to try anyway.

It's almost impossible to see Liz now. The rain is coming down so hard, the creek is risin', the ghost canoes, the floating bones, the soup keeps ladling down on top of him.

Metal spoon, lightning bolt.

Waterfall crash, thundershot.

In the midst of the torrent, a knockout bell.

Eyes forced open. Reach for the phone.

"You want me to come by and pick you up or you want to meet me at the motel?"

Still groggy. "What?"

"You mean you're not even up yet, Harter? It's Monday morning. This is Dave McManaway. The driver's license photo in the newspaper paid off. A guy called an hour ago. We know where Roger Wilton spent Friday night. We're checking for prints now. I left a message at headquarters for you, but I was starting to worry."

"Where are you?"

"The Goodnight Motel."

"On Gap Street?"

"You got it."

"I'll be there in twenty minutes."

He dropped the phone into its rack, gave his eyes a rub, then threw back the covers, swung his legs out of bed, and headed straight for the kitchen. He turned up the burner to reheat last night's coffee, still in the pot.

In the living room, he lit a cigarette and thumbed through the phone book for Flathead Nash's number. He'd have to postpone his visit with Nash for a few hours. He wondered whether Nash already knew about his nephew's death, or whether he'd be the one to break the news as he had with the Merrills.

Dialing, he glanced out the window, down toward the top floor and roof of the old passenger station, *the museum.* Off in the West Side distance, he could see the spire of the church near Pete Epstein's office. Looking a little south, he could almost see the roof of Liz's studio. It wasn't even raining.

18

THE GOODNIGHT MOTEL wouldn't have made any travel guide's list of five-star accommodations. The place might have seemed comfortable enough in the late 1940s when it was built, but somewhere down the years it had dropped into dinginess. There was no way it could compete with the new Holiday Inn or any of a half-dozen other lodging establishments in the city. You almost expected the neon sign out front to blast CHEAP ROOMS on and off. Harter guessed that was why Roger Wilton had registered there. Roger had to make his couple hundred bucks last. Then again, Roger had been away for more than seventeen years, so the Goodnight could have been the only motel he remembered.

Even with its cheap rooms, Harter didn't believe the motel was going to benefit much from all those tourists Shawnee was supposed to attract in the future. It wasn't near the new railroad museum, or the park, or the big Victorian homes in the West Side, or any other spot that was likely to draw a crowd. The Goodnight was just inside the city line in South Shawnee, not far from the railroad yards and offices. Maybe that was another reason Roger had picked the place. It was close to Shantytown.

The customers in the motel's best days had probably been people in town on railroad business. But later it had become little more than a string of rooms let for the evening. You could drive by almost any night, check out the license plates, and learn who was screwing who. Some of Shawnee's most illustrious citizens had rolled and tumbled on those lumpy mattresses. If you put cameras behind the mirrors on the walls, you could easily come up with the stuff of pornography or blackmail, but the camera lenses would have to be strong enough to shoot through the deposit of perspiration and semen on the cracked mirror glass.

McManaway was sitting on a plastic chair next to the bed, sorting through a tan travel bag, when Harter came in.

"About time you got here. They took the fingerprints down to the lab a few minutes ago. I don't hold out much hope of them helping a lot. Could all belong to Roger Wilton. The motel owner says he didn't see anyone visit the room. Hell, with this place, the prints could belong to somebody who was here for an hour the night before Wilton showed up."

"When did Roger check in?" Harter asked.

"Friday night. He apparently went off a few times on Saturday. The owner says the last time he saw Wilton was about seven-thirty Saturday evening. He drove away and never came back. The guy's in his office if you want to talk to him."

"I'll get to him. What about the car?"

"A 'seventy-nine Subaru with North Carolina tags. We haven't found it, or the keys either. I've put out a bulletin."

"Good," said Harter, sitting on the edge of the unmade bed. He pointed to the tan plastic bag. "Anything in there?"

"Clothes. An extra pair of jeans, a couple clean shirts, underwear, socks. I guess he figured he might be here a while. There's a toothbrush and a razor in the bathroom. Nothing unusual."

"No drugs?"

"Haven't found any."

"No notebook or letters or phone numbers or anything like that?"

McManaway shook his head.

On the stand beside the bed, next to a green glass ashtray, was a cassette tape recorder and a pile of cassettes. "Did he have good taste in music?" Harter asked. "Any John Lennon?"

McManaway smiled. "Mostly sixties stuff. That's probably what he listened to. I'm like that. We like the music we grew up with. I'll bet his car didn't have a tape player so he brought that along for the ride."

Harter looked through the plastic cassette boxes. *Beatles. Cream. Grateful Dead. Rolling Stones. Jimi Hendrix.* He pressed the play button on the machine to hear what Roger had been listening to shortly before his death. The player immediately clicked off. Harter pushed EJECT and, when the door flipped up, removed the tape. It was a Maxell cassette, not a prerecorded one, and it was unmarked. He slid the plastic container back into the recorder, punched REWIND, and watched the little reels turn until the left one was full and the right one empty. He hit PLAY again, and turned up the volume.

At first there was only the static of blank tape. Then came the words.

What the fuck am I doing Didn't want to do it then either

It was a male voice. Soft, not rough. Slightly southern, perhaps from years spent in North Carolina. Harter had no doubt he was listening to Roger Wilton. He was sure it was the same person who'd wanted to meet him at the station.

Just talking into this damn box Trying to get my thoughts ordered Hard to line all the ducks in a row

The space between phrases heightened the uncertainty— the sadness—in Roger's voice. Harter could picture him lying on the motel bed late Friday night or Saturday afternoon, talking to himself, almost psychoanalyzing himself as the cassette recorder's built-in microphone picked up his words.

Didn't know what to do that night either Nineteen sixty-seven Mom In the shed Lucky the old man was away They'd called him out to a train wreck in the country someplace and be was gone every night that week

We knew we had to do it then The old bastard never would have understood He'd have climbed on his high horse

The "old man" had to be Wheat Wilton. Matt Curry had told Harter that Roger's father had also been away the night Nan Wilton was killed. Whatever the old man would or wouldn't have understood in 1967 was a dead point. Wilton surely couldn't understand much now.

Mom said it wasn't good but it was the right thing She promised to help so it didn't happen to me what—

A loud truck went by, blotting out the words. Harter pushed STOP, then REWIND to take the tape back a bit.

—tard never would have understood He'd have climbed on his high horse Mom said it wasn't good but it was the right thing She promised to help so it didn't happen to me what—

There was the damn truck again. It was on the tape. Missing words, like a Richard Nixon Special. Truck passing.

—Night In the shed We pushed We moved everything out of the way and kept dampening the ground so it was easier to dig So the same thing didn't happen to me Christ I can't do this Can't risk putting this down on tape Got people to see Can't use their names Have to change all the names like Dylan sang in "Desolation Row" She—

There was a click and, once more, only the hiss of blank tape.

After a while, McManaway said, "He's probably erased the rest, if there was anything there to start with. What do you make of it?"

"I picture him lying in bed, all by himself, trying to make some sense of why he'd come back to Shawnee," said Harter. "Recording his words somehow helped him to think. Some people keep diaries, I suppose. Don't you ever talk to yourself like that?"

"Once in a while."

"Sometimes I have to change all the names, throw them all in a pot, stir them up and see what brews, too," Harter said, thinking of his trips to the overlook. "I'd say we now know a few things, though. Roger sure as hell knew who was buried in that shed, since he and his mother did the burying. His father was away, so I'd almost bet it was December Nineteen sixty-seven, about the time Nan Wilton was killed in the hit-and-run. When you get back to headquarters, I want you to really comb Caruthers' report of the accident. I have to go see Nan's brother, then I'll be down. Take the tape and the recorder. Play the whole thing through just to be sure there's not something later on."

There was a rap at the door and Harter turned off the recorder before he motioned for McManaway to see who it was.

Who it was, was Sgt. Wayne Smith of the state police, and what he said was, "Thought I'd check this out myself, Harter. I shared our info with you. Now it's your turn."

"Look around all you like, Wayne. Nothing much here. The motel owner saw Roger Wilton's picture in the paper. I told you that might be worth a shot. You know, we can cuss the media all we like, but we use them, too. Sometimes they make our job easier. Have you heard anything from North Carolina?"

"It's taking shape," Smith said. "Wilton lived in an apartment in Charlotte. Police down there didn't find much when they got in the place, but they've talked to a few people. Landlady says Wilton left Friday morning, which jibes with him showing up here that night. He didn't tell her where he was going or why. Apparently, he changed jobs a lot. He's been working recently as a groundskeeper at a golf course."

"Any family?"

"Divorced. His ex-wife says they were married in Nineteen seventy-eight and separated two years later—right after their daughter was born. She believes Wilton couldn't handle being a father. Everything was fine before the baby, but then he went crazy just going to work, coming home, and tending the kid. I guess some men are like that."

"Some men, maybe," said McManaway, the expectant father.

"Did she say whether Roger ever mentioned Shawnee?" Harter asked.

"She knew he'd grown up in the mountains, and that was about it. She hadn't heard about the bones being found here. He told her he left Shawnee in the late sixties and hitchhiked across country a couple times, eventually landing in North Carolina. He led her to believe all his close relatives were dead."

"Maybe they were," said Harter, thinking of the photo of Roger and his mother.

"The ex-wife claims she hasn't seen much of him for years. Other than holidays, he didn't visit the daughter a whole lot. She had no idea he had come up here. She doesn't know if he had a girlfriend. We're trying to check on it."

"You know we haven't located his car yet?" said Harter. "A Nineteen seventy-nine Subaru."

Smith nodded. "My troopers are keeping their eyes open. I take it you'll see I get any reports on fingerprints and whatever you found here."

"Sure," said Harter, glancing over at the tape recorder. "How about Roger Wilton's autopsy results?"

"Epstein says he'll have it this afternoon. You'll get a copy." Smith looked around the room. "If this place is a washout, I'd at least like to talk to the motel owner while I'm here."

The springs rattled as Harter pushed himself up from the bed. "I was just about to do that myself. Guy runs a nice place, doesn't he?"

"Wouldn't know," Smith said as they stepped out on the porch that fringed the row of boxes.

"Wait a minute," Harter said, and he ducked back in the motel room. Whispering, so Smith couldn't hear, he told McManaway, "Make a couple copies of that tape and send one to Wayne."

19

THE PROPRIETOR of the Goodnight Motel wasn't any more pleasant than the establishment he ran. He had a slight accent that Harter decided was English worn away from years in Shawnee. Every time the guy spoke, a spray of spit emerged with his words, making you want to stand on the far side of the drab office from him. What he had to offer wasn't worth the danger of being infected with his germs.

Roger Wilton had arrived after ten on Friday night, November 8. He'd paid in cash for three nights and suggested he might stay longer. He wasn't concerned with luxuries, just wanted the cheapest room available. He'd taken a few things out of his green Subaru and disappeared into number 14. The owner hadn't noticed any visitors, but he wasn't in the business of keeping track of such things. As far as calls, the rooms didn't have phones, so maybe Roger used the pay phone, he didn't know.

Saturday morning, Roger had come into the office for a cup of coffee before driving off somewhere. By mid-afternoon he was back, and then he'd gone out again in the evening, about seven-thirty. The Subaru was still gone Sunday morning, but the proprietor didn't worry. He had his money up front. Besides, he never questioned people going about their business, and he never questioned their business. Wasn't until he saw the photo in the morning paper that he gave it much thought. He had no doubt the man in the picture—the man whose body had been found on Black's Mountain—had been his customer, so he'd phoned the cops. He hadn't touched anything in the room. He'd never laid eyes on Roger Wilton before Friday night, he insisted over and over, as if Harter and Sgt. Smith were trying to blame him for something. He was only being a good citizen.

From the motel, Harter drove to Flathead Nash's house. He hoped Nan's younger brother was also going to play the good citizen. The little he'd seen of David Nash at the museum opening hadn't been inspiring. When told that Harter wanted to ask him a few questions, his response had been, *Well, you can ask.* Any idiot could ask. Breaking through Nash's tough-guy act might be tough.

Harter drove up the hill that divided South Shawnee and the East End. On the down side, he passed the elementary school where he had spent six years. Each morning, rain, snow, or shine, he'd hiked up the steep grade to school, but now, like so much of his childhood, it was gone. Or rather, it still stood there, like the passenger station, but it no longer served as a grade school. It was now a senior citizens' center. You could spend both your first and your second childhoods there.

He turned onto the road that ran up to the hospital. Just past the huge building, he turned again and steered down a narrow street until he figured he was close to Nash's house. He parked in the first spot he came to, got out and began checking numbers.

Matt Curry had told him this was the neighborhood where Nan Wilton—*Nan Nash*—had grown up. Harter wondered what it would have been like fifty years before, and decided it would have been much the same. With one or two exceptions, the houses were older dwellings, two-story brick affairs crammed close together on the hilly, thin street. Most of the homes seemed well taken care of. Some of the tiny yards had the look of generations of tending.

Flathead Nash's place wasn't much different from the rest, though the windows could have used a washing and the white trimwork needed a paint job.

When Harter had called Nash that morning to postpone their meeting, Nash had acted as if he didn't know his nephew's body had been found. He hadn't yet seen a newspaper and the Merrills hadn't bothered to let him know. There'd been a pronounced pause after Harter had dropped the knowledge on him. Harter had pondered whether he should call Matt Curry, too, but he wasn't sure why. Maybe Nash already had.

The Flathead Nash who opened the door didn't appear any more morose or depressed than the Flathead Nash he'd run into at the station on Saturday. The big guy motioned him in without a word and led him through the front room and back to the kitchen. Nash wasn't the worst housekeeper that Harter had ever seen. A few newspapers littered the living room and there was a bit of dust atop the coffee table, but the disarray wasn't out of control. Nash was wearing the same pants and shirt he had at the museum opening. There was something almost swaggering, or staggering, about his gait as he padded through the house in his slippers.

Nash sat at the kitchen table in the same spot he'd obviously been vegetating before Harter had knocked. A beer, a pack of cigarettes, and an ashtray were laid out in front of him. Pushed off to one side was a plate that showed the remains of egg yoke.

Without invitation, Harter sat across from him, near the back door. "This your family place? This where you and your sister grew up?" he asked.

"No, that's a few doors up the street," Nash answered in his rough voice. He lit an unfiltered Camel. "Want a beer?"

"I'll take some coffee if you got it," said Harter, lighting his own cigarette.

"Have to be instant."

"Fine with me."

Nash got up, went over to the stove, and turned on the burner under a teakettle that was next to an unwashed skillet with a spatula in it.

Harter watched him lift a cup off the drainboard, then find a clean spoon and a jar of instant coffee. "You still work for the railroad?"

"I don't work no more," said Nash without looking at him. "Bad back. I do a few odd jobs now and again. I make ends meet. The house is paid off."

"Everybody seems to have worked for the railroad. You, Matt Curry, your brother-in-law Wheat."

"What else was there to do around here?"

There mustn't have been much water in the kettle because it was already whistling. Nash took a drag on his Camel, then poured hot water into the cup and brought the cup over to the table. He pointed toward a sugar bowl and a container of milk.

"Black," Harter said.

"Eats out your insides," said Nash, reaching for his beer.

"Sorry I surprised you with the news of your nephew."

"It was a surprise and it wasn't. Never figured I'd hear of him again, but I always figured he'd end in a bad way."

"What do you mean?"

"I mean what I said. After he drifted off years ago, I knew we'd hear some day that he was dead. I'm sure plenty of people always figured I'd end in a bad way, too, but I'm still here, cussing and grouching."

"Roger didn't try to contact you Friday night or Saturday, did he?"

"Don't know if he tried or not. Never got me if he did."

"What'd you think of your nephew?"

"I think he did what the hell he wanted, and I ain't going to jump on him for that. If you ask me, he should have gone in the Marines, but that's water over the dam. Nan spoiled him, but Roger and I always got along."

"I hear she'd go along with whatever he wanted."

"You heard right."

"But Wheat wouldn't."

"Don't see Wheat as no kind of hero. Nan was the one with the hot temper, but Wheat could be cold-hearted mean. He wasn't the sort whose blood boiled. He was one of them that calculated everything."

"Did he and Nan fight?"

"Don't know what went on when they was in private. No business of mine."

"How'd they get together, the two of them?"

"I was little and didn't pay much attention. Nan was eight years older than me. She was working in the union office when she met him, and then she got pregnant, though my mother never wanted none of us to say it out loud. So they got hitched, that's all. Wasn't the way Ma wanted it."

"What do you mean?"

"Ma wanted Nan to be a nurse, 'cause she herself always wanted to be a real nurse. See, Ma was sort of a midwife. This was a long time ago, you know. Women didn't have all their babies in hospitals, particularly in South Shawnee and out in the country. They couldn't afford to in the thirties, so they'd call Ma and she'd help deliver 'em. I always judged that's why she wanted a house up here by the hospital. It made her feel almost official somehow, being up here near doctors and nurses. Anyway, Ma wanted Nan to be a nurse. She was supposed to work in the union office a couple years, save her money and then go to nursing school, but she got knocked up and wound up with Wheat."

"Did your sister ever try to go back to school after she was married?"

"She had Dorothy, then Roger, and Wheat wouldn't hear of it. A man's supposed to support his family, as he saw it. I know what he meant, but she would have been a good nurse. So would Ma. Nan was a hell of a lot brighter than Wheat. She got all the brains in the family, not me. Roger was smart, too, but he didn't always show it."

"You're not very fond of your brother-in-law, are you?"'

"Just because Wheat's old and sick don't mean he ain't an asshole."

"There was a newspaper article a year or two ago about two brothers in Massachusetts who didn't speak for twenty-five years, then died on the same day."

"You wishing a stroke on me? No matter what I thought of him, Wheat's goddamn sad enough now. I saw him the other day."

"The Merrills told me you were there. Why?"

"The bones, I guess. They made me think of him and Nan."

"You have any ideas about the bones?"

Flathead shook his head and reached for another Camel.

"How about Roger? Any ideas about him?" Harter asked.

"Don't believe I seen him since Nan's funeral."

"Saturday, you told me you were out of town when she was run down."

"Yeah, but I was back in time for the burying."

"Your brother-in-law was out of town the night it happened, too, wasn't he? Must have been a big shock to come home and find her dead."

"It was a shock for all of us."

"Roger was going to the community college at the time, right?"

"So they say. Never knew the details myself."

"Was he upset at the funeral?"

"About as upset as anyone that's mother just got run over. What the hell kind of question is that?"

"Sorry. It was a bum thing to ask. But tell me, did you ever meet any of Roger's friends? Do you know if he had a girlfriend?"

"Wouldn't know no names or faces after all these years. Not sure I ever did. The couple times I saw him, his hair kept getting longer and he was hanging around with others like that. No one paid me to keep tabs on him. I wasn't his old man."

"How did he get along with his sister and her husband?"

"Wouldn't know. Never stayed in touch with 'em."

"Dorothy seems to have been closer to her father than her mother."

Flathead gave a shrug, and Harter knew he'd just about pulled everything out of him that he was going to be able to. "Thanks."

"For what?" asked Nash.

"For the chat," said Harter, getting up from the table.

"No need to thank me. I ain't exactly inviting you to drop in whenever the hell you please."

"I ain't asking you to."

They were halfway through the front room to the door when Flathead stopped cold and pointed at a picture on the wall. "That's us, the whole clan. Ma, and my father, and me, and everyone on the day Nan graduated high school. I'm the little one, you believe that? Hair combed and shoes shined. Times change."

Harter stared at the hand-tinted photograph. Nan Nash, wearing a cap and gown, stood next to her proud mother. Clumped around them were the rest of the Nash family. It *was* hard to believe Flathead Nash had ever been a cheery-faced kid.

Nan was twelve or fifteen years younger than in the photo of her and Roger on the porch on Egypt Street, but he'd studied the other picture enough times to recognize her. If the colorist had it right, her long hair and clear eyes were both dark brown. Her bright red lips were curved into an enormous smile.

She looked like she had the whole world ahead of her.

20

HARTER COULDN'T GET Nan Wilton's pretty face out of his head as he left her brother's house. He kept seeing her as he got in his car and pulled away from the curb. But he'd barely driven a block before they called him on the police radio and her image evaporated.

They'd located Roger Wilton's car on the street in front of the high school, not far away. He turned onto the road that circled by the hospital's emergency entrance and twisted its way uphill until it came out across from the school's football stadium. He knew the entwined streets as well as he knew the lines on his palm, and he knew where they broke off or hit dead ends.

Wilton's green Subaru was parked almost straight across from the main doors of East Shawnee High, near three police cars. Uniformed cops surrounded the vehicle.

"No idea how long it's been there," a neighborhood man was telling McManaway as Harter walked up. "No way to keep track of all the cars on this street. They had a football game Friday night, then some goings-on, a dance or something Saturday night, and on weekdays the whole damn block is filled with students' and teachers' cars. You just can't worry about who's parked up here."

"What time was the dance over on Saturday night?" Harter asked.

"I don't know. Eleven, eleven-thirty. Before midnight," the man said. "Unless there's a ruckus, none of us pay much mind. It's the price you pay for living near the high school."

"Thanks," McManaway said to the guy.

Then, as they walked toward the Subaru, he said to Harter, "At least the mystery of the missing keys is over. They were in the ignition. But I doubt Wilton drove the thing up here, unless he was pretty disconnected that night. The keys were inside and the doors were locked. I'd bet Wilton met his killer somewhere else and the car was parked here early Sunday morning, after the body was dumped on the mountain. The killer just locked the doors and walked away. Of course, it could be different. Maybe Wilton was meeting an old high school friend and this seemed like a good place to get together."

"Maybe," said Harter. "But I'd go with your first impulse. Let's say the car was dropped here later. So the murderer either lived close enough to walk home in the middle of the night, or had an accomplice who picked him up."

"Or *her,"* said McManaway, smiling.

Harter drummed his fingers on the green metal of the car and stared through the windshield at the driver's seat. "They took prints, huh?"

"Yeah."

"I see we're the big show. Look over at the high school."

Despite the fact that it was November, the classroom windows were wide open, and teenage bodies were leaning out, trying to get a better view of whatever the police were doing.

"Like a snowstorm," McManaway said.

"What?"

"Don't you remember being in elementary school and crowding around the windows all excited when it started to snow?"

Suddenly, Harter got the urge to go inside the building. If he was serious about tracking Roger Wilton's days in Shawnee, he might end up there eventually, so it might as well be now. He'd wandered halfway across the street before he thought to call back to McManaway, "I'll be down at headquarters later."

"I left a copy of the tape and the autopsy on your desk," said McManaway, but by then Harter was climbing the bank of steps that led up to the stone plaza and the flagpole in front of East Shawnee High.

One step inside the doors, and he was no longer sure where he was going. Though he'd spent six years at East Shawnee, the school no longer belonged to him, and he felt like an alien. A sign inside the entrance reinforced the feeling: VISITORS MUST REPORT TO OFFICE. He hoped they hadn't moved the office. Two boys gave him long glances as he passed them in the locker-lined hall.

The furniture was newer and the long-legged secretary was sure prettier, but the office didn't look all that different than he remembered. After he'd introduced himself, the secretary had gone down a corridor and, before long, a man in a gray suit was standing across the counter from him, holding out a hand to shake.

"Edward, isn't it? Edward . . ."

"Harter."

Mr. Adams, the principal, had always had a formal streak, had always refused to use nicknames. Adams had been Harter's eleventh-grade history teacher, and the students were all Edward, William, or Susan, never Ed, Mouthy, or Suzie.

"What year was it you graduated?"

Harter got the impression that Mr. Adams opened many a conversation with that question. "Nineteen sixty."

"My, my. I must have taught you my third year here. Seems so long ago, but I guess it's been twenty-five years, hasn't it? I never had an inkling in those days that I'd become principal."

Nor had Harter. As he recalled, discipline in the history teacher's class had been far less than shipshape. It was one of those rooms where the air was filled with spitballs and sometimes with textbooks. He'd always believed Adams had become principal by default. Either that, or he'd just piled up so many education courses and so much seniority that they couldn't deny him the job.

"You're with the police now, aren't you?" Adams always seemed to ask that question whenever Harter ran into him.

"Yes."

"Well, what are they doing outside? Everyone wants to know. It's quite disrupted our day."

"It's a murder."

"A murder?" Adams sounded shocked, like he was worried that one of his students had bumped someone off.

"You didn't happen to notice the story in the paper this morning about the body found on Black's Mountain, did you?"

"Yes, I did."

"The Subaru parked out front belonged to the victim, Roger Wilton. He graduated from here, too. We believe he might have been killed because of something that happened almost twenty years ago."

"Does it have something to do with those bones they found in South Shawnee? Isn't that what the article insinuated?"

"We're not sure, but since I was here, I thought I'd drop in and see if anyone can remember anything about Wilton and who his friends might have been."

"Roger Wilton . . . The name sounds familiar. I might have taught him myself. When would he have graduated, Edward?"

"Nineteen sixty-six, I think."

"These days there aren't many of us here who might remember him. We've had more than our share of retirements and turnover in the past twenty years. Mr. Webster still teaches biology—I'm sure you recall him—and Mrs. Robbins is still the librarian, but they're about the only ones. It's all so long ago, you understand—Nineteen sixty, Nineteen sixty-six—that's like the distant past. Before all the turmoil. In those days, we didn't worry about students smoking marijuana in the lavatories, and we could send girls home when their skirts were too short. It's a different world now, Edward."

"Where might I find Mr. Webster?" asked Harter, trying to avoid a nostalgia sermon.

"I believe he has classes until the end of the day. Why don't you go to the library and see Mrs. Robbins? She has a set of yearbooks up there. They could be of some help. I'll send a note to Mr. Webster's room and ask him to stop in and see you when school's over. There's only an hour left. I'll try to get you a transcript of Roger Wilton's classes and grades, if you'd like. That's about all I can do."

"Fine," said Harter. "One more thing."

"Yes?"

"Was there a school dance Saturday night?"

"It was Homecoming."

"What time was it over?"

"I'm sure everyone was out by eleven-thirty, unless the band was still packing up their equipment. The cleanup committee came back yesterday afternoon to take down the decorations."

Harter nodded, started to leave the office, then turned back. "The library's where it used to be, isn't it?"

"Yes."

For some reason he didn't fully understand, he found himself taking the long way through the building. As he passed the gym, where flood victims had slept on cots for two nights the week before, a bell rang and kids swarmed out of the locker rooms. He was almost carried upstairs by the press of them, all the while feeling their eyes on him. He was glad when he found the library.

He recognized Mrs. Robbins, though he doubted he'd have known her if they'd met in the grocery store. It hit him that she must have been very attractive in the late 1950s. He'd thought of her as older, but he guessed that was how kids usually saw adults. Now she was probably in her early fifties, her hair was still blond, and she wore a trim, tailored red suit.

An English teacher was about to bring in her last-period class for a research project, she told him. But if he wanted to look through the old yearbooks, he was welcome, and she'd join him when she could. She pointed out the yearbooks, all neatly arranged on two shelves. "The history of East Shawnee High," she informed him before moving off to greet the students filing in.

Just as he'd had the urge to enter the high school and take the roundabout route through the halls, Harter had an urge to look up his own graduating class, but he fought it off. Instead, he pulled 1965 and 1966 from a shelf and took the volumes into Mrs. Robbins' glass-walled office. Before he sat down, he had another urge and returned to the shelves to collect 1940 and 1941. East Shawnee High, built in the Depression as a public works project, was only a few years old then. He figured he'd find Nan Wilton there.

Sure enough, there was Nancy Nash, 1941, pearls around her neck, like the other girls. She hadn't been valedictorian or salutatorian or class president, but, despite the lack of glamorous titles, her peers had selected her *Most Likely to Succeed.* There must have been something about her, some drive, some vibration, some innate intelligence. He guessed everyone believed she'd be a heck of a nurse, like her mother wanted. Flathead and Matt Curry had said she was smart, and according to the yearbook, she'd been in the Honor Society. She'd also been on the girls' basketball team and, in her junior year, in the Thespians.

No academic, athletic or extracurricular credits were listed under her son's name in 1966. He had won one distinction, however. *Best-Looking*

Boy. With his dark eyes and long dark hair, it wasn't hard to see why. Like the other boys, he wore a dark suit and tie in his photo, but the hair seemed to cry out, *Don't let the Sunday clothes fool you.* Harter imagined Roger had some sort of wild appeal to the girls of 1966.

"I see you've found what you were after," said Mrs. Robbins, taking a seat next to him. "They're settled down out there for a while. At least, they're pretending to copy things out of encyclopedias."

"Do you remember Roger Wilton?" Harter asked.

"I think so." She slid the yearbook over in front of her and glanced down at the picture. "You realize, I've never seen students every day, like their regular teachers, and I never learn everyone's name, but I've been racking my brain, and there's something, if this is the right year." She slipped back a few pages. "There she is."

"Who?"

"Joyce Dillard. She was my library assistant for a couple of years, and she was crazy about this Wilton boy. Joyce went all moony-eyed over him. They'd walk through the halls hugging and holding hands. I can see myself telling them to separate. You remember the old 'daylight rule,' I guess. But when it came time for the senior prom, the Wilton boy asked someone else. Joyce was awfully upset. More than once, they argued in the hall and Joyce broke into tears."

"You don't remember who he took to the prom, do you?"

"Yes, I do. That's one more reason the whole thing sticks in my mind. It was a Malcolm girl. I don't know her first name."

Harter glanced down at Joyce Dillard's photo, then started to turn to the M's in the yearbook.

"Oh, you won't find the other girl there," said Mrs. Rob-bins. "She didn't attend East Shawnee. She went to the Catholic school, which was odd because her father taught here, or maybe that's why he sent her to parochial school. It's not good for a parent and child, or husband and wife, if you ask me, to be in the same school. You may remember her father—Gerald Malcolm."

"He taught me algebra," said Harter. "Is he retired?"

"Six or seven years ago."

"I wonder where his daughter is."

"She's dead," said Mrs. Robbins.

"When?"

"If I'm right, it would have been a year or two before Gerald retired. Tragic. Some devastating illness. She was still in her twenties. She'd been living in California for years. San Francisco, I believe. Gerald never talked about her much. I think he was hurt that she never came back home."

"Strange," said Harter. "You know, Roger Wilton took off for somewhere, maybe California, early in 1968. What about Joyce Dillard? What became of her?"

"Oh, she's easy to locate. She's the librarian at the community college." Mrs. Robbins smiled. "I suppose we sometimes influence our students in a positive way. Joyce is married now. Her husband is a professor. She's Joyce Bertoia now."

"I'll look her up. I have to go out to the campus anyway. Roger Wilton was a student there until just before he left Shawnee."

"Of course, this may all mean nothing."

"That's the way it always is."

"Mrs. Robbins—" A girl in a blue sweater and tight jeans stood in the doorway to the office. "Would you help me?"

"I'll be back in a minute," the librarian told him as she got up to follow the girl into the main room.

Harter turned the yearbook pages, thinking about what she'd said. Roger was involved with a girl who'd also headed to California in the sixties. But that meant they weren't her bones in Egypt Street. Nor were they Joyce Dillard's. Hell, the Best-Looking Boy probably had girlfriends aplenty.

He slowly turned his head from Nan Nash to Roger Wilton, from mother to son. They looked a lot alike, and they were both dead.

21

THE HALLS were nearly empty by the time Harter finished with the biology teacher. Mr. Webster had always given off the aura that he was floating above it all, and the vibrations had gotten stronger over the years. Not only didn't he recall Roger Wilton, or Harter for that matter, but you could almost believe he didn't even have a memory of Gerald Malcolm, a man he'd taught with for decades.

But then, as Harter pictured Webster puttering around the science lab on his free periods, he knew that Webster's distance from the rest of East Shawnee High probably wasn't fabricated. Day after day, year after year, he'd carried his thermos and his lunch in a brown sack, so he hadn't even gone to the teacher's lounge for coffee or to the cafeteria for food. He'd never been privy to any of the school gossip.

Yearbooks for 1941 and 1966 were under Harter's arm as he left the building. Mrs. Robbins had said he could borrow them, though he didn't exactly know why he'd asked. Like the transcript he'd picked up at the principal's office, he didn't know what good they'd be. Still, collecting it all made him feel like he was laboring away, and all the paper and the photos gave him something to stare at, something to concentrate on as he tried to think things through.

He climbed in his car, dropped the yearbooks and transcript on the seat next to him, and, before turning the ignition, reached for a cigarette. He was puffing on the thing when, a block from the high school, he passed an alley. A bunch of boys were congregated there off the main street, lighting cigarettes now that their school day was over. He, too, had had his first smoke in that alley. He'd stood there and felt the dizziness hit his head, the dizziness that only comes when you don't smoke regularly.

He rubbed his cigarette out in the ashtray. The damn thing didn't taste so good anymore. Liz had always been after him to quit. Maybe he would. *With her or without her.*

Or maybe today's boys weren't smoking tobacco. Maybe they were getting their dizziness some other way. Mr. Adams had mentioned "the turmoil." There'd been no marijuana when Harter was in school—none available in Shawnee that he'd known of. Those were the Eisenhower fifties, days of Elvis "Jailhouse Rock," Chuck Berry "Rock and Roll Music," Carl Perkins "Blue Suede Shoes," not heavy metal, not "Mind

Games," not psychedelia, no matter how threatening the music had seemed at the time.

But Shawnee in the 1950s hadn't been all "Ozzie and Harriet" either, or "Father Knows Best," or any of those neat, clean TV shows. Those television families had always seemed to live in comfortable households where Dad left each morning in a tie and white shirt and returned undisheveled with a smile and a bit of wisdom. Where the trains didn't rumble through. Where the garbage men didn't rattle the trashcan lids at six in the morning, and no one's father actually worked on the garbage truck. Hell, there wasn't even any garbage for them to pick up. And, no one worried about how to pay the bills. Mom cooked breakfast on a modern range, cleaned house in high heels, went to Ladies Club luncheons, and was there with milk and cookies when the kids came home.

Harter had never lived in that world. *Nor had Roger Wilton.*

Roger, growing up in Shantytown, spoiled or not, must have survived his share of troubles. Even if he turned into a hippie in 1966 and 1967, Roger had been a kid in the fifties. Younger than Harter, younger than his sister Dorothy, probably more rebellious, arguing with his father. But Harter had, too. Fifties slide into sixties, with no one completely understanding how people change. *Times change,* Flathead Nash had said. Sixties slide into seventies, and seventies into eighties. People age. They fall in and out of love. Kids smoking in alleys become middle-aged men with habits. Stations turn into museums. Schools become senior centers. Floodwaters rise and fall. Bones surface. *Strange homecomings.*

Harter lit another cigarette.

MCMANAWAY had gone by the time Harter walked into headquarters. Just as well. He'd had enough talk for one day.

His desk was becoming so cluttered that he had to push junk aside to make room for the transcript and yearbooks. There were notes from McManaway, a copy of Caruthers' report on the 1967 hit-and-run that killed Nan Wilton, Roger Wilton's autopsy report, a summary of the findings about the girl's bones, a half-moon earring, a printout from North Carolina on the Subaru, photos, newspaper clippings, a cassette tape, a tape recorder, and a pile of messages from another day's flurry of phone calls.

Apart from some hamburger wrappers and a few road maps, nothing had been found in Roger's car, according to one of McManaway's notes. The car, by the way, had no tape player and its radio didn't work, hence the tape recorder. Roger had purchased the Subaru used in 1983. McManaway hadn't turned up any criminal record on him or on any of the other people Harter had asked him to check out.

Pete Epstein's autopsy on Roger didn't contribute much. Wilton had, indeed, been shot twice in the chest, as Epstein had said Sunday morning. The time was estimated as shortly after nine on Saturday night. Epstein still believed the shooting had taken place somewhere else and the body dumped behind the picnic table on Black's Mountain.

The university expert hadn't been back in touch with anything new about the bones.

For what it was worth, the earring was probably untraceable after all these years.

The tape had nothing on it other than what they'd heard in the motel room that morning. McManaway had made copies and had sent one to Sgt. Smith, who hadn't communicated anything fresh and startling, either.

From the clipped tone of McManaway's scribbles, Harter could tell the younger cop was beginning to wear down from crossing t's and dotting i's. And he'd been the one who'd left so many thankless tasks for McManaway. but you had to learn some way. Someone had to deal with the fine points while someone else mined the people. Mining the people in a case was usually pretty unscientific. Maybe that was why Harter liked it. Fingerprints, tire marks, autopsies only took you so far. He just hoped that Dave McManaway wouldn't come to hate him.

He picked up the cassette tape and slid it into the tape player. Soon he was hearing Roger's soft voice again.

What the fuck am I doing Didn't want to do it then either Just talking into this damn box Trying to get my thoughts ordered Hard to line all the ducks in a row Didn't know what to do that night either Nineteen sixty-seven Mom In the shed Lucky the old man was away They'd called him out to a train wreck in the country someplace and he was gone every night that week We knew we had to do it then The old bastard never would have understood He'd have climbed on his high horse Mom said it wasn't good but it was the right thing She promised to help so it didn't happen to me what—

And then a truck outside the Goodnight Motel blotted out whatever "what" was.

It didn't happen to me what—

22

> NEXT MORNING it was all in the newspapers in the minutest detail. It even had additions—consisting of Detective This, Detective That, and Detective The Other's "Theory" as to how the robbery was done, who the robbers were, and whither they had flown with their booty. There were eleven of these theories, and they covered all the possibilities, and this single fact shows what independent thinkers detectives are. No two theories were alike, or even much resembled each other, save in one striking particular, and in that one all the eleven theories were absolutely agreed. That was, that although the rear of my building was torn out and the only door remained locked, the elephant had not been removed through the rent, but by some other (undiscovered) outlet. All agreed that the robbers had made that rent only to mislead the detectives. That never would have occurred to me or to any other layman, perhaps, but it had not deceived the detectives for a moment. Thus, what I had supposed was the only thing that had no mystery about it was in fact the very thing I had gone furthest astray in.

After he got off the phone with Flathead Nash, Matt Curry pulled a battered old book off the parlor shelf and flipped through the dog-eared pages for Mark Twain's story "The Stolen White Elephant." He'd read Twain's yarn many times, Samuel Clemens fan that he was. He'd read the tale in cabooses as trains powered along, chuckling over the humorous account of the search for a missing pachyderm. Now, he hoped the story would make him feel better about how detectives went about their business, how their minds worked, what they were apt to miss. He hoped the tale would make him feel better, but it didn't.

The words swam in front of his tired, dark eyes. Instead of making him relax, they made him realize even more that what was going on wasn't humor or satire, wasn't some fiction about inept dicks and an elephant. It was a real life tragedy.

The bones, the death of Nan, now the killing of the boy. All tragedy. Not tall-tale stuff. As real as the floodwater lapping at his porch steps, leaving the guts of his house damp and chill.

Harter wasn't Detective This or Detective That, loaded down with crazy theories. He was a hard-nosed cop and what he might find scared the old man.

"What'd he want to know?" Curry had asked Flathead on the phone.

"Mostly about Nan and the boy."

"What'd you tell him?"

"That I wasn't around when none of it happened."

Which was true as far as it went. Flathead usually told the truth, within his limits.

The boy. Who'd have figured Roger would come back to Shawnee?

Curry looked out the window, over at the Wilton place, just across Egypt Street, not very far, though sometimes it had seemed so distant, like the night Nan had crossed—had *tried* to cross. She'd only been crossing the street. She shouldn't have been in danger. Should have been something he could have done to save her. He hadn't even heard it happen.

Outside, the darkness was almost complete. It was cloudy again. He hoped it wouldn't rain.

His eyes returned to the book on his lap. He turned back to the start of Twain's elephant saga.

> The following curious history was related to me by a chance railway acquaintance. He was a gentleman more than seventy years of age, and his thoroughly good and gentle face and earnest and sincere manner imprinted the unmistakable stamp of truth upon every statement which fell from his lips.

He hoped that was how Harter saw him: thoroughly good, gentle, earnest, sincere, truthful. That there could be more to him, or anyone, was beside the point. For the time being, it was all about what people—*what Harter*—believed. If the cop dug too deep, it couldn't help anyone.

Curry closed the book, tossed it over on the daybed, pushed himself up from his soft chair. He commanded his stiff legs to maneuver the stairs to his bedroom. Once he got there, he pulled open a dresser drawer with some difficulty. The drawer was as affected by dampness, as temperamental, as arthritic, as hard to move as his legs. He rooted around until he found the box, then lifted it out, placed it on top of the dresser, and removed the lid. His clumsy fingers sifted through the small pieces—the cufflinks that had belonged to his father before he'd disappeared, the wedding ring that had been his mother's, the tiepin he'd worn as a young man, the earring, all knots on a long heavy rope that twisted its way back into the past.

Tug on the rope and it was like you were pulling the past into the present, all those knots linked together like boxcars and gondolas on a freight train stretched long on the tracks through the mountains, ready to wreck if something went wrong, pennies on a rail. *Falling rock.* Old men argue. After a while, he and Wheat were no longer those two young buddies playing among canal boat hulls, and Egypt Street grew wider between their houses, until sometimes it was like the Red Sea and you needed God himself to part the waters so you could get across. *Pharaoh's army got drown-dead.* But, no, it had been Nan who drowned.

He stared down at the earring in his hand. He'd known the night he found it that it wasn't hers, so he'd picked it up, put it in his pocket, and later he hid it in his drawer. *December 1967.* The night after she'd died. Wheat and Roger had been at the funeral home and Curry had wandered over and circled around the Wilton house, taking it in, as if he'd never see the place again, though it was directly across the street from his.

He'd opened the shed to see if the floor looked too disturbed, too suspicious, and he'd spotted the earring, a half-moon of a thing. He'd known it wasn't Nan's. Her ears weren't pierced, and when she wore jewelry, she liked jewelry that sparkled, like her eyes, and the earring didn't.

Still holding it, he sat on the corner of his bed. The earring couldn't have done anyone any good then—and couldn't now. It would just ruin reputations, memories. Nan had told him about the girl the night it happened, just two nights before she was hit by the truck. *God, there should have been something he could have done.*

They'd been lying on the bed, this bed, and she'd told him what had happened, just as she'd told him so many things through the years. And, as she'd done so often, she pledged him to secrecy. He'd tried not to show his shock, tried to accept her confession with grace.

She was upset, and he'd reached over and put his arm around her. They'd been fully clothed, and she was worn out and upset from burying the girl. Lying on the bed, fully dressed, talking serious. Sometimes it had been like that. And other times . . .

She hadn't expected, hadn't wanted, it to happen like it did. She'd had only the best intentions. He'd put his arm around her and told her, yes, he believed her. He didn't believe Nan and Roger would murder anyone. It was the times. And now, years later, there was no sense muddying names, not hers. Harter would have to sort it out by himself. He'd pledged himself to secrecy.

He had broken that pledge once—but only once. Flathead had come to Egypt Street months after it happened, drunk as he often was. Drunk and angry, ready to beat someone up. Down in his cups over the killing of his sister. Filled with his own theories about what had happened, just like those eleven detectives with their wild theories about the missing elephant. It had been soon after Roger left town to escape Wheat, and Flathead was sure the boy had something to do with it. He ranted about going to the police. He ranted about Wheat. Finally, Curry had calmed him a trifle, sat him down, poured coffee down his throat, and then told him what he knew, what Nan had confessed. He knew Flathead wouldn't do anything to hurt his sister. Even in his craziest moments, Flathead loved his sister. So it became a secret two men shared, and now someone else was digging for it. Roger hadn't helped by coming back to Shawnee. He'd only added more shovels.

He could still see the cops over behind Nan's house the week before, digging up the bones. He could see Harter crossing the street toward him for the first visit on Wednesday morning. Like Nan had so many times.

Those years of crossing Egypt Street at night, at odd hours, when Wheat was away working a wreck or on some job, when Curry and Nan could arrange the time without raising eyebrows. All those times, knots in a long heavy rope. He could feel them still. Falling rocks, and the mountains change shape.

The first time was so long ago, he couldn't recall it. You'd think you'd remember the first time, but he really couldn't. It had just come about slow and natural, a word dropped here, a glance there, and then she'd started walking over with a piece of pie or cookies, and then she was telling Curry it should have been him she married in 1942, and not Wheat.

The years went by, and first Wheat argued with him about any subject that came up, and then they stopped talking altogether. They would never again build a shed together.

He could see her standing by the dresser, near the bed, unbuttoning the front of her dress, then sliding the dress from her shoulders, and after it dropped down her body to the floor, she bent her knee to lift her foot free of it. In her white lace-edged slip, she came over to him, her arms reaching out, and his to hers. He pulled her down on top of him and rubbed at her smooth back, down to her buttocks. Never could have imagined it. There'd been a time he never could have imagined it. When he'd thought he'd lost her for good. So soft against his hard. She never seemed to age. She was always as attractive to him as she'd been when he first saw her in the thin summer dress with the high heels strapped across her ankles at the bus stop that warm day, 1941. Always that attractive to him, year after year.

He'd never do anything to hurt her.

23

HARTER TURNED the corner at the SHAWNEE COMMUNITY COLLEGE sign and drove past a baseball field, unused this November morning. Ahead of him, the hollow between the ridges was filled with a complex of red brick buildings and parking lots. Built in the early sixties for a small student population, the tiny college with no dormitories had always struck him as little more than a glorified high school. Still, before Shawnee Community, there'd been no place in town for anyone to get any sort of "higher education."

In the early 1970s, when the powers-that-be had decided cops should be more humane and well rounded, Harter had attended night courses in sociology, psychology and criminology in the main building. The classes had, by and large, been junk. He kept believing he was back at East Shawnee High. He bet many of the kids on campus developed the same feeling. Roger Wilton, Class A rebel, probably had.

He parked near the student union and debated whether to go inside for another cup of coffee before hitting the registrar's office and the library. It had been in the student center one night that he'd met Liz. Then, as now, she was a part-time instructor in dance and exercise. Teaching a few mornings and evenings at the community college was about the only way she could eke out a living giving dance lessons in Shawnee. Sometimes he wondered if she ever had second thoughts about moving back home from New York City.

He decided against an umpteenth cup of coffee. He didn't need it, and there was no point in taking the chance of running into Liz. Tuesday morning was one of the times she was likely to be on campus, and part of him wondered if that wasn't why he'd picked this time to come.

Liz was still on his mind when he showed his badge to the woman in the registrar's office and requested whatever info they had on Roger Wilton. The secretary was obviously not one who'd been there eighteen years before, and there was no reason why she'd remember Roger even if she had been.

Roger had enrolled in 1966, the fall after he'd graduated from high school, according to his transcript. He'd attended classes for a year and a half, until January 1968, and there the trail ended. His courses were a mishmash. Some he'd dropped, others he'd failed, and if he'd been a success at anything, it had been a freshman writing course where he'd gotten a B. His final semester had been a total washout, but Harter guessed that was to be expected. Roger had apparently been turning hippier and hippier, and he certainly must have been affected by the death of his mother in December, not to mention battles with his father and whatever else had happened. During his last days at Shawnee Community College, he might even have been planning his own disappearance. Draft calls would have been high in 1967-68. Harter wondered if Roger had bothered to inform the Selective Service of his cutting out.

He folded the copy of the transcript, stuck it in his jacket pocket, and left the administration building. Outside, students and professors rushed about as he headed to the library. Up ahead, he spotted a woman in black tights. She had short, dark hair and a dancer's body. At first he was convinced she was Liz, and he didn't know whether to speed up to catch her or slow down to avoid her. On second look, he noticed she was young and her hair was teased up and had a red streak through it. She wore a slick gold jacket covered with crazy pins and patches, and barely sticking out below the jacket was the fringe of a short, short black skirt. She had on spike heels, not dancing shoes. If she'd worn such an outfit to East Shawnee High when he'd been a student, *before the turmoil*, the principal would have shipped her home for a haircombing and more ladylike attire, like Mr. Adams wished he still could.

Well, there was no reason she shouldn't show off those legs. Girls would wear whatever they thought would attract boys, and this one must earn a lot of glances. Enough years of being a responsible adult stretched gray and long in front of her, Harter thought.

She turned up the sidewalk to the library and he followed. She wasn't used to the tall, thin heels and wobbled a little as she negotiated the steps. Inside, she went over to a table where two other girls with wild hair and heavily made-up eyes sat with a mass of papers and books spread out before them. Harter walked to the desk and asked about Joyce Dillard, Class of 1966.

Joyce Dillard Bertoia seemed upset that a detective had come to see her at work. It was like she feared he'd lead her out of the library in handcuffs while students formed a gauntlet all the way to the paddy wagon. She didn't look much like her picture in the old yearbook. She was thirty-six or thirty-seven now, and with her hair pulled back and a skirt that dropped nearly to her ankles, it was hard to picture her as a boy-struck teenager clutching Roger Wilton in the hall.

Her blue eyes scanned the room as they talked, and eventually she led him back to a storage room loaded with books on shelves and in crates. Harter didn't need a Ph.D. in psychology to grasp that she didn't want to discuss Roger. Yes, she'd read about his death, but she knew nothing, she said. And he believed her.

"I don't know why you came to see me. I've not seen him since before he left Shawnee," she insisted.

"I understand you used to date him. I'm interested in who he knew back then. It's a long shot, but I figure he must have looked up some old friends after he came back. There has to be a reason for his return."

"Don't you think it had something to do with the skeleton they found last week? I read about that, too."

"We figure it does."

"Well, he certainly didn't come to visit me," she said. "We stopped dating in high school. He was getting pretty weird."

"What do you mean—*weird*?"

"Weird . . . Not normal . . . But I didn't actually see it very clearly at the time. It was hard to see things clearly in the Nineteen sixties."

"You mean he took drugs?"

"No, not in high school. Not when he was around me, at least. Maybe later—I imagine he did later. What I mean is that he acted weird, did lunatic things at times. You couldn't predict him. Like the time—"

"What time?"

Mrs. Bertoia looked down at her lap. The fingers of her right hand were nervously twisting her wedding ring around and around.

"One night in a cemetery . . ." She shook her head.

"Come on. Tell me about it."

"It was the fall we were going together. The fall before we graduated from East Shawnee. There was some crazy story about how a statue in a cemetery moved, and he got the idea he wanted to see it. We'd been to a Halloween party, and then we drove out in the country to the graveyard."

"And?"

"Roger would get these notions in his head. He was convinced that if the statue really did move, it would happen at midnight on Halloween. When we got out there, we had to walk quite a distance through the grave markers. I was dressed up for the party, and my heels kept sticking in the mud. He had a flashlight, and he'd shine it ahead of us. Finally we came to this memorial, this angel sitting on a chair—a throne, I guess—over a grave. He told me to sit in its lap and—this is painful, Mr. Harter—"

"And you sat on the statue?"

She nodded. "I wanted him to sit there first, but he said the thing only moved when a girl sat on its lap. I'd have done almost anything for him. I was so dumb in those days. After I sat down, he switched off the flashlight and we stayed there in the dark awhile. I remember the concrete was cold against the backs of my legs, and after a few minutes I told him I wanted to leave. But he didn't answer. I told him again that I'd had enough of this silliness, but he didn't even seem to be there. I got scared, sitting on the grave, the clamminess and all, and I started screaming, but there was no sign of him. I jumped up and started running. It was dark, and I kept tripping and falling in the mud. I rammed into a tombstone and ripped my nylons—Why am I telling you this?—"

"You're honest, and I asked."

"Some animal was howling in the woods. I thought it was a wildcat. I took off my shoes so I could run better, but I kept running into headstones, like the graves were a maze. When I got back to the car, it was all locked up and I didn't know what to do. I just stood there, no shoes, my feet and stockings wet and dirty, my clothes muddy and torn, crying, wailing. Then Roger leaped out of the bushes and yelled *Boo!* and laughed and—"

"Nice guy."

"He could be," she said, suddenly defensive, as if she'd bared too much. "I can't begin to explain, but if he'd asked me to go out there with him again the next week, I probably would have."

"You dated him for quite a while after the scene in the graveyard, didn't you?"

"We went together until spring, when he—when he met someone else."

"A Malcolm girl? The daughter of Mr. Malcolm, the school teacher?"

"Yes."

"Did you know her?"

"Not really, but from what I saw she was more like Roger than I was. More in his line. She was willing to do anything."

"What do you mean?" asked Harter, though he knew the question was touchy.

"I . . . I don't really know what went on between them, Mr. Harter. I wouldn't want to guess. Talk to her."

"I can't. She's dead."

"Oh—I didn't know."

"I'm going to see her parents, in case they remember anything."

"Mr. Malcolm always seemed like a kind man," said Mrs. Bertoia, obviously happy to change the subject.

"Yeah, he did. How about anyone else—maybe a friend Roger might have looked up when he came back here last week?"

"I'm at a loss. I don't know. Possibly Len."

"Who's he?"

"Len Schiller."

"The guy in his thirties who lives over on Billings Street?"

She shrugged. "I don't keep in contact with him, or with most people from those days. Len had dropped out of high school and had an apartment. We'd go visit him sometimes. Do you know him?"

"I've busted him. Possession and burglary. Couldn't pin anything more on him, though he always seems to be around trouble."

"After Roger and I broke up, he was with Len Schiller or Christy Malcolm almost every time I'd run into him. He wasn't one to have a lot of close friends. Only a couple at a time."

"I'll check Schiller out. How about Roger's parents? Did you ever meet them?"

"I met his mother a few times. She was just about the only person he'd listen to at all, but she wasn't one to come down on him hard."

"How about his father?"

"He hardly ever mentioned his father."

"Look, if something else pops into your mind, give me a call. You've been a lot of help."

"I hope nothing else pops into my mind," she said, showing a sliver of a smile for the first time. He supposed Joyce Bertoia could relax now that he was leaving.

She was chatting with another librarian at the front counter when he went out the library door. The other woman might be asking her why a cop had come to see her. If so, Harter was sure she wasn't having a lot of fun explaining. It wouldn't be much more pleasant than sitting in the lap of a cold, clammy concrete angel on a black Halloween night, waiting for the statue to move. Sometimes it was hard to tell the quick from the dead.

He was opening his car door when he saw Liz strolling across the parking lot to her car. Swinging her tote bag, her dancer's legs striding, her dark hair blowing a bit, she looked carefree as hell. He started to walk over to her, then froze.

She hadn't spotted him, so he climbed in his car and turned the key. He was two cars behind her when she pulled off campus and onto the highway back to town. As they braked for the second traffic light, a blue Shawnee-Potomac Railroad truck swung in ahead of him, adding another vehicle length between them.

The light changed, and Liz turned right, toward her West Side studio and her afternoon aerobics class for the Shawnee Women's Society. Harter, like the blue railroad truck, turned left. He never was very good at following her lead.

24

GERALD MALCOLM lived off the Old Pennsylvania Pike on the north side of Shawnee in a white house that, once upon a time, had been the center of a prosperous farm. Now a string of new brick and aluminum-sided residences lined the road into the place, but behind the retired teacher's home, a red barn still rose tall from a stone foundation. Harter parked beside a green pickup truck and, walking toward the front porch, noticed that the barn and the large garden plot nearby looked like they were in active use. He wasn't much of a farm boy, but he'd seen enough apple trees to recognize a small orchard on the hillside. It, too, appeared well tended.

Malcolm exuded cheeriness when Harter introduced himself, former student to former algebra instructor. They small-talked for a few minutes about East Shawnee High, and then Mr. Malcolm's smile turned down when Harter explained why he'd come. Like Joyce Bertoia, Malcolm seemed surprised, even shocked. Or maybe, thought Harter, he was misinterpreting the expression. Maybe the mention of Christy Malcolm had brought back a pain her father had fought hard to get over.

A few steps inside the house, Malcolm started to lead Harter into the living room, then froze, as if he was tossed up about which room to use. The girl on the couch was confused, too. She dropped her magazine on the coffee table and stood up like she was about to leave the room to them. She was black, maybe sixteen or seventeen, and her swollen belly pressed tight against an oversize T-shirt.

"Just someone to see me, Karen," said Malcolm, motioning her back to the couch. Then he led Harter down the hall and into a sort of office.

The room was clearly divided in halves. Harter got the impression it was probably the most-used room in the house. Malcolm's age showed as he dropped into a swivel chair beside an old-fashioned rolltop desk. The top was open and Harter could see that each of the desk's cubbyholes was crammed with letters, bills, and what looked like agricultural publications. "This your farm office?" he asked.

Malcolm ran his hand back over his bald head. "Farming is a losing proposition, but it gives me something to do. I sold some of the land for development years ago, but I kept fifty acres. That's more than I can handle. Sit down, Ed—*Detective.*"

Harter did, and leaned his arm on the edge of a gray metal desk, much like the one in his own office. The flat surface was as full of papers, mail, and magazines as the rolltop desk across the room. Amid the clutter,

Harter spotted a big sheet of tagboard next to Magic Markers of different colors. Someone had started to print a poster but hadn't gotten any farther than BENEFIT in red block letters.

"My wife," said Malcolm. "The poster you're staring at, that's her project. You've probably never met Connie, but that's how she spends her days."

"What's the benefit for?"

"The Allegheny Unwed Mothers' Home. Connie does volunteer work for them. Sometimes she puts in forty or fifty hours a week."

"Sounds like a worthwhile cause," said Harter, happy to give Malcolm his head for a while, hoping he would relax.

"Quite worthwhile, I'd say, and important. Every young woman who carries her baby full-term means one who doesn't turn to abortion. That's the main thing to us. That's how Connie got involved with the home. She's Catholic and takes it very seriously. I'm not myself, but we always sent our daughter to parochial school for the strong moral background. Connie joined the local Right to Life chapter years ago, and she's gone to Washington for demonstrations and national meetings. She was always angry over all those babies being aborted, murdered. After Christy's death, she became even more aware of the children who aren't allowed to be born, and of the people who want kids but can't find one. That led her to work with the home for unwed mothers. When they have more young women than they can handle, we keep some of them here."

"Like the girl in the living room?"

"Yes. I suppose the most we ever took in at one time was three, and that was some houseful, I'll tell you. But it does Connie a world of good to help the girls through their rough spots. The girls become like daughters to us, like the daughter we lost at such a young age. We grow attached to some of them, and they write us for years afterwards. And it keeps Connie sane."

"I guess the babies are put up for adoption?"

"In most cases. Oh, a few girls decide to keep their babies, but mostly they're adopted out. There are so many couples unable to have children, Detective. There's quite a waiting list, though it's a shame that sometimes it's hard to place black babies. The Allegheny Home takes care of everything. They think they've found a family for Karen's, just in the nick of time. She's due in a month. That's where Connie is right now. She often visits the adopting families beforehand to be sure they're the right kind of people."

"Sounds like good work," said Harter, but he was just filling space. His mind had drifted to Dave and Sally McManaway, about to have a baby they wanted.

"We try to do good works."

Harter stared over at the ex-teacher and tried to look through Malcolm's glasses, past the thick lenses, at his eyes. He felt like a jerk when he pulled the conversation back on the road. "I guess I can understand your wife's dedication. Your daughter *was* young when she died, wasn't she?"

"Twenty-eight. It was in March Nineteen seventy-eight, just two months before her twenty-ninth birthday."

"She died from—"

"A brain tumor. No one knew she had it until it was too late."

"And she was living in San Francisco?"

"Yes. Christy moved out there the fall after she graduated from high school. She attended college there and liked the West Coast so well that she decided to stay."

"You must have made a number of trips out there over the years, especially when she was ill."

"Not enough, I'm afraid. I'd say that's part of the reason for some of the emptiness that . . . that Connie is trying to overcome. It's hard on mothers to lose their children. It's even harder when you're not prepared for the death. As I said, Christy didn't know about the tumor until it was too late. She informed us only a week before she died. She was like that—quite independent."

"Was she married?"

"No. She'd thrown everything into her career. She worked for an investment firm out there. Had a bright future."

"She'd have graduated here in, what, Nineteen sixty-six?"

"It was 'sixty-seven, actually."

"Then she was a year younger than Roger Wilton?"

"I believe so."

"And she left for California early in Nineteen sixty-eight, about the same time he did?"

"It wasn't like that at all." Malcolm took off his glasses and placed them on the desk. Turning back to Harter, he squinted and said, "If you want the truth, Christy went to California to get away from the Wilton boy. Believe me, that was the only reason Connie and I would have allowed her to go out there on her own. We were quite protective parents."

'Why did she have to get away from him?"

"They'd broken up, which made Connie and me happy, but he wouldn't stop calling her at all hours. More than once, he sat in a car at the end of the driveway and waited for her to go to work or go out. If you're suggesting she ran away with him, you're dead wrong, Detective. She had the good sense to want to free herself from a bad influence."

"You and your wife didn't approve of Roger Wilton?"

"That was no secret."

"Any particular reason?"

"He was wild, had no standards. And from what we learned of the family, they weren't the best, either."

"He was a hippie and your daughter found him attractive?"

"You could put it like that."

"In Nineteen sixty-seven, San Francisco was the hippie capital of the world. Why did she choose to go there?"

"She was accepted in college there. She spent the summer and fall of 'sixty-seven here in Shawnee, working at a store downtown and saving money for school. Just after Thanksgiving, she flew out to San Francisco so she could get situated for the second semester. Connie and I went out at Christmas to see her apartment and spend the holidays with her. I have no idea why the Wilton boy ran off to California, or even if he did. But if it was to find Christy, he must have been quite disappointed. She never mentioned him again." Malcolm put his glasses back on, but the thick lenses couldn't cover up the anger shooting from his eyes. "Are you investigating my daughter, Detective, or are you investigating the murder of Roger Wilton?"

"I'm sorry."

The words came out like a reflex reaction. Over and over, Harter felt the need to apologize. He kept overstepping bounds, digging into private tender spots that didn't, on the surface at least, have much to do with the case. He'd already done it that day with Joyce Bertoia, and he'd done it with Dorothy Merrill and maybe with Matt Curry. Then, there'd been Paul Keith, the gentleman from Pittsburgh who'd lost track of his wife during World War II. Seemed like so long ago that Keith had called him, but it had actually been less than a week. Some cases were like that—sometimes you seemed to rough up people's emotions. He hoped no one would force him to give a good reason why.

Karen, the pregnant black girl, watched nervously as he passed the living room on his way to the front door. Gerald Malcolm stood on the porch and watched as Harter started out the driveway, as if he was making sure that the detective was really leaving.

Harter was almost to the road when a beige station wagon pulled in toward him. He glanced over and saw a round-faced woman with gray hair in the driver's seat. He figured she was Connie Malcolm and, for a second, it seemed like she was about to roll down her window and say something to him, but instead she edged on past. In his rearview mirror, he could see the bumper sticker on the back of her station wagon.

SAVE THE BABIES

He could picture Mrs. Malcolm going into the farmhouse and then into the office to finish the poster for the Allegheny Unwed Mothers Home. He pictured her grieving for her daughter and trying to work out her grief by throwing herself into a cause.

Why did he feel like he was bulldozing over good people?

At least when he found Roger's old friend Len Schiller he wouldn't have to feel guilty. Schiller deserved to be flattened out now and again.

25

THE FIRST TIME Harter arrested him, Len Schiller had been standing outside a bar smoking a joint. Harter had been working a car theft and had gone to the tavern to find one of the suspects and take him for a ride.

It had been the early seventies, and the unspoken policy was to bust only dealers and serious drug offenders, not the guy with the small stash. As Harter had come up the street that night, he'd hadn't earned so much as an eyeball from Schiller. He'd ignored the marijuana smoke and ducked in the bar, but his man wasn't there. When he'd emerged a few minutes later, Schiller was still on the corner, talking to a teenage girl, a fresh joint in his hand, marijuana smoke drifting above his head, cocky as hell, and it was more than Harter could take. So he busted him, amid a lot of squawking about police brutality. Schiller served thirty days for possession.

The second time Harter arrested him, Len Schiller's apartment had looked like a warehouse for stolen goods. He had a TV for every channel and two stereos for every room. Schiller's lawyer had argued that his client had simply bought the hot stuff from other guys and didn't have any notion where it came from. Maybe his client was dumb, maybe he couldn't pass up a good deal, but he was no thief, according to the attorney. Schiller ended up serving five months in the local jail on a plea bargain. He told the jailers that he'd needed a rest anyway.

To Harter, Schiller wasn't as stupid as his lawyer would have it, and he *was* a thief, pure and simple. He was one of those jerks you saw everywhere around town but couldn't quite grasp what they were doing there, or how they made a living. It was hard to pin anything on him that was worth the effort. At some point, you crossed the line into harassment if you stayed on him, or so a shyster would claim.

Back in the sixties, when Roger Wilton would have known him, Schiller might have appeared to be a romantic, outside-the-law hero with long hair and a drooping mustache, but eventually the outlaw streak had deepened and taken over altogether. Harter never saw him any longer in the company of anyone who worked for a paycheck. Over the years, he'd grown dirtier and tougher.

Schiller's place on Billings Street was much more than a three-room apartment. He lived in the corner fifth of a huge brick building that ate up an odd triangular city block. Four stories tall, the joint sort of faced west at the tracks and the downtown, in a catty-cornered way. The upper floors had once been rooms for railroad workers while the street level had been lined with shops—a cobbler, a dry cleaner, a ma-and-pa grocery, a liquor store and others. The structure had been earmarked for demolition in a lame 1960s urban renewal project that mostly fell apart. Aside from Schiller and a tenant at the other end, the building had long been vacant, and the jagged-glass, half-boarded-up windows of the upper stories testified to its uncertain future.

Each time Harter passed the building, he got the feeling that a movie director could make good use of it. There were plenty of spots around Shawnee like that. Maybe the tourist-seeking town fathers should get in touch with Hollywood. Alfred Hitchcock would have loved the building's menace. Jimmy Stewart would have had a vertigo attack if he'd been forced to climb the winding staircases inside. Hitchcock could have filmed *Psycho* there, too, though it would have been a different movie. The sprawling Billings Street monster was surely someplace the molemen might hang out, as well, and Len Schiller was surely one of the molemen.

Harter rapped at the front door, and when no one answered he rapped harder. His pounding seemed to echo off the building across the street. He could have sworn someone was inside. It was just one of those intuitions you get, just one of those inklings that his life so often depended on.

He went around the side in time to see a gray van tear up the potholed alley. He rapped on the back door and the door pushed open from the force of his knock. Schiller, or someone, had been in such a hurry that he hadn't pulled it shut tight. He waited for a minute, then entered.

The kitchen was as he remembered, though it seemed cleaner and more modern than when he'd last seen it. The outside of the building was deceptive. You expected some poverty-stricken, run-down flat and what you found was a well-equipped, fairly comfortable residence. The microwave oven, refrigerator and other appliances were new. The walls had been painted in the not-so-distant past, but every inch of space over the kitchen table was still covered with snapshots of Schiller and his friends, pictures torn from magazines and newspapers, posters of rock stars, and a few Playmates of the Month.

Harter wandered into the living room and noted a new rack-system stereo, a large color TV, a videocassette recorder, and other trappings of a middle-class life. Missing was the clutter of obviously stolen goods that he'd found the second time he'd busted Schiller. Nor did there seem to be drugs, baggies or paraphernalia sitting around.

He opened a door that led to a hallway and stairs up to the second floor. Given the immensity of the near-vacant building, he wondered if Schiller was using one of the upstairs rooms for his warehouse, so his lawyer could argue that he was totally unaware of what was up there. Harter was about to go up and check it out when he heard the car. He closed the hall door and peeked through the living room curtains.

A Toyota had pulled to the curb and two clean-cut teenagers were climbing out. Harter glanced down at his watch. Three thirty-five. School would have ended a short time before.

The boys made for the front door and he retreated to the kitchen. As he hoped, they knocked rather than walked in. Waiting them out, he leaned on the table and stared at the collage Schiller had put together over the years. Some of the stuff on the wall overlapped other stuff like layers of years, and some of it was faded with age.

The boys stayed at the door a long while, like they were used to Schiller keeping them waiting. Finally, after Harter heard the car engine start up and the Toyota drive up Billings Street, he went out the back door, leaving it slightly ajar.

He was most of the way to headquarters when he decided to make a detour.

FROM THE OVERLOOK, Shawnee didn't look all that different than it had when, as a kid, he'd camped on the mountain with his father. The river and the canal still defended the south side, and the Shawnee-Potomac mainline still cut through the crotch of the city. The big buildings that stood out from a distance were, by and large, the same ones that had always stood out. What had changed was what went on inside those buildings. What had changed was the people. What had changed was the content, not the form. It was more mental than physical.

Still, turning west, facing beyond the city toward the high mountains, you could almost believe nothing had changed. Those mountains—from the overlook there were rows of them—mile after mile of Allegheny ridges, blue and occasionally purple. You could only ever see the tops of them, one behind another. Just the very tops. They hid each other, shielded each other from close scrutiny. They prevented anyone from seeing what really went on between them.

26

THE OFFICE was empty when Harter walked in with a hoagie in one hand and, in the other, a Styrofoam cup full of water from the hall cooler. He pushed aside papers and messages to make a spot to eat.

The spicy aroma of salami and olive-oil-drenched lettuce burst into the room as he unwrapped the white paper. Caruthers had always accused him of stinking up their office whenever he brought in one of Mattioni's hoagies. So there'd been days when Harter had bought one for the hell of it, just as he'd sometimes blown cigarette smoke Caruthers' way to jag at him. Now Caruthers was in Florida. How long would it take for the edge to wear off, for Harter to erase the former detective from his mind?

All around, there were reminders of Caruthers. Like those damn filing cabinets, filled with old cases. Like the 1967 report sitting on the corner of his desk, the report on the death of Nan Wilton. Maybe he should move all the furniture around and clean house to clear away the years. Maybe, one day, he'd even be able to forget the night Caruthers had been slow in coming to his rescue after a cane-wielding madman had disarmed him with a blow from his weighted stick. He had no doubt that Dave McManaway would be better.

Harter took another bite of hoagie and sifted through Tuesday's accumulation of paper. On top was a note from McManaway: "Call me at home. You won't believe this." He decided to put off the call until he was done eating.

Another note informed him that Sgt. Wayne Smith had been in touch. The state police were giving up on the North Carolina angle. They hadn't turned up so much as a hint that Roger's murder had anything to do with anyone down there.

Then there was the morning's newspaper, which Harter hadn't bothered to read before he'd headed out to Shawnee Community College. The brief item in the local section reported only that Roger's car had been found near the high school and police continued to investigate the case. There was no mention of the Goodnight Motel or other details. McManaway had obviously been choosy about the facts he gave out. Score another one for Dave.

Finally, there was a fingerprint report with yet another note paper-clipped to it. McManaway had saved him the trouble of reading the entire thing by summarizing: "Roger Wilton's were the only prints found in the motel room or the Subaru."

All this paper, all this work, to find out who murdered a guy no one particularly cared about. To identify some bones that were nearly twenty years old. Maybe, to delve back into a 1967 hit-and-run.

But you couldn't look at it that way. No one had the right to go around shooting people, or bury bodies in the backyard, or run people down. And whoever had done those things might still be walking Shawnee streets.

He balled up the hoagie wrapper and tossed it at the trash can, then reached for the phone. Sally McManaway sounded cheery as hell when she answered. He tried to be equally upbeat. "How you doing, Sally?"

"Fine."

"No labor pains?"

"Not yet, but we're getting down to the last few days."

"Dave's told me. I suppose you have a bag all packed and waiting by the door."

"Oh, a brand-new one. Dave bought it for me." She laughed. "He keeps coming home with all sorts of things. He even bought pickles and ice cream. But there must be something wrong with me. I don't have a craving for them, so they just sit in the refrigerator. Do you want to talk to him?"

"Unless the two of you are in the middle of a practice run to the hospital."

"We've already done that. I'll get him."

Harter heard the bump of the phone against a table. As he waited, he wished he'd had more to say to her, but babies weren't exactly his subject. He'd never had a kid. He had no bits of wisdom to impart. He might have tried to ease her mind about her husband becoming a detective, he guessed. But that was between Sally and Dave.

"So you found my note?" McManaway asked.

"Yeah. What's it about?"

"I was out by the viaduct this morning and I saw Darrell Phillips puttering around in front of his store. Turns out his wife signed him out of the mental health center after just one day."

"Not surprising, is it? Ask her, and she'll give you the story about her husband having an appointment with a private psychiatrist."

"That's not the thing. Seeing Phillips made me remember you wanted me to check on his military record when I had a chance. I made a few calls. It wasn't as difficult as I feared. I must be getting good at doing your hackwork."

"And?"

"Harter, you won't believe this."

TUESDAY WAS Darrell Phillips' club night and he'd already left, Vi Phillips told Harter as he followed her up the stairs to the apartment over the appliance dealership. Both she and the apartment gave off a feeling of spotlessness and tidiness. This wasn't an early-morning distress call, and Mrs. Phillips was considerably more composed than the previous times he'd seen her. Her red hair looked like she'd just come from the beauty parlor.

Harter thought twice about sitting on the white couch, not wanting to leave a smudge, but most of the other furniture was white, too, and the tables were all covered with frilly doilies and fragile bric-a-brac, so he supposed the sofa was as good a place to drop as anywhere else. He declined the coffee she offered and waited for her to sit down before he began.

As if to cut him off at the pass, she explained that her husband had spent Sunday night at Shawnee Mental Health Center, and on Monday she'd taken Darrell to his own doctor, who saw no reason he couldn't come home. Whatever was troubling him, he wasn't dangerous, she insisted. The last two days he'd been perfectly normal.

"I'm not here to hassle you over signing him out," said Harter. "It's about your husband's military record. His time in Vietnam has been mentioned several times."

"That's not unusual, is it? If we're to believe what we hear, a lot of veterans have difficulty forgetting Vietnam."

"But, usually they've been there."

"What?"

"The ones who have trouble forgetting are usually the ones with something to forget. Your husband was never in Vietnam."

"Then—"

"Then what?"

"There must be some mistake." She was obviously shaken. Her voice had become high and thin.

"I don't think so. We made a number of calls today. We've asked for verification in writing, but, if you know the Army, that may take a while. I thought you ought to know sooner."

"This doesn't make any sense."

"No, it doesn't. What did he ever tell you about his service record?"

"He doesn't speak much about it, at least not about the details, but he did say he was there and it was awful. Darrell and I have been married for six years. It's the second marriage for both of us. I met him when I came here as office manager for a construction company in 1978. After my divorce, I wanted to get out of my hometown. I imagine I never really felt the need to probe him about the war. Of course, I'd listen if he mentioned something."

"Have any of his old army buddies ever come to visit?"

She seemed to think for a second, then answered, "No."

"Thing is, it's not just that he wasn't in Vietnam. There's no record that he was ever in the service."

"I don't know what to say."

"Neither do I. Do you remember him ever bringing up Vietnam with anyone else? Maybe his ex-wife would know."

"She—she doesn't live in Shawnee any longer. As far as others, I just don't know. I took whatever he said at face value. By the time we married, both of his parents were dead, and I had no reason to doubt anything he said. Actually, I don't believe he mentioned Vietnam until the last couple of years. I was a little surprised myself when it first came up. Mostly he talked in generalities about how terrible it had been."

"But he never talked about it in front of other people?"

"Not that I recall."

"Did something happen two or three years ago—some bad situation like the flood—something that could have unnerved him?"

"You mean something to start him talking about the war?"

"Yeah."

Again, she seemed to think for a minute, then shook her head no. "Unless it was the recession. That's when our business began to drop off."

"Your marriage wasn't on the rocks, was it? Was either of you seeing someone else?" *There, he'd asked it.* "He does keep confessing to shooting you, you know."

"Those things are none of your business, but, no, there's nothing like that."

Her voice had become a husky whisper, and he could tell how hurt she was by the question. *Why did he feel like he was bulldozing over good people?* He rubbed his fingers against the soft white fabric of the couch. "You say your husband doesn't have a drug or alcohol problem?"

"Definitely not." Her voice was louder. The hurt was turning into anger.

"And he has no gun?"

"No," she said emphatically.

"Would you like me to wait until he comes home and we could take him over to the mental health center again?"

"What I'd like is for you to leave, Detective Harter. Darrell isn't violent. He may be mixed up right now, but he'd never hurt anybody. He's been a perfect husband. He's just upset by the flood and our business. I'll call his doctor tonight and we'll decide what to do."

"I don't want to feel responsible if anything happens to you."

"Nothing is going to happen to me. Darrell and I will work this out. I wouldn't have him committed to Crimpton State Hospital for anything. And I won't wreck everything we've struggled for."

"Do you think, perhaps, he feels guilty about not going to Vietnam?"

"I think you better leave. Darrell's done nothing." Though her voice was white hot, her eyes were nearly as red as her hair. She was ready to start bawling the minute he left. "Please go, Detective. Darrell and I will solve whatever problems he has."

He stared across the room at her for nearly a full minute before he stood up. "If that's what you want, Mrs. Phillips."

"That's what I want."

"Call me if anything happens, if it even looks like something might happen."

"What if they're wrong? What if the Army made some mistake, simply lost Darrell's files or checked on the wrong name?"

"I told you, we're expecting a written statement."

Mrs. Phillips just sat in her white chair, watching him edge toward the door, making no move to escort him, holding herself in until he was gone.

Outside, in his car, he couldn't decide if he was doing the right thing by driving away. One part of him wanted to wait there until Darrell Phillips came back from his club meeting, wait there all night if need be. Another part told him that he couldn't just sit outside the appliance store night after night. What if she was right? What if the Army was wrong? Wouldn't be the first time.

He lit a cigarette but barely puffed on it. Just held it between his fingers as it burned down to the filter. The streetlights bounced off the old viaduct across from the store. The night was clear and the moon was fattening toward full belly.

After ten or fifteen minutes, he turned the key. Maybe Len Schiller was home.

27

THE ALLEY was a narrow one-way street, but he wasn't about to have Schiller leave him in the dust again, so he pulled in the wrong way. He wasn't going to park out on Billings Street and stroll mannerly up to the front door so the goddamn punk could slip out the back another time. If Len Schiller escaped this time, he'd be hoofing it.

He dodged a world-class collection of potholes at the alley's mouth, and then his headlights were shooting straight into the headlights of a van parked behind the big brick white elephant, the gray van that had speeded away earlier. Looked like the vehicle's rear doors were open. Suddenly a girl came around from the back and stood sentry. He left his engine running and his lights on. She eyed him as he walked toward her.

At first, she reminded him of the girl he'd seen that morning at the community college, the one with the black tights and frizzed-up hair. This one, too, wore a slick, shiny jacket, and her hair was mussed like she'd slept on the same side of her head for three nights' running. Drawing closer, he saw there really wasn't much other similarity. *Girl* wasn't even the right word. She looked to be in her late thirties. Her distrusting glare, combined with the alley shadows and harsh headlights, made her pale face appear even harder, more lined, more tired than it probably did on a good day.

"You'll have to move," she said. "You're blocking us in."

He stepped around her and inspected the rear of the van. It was two-thirds loaded with stereo and TV equipment, cardboard boxes of stuff, clothes, and small furniture. "Does Schiller let you do all the lifting and hauling?" he asked. "Where is he?"

"You a cop or what?"

"Or what."

"He's inside."

Before he crossed the tiny backyard to the kitchen, Harter side-tripped to his car, turned off the motor and lights, and removed his keys.

The door was wide open and he saw Schiller before Schiller saw him. They hadn't taken away all the kitchen furniture yet, and Roger Wilton's old buddy was sitting at the table, back to the door, busy on the phone. He was decked out in full costume, black jeans and leather jacket, and looked like he'd gained a few pounds since Harter had last seen him.

"We'll be out of here in an hour or two," he said to someone.

"Len—" The woman pushed past Harter, into the kitchen. "Len—"

Schiller turned, saw Harter in the doorway, and cut off the phone talk fast. "What the fuck do you want?"

"Just walking my beat," Harter said. "Saw your van out there and wanted to be sure no one was ripping you off while you were out earning an honest buck. Just protecting upstanding citizens."

"Don't get fucking sarcastic with me, Harter."

"So he is a cop?" the woman asked. "Gave me a smart-ass answer when I asked. He's got the alley blocked. He seemed to know you."

"He's a cop all right,, and he likes to think he knows me. Likes to think he knows everyone and everything. Makes up shit about people, about them breaking the precious law," Schiller told her.

"We're still leaving tonight, aren't we?" she asked.

"No sweat, Patty. He's just a sixty-second man. Make another trip through the place to be sure we ain't leaving nothing important behind, and I'll take care of him."

"She your wife or girlfriend?" Harter asked as soon as Patty was gone.

"None of your business." Schiller replied.

"Same old warm Len."

"You didn't come here to share a beer. I asked before—what do you want?"

"Actually you asked me what the *fuck* I wanted. Someone should teach you to speak civilly."

"You ain't the one to teach me nothing."

"Can I come in, or do I just stand here in the doorway?"

"Got a search warrant?"

"No warrant, but I'll get one if you want. And I came by myself. For a chat. Call it deep background. Isn't that what the politicians and reporters say? I want to know about Roger Wilton."

"Is he the one they found dead out on the mountain the other day?"

"One and the same. I hear you used to know him well."

"Maybe. I'm like you, Harter. I know a shitload of people. They come and they go. If it's the guy I'm thinking of, I haven't seen him since the sixties. Never gave him a thought till I read about him being shot. You sure he didn't OD or something?"

"Shot twice in the chest." Harter stepped into the room and, when Schiller didn't protest, crossed to the far end of the table and sat down. "Why do you think he might have overdosed?"

"Just small talk, just remembering a guy I once knew."

"Was he into drugs in those days?"

"Lots of people were into lots of shit in those days. There's people who are judges and stockbrokers now and were hippies then. What'd Roger turn out to be?"

"A groundskeeper."

"Figures."

"Looks like he came back to town last Friday after hearing about the bones being found at his family's house in Shantytown. Guess you know about that, too?"

"Seems like I heard it. Last week's news, wasn't it? Long time ago, last week."

"The bones date to the sixties. Like your friendship with Roger Wilton."

"Lots of skeletons date to the sixties. What's it got to do with me? You accusing me of shooting Wilton or burying a body twenty years ago or something?"

"For such a goddamn innocent, you're pretty touchy, Schiller."

"I'm tired of you assholes harassing me all the fucking time. That's why Patty and me are leaving. Going to start fresh in a new place."

"Sure you're not packing up because you saw me come by this afternoon? I saw the van scoot away. You got a condo waiting for you in Miami?"

"I'm clean, you son of a bitch. Haven't been in trouble for a long time. Can't a man improve himself? We're just getting out of Shawnee. Got to be out of this hole by the fifteenth or pay another month's rent. Patty and me are moving to a farm in southern West Virginia. Should have moved to the country ten years ago when the notion first struck me."

"Back to nature, huh?"

"Something wrong with that?"

"I don't picture you as a country boy. You'd be out of your element."

"Don't fucking bait me, Harter. Shit, I let you come in my house and you insult me over and over. I should call my goddamn lawyer."

"Can we finish moving shit?" asked Patty from the doorway behind Harter. "Isn't he gone yet?"

"Go back in the other room," Schiller told her.

Harter sat silent for minute, studying the wall above the table, the wall with all the old photos and posters plastered over it. "You don't happen to have a picture of Roger Wilton, do you? Some of these look as old as the sixties."

"Hell, I don't know what you'll find stuck there. I keep telling you I haven't seen Wilton since—what was it?—'sixty-seven or 'sixty-eight."

"Since he left town after his mother was killed."

"You trying to pin that on me, too?"

"Did you ever meet his mother or any of his family?"

"Maybe. I don't know. Nothing about them sticks with me. Christ, I can't even remember half of my own aunts and uncles."

"They're probably happy about that."

"Stop fucking insulting me!"

"How about any of the girls he hung out with? Maybe a Joyce Dillard or a Christine Malcolm. They called her Christy, and she was the one he'd have been seeing at the end. She went away to California that fall."

"Was she the one with the big tits and tight little moneymaker?"

Harter pictured Gerald Malcolm at his desk, still sad about his daughter's death, and it was all he could do to keep from reaching over and grabbing Schiller by his long greasy hair.

Schiller must have sensed his anger, for he was more careful when he spoke again. "So, her name was Malcolm, was it? We didn't use last names much. It was Roger and Len and Christy. Never knew much about her. Any more blasts from the past? I need to get out of here."

"I'd prefer you stay around for a while. I may want to talk to you again."

Schiller shook his head. "Told you. Got to be out by the fifteenth. You going to pay my next month's rent?"

"You've got a couple days. You'll be a hell of a lot more comfortable here than in jail. I'm sure I could come up with a reason to hold you for forty-eight hours."

"Goddamn, Harter. More of your fucking harassment. I don't know nothing about no bones or Roger Wilton's mother or no Malcolm girl."

"And you never saw Roger over the weekend? He didn't call you from the motel Friday night or Saturday after he came back?"

"Never saw the son of a bitch for the last seventeen years, almost half my life. He never called me from the Goodnight Motel or anywhere else."

"How'd you know that?"

"What?"

"How'd you know Roger stayed at the Goodnight Motel?"

"Read it in the paper."

"No. All the paper mentioned was finding his car by the high school."

"Look, Harter, it's all over the fucking street, about the motel. There's other ways of finding shit out."

"It's still a good reason to hold you a while. You want to hear your rights now?"

"Put your hands on the table," ordered Patty.

Harter felt pretty dumb when he looked over his shoulder and saw the pistol in her hand. He'd ignored all the rules, bypassed common sense. Showed up alone. Forgotten that anything could happen. Forgotten about the molemen. And they'd come.

Schiller was moving around the table now, keeping his distance from Harter. When he got beside Patty, she gave him the gun. "He's got his under his jacket," Schiller told her. "Reach under and take it." She seemed a little reluctant.

"You going to dump me on Black's Mountain, too?" Harter asked. "Going to abandon my car up by East Shawnee High?"

"Get his gun," Schiller ordered again.

Harter waited for Patty to lean over and reach inside his jacket. He knew he'd only have the one chance. One chance to put every muscle in action, to throw her behind him, between Schiller and him, between the gun and his back. If Schiller was fast on the trigger, if Patty was harder to toss than he suspected, it was all over.

Patty bent forward slightly and, as she started to slide her hand in for his gun, Harter scraped his chair back like he was giving her more room. Then, in one long motion, he grabbed her by the waist, rolled to the linoleum and shoved her toward Schiller with all the strength he could manage.

He was pulling out his gun when Schiller's went off, and Patty was falling heavy on top of him. At first he thought she'd been shot in the mix-up, but then she was screaming and banging her fists against him and he realized Schiller had just thrown her at him like he'd thrown her at Schiller.

He pushed Patty off him so rough that he heard her body slam against the cabinet beneath the sink. He pointed his gun at the doorway, but Schiller was gone.

He climbed to his feet and headed cautiously for the living room. The hall door was open and he could hear the punk scrambling up the steps into the huge building's maze of empty rooms.

The steps creaked as Harter followed. Step by step, creak by creak. Up to the third floor. At least it wasn't as dark as he feared. Along the derelict hall, doors were open or missing, allowing in streaks of light from the moon and the streetlights out front.

The first room was the toughest. He flattened himself against the wall just outside the door, like they taught you in police school, and then he jumped in, ready to fire, but no one was there.

Room by room, he worked his way down the hall, revolver ready. Never anyone there.

It was a long hall and he was almost convinced Schiller had escaped, had ran down the stairs at the far end, when he heard glass break in a room on the alley side.

He rushed through the doorway in time to see Schiller leap down onto the roof of a lean-to, a shed that abutted the building. The punk hit the tin roof hard and took a while to straighten up. When he did, he spotted Harter in the window and pulled off a shot.

Harter aimed for his gun hand, but then Schiller moved and his chest seemed to explode when the bullet cut into it. There was a long moan and then Schiller fell off the lean-to and thudded against the ground.

Patty was a good driver. She backed the van out of the alley as fast as anyone would have dared to drive it forward. All Harter could do was watch her go.

28

HIS FINGERS drummed on the edge of Len Schiller's kitchen table. He kept telling himself how stupid he'd been to have fallen into such a hole.

"She won't get far," said Sgt. Wayne Smith. "Schiller had more than ten thousand dollars on him. He must have been carrying most of the cash. Probably didn't trust her. She's in that gas-eating van and she'll have to be stopping to fill up. She'll be easy to spot."

"She might be heading into West Virginia," said Harter, staring up at the collage over the table. "Schiller talked about moving to the southern end of the state."

"Tough country down there for strangers," said the state cop.

"Of course, he may have been lying." Harter reached up and lifted a clipping to see what was underneath it.

"When we find her, she'll pour it out to save herself," Smith said. "If you're right, if Wilton called Schiller from the motel and Schiller bumped him off for some reason, then she had to help, at least with moving vehicles around."

"Yeah, but what does it all have to do with the bones on Egypt Street?" Harter asked.

"Who knows? But I bet you're right that it was Wilton who wanted to meet you at the train station Saturday night. We know from the tape he could have explained things. Schiller just got to him first. Hell, he might have shot Wilton right here. We'll look around upstairs tomorrow morning in the daylight. The van was perfect for hauling the body out to Black's Mountain. It all fits."

"Nothing fits." Harter stood up for a better view of an old photo of a group of long-haired kids. "There's no reason. No motive. It's not like the movies where it's boom-boom, the bad guys get blown away, and everything's suddenly crystal clear. We don't know a hell of a lot more than we did a few hours ago."

"We know Schiller and Patty are connected somehow with Wilton's murder," said Dave McManaway. He'd been pretty quiet since showing up. "They wouldn't have pulled a gun on you if they weren't worried. I wish I'd been with you."

"It's got to be them," said Harter.

"Sure it does. We'll get them," Smith said.

"I mean this photo." Harter reached up and pulled the old snapshot off the wall. "It's got to be them. I've studied Roger's face enough times to recognize him. He's got his arm around a girl, and it's not Joyce Dillard. I bet it's Christy Malcolm. That's Schiller on the other side of her. Christ, he looks eighteen or nineteen, almost human, like maybe he really had a mother. What the hell happened to these people?"

"You're getting punch drunk," Sgt. Smith said. "Go home and sleep as long as you want. We'll finish up here."

Harter didn't bother to argue. He went out the door with the picture in his hand.

—NIGHT In the shed We pushed We moved everything out of the way and kept dampening the ground so it was easier to dig So the same thing didn't happen to me Christ I can't do this Can't risk putting this down on tape Got people to see Can't use their names Have to change all the names like Dylan sang in "Desolation Row" She—

She what?

She who?

Roger's mother?

The girl they were burying?

All tangled up, these people. The more he stared at the photos he'd collected, the more he listened to the tape from the motel room, the more he ran back over what he'd learned from the people he'd questioned, the more tangled up they got. Mother and son and girlfriends and jerks and old men. Generations swirling in floodwater together. 1940s/1960s/1980s. One thing leads to another. Middle-aged men with habits.

Harter could see Roger Wilton talking into the tape recorder at the Goodnight Motel, could see him struggling with the past, and with the future, with what he would do.

He leaned forward and switched off the cassette player on the coffee table in front of his couch. He reached for his cigarettes, lit one, then glanced again at the pictures, the yearbooks, the reports, the notes, all spread around his table and carpet. He'd spent the morning sifting through it all, and now it was lunchtime. Now it was time to get something in his stomach other than caffeine.

He'd slept badly Tuesday night. Kept being surprised by Patty with a gun in her hand. Kept going down a dark corridor, room to room in the innards of the old building. Kept seeing Schiller falling from the lean-to roof with a hole in his chest. Hadn't meant to kill him. Kept seeing Patty drive off. Time after time. Kept wondering why nothing fit.

He'd thought about going to Liz's after Wayne Smith had sent him away from Schiller's. Wanted to have her put her arms around him and not say a damn thing, just wanted to feel her, make sure she was still alive, find some other way to communicate with her than words. But then he'd thought better of it and gone home.

He rubbed out his cigarette and found himself staring at Roger Wilton's graduation photo and, from the yearbook page, Roger stared back. *Best-Looking Boy, 1966*. Devilish, or worse, in his tie. The sort to play graveyard pranks. Dark eyes like his mother's.

Nan Nash, East Shawnee class of 1941, black sweater and pearls, big smile. *Most Likely to Succeed.* To be a nurse. Nurses and schoolteachers, the paths open to women in those days.

Roger and Nan on the porch of the Egypt Street house on a fifties afternoon, only yards away from where a body would be buried years later.

Roger with his hippie friends, 1967, before he'd left town. His arm around a girl. Had to be Christy Malcolm. Who'd gone to San Francisco late in 1967. Who, according to her father, had gone away to escape the Wilton boy, who had also run away to escape something. Or someone. Schiller said Christy had big tits and a tight little moneymaker. He was in the photo, too. Schiller, his eyes on Christy, but she was turned away from him, turned toward Roger.

Harter picked up his magnifying glass and held it over the girl's pretty face. Her lips were parted like she was whispering to Roger. Maybe she was saying, "Let's get away from this guy Len." Her long dark hair was tucked behind her left ear. There was an earring. Light-colored. Shaped like a semicircle. Like a half-moon.

He looked at the girl and the earring a long time before he put down the magnifying glass and picked up the phone. A young woman answered and he figured she was Karen, the pregnant black girl. Once Gerald Malcolm was on the line, he told him he was working on his investigation report and needed to tie up a few strands. He wanted the report to be as complete as possible so no one would ever have to go down the same blind alleys he had. What college, he wondered, had Christy moved to San Francisco to attend?

After that, he called Dave McManaway and Pete Epstein and told them what he wanted them to do.

People set in motion, he went out the door, down the two flights of steps, and outside to his car. The Wednesday afternoon traffic was light as he drove the Avenue to South Shawnee.

He wasn't exactly sure what he was after, but he was running on feeling. He felt like he should visit Shantytown again. Sometimes he just had to see things again, like looking at old photos, like trying to resurrect the moments trapped in them.

The leavings of the flood were still apparent as he drove along Egypt Street. Only a little more than a week before, the street had been underwater, the shed had floated away, the bones had been exposed, and this had all begun. No matter how fast life seemed to move these days, a week wasn't very long.

29

"GOD SPARED US," said Spilky. He'd opened his door to let out his cat and seen Harter getting out of his car. Or maybe he'd seen Harter climb out of his car, so he'd opened the door to let the cat out. Anyway, Matt Curry's neighbor had asked Harter about the investigation, then launched into his spiel.

"Didn't seem possible a week ago, but now everything's returning to normal. We were discussing it at church Sunday," Spilky said. "The pastor said God must have plans for us and let us off light this time. In Bible class, a man said maybe the reason for the flood was to uncover those bones so the killer would be punished for his past sins. God works in mysterious ways."

"You really believe folks lost their homes, and three dozen people drowned so an old score could be settled?" Harter asked. "The flood was just chance. Too much rain at the wrong time. All just chance."

"There has to be some meaning," Spilky insisted.

"No, there doesn't," said Harter, turning away.

As he headed down the bank to the Wilton house, Harter wished he hadn't opened his mouth. All he needed was a call to the police commissioner complaining about his irreverence. The powers-that-be were always sensitive as hell whenever God got dragged into it. He usually kept his opinions about politics and religion, those deadly subjects. to himself when dealing with the public. But Spilky had caught him off guard. Like so much had recently. Like Patty and Len Schiller.

He'd better do a repair job on his guard. The damn thing kept falling off.

FROM HIS FRONT WINDOW, Matt Curry watched Harter go around the side of the Wilton place. The cop seemed distracted. Had Spilky said something important to him?

Harter stopped near the roped-off hole where the shed had been and stood there, staring into the hole for a long time. Not budging. Frozen in place like the ancient threesome in his memory of the old farmhouse at the edge of town. Like he was waiting for the rocks to fall.

Curry had stood by the hole himself two nights before, after learning about Roger's death, after talking to Flathead about what Harter had wanted to know. He'd tried to sleep, but couldn't. Tried to read Mark

Twain until his eyes fell shut, but they didn't. Kept picking up the earring he'd found in the shed shortly after Nan had been run down. Kept going over what he knew, and what he didn't, and telling himself he ought to call Harter, then deciding not to.

He'd crossed Egypt Street in the middle of the night and shined a flashlight down into the grave, as if there was something to see, something he'd missed all along, something that added up to sense, but the only thing that kept coming to him was that he didn't want to hurt her. He and Flathead had pledged themselves not to damage her. He'd never do anything to hurt Nan. Not even now.

But the bones had been found after all these years, and Roger was dead, and the detective kept returning to Shantytown, kept staring into the grave, kept asking questions.

Something he'd told Harter nagged at him. He'd put Nan in a bad light and he shouldn't have. He didn't know why he'd done it, except that once the story started to come out, he'd found himself cutting back on the details to cover up. He'd even said Wheat had been the one who'd told him, but really it had been Nan. She'd come to his house that night with a purple bruise beneath her eye and confessed she'd been ready to kill Wheat.

Wheat had hit her. He'd accused her of being unfaithful, and he'd hit her. Wheat didn't know who her lover was—at least, that's what Nan had said—but he could feel in his bones that his wife had a lover.

Lover. She came over to him, her arms reaching out, and his to hers. He pulled her down on top of him and rubbed at her smooth back, down to the valley above her buttocks. So soft against his hard. Touching him down there where no one else ever had. And then, sliding into her so easy. Never anyone else but her. Wrapped in her warm wetness, like he was born to be there, like nothing mattered more than those moments.

Lovers.

Wheat had hit her. Then, after supper the next evening, he'd started in again. Yelling, accusing. She was washing the dishes and she had this knife in her hand and she turned and threw it. She hadn't meant to kill him. Nan never would have hurt anyone intentionally. If she'd really wanted to, she'd have got him with the knife, but she didn't. She'd never kill anyone. Curry wished there was a way to get the point across to Harter without having to bring up all sorts of other questions.

Harter stood by the hole, like the earth was telling him something. Not far from the cop, another spectator had staked out a position. The Spilkys' cat had wandered across the street and seemed to be watching the detective watch the grave. It wasn't a bad-luck black cat, rather an orangish mixed breed, and Curry liked it better than he liked his neighbors.

After a while, the cat rose from its sprawl and prowled around a little, moving with that shoulder strut that cats have. The creature circled a spot a couple times. Then, after it had done its business, it began pawing at the ground, shoveling soft, muddy soil over its waste, like it didn't want anyone to know what it had done.

A pickup truck with a camper top came down Egypt Street and parked in front of his house. Curry didn't recognize Bill Merrill at first. He didn't know when he'd last seen Wheat's son-in-law, but, as Bill made his way toward Harter, he decided that was who it was. Nan had never liked Bill. No, it wasn't so much that she didn't like him as that she hadn't wanted Dorothy to marry so young. She'd hoped the girl would finish school and become the nurse she never was, the one her mother had wanted her to be. She'd had huge hopes for Roger, too.

Why didn't things ever work out?

Lovers.

AS HARTER walked to the front of the house to meet Bill Merrill, he noticed the expression on Merrill's face tighten in surprise. He obviously hadn't expected to run into the detective.

"Day off?" Harter asked.

"I finagled the afternoon," said Merrill. 'Truth is, I haven't been here since the flood. I've been working and I kept putting it off. Didn't want to face it. Besides, after the news about the woman buried here, Dorothy and I thought it might be best to stay away a few days. So, this is the place?"

Harter nodded.

"My son and a friend of his are coming down after school. We won't be getting in your way by going inside the house, will we?" Merrill asked. "We wanted to check the house out and decide what to do with it. My vote's to tear it down, but it's not my homeplace. I'm not sentimental about the thing like Dorothy and Wheat. To me, it's an albatross. Sure as hell won't sell now."

"You won't get in my way," said Harter. "Just let me know if you find more bones."

Merrill gave him a strange stare. "Are you expecting more bones?"

Harter shrugged. "How are Wheat and Dorothy doing?"

"About the same as on Sunday. Dorothy's a little depressed. First, the skeleton, then her brother's murder. She worries what our friends are thinking. Wheat may be a little weaker than a week ago. I don't know how much he understands about the flood and the bones, but he seems to be deteriorating. Could be he's just another week older. We never bothered to explain to him about Roger. Didn't see much reason."

"I know you didn't think much of Roger, but I'm looking into some of his friends from the sixties. Did you ever hear of a guy named Len Schiller?"

Merrill shook his head without saying anything. Harter found it odd he didn't have more curiosity. Merrill didn't appear at all concerned what might have happened to his brother-in-law, so Harter didn't offer anything about Tuesday night at Schiller's. The shooting had been too late for the morning paper, and not many people knew about it.

"How about a girl named Christy Malcolm?" he asked. "Roger seems to have seen a lot of her in Nineteen sixty-six and 'sixty-seven."

"Keep telling you, I had no use for him," Merrill said. "But *Malcolm*... The name sounds familiar somehow."

Harter remembered sitting in the Merrills' kitchen on Thursday, and a remark from Dorothy about her husband's school days. "Maybe you know the name from church. Christy Malcolm would have gone to the same Catholic school you did, though she'd have been there years later. Her father, Gerald Malcolm, used to be a math teacher at East Shawnee High."

"Maybe that's it, then. I could know the family from church, not that I go much anymore. Can't really tell you much about them. What's the Malcolm girl got to do with Roger's killing, anyway?"

"I don't know."

"Well, whatever you know is probably more than I do. I just married into the Wilton clan. They aren't exactly my people. I never really got along with Nan, and I couldn't tolerate Roger. When they all lived here, I visited this house as little as possible. It's a pain to have to deal with it now. Wheat's all right, as far as I'm concerned, but Nan was something else. Over the years, I've grown to like Wheat, and you must have noticed that Dorothy is absolutely devoted to him. Wheat never gave me trouble like Nan did."

"Your wife seems to have mixed feelings about her mother, too."

"We went over this the other day, didn't we? I don't see how it's any of your business, Detective."

How many times had Harter heard that line? How many times in the last week had he replied that he wasn't sure what was his business and what wasn't? How many times had he simply plowed ahead? *Bulldozing over good people.*

"What was wrong between your wife and her mother?"

Merrill avoided an answer as long as he could, but finally he must have realized that Harter would stand at his elbow the rest of the day if he didn't open up.

"Nan didn't want Dorothy and me to get married," he said. "She tried everything she could think of to stop us."

"Why?" The big uncomfortable question.

"I was out of school when we started going together, but Dorothy wasn't. Nan wanted her to graduate and go on to college, but Dorothy got pregnant. We don't really talk about it, but it was no secret. I don't know what it's like these days, but twenty-five years ago they didn't want pregnant girls to attend classes at the high school. I don't know if there was a law against it, but they certainly discouraged it. They didn't want the other girls tainted, I guess, as if none of the others ever spread their legs. You can see it still makes me mad. Anyway, Dorothy would have had to quit school, and Nan didn't want her to. My folks were real religious and they were pressuring me to marry her, but Nan wouldn't give her consent. Finally, Wheat did."

"And Nan never gave in?"

"No. She was bullheaded as hell. You had to know her to understand. She kept telling Dorothy that marrying me would wreck her life, that she was too young to be *trapped* like that. One night Nan told her she'd been pregnant when she'd married Wheat and she'd always regretted it. It was a crummy thing to unload on your daughter, especially since it was Dorothy who Nan had been carrying. She insinuated she'd had an unhappy life and wished she'd never married Wheat. Dorothy still cries when she thinks about it. Here was her own mother telling her she wished she'd never married her father."

"Must have been rough," sympathized Harter. "Back then, there was certainly a lot of stigma attached to an unmarried girl having a baby. Your wife was caught in a real bind."

"Oh, Nan didn't want her to have the baby."

"She didn't?"

"She offered Dorothy an abortion."

"An abortion? They were illegal then."

"Yeah. A woman couldn't just stroll into some clinic, have it done, and stroll out again the same day. It was all back-alley stuff. Nan claimed she knew how to do it. Nan's mother had been a midwife, and growing up, she'd picked up a lot about childbearing and all sorts of old wives' tales about how to end a pregnancy. She had books, too."

"Her brother told me she wanted to be a nurse," said Harter.

Merrill nodded.

"Dorothy refused the abortion, and you two got married?"

"Right. And Nan was wrong. Dorothy and I are still together. She'd kill me if she found out I told you all this."

"Do you know if Nan Wilton ever performed abortions for other women?"

"I have no idea."

Harter glanced across Egypt Street at Matt Curry's house. In his mind, a whole new set of questions for the old man was forming.

30

HARD TO LINE all the ducks in a row Didn't know what to do that night either Nineteen sixty-seven Mom In the shed Lucky the old man was away They'd called him out to a train wreck in the country someplace and he was gone every night that week We knew we had to do it then The old bastard never would have understood He'd have climbed on his high horse Mom said it wasn't good but it was the right thing She promised to help so it didn't happen to me what (roar of a truck) *Night In* the *shed We pushed We moved everything out of the way and kept dampening the ground so it was easier to dig So the same thing didn't happen to me Christ I can't do this Can't risk putting this down on tape Got people to see Can't use their names Have to change all the names like Dylan sang in "Desolation Row" She* (click)

"Dylan. My daughter had all of his records," said Pete Epstein. "He was like a god to the kids twenty years ago. First it was Elvis, then the Beatles, then Bob Dylan. I wonder who their gods are today?"

"Bruce Springsteen, Madonna, Michael Jackson?" said Dave McManaway with an uncertainty in his voice.

Dr. Epstein leaned his elbows on his autopsy table, the table where Roger Wilton's body had been stretched out a few days before, the table where the girl's bones had been arranged the last time Harter had been in the medical examiner's office.

"Sounds to me like you've figured it out right," Epstein said. "It all makes some sort of sense. From what Bill Merrill told you yesterday, even the tape adds up. What was it Wilton said? His mother insisted what they were doing wasn't *good* but it was *right."*

"She didn't want the same thing to happen to him that happened to her," added Harter. "She didn't want it to happen to Dorothy, either. Nan Wilton must have felt awful trapped and frustrated."

"A hell of a lot of women wouldn't choose to go back to the sixties or before," Epstein said. "When people talk of the good old days, they often forget what they were really like. I imagine Nan Wilton's feelings about her life weren't so singular."

Harter reached in his pocket for a cigarette. He'd no sooner put the filter between his lips and struck a match than Epstein was saying, "Wish you wouldn't do that in here. I'm a doctor, you know. I'm supposed to warn people against smoking."

"Some people drink," Harter said, but he blew out the match, stuck the cigarette back in his pocket, and mentally scrawled Pete Epstein's name right below Liz's on the list of those trying to save him from himself. "There's no doubt the teeth match?"

"No question. It was a lucky break to find the right dentist so fast. Could have taken weeks."

"So, we finally got one lucky break," said Harter.

"Sad, isn't it? She wouldn't have died today. And, then, Roger Wilton would probably be alive, too. Both of their lives would have turned out differently."

"There's nothing about the skeleton that would confirm or deny the girl was pregnant?"

"No. Most likely, she was only a few months along."

"I still don't get what Len Schiller had to do with it," said McManaway, who seemed ill at ease.

Harter wondered if the father-to-be was upset by the idea that Nan Wilton had been more than willing to abort a fetus if, in her opinion, it kept a girl from wrecking her life, or kept her son from wrecking his in a forced marriage. She must have really regretted marrying Wheat.

"These things happened. Don't let it play tricks on you. Don't let it, for instance, set you against midwives," said Epstein, spinning off in a new direction. "I'm not one of those who want to lock the medical profession's door too tightly. There's a use for midwives. Hell, hundreds of doctors did the same thing back when abortions were illegal. I knew a few, and they weren't criminals. They simply said yes when some poor girl showed up at their door one night. Seems to me that was better than just letting the baby die after it was born. That happened, too. You've heard the stories. A little old lady passes away, the pillar of her church, and a baby's remains are found in a trunk in her attic. This time, it was the mother who died. Nan Wilton might have believed she knew what to do, but she obviously didn't." He glanced across the autopsy table at McManaway. "It's damn hard to be as heated up for the right to abortion as the Right-to-Lifers are against it, but . . . God, I sound like a liberal. Save me. Shut me up or I never will be able to get into politics."

"I promised to vote for you, Pete," Harter said. "You'll be great cutting ribbons at museum openings." He looked over at McManaway. "Ready?"

OUTSIDE, MOTHER NATURE had put on her makeup and was disguising herself as a sexy young dazzler rather than a stormy withered bitch. Her bumps were covered up so her complexion appeared smooth and clear from a distance. Her bright lipstick made the sun feel warm and inviting for a November afternoon. It was like she wanted to seduce you one last time before winter.

They pulled out of Dr. Epstein's parking lot, headed down the hill past the Episcopal Church, drove through the downtown, over the tracks and into the East End, past rows of houses, and then north out of town, neither of them saying much. Harter wondered if McManaway's mind was on Sally, ready to give birth to their first child at any moment. But his was with an old man.

After he'd left Bill Merrill the day before, he'd gone across the street to Matt Curry's. It had taken a while, but the retired railroader finally started talking. *And talking.* Harter wasn't sure what had forced open the rusted floodgates, but he sensed Curry had been waiting for a long time to tell someone some things. He wanted Harter to know that, say what you would about her, Nan wasn't evil. Curry would never put up with evil. *He loved her.*

They turned off the Old Pennsylvania Pike and into the lane that led back to the farmhouse. Connie Malcolm's station wagon was gone again. Perhaps she was on another mission of mercy, as she had been two days earlier. They parked beside Gerald Malcolm's green pickup and slowly got out of their car.

"I'm not looking forward to this," said McManaway as they walked to the porch.

"Neither am I," said Harter.

31

"ME, AGAIN." Harter tried to sound as friendly as he could when Karen cracked open the front door. "Is Mr. Malcolm in?"

The pregnant black girl pulled the door open wider and let them step inside. She led them halfway down the hall before Gerald Malcolm emerged from his office. "I thought I heard someone ring the bell. Guess I was too deep in farm accounts for it to really register."

"I wasn't sure I should bring them back," Karen said nervously.

"No, it's fine. You can get back to whatever you were doing, Karen." As the girl turned away, Malcolm looked at Harter. "What's on your mind today?"

"A few more questions. Told you yesterday that I'm trying to tie up loose ends so they stay tied. This is Dave McManaway. He's been assisting me with the case."

"You may not remember, but I sat in your classroom for two years," McManaway said to Malcolm.

"I'm afraid I don't remember. After a few years, all those student faces tended to blend together. Sometimes it seems half of Shawnee must have sat in my classroom. I hope a few people learned a little algebra. Good to see you again, anyway."

Malcolm's tone wasn't very convincing that he was really glad to see McManaway again. Not any more than he wanted to see Harter another time.

Gerald Malcolm's office looked much as it had on Tuesday afternoon. Assorted papers still cluttered Malcolm's desk, but there was no unfinished poster on his wife's. By now, the poster was probably on display in a store window, plugging the benefit for the Allegheny Unwed Mothers Home.

Malcolm motioned for the two detectives to be seated When neither Harter nor McManaway piped up fast with a question, he said, "I thought you told me on the phone yesterday that your investigation was winding down. You mentioned this fellow Schiller. I read about the shooting in this morning's paper. He sounds like an unsavory sort."

"He was one of the bad guys," Harter said.

"And he was the one who murdered Roger Wilton?"

"We believe so, but we're not sure why."

"I certainly can't help you with that one, Detective. *The News* seemed to suggest Schiller was heavy in the drug trade. Could it have had something along those lines? Or maybe he and Wilton argued over something that happened when they were young."

"Roger left Shawnee in 'sixty-eight. Seventeen years is a long time to keep a grudge so alive you'd be willing to kill someone over it." Harter reached in his pocket and pulled out a photo. "We found this picture at Schiller's and wanted to know if you recognize anyone in it. Len Schiller's the one on the far right, next to the girl. Roger Wilton's on the other side of her, with his arm around her. I wondered if the girl was Christy, and whether you could identify any of the others. Looks like it might have been taken in Nineteen sixty-seven."

Malcolm half-rose from his chair and leaned forward to reach for the photograph. His slow, deliberate movement reminded Harter that he was dealing with an older man, not a tough jerk like Schiller.

Malcolm peered through his thick lenses at the snapshot for a full minute before saying, "Yes, that's Christy. If you hadn't told me it was the Wilton boy, I might not have known him. I certainly can't put names to any of the rest of them. I didn't approve of the crowd my daughter was running with in those days, Detective. That's why Connie and I encouraged her to go out to San Francisco to attend college. We hoped she'd start again and find new friends. But I explained all that to you Tuesday, didn't I?"

"Your daughter was a pretty girl. I studied the picture a long time, too, and I noticed her earring." Harter reached in his jacket pocket again. "It was a lot like these."

Malcolm squinted across the office at the ivory half-moons in Harter's hand, then glanced down again at the photo. "I'm afraid I can't tell if they're similar. I'll take your word for it, if it matters."

"I think it matters, Mr. Malcolm. One of these was found last week at the Wilton house in Shantytown, in the hole where the skeleton was. The other was given to me yesterday by a neighbor who'd picked it up near the same spot in December of 'sixty-seven."

As Malcolm handed the picture back to Harter, he suddenly seemed even older than he had a few minutes earlier. He almost seemed to creak, like the steps in the old building on Billings Street where Schiller had lived.

"A couple other things have also turned up, and they don't make sense," Harter said. "We learned your daughter's dental records match the teeth of the skeleton. And, after calling you yesterday, I asked McManaway to check Christy's college records. He learned she was accepted for admission, but never actually registered. She never attended a class there. Couldn't have graduated. We couldn't find any verification that she died in San Francisco in Nineteen seventy-eight, either."

"It was Nineteen seventy-seven," said Malcolm.

"Two days ago, you told me it was March Nineteen seventy-eight, just before her twenty-ninth birthday."

"One of us must have been confused. Perhaps I misspoke. Connie and I don't talk about Christy much. It's painful, even now."

"I imagine it is," said Harter. "I'm sorry to keep bringing it up. We'll check on Nineteen seventy-seven then."

Malcolm tilted his head down so his eyes shot at the rug. "You don't have to."

"You can stop talking to us at any time," warned Dave McManaway. "You have rights."

"You have to understand—I didn't kill anyone."

"You have the right to—"

"I didn't kill anyone!"

"So, what happened?" asked Harter, waving off McManaway.

His eyes still facing the floor, Malcolm said, "It *was* Christy who was buried by the Wilton house, just as you suspect. Doesn't do much good to claim otherwise, does it? She didn't die in Nineteen seventy-eight. Connie and I invented the story about the brain tumor because we couldn't continue pretending Christy was doing well on the West Coast. Everyone was always inquiring about her. They wondered why she never came home for a visit."

"How did your daughter really die?"

"An abortion that went wrong."

"Performed by Nan Wilton in December, Nineteen sixty-seven?"

Malcolm lifted his head and stared across the room at Harter. "Christy should never have gotten involved with the boy. He was a bad one."

"I'm not going to sit in judgment on how bad Roger Wilton was twenty years ago," Harter said.

"God, the awful things that happened to kids in the sixties," said Malcolm, his voice low and sad. "I saw my students change, and I saw Christy change. They seemed to change overnight. It was like the world turned upside down and there was no gravity so all standards and morality fell off into space. Christy wasn't like that before."

Wasn't like that before. Harter remembered what Mr. Adams, principal of East Shawnee High, had said. *Before the turmoil.*

"Did you know your daughter was planning to get an abortion?"

"Lord, no. We didn't even know she was pregnant. I wish we had, but Christy told us nothing. She was probably afraid of how we'd react. We didn't bring her up like that. She wasn't a bad girl."

"I'm sure she wasn't," said Harter, but something Joyce Dillard Bertoia had said returned to him, too. *Christy was willing* to *do anything* to *please Roger,* and Joyce wasn't. "The people who knew her well say Nan Wilton wasn't a bad person either. She just wanted her son to finish college. She didn't want him to marry your daughter any more than you wanted Christy to marry him. It's a shame the two of you couldn't have gotten together. Did you ever meet her?"

"No."

Harter considered telling Malcolm more about Nan and the Wiltons. How she had hopes for her son just as he had hopes for his daughter. How everything in her life kept falling apart. First she got knocked up, as her brother Flathead had put it. Then her daughter did. Finally, her son got a girl in trouble. He didn't know what they called it now, but that was what they'd called it then. *Got a girl in trouble.* It happened to one after another of the Wiltons, like there was something in their blood that made it inevitable. Almost unbelievable—except it had happened. He decided not to go into it all. Malcolm would only use it to justify why Christy should never have gotten involved with Roger and his family. It was too late to explain things away.

"When did you learn your daughter was dead?" Harter asked.

"It must have been two days later."

"You didn't know where she was for two days?"

Malcolm looked like the question dazed him a little. "It wasn't like that at all. We thought she was spending the night with a friend—a girl-friend—so we weren't worried at first. When she wasn't home by the next evening, Connie called to check up on her and we were told she'd only visited the afternoon before for an hour or so. Then I called Roger Wilton, and he said he hadn't seen Christy for several days. He said they'd broken up. I felt like he was lying, and, of course, now I know he was. I told him I was going to contact the police and report her missing."

"Did you?"

"Yes, but they were no help. Whoever it was asked me how old she was, and when I told him, he said, 'Well, she's of age.' Then he asked how long she'd been gone, and when I said since the night before, he said to give her a little more time. He suggested she might have run away, as a lot of young people did in the sixties. He wanted to know if I had any reason to believe harm had come to her, and of course I didn't. He told me to call back in a few days if she was still missing."

Harter nodded. Over the years, he'd given the same response on more than one missing-persons call himself. Usually the person turned up and that was as far as it went. "You never called back?"

"No."

"Why?" asked McManaway.

"Early the next morning we got a call from a woman who said Christy had died from an abortion. She said the body was buried where no one would find it."

"Any idea who the woman was?"

"She wouldn't identify herself, but I imagine it was Roger's mother. I'd never have recognized her voice. At first, Connie and I wondered if it was a cruel prank, and we kept waiting for Christy to get in touch."

"I can't believe you didn't tell the police." McManaway sounded almost angry.

"Tell them what? That a mysterious caller claimed my daughter had died from an illegal abortion? I was a school teacher and my wife was active with church groups. We decided to wait and see what happened. I can't explain it. Why do people do what they do sometimes? The longer we kept it quiet, the harder it was to tell anyone. You understand we really weren't certain what had happened. They were different times."

"So, you eventually concocted the story about her going to San Francisco?" asked Harter.

"Everyone knew she'd planned to go out there in a few weeks anyway. I suppose she wanted to have the abortion before she left."

"Then you did believe she died from an abortion?"

"I'm afraid so. For a while, we feared the body would turn up in an alley someplace, but the days became years and nothing happened. Not until the flood, at least. We did believe it had something to do with Roger, though we didn't know about his mother at the time. If Roger had come to this house that winter, I'd have killed him. I'm not proud of it, but I would have."

"But you didn't kill him Saturday?"

"No. Believe me. It must have been Schiller. He . . ."

"He what?"

"He showed up at the door Saturday afternoon, a few hours after Roger left. Karen answered and she was quite frightened by him. She made him stand outside while she came to get me."

"You say Schiller was here after Roger left. So Roger visited you, too?"

Malcolm ran his hand back over his bald head and began rubbing at the base of his neck. "Roger came back to Shawnee after he heard about the body. Of course, he knew it was Christy's, and, of course, Connie and I suspected it was, too. We hadn't talked to him since I called him to question him about Christy all those years ago. We'd read about his mother being killed in an accident, but until he came here Saturday, we didn't know she was the one who performed the abortion."

"Roger told you everything Saturday?"

Malcolm's head bobbed. "He didn't want anyone to think he or his mother had committed a murder. That's why he came back. He wanted to arrange a meeting with the police so he could tell them the truth. Then he hoped he could slip out of town and get lost again. I argued that the truth wouldn't do anyone any good, but he kept insisting he and his mother never meant to hurt Christy. Christy wanted the abortion, he said. He wanted to get it off his conscience."

Get it off his conscience. Everyone seemed to want to paint Roger so black that he had no conscience, but he obviously did. He'd never been able to escape the memory of his girlfriend's death in 1967. And he might have been spoiled, but he cared enough about his mother to carry around that snapshot of the two of them on the Egypt Street porch.

"Roger made an appointment to meet me Saturday night, but he didn't keep it," Harter said. "Schiller had apparently shot him by then. His body was probably on its way to Black's Mountain. Was that the plan you and Schiller came up with?"

Malcolm's lips tightened. "There was no plan. I didn't mean for him to kill Roger. I didn't know he was going to do it. Schiller just seemed to know so much. He acted as if he'd known it all in Nineteen sixty-seven, too, as if Roger might have filled him in before he ran away. Schiller said he'd also heard from Roger that morning and he knew Roger intended to tell the police everything. He said he was sure my wife and I didn't want the whole world to know what happened to Christy, and he promised to keep it from happening."

"By murdering Roger Wilton?"

"No. He was going to buy Roger off. He said Roger didn't have anything, so it wouldn't take much to make him keep his mouth shut."

"This doesn't sound like the Len Schiller I knew," said Harter. "What was in it for him?"

"Money."

"How much?"

"Two thousand dollars. He wanted twelve, and said he was going to offer ten thousand to Roger to go away. He promised I'd never hear from him again. I guess I felt he was sleazy, but I didn't realize he was such a criminal. At first, I didn't want any part of what he was suggesting, but he was very convincing. He knew all the details and seemed to be very familiar with Roger. I kept thinking about the alternatives, about the truth coming out, and finally I gave in. If he could get Roger to keep quiet and go away, it was worth twelve thousand dollars to me."

"People have been killed for less," said Harter.

"You have to believe me. I didn't know Schiller would murder him. I'd never have gone along with it if I'd had an inkling," pleaded Malcolm. "Roger had disappeared before, and I thought he might be willing to disappear again. I didn't kill anyone. I've never killed anybody in my life."

"Did you pay Schiller on the spot?" asked Harter, remembering the large amount of cash on Schiller's body.

"I don't keep that kind of cash around. I gave him a check."

"Didn't it occur to you that a canceled check might tie you to the murder?"

"I told you—I didn't know there was going to be a murder. Believe me. Schiller said the banks were closed for the weekend, so I had until Monday afternoon to stop payment. Meanwhile, he had the rest of Saturday and Sunday to talk Roger into leaving. He promised I'd get a call one way or another."

"Did you?"

Malcolm nodded. "I'd expected to hear from Roger, but Schiller phoned Sunday and said Roger had already left town. Then Monday morning I read that he was dead."

"Why didn't you contact the police?"

Malcolm said nothing.

"I take it you made no attempt to stop the check," said Harter. "Schiller kept his half of the bargain, didn't he? Roger was out of the way, and he never got a chance to talk to me. I can't get rid of the feeling that the blood's on your hands, Mr. Malcolm. Did your wife go along with this conspiracy?"

"My God, no. Connie knows nothing about it, not even now. She was away when both Roger and Schiller came to the house. Perhaps, if she'd been here, she would have talked me out of it. Look, I even wrote the check on the farm account as so she'd never see it."

"But she went along with the cover-up story all these years."

"How many times do I have to tell you? I never intended anyone would die."

"Not Nan Wilton, either?"

"Are you suggesting I had something to do with her death?"

"She was hit by a truck in Nineteen sixty-seven, only a day or so after the botched abortion. You're saying you know nothing about it, either?"

"I don't." Malcolm's voice was becoming a whine. "If I didn't kill the boy in Nineteen sixty-seven, why would I kill his mother?"

"I have no way of knowing when you're telling the truth and when you're not. You didn't call the police and tell them about your daughter eighteen years ago. You concocted a lie and held to it all this time. You didn't tell me about Roger and Schiller visiting you when I was here Tuesday."

"Who'd want everyone to know their daughter died like Christy did? The truth doesn't really matter after all these years, does it? It can only destroy people. Connie and I have always tried to do good. Why do you think we take in girls like Karen? We've tried to pay our penance."

Harter shook his head in disgust. "Looks like a big bill to me. I hope you've got enough time left to get out of debt."

"We're not the reason our daughter died, Detective. The full truth couldn't have helped anyone. Not us, not the Wilton family. Who cared?"

"Roger did," said Harter. "Roger Wilton obviously did."

32

"I SHOT HER."

Friday morning. *Early.* For the third time, Harter sat across the interrogation table from Darrell Phillips and listened to Phillips confess. Both of them had Styrofoam cups of coffee in front of them.

As he watched the appliance dealer, Harter considered asking about his war record. Considered opening up the touchy subject of whether Phillips had actually been in Vietnam and what terrors he'd seen there, or whether it had all been a tall tale, or whether Phillips was so deluded he believed he'd been in a war that he hadn't.

But Harter didn't ask. Said nothing. He was no shrink. And he was worn out. Floods and bones. Molemen and bulldozers. Abortions and murders. Mind games and tapes of disembodied voices. He decided he'd wait for Dave McManaway and Vi Phillips to show. He'd see what they had to say, what *she* had to say. See if she had any doubts yet about her husband's sanity. See if she was ready yet to sign him into Shawnee Mental Health Center for more than twenty-four hours. For long enough that someone with proper training might figure out how to help him.

Somehow he felt Vi Phillips would never be ready. He pictured her Tuesday night—before he'd left her white apartment and gone to Schiller's bloody one—pictured her insisting that he leave, that he leave her and her husband alone to solve their problems. Over and over, so many pictures from the past ten days—the past forty years, for that matter—kept reappearing to him. Pictures and words.

Vi Phillips was never going to be ready. But he was. Ready to do whatever legal junk had to be done to stop Phillips from strolling in and confessing another morning. Ready to put an end to it.

But it was up to the prosecuting attorney as well. And that was no sure bet. He and McManaway hadn't had any luck when they'd gone to the prosecutor's office Thursday evening after leaving Gerald Malcolm's house. The prosecutor had patiently heard them out, but in the end he'd announced it would be tough to convince a jury to punish the retired schoolteacher. Malcolm was respected. The death of his daughter would cause sympathy in as many people as would be outraged by the cover-up. There was no one to testify that Malcolm wasn't telling the truth when he said he didn't realize Schiller would murder Roger Wilton. The prosecuting attorney didn't like weak cases and he didn't like mistrials and hung juries. He didn't like to lose and he didn't like bad press.

Harter pulled out his cigarettes, lit one, asked Phillips, "You want a smoke?"

Phillips' head was buried in his puffy hands, but it seemed to sway no.

The small interrogation room filled fast with smoke and, for some reason, Harter thought about how much Liz would hate it, would hate the way he worked. No matter what he did, he always seemed to end up irritating her, getting on her nerves. The small things, they added up, and each one added an inch until the distance between them was measured in yards, more yards than he could ever long-jump, even with a running start. Why they couldn't move toward each other, he couldn't understand.

When the knock hit the door, he hurried out to the hall to hear what Vi Phillips had to say this morning, but the redhead wasn't there.

McManaway looked pale and shaky. Finally he got his lips going.

"She's dead," he said. "He shot her."

A YOUNG uniformed cop was standing guard when Harter and McManaway showed up at the apartment over the appliance store. McManaway had posted the officer at the door when, confused, he'd gone down to headquarters to tell Harter the news in person.

Upstairs, the television set still blared in the living room, just as McManaway had found it when he'd first walked in. In the middle of the carpet lay the pistol that Vi Phillips had claimed her husband hadn't owned. Her husband, by now, was in a cell, and the prosecuting attorney and mental health center had been notified, for whatever good they could do.

McManaway was still upset. He kept repeating the story of how he'd found her sprawled on the double bed in her blood-soaked nightgown. "I never believed he'd really do it," he said.

"Anything can happen," Harter mumbled.

"You mean you actually thought he'd shoot her?"

"They're all wounded and they live lies."

"Phillips?"

"Phillips. The Malcolms. The Wilton family, too. All of them."

"What can we do about it?"

"Not a goddamned thing that I know of. Just wait for the next flood and see what it turns up. See who else's troubles surface. Hell, don't pay any attention to me. I'm tired."

"So am I," said the younger detective.

When the phone rang, neither of them reached for it immediately. Finally, McManaway, either because he couldn't stand the nagging noise or didn't want the beat cop to come upstairs, walked over to the end table and picked up the receiver. The conversation was brief, and after he'd hung up, he said "Damn," and started for the door.

"What's the matter?" Harter asked.

"It's Sally. Her mother's taken her to the hospital. She's in labor. God, I didn't want it to be like this. I thought we had a couple more days. I wanted to be there, Harter. I wanted to drive her up to the hospital myself and stay with her every minute. Doesn't anything ever work out?"

33

A ROW OF FRANKFURTER BUNS stretched up Al's arm, and Harter watched him slop mustard on the wieners. The crowd was thicker than usual for a Friday afternoon, and it was all Al could do to keep up with the orders.

As they'd walked from headquarters to the restaurant, Harter had poured out the Darrell Phillips saga to Sgt. Wayne Smith. The tale was new to the state cop and he seemed to accept that Harter's sadness and frustration were multiplied by the other events of the last ten days.

Inside Al's, Harter had staked out a seat in the rear corner, his back to the wall, his eyes facing the hot dog factory by the front window. He'd gulped down his wieners fast, but Smith ate much slower. After each bite, Smith chewed thoroughly and then he would talk a little before chomping off another length. Harter wasn't truly listening to what he was saying. For some reason, his mind was more with the onions being spooned on the dogs. Al was at least doing something solid, an action that had an end and left a satisfied customer.

Harter slid around on the wooden bench and managed to tune in on Sgt. Smith's voice in time to hear, "So, anyway, they found the gray van about a hundred miles into Ohio, but there's no sign of Schiller's girlfriend. Patty probably hiked up her skirt and hitched a ride. Christ, we don't even know her last name. All we can hope is they get good prints and she's been booked before."

"What's it matter?" mumbled Harter.

"Ah, come on. Don't act like you don't care if we pick her up. She pulled a gun on you!"

"She's an accessory at best, if we can even prove that. Hell, she'd say the gun just happened to be in her hand because she was taking it out to the van. Our esteemed prosecutor was loud and clear about his legal philosophy on weak cases last night. He doesn't like to lose cases."

"Don't be such a fucking martyr, Harter. You did all the police work, and it led you to Gerald Malcolm. You figured everything out. Sometimes it just doesn't lead to a conviction. We've all been there. You know as well as I do that the prosecutor might be right. A jury's more apt to buy the story that Malcolm was only trying to pay Wilton to go away. For all we know, Schiller could have really intended it like that. He just wanted an easy two thousand bucks. Maybe Roger Wilton wouldn't disappear and they started arguing and Schiller shot him. Anyway, no jury is going to blame Malcolm for how his daughter died, even if he did help cover it up. Just let it drop for now. Schiller's girlfriend might give us a new angle, if we find her."

"Or she could say she only knew Schiller for a week and she never laid eyes on Roger or Gerald Malcolm."

Smith shrugged. "Look. You got Schiller, and Malcolm has to be all torn up inside. Right now, he doesn't know what the prosecutor intends to do. He and his wife are probably living in dread of what might come out in the papers."

"They lived a lie a long time. I guess they can live in dread a little while longer," said Harter, rubbing his index finger around the rim of the empty plate in front of him. "They must have known someone would find out someday."

"You'd think so." Smith stuffed the last of his third hot dog in his mouth and chewed. "Took long enough for the truth to be told, though."

"All the truth except what happened to Nan Wilton. Malcolm claims he had nothing to do with that, either."

"Do you think he did?"

"Got me."

"Did you ever consider maybe it really was an accident, like Caruthers wrote it off at the time? You know, Caruthers wasn't as bad as you make him out. He could be pretty meticulous. Hell, Harter, you're the one always rattling on about chance. Could just be chance that Nan Wilton was run over a few days after the abortion. She might have been just crossing the street at the wrong moment."

"And they built the pyramids over the pharaohs by chance, too."

"What's that supposed to mean?"

"Something Pete Epstein said last week."

"Sounds like Epstein. So, what did Caruthers have to go on back in Nineteen sixty-seven, anyway? I haven't seen the old report."

Harter noticed the guy sitting in the booth behind Wayne Smith had his head cocked like he was listening to them. "Let's get out of here," he said.

They paid at the cash register and were halfway to the corner before Harter opened up. "Caruthers decided she was hit by a pickup truck."

"Not much help now."

"He thought it might have been blue. Apparently there was a smudge of paint on her robe."

"A blue pickup." Smith gave a soft laugh as they started across the quiet downtown street.

"What's funny?" asked Harter.

"You remember standing on the corner when you were a kid and watching the traffic? We used to make penny bets about what would come along next, or who could recognize the make and model soonest."

"Or whether it would have out-of-state tags or what color it would be."

"Right."

"I'm sure kids today have more high-tech ways to pass their time. No one even had a TV when I was little."

"Well, Smart Jack, tell me how many blue pickups you remember."

"Got me."

"First off, there weren't as many trucks as today," Smith said as they walked through the parking lot near the police department. "Everyone and his brother wasn't driving around in a pickup with a camper top. Not in this town at least. And seems to me nearly all of them were red. Farmers came into Shawnee in red pickups. Remember?"

"Guess so. Except for the Shawnee-Potomac Railroad trucks." Harter saw himself pulling out of Shawnee Community College behind Liz on Tuesday. Saw the blue railroad truck sliding in between them. "They've always been blue with a silver insignia like they are now."

Smith nodded as he opened the headquarters door. "State Roads trucks were blue a couple years, but mostly the blue pickups you saw were railroad vehicles." He followed Harter into the building and down the hall to the detective's office. "Roger Wilton's old man worked for the railroad, didn't he? On the tape from the motel room, Wilton said his father was out of town the week of the abortion, which would also have been about the time of the hit-and-run."

"Yeah. Wheat Wilton worked for the Shawnee-Potomac and was supposed to be working at a train wreck site that week," Harter said as he dropped into his chair.

"Did you ever get in touch with the railroad and see what you could find out about that wreck?"

Harter looked up at Smith and for the first time that day his eyes seemed to have been plugged in. "I know a guy at the Shawnee-Potomac personnel office at the yards. I bet when they went conglomerate and moved the corporate office to Florida, or wherever the hell it is these days, they didn't bother to take all the old records. It's a chance. It's worth a Friday afternoon. You're not such a bad cop, Wayne."

"Thanks for the endorsement, Harter. I'm nice to women and children, too. In fact, I'll tell you a real secret if you keep it quiet. I've got a bird feeder in my yard, and sometimes I sit by my picture window and watch the birds."

But Harter's mind was already moving on. "Darrell Phillips killed his wife," he said.

"He's not the first man ever did," said Wayne Smith.

34

FLATHEAD NASH'S house looked just as it had five days earlier. The same newspapers rested on the living room rug. The dust on the furniture was about the same. The picture from Nan Wilton's high school graduation hung on the wall as Nash led Harter and Matt Curry through the front room. On the kitchen table was another plate with egg yolk dried on it. Nash himself wore the same faded flannel shirt, though he had changed his trousers. Once again he spooned instant coffee from the same jar, though he'd soon need to buy a new one.

Harter was playing it all by ear. There were times when the years of experience didn't mean much. In elementary school, they taught you how to check your answers by toting them up the other way, but he couldn't figure out how to double-check this case.

He'd spent the previous afternoon in a room filled with the Shawnee-Potomac Railroad's dead paper. That night from his apartment, he'd called Matt Curry and arranged to pick him up Saturday morning. They'd driven crosstown to Nash's house near the hospital. Near the hospital where Dave and Sally McManaway's baby had been born on Friday. Once this was over, Harter should go and inspect it.

Flathead Nash brought coffee cups to the table and sat down at the end of it, between Curry and Harter, who took seats across from each other. The old men waited for the cop to talk first, and for a second Harter thought maybe he'd made a mistake. What good was it to tell them his suppositions? What good was it to say things that could never be proven? The old man . . . like Gerald Malcolm, no one was going to put him in jail.

He plowed ahead anyway. Trying to build up to it logically, Harter began talking about what had happened to Roger. The abortion story was no surprise to either of the old railroaders, but the connection between Len Schiller and Gerald Malcolm was. He tried to explain why Malcolm would probably never be charged with a crime, tried to explain the prosecutor's reasoning, but he didn't sound convincing even to himself. He could read from their faces that Curry and Nash weren't interested in legal manipulations.

"Goddamn prostituting attorney," said Curry.

"What?" asked Nash.

"That's what Twain wrote one place. Tom and Huck are in a courtroom and one of them complains about the *prostituting* attorney. That's what it bubbles down to."

Harter wasn't in the mood to defend the criminal justice system. He began leading them back to December 1967, when Nan had been run down, when the abortion had gone wrong, when the molemen had arrived. He told Nash and Curry about the tape and how Roger had said Wheat was away at a train wreck, and how the railroad's records confirmed it. He told them about Caruthers' report on the hit-and-run, and about the blue paint—*the blue pickup*—the Shawnee-Potomac truck, *maybe*.

He tried to make it clear he was sliding into what-ifs, and they seemed to stay with him at every bend. The wreck had been less than fifteen miles from Shawnee. In a narrow cut west of town. Two trains misrouted on the same track. Head-on collision. Two men dead. Main line blocked. They'd worked around the clock for four days to get rail traffic moving right. They'd brought in a cook and put sleeping cars on the siding so the laborers didn't have to leave the site.

Harter knew enough about working at night, about railroad crews at accident sites—knew enough to realize a person could slip away for a couple of hours. Could drive a truck to town and back. And if there was a dent in the hood or the bumper, well, hell, they *were* working around wreckage. Maybe the damned thing just rammed into a pile of pulled-up railroad ties. Flathead Nash and Matt Curry understood, too.

Harter had learned that Wheat Wilton was authorized to drive a railroad truck. He'd come across a file from 1970. Wheat had been involved in a minor accident at a crossing, and there was a statement saying he'd had a spotless driving record until then. His work record in general was clean, though he'd been passed over for promotions more than once.

"The son of a bitch ain't never been worth a nickel of cat's meat," proclaimed Flathead.

"Remember, I'm just laying out what *could* have happened," Harter cautioned. "We'll never know for sure. We can't make Wheat Wilton say anything. We can't read his mind. No one will ever put him on trial. He'd be declared incompetent as soon as a charge was placed."

Harter took a sip of lukewarm coffee, and the word *incompetent* rolled around in his brain. Darrell Phillips might damn well be incompetent, too.

"I always felt it was Wheat, but how could I prove it?" Curry mumbled.

"I can't really prove it now," Harter said.

"We ought to strangle the bastard," said Flathead.

"Nan told me they were arguing all the time those days," said Curry. "Wheat had hit her. He was calling her from the wreck in the middle of the night and . . ." He twisted his neck and glanced from Harter to Flathead. "And sometimes she wasn't home. The night Roger and her buried the Malcolm girl, Nan said she heard the phone ring inside, but they were out in the shed and she couldn't get to it in time. Other times, she was with—"

Flathead cut him off. "I want to slug the old asshole."

"You'd wind up in court, and you'd lose," Harter said. "You can't go around hitting people, especially elderly people in the shape Wilton is." He turned back to Curry. "What else did Nan tell you?"

"She'd been looking for a way to get Wheat out of the house so she could do the abortion. She even thought of renting a room somewhere, but then the train wreck happened. Wheat didn't know about the girl being pregnant. Nan kept it from him because it would have just been another reason for him to come down on Roger."

"We ought to push the son of a bitch out his window and let him lay in the middle of the Avenue so the trucks run over him," snarled Flathead.

"It wouldn't bring Nan back," Curry said.

"Well, we ought to at least go down there and let the bastard know we know what he did. Maybe he'd just keel over."

"It won't bring her back, no matter what we do. I always knew it was Wheat. I felt it in my gut. He was turning more jealous each day."

Flathead slammed his fist into the table and the coffee cups jumped. "The cocksucker!"

"What about Nan's daughter?" asked Harter. "Every time I run through what to do, I think of Dorothy. Why put her through the pain at this point? She loves her father."

"And hates her mother," said Flathead.

"She shouldn't hate Nan," Curry said. "If Dorothy knew the whole truth, she'd feel different. You're not supposed to hate your mother."

Harter stared across the kitchen table at Matt Curry. "You think Dorothy would feel better if we spread all this out in front of her? None of this is her fault. The abortion. Why Nan was crossing the street in the middle of the night. Why you and Wheat couldn't get along. Dorothy already has to deal with her father being a vegetable, and sooner or later she's going to walk in his room one morning and find him dead."

"We ought to help him along," said Flathead.

"Let the bastard live with it," said Curry. "Let Wheat sit there frozen, running his sins through his mind."

"If the bastard has any mind left," said Flathead. Some of the fury blew out of his voice in mid-sentence as what he was saying dawned on him. He reached for his Camels, put one in his mouth, and lit it.

"Sometimes you hope there's really a hell, because even this life isn't bad enough for some people," Curry said.

LATER, Matt Curry thought maybe he was wrong. This life could be bad enough. He'd loved Nan, and she'd done a terrible thing, and then she'd been murdered. He'd always known it had been Wheat. But like Harter, he couldn't prove it. Couldn't find the piece that said it all. Many times he'd imagined Wheat sitting in a truck, parked up Egypt Street from his house, waiting for Nan to make her way across. He'd always felt it, but he'd always sealed it in. Hadn't wanted anyone to know about him and her. Would never do anything to hurt her. Wheat had hurt her enough, all those years. Had hurt him, too.

Then Harter had come back for the third time on Wednesday afternoon. The cop had walked in like he was in charge, like he knew something, like railroad brass. Curry had listened to his hard questions, and slowly he had decided. The truth had to have less sting than the ghosts.

Thou shalt not commit adultery, his mother would have preached. He could see her. But thou shalt not commit murder, either. Some sins were worse than others. Had to be worse than others. Some sins could not be forgiven. Nan never meant to kill the Malcolm girl, but Wheat had meant to kill Nan.

He and Wheat, two boys playing along the tracks, among the canal boat ruins. Then they were young men building a shed beside the Wilton place. Then they were courting the same woman. *He loved her.* Then one day they didn't speak any longer.

She was wearing one of those dresses so thin you could see her body move through it, with shiny stockings and high-heel shoes that strapped across her slender ankles. He always remembered her like that. She smelled so clean. Then years later her dress was sliding from her shoulders and she was bending her knee to step free of it. In her lace-edged slip, she crossed the room to him, her arms reaching out. Then one night she was dead.

There wasn't a damn thing he could do to set any of it right.

Old man frozen in place.

35

AFTER HE WATCHED Matt Curry struggle up the steps to his front door, Harter drove back through Shantytown and out toward the railroad yards. For an instant at the light, he considered turning south and heading to the overlook, but instead he turned the other way on the Avenue and went to headquarters.

He still wasn't certain he'd done the right thing by unloading his conjectures on Curry and Nash. It was too much like weather prognostication in an old almanac, too much guesswork. But somehow he felt better for having done it. As he'd driven Curry home to Egypt Street, he sensed a relief in the old conductor, too. It was like, right or wrong, there was an end to old mysteries. No one had to live with secrets anymore, though there was still plenty of pain.

Herr, the desk cop, was on the telephone when Harter walked through the door. There was one of those you-won't-believe-this looks on Herr's face, but Harter was prepared to ignore it. He'd had that feeling himself too many times lately.

"Wait a minute," Herr said to whoever was on the line. So Harter got the message, Herr tilted his head and added, "One of the detectives has just come in. I'll let you talk to him."

Harter pointed down the hall and hurried toward his office.

"Well, what are you going to do about it?" demanded a woman as soon as he picked up the receiver.

"About what?" he asked.

"How many times do I have to explain? I've been calling all day." She was pretty damn mad.

"You haven't explained it to me yet."

"How are you going to help those people?"

"What people?"

"The ones on the moon."

No wonder Herr had been glad to see him come in. "Back up. I don't know what you're talking about, lady."

"Didn't the other cop tell you? There's people stranded up on the moon."

"How do you know?"

"I saw them. I always look at the full moon with my telescope, just to make sure it's as bright as it should be. Last night was a full moon and I focused in and I saw the people up there. I was so upset I couldn't sleep. No one wants to help them."

"How many people were up there?" Harter asked, a little amazed at his own question.

"At least four. I saw four. Two men and two women. There could have been others on the dark side. They were just standing there, staring back at Earth, staring back at me, with big pleading eyes. They were so worried and lonely. They made me so sad. I don't think they can get back down. They're stuck up there. It's like they're hostages or something."

"You could actually see their faces?"

"Of course. I have a very strong telescope. Why, it cost almost a hundred dollars. They didn't have any food or water with them. They'll die if they can't get home soon. They were begging me to save them."

"You heard them?"

"Don't be silly. It was more like they were thinking an SOS to me, like they were sending brainwaves. Am I the only one who cares?"

"If they could get up there, I'm sure they can get back. It's like a cat in a tree, isn't it?"

"But they're out of fuel. They were like Noah and his Ark. They were trying to escape the flood, and they ended up on the moon, and now they're out of fuel."

"I don't know what to say. All of our spaceships are busy right now."

"Don't make fun of me, Detective."

"Look, I'm just one of two detectives here. The police department has enough trouble keeping patrol cars on the road. I don't know how to get to the moon to save anyone."

"A hell of a cop you are!"

Sometimes he was apt to agree with her. "What you need to do is get hold of someone in the federal government. Try the White House."

"I've tried," she said, more belligerent than ever. "It's a weekend. The president's at his ranch. Those people need help now or they'll die up there. There's no oxygen. They can't last long."

"Did you try NASA?"

"NASA?"

"They're in charge of space, aren't they? They're the ones who send astronauts to the moon."

There was a long pause, and then she said, "You're right. I'll call them." He heard a click and a dial tone came on.

He dropped the phone into its cradle and pulled out his cigarettes. He had no idea how to rescue people from the moon. He surely wasn't the Wise Old Man of the Mountains. He didn't even know what he was going to have for supper.

He stared at all the papers on his desk, took a second long drag, then snubbed out the cigarette. He thought that if he could clear away all that paper, stuff it in a filing cabinet or something, get it out of his sight, maybe Monday would be different. But he really didn't feel like spending Saturday afternoon moving the junk around.

He glanced over at Caruthers' desk, the one McManaway was using, and he remembered a new baby was in the world. He thought perhaps he'd go up to the hospital and have a look at it, and find McManaway and tell him all that had happened, and then he might drive over the bridge into the West Side and see Liz. If all went well, they might go somewhere on Saturday night and check out the moon and see if the people had gotten down yet.

RAMBLE HOUSE's

HARRY STEPHEN KEELER WEBWORK MYSTERIES

(RH) indicates the title is available ONLY in the **RAMBLE HOUSE** edition

The Ace of Spades Murder
The Affair of the Bottled Deuce (RH)
The Amazing Web
The Barking Clock
Behind That Mask
The Book with the Orange Leaves
The Bottle with the Green Wax Seal
The Box from Japan
The Case of the Canny Killer
The Case of the Crazy Corpse (RH)
The Case of the Flying Hands (RH)
The Case of the Ivory Arrow
The Case of the Jeweled Ragpicker
The Case of the Lavender Gripsack
The Case of the Mysterious Moll
The Case of the 16 Beans
The Case of the Transparent Nude (RH)
The Case of the Transposed Legs
The Case of the Two-Headed Idiot (RH)
The Case of the Two Strange Ladies
The Circus Stealers (RH)
Cleopatra's Tears
A Copy of Beowulf (RH)
The Crimson Cube (RH)
The Face of the Man From Saturn
Find the Clock
The Five Silver Buddhas
The 4th King
The Gallows Waits, My Lord! (RH)
The Green Jade Hand
Finger! Finger!
Hangman's Nights (RH)
I, Chameleon (RH)
I Killed Lincoln at 10:13! (RH)
The Iron Ring
The Man Who Changed His Skin (RH)
The Man with the Crimson Box
The Man with the Magic Eardrums
The Man with the Wooden Spectacles
The Marceau Case
The Matilda Hunter Murder
The Monocled Monster
The Murder of London Lew
The Murdered Mathematician
The Mysterious Card (RH)
The Mysterious Ivory Ball of Wong Shing Li (RH)
The Mystery of the Fiddling Cracksman
The Peacock Fan
The Photo of Lady X (RH)
The Portrait of Jirjohn Cobb
Report on Vanessa Hewstone (RH)
Riddle of the Travelling Skull
Riddle of the Wooden Parrakeet (RH)
The Scarlet Mummy (RH)
The Search for X-Y-Z
The Sharkskin Book
Sing Sing Nights
The Six From Nowhere (RH)
The Skull of the Waltzing Clown
The Spectacles of Mr. Cagliostro
Stand By—London Calling!
The Steeltown Strangler
The Stolen Gravestone (RH)
Strange Journey (RH)
The Strange Will
The Straw Hat Murders (RH)
The Street of 1000 Eyes (RH)
Thieves' Nights
Three Novellos (RH)
The Tiger Snake
The Trap (RH)
Vagabond Nights (Defrauded Yeggman)
Vagabond Nights 2 (10 Hours)
The Vanishing Gold Truck
The Voice of the Seven Sparrows
The Washington Square Enigma
When Thief Meets Thief
The White Circle (RH)
The Wonderful Scheme of Mr. Christopher Thorne
X. Jones—of Scotland Yard
Y. Cheung, Business Detective

Keeler Related Works

A To Izzard: A Harry Stephen Keeler Companion by Fender Tucker — Articles and stories about Harry, by Harry, and in his style. Included is a compleat bibliography.

Wild About Harry: Reviews of Keeler Novels — Edited by Richard Polt & Fender Tucker — 22 reviews of works by Harry Stephen Keeler from *Keeler News.* A perfect introduction to the author.

The Keeler Keyhole Collection: Annotated newsletter rants from Harry Stephen Keeler, edited by Francis M. Nevins. Over 400 pages of incredibly personal Keeleriana.

Fakealoo — Pastiches of the style of Harry Stephen Keeler by selected demented members of the HSK Society. Updated every year with the new winner.

Five Jack Mann Novels — Strange murder in the English countryside. *Gees' First Case, Nightmare Farm, Grey Shapes, The Ninth Life, The Glass Too Many.*

Seven Max Afford Novels — *Owl of Darkness, Death's Mannikins, Blood on His Hands, The Dead Are Blind, The Sheep and the Wolves, Sinners in Paradise* and *Two Locked Room Mysteries and a Ripping Yarn* by one of Australia's finest novelists.

Five Joseph Shallit Novels — *The Case of the Billion Dollar Body, Lady Don't Die on My Doorstep, Kiss the Killer, Yell Bloody Murder, Take Your Last Look.* One of America's best 50's authors.

Two Crimson Clown Novels — By Johnston McCulley, author of the Zorro novels, *The Crimson Clown* and *The Crimson Clown Again.*

The Best of 10-Story Book — edited by Chris Mikul, over 35 stories from the literary magazine Harry Stephen Keeler edited.

A Young Man's Heart — A forgotten early classic by Cornell Woolrich

The Anthony Boucher Chronicles — edited by Francis M. Nevins
Book reviews by Anthony Boucher written for the *San Francisco Chronicle,* 1942 – 1947. Essential and fascinating reading.

Muddled Mind: Complete Works of Ed Wood, Jr. — David Hayes and Hayden Davis deconstruct the life and works of a mad genius.

Gadsby — A lipogram (a novel without the letter E). Ernest Vincent Wright's last work, published in 1939 right before his death.

My First Time: The One Experience You Never Forget — Michael Birchwood — 64 true first-person narratives of how they lost it.

Automaton — Brilliant treatise on robotics: 1928-style! By H. Stafford Hatfield

The Incredible Adventures of Rowland Hern — Rousing 1928 impossible crimes by Nicholas Olde.

Slammer Days — Two full-length prison memoirs: *Men into Beasts* (1952) by George Sylvester Viereck and *Home Away From Home* (1962) by Jack Woodford

Murder in Black and White — 1931 classic tennis whodunit by Evelyn Elder

Killer's Caress — Cary Moran's 1936 hardboiled thriller

The Golden Dagger — 1951 Scotland Yard yarn by E. R. Punshon

Beat Books #1 — Two beatnik classics, *A Sea of Thighs* by Ray Kainen and *Village Hipster* by J.X. Williams

A Smell of Smoke — 1951 English countryside thriller by Miles Burton

Ruled By Radio — 1925 futuristic novel by Robert L. Hadfield & Frank E. Farncombe

Murder in Silk — A 1937 Yellow Peril novel of the silk trade by Ralph Trevor

The Case of the Withered Hand — 1936 potboiler by John G. Brandon

Finger-prints Never Lie — A 1939 classic detective novel by John G. Brandon

Inclination to Murder — 1966 thriller by New Zealand's Harriet Hunter

Invaders from the Dark — Classic werewolf tale from Greye La Spina

Fatal Accident — Murder by automobile, a 1936 mystery by Cecil M. Wills

The Devil Drives — A prison and lost treasure novel by Virgil Markham

Dr. Odin — Douglas Newton's 1933 potboiler comes back to life.

The Chinese Jar Mystery — Murder in the manor by John Stephen Strange, 1934

The Julius Caesar Murder Case — A classic 1935 re-telling of the assassination by Wallace Irwin that's much more fun than the Shakespeare version

West Texas War and Other Western Stories — by Gary Lovisi

The Contested Earth and Other SF Stories — A never-before published space opera and seven short stories by Jim Harmon.

Tales of the Macabre and Ordinary — Modern twisted horror by Chris Mikul, author of the *Bizarrism* series.

The Gold Star Line — Seaboard adventure from L.T. Reade and Robert Eustace.

The Werewolf vs the Vampire Woman — Hard to believe ultraviolence by either Arthur M. Scarm or Arthur M. Scram.

Black Hogan Strikes Again — Australia's Peter Renwick pens a tale of the outback.

Don Diablo: Book of a Lost Film — Two-volume treatment of a western by Paul Landres, with diagrams. Intro by Francis M. Nevins.

The Charlie Chaplin Murder Mystery — Movie hijinks by Wes D. Gehring

The Koky Comics — A collection of all of the 1978-1981 Sunday and daily comic strips by Richard O'Brien and Mort Gerberg, in two volumes.

Suzy — Another collection of comic strips from Richard O'Brien and Bob Vojtko

Dime Novels: Ramble House's 10-Cent Books — *Knife in the Dark* by Robert Leslie Bellem, *Hot Lead* and *Song of Death* by Ed Earl Repp, *A Hashish House in New York* by H.H. Kane, and five more.

Blood in a Snap — The *Finnegan's Wake* of the 21st century, by Jim Weiler and Al Gorithm

Stakeout on Millennium Drive — Award-winning Indianapolis Noir — Ian Woollen.

Dope Tales #1 — Two dope-riddled classics; *Dope Runners* by Gerald Grantham and *Death Takes the Joystick* by Phillip Condé.
Dope Tales #2 — Two more narco-classics; *The Invisible Hand* by Rex Dark and *The Smokers of Hashish* by Norman Berrow.
Dope Tales #3 — Two enchanting novels of opium by the master, Sax Rohmer. *Dope* and *The Yellow Claw.*
Tenebrae — Ernest G. Henham's 1898 horror tale brought back.
The Singular Problem of the Stygian House-Boat — Two classic tales by John Kendrick Bangs about the denizens of Hades.
Tiresias — Psychotic modern horror novel by Jonathan M. Sweet.
The One After Snelling — Kickass modern noir from Richard O'Brien.
The Sign of the Scorpion — 1935 Edmund Snell tale of oriental evil.
The House of the Vampire — 1907 poetic thriller by George S. Viereck.
An Angel in the Street — Modern hardboiled noir by Peter Genovese.
The Devil's Mistress — Scottish gothic tale by J. W. Brodie-Innes.
The Lord of Terror — 1925 mystery with master-criminal, Fantômas.
The Lady of the Terraces — 1925 adventure by E. Charles Vivian.
My Deadly Angel — 1955 Cold War drama by John Chelton
Prose Bowl — Futuristic satire — Bill Pronzini & Barry N. Malzberg .
Satan's Den Exposed — True crime in Truth or Consequences New Mexico — Award-winning journalism by the *Desert Journal*.
The Amorous Intrigues & Adventures of Aaron Burr — by Anonymous — Hot historical action.
I Stole $16,000,000 — A true story by cracksman Herbert E. Wilson.
The Black Dark Murders — Vintage 50s college murder yarn by Milt Ozaki, writing as Robert O. Saber.
Sex Slave — Potboiler of lust in the days of Cleopatra — Dion Leclerq.
You'll Die Laughing — Bruce Elliott's 1945 novel of murder at a practical joker's English countryside manor.
The Private Journal & Diary of John H. Surratt — The memoirs of the man who conspired to assassinate President Lincoln.
Dead Man Talks Too Much — Hollywood boozer by Weed Dickenson
Red Light — History of legal prostitution in Shreveport Louisiana by Eric Brock. Includes wonderful photos of the houses and the ladies.
A Snark Selection — Lewis Carroll's *The Hunting of the Snark* with two Snarkian chapters by Harry Stephen Keeler — Illustrated by Gavin L. O'Keefe.
Ripped from the Headlines! — The Jack the Ripper story as told in the newspaper articles in the *New York* and *London Times.*
Geronimo — S. M. Barrett's 1905 autobiography of a noble American.
The White Peril in the Far East — Sidney Lewis Gulick's 1905 indictment of the West and assurance that Japan would never attack the U.S.
The Compleat Calhoon — All of Fender Tucker's works: Includes *The Totah Trilogy, Weed, Women and Song* and *Tales from the Tower,* plus a CD of all of his songs.

RAMBLE HOUSE
Fender Tucker, Prop.
www.ramblehouse.com fender@ramblehouse.com
228-826-1783 10329 Sheephead Drive, Vancleave MS 39565

Made in the USA